The Best
AMERICAN
ESSAYS
2020

The Best
AMERICAN
ESSAYS®
2020

Edited and with an Introduction
by ANDRÉ ACIMAN

Robert Atwan, Series Editor

MARINER BOOKS

HOUGHTON MIFFLIN HARCOURT

BOSTON • NEW YORK 2020

ISSN 0888-3742 (print)   ISSN 2573-3885 (e-book)
ISBN 978-0-358-35991-3 (print)   ISBN 978-0-358-35858-9 (e-book)

Printed in the United States of America
DOC 10 9 8 7 6 5 4 3 2 1

Contents

Contents

Foreword

All life is an experiment. The more experiments you make the better.

—Ralph Waldo Emerson, *Journals*

The best prose shines with the luster, vigor, and boldness of poetry.

—Montaigne, *Of Vanity*

No, said Brewsie, I wont remember but I will find it out again.

—Gertrude Stein, *Brewsie and Willie*

BACK IN THE late 1970s, I cohosted with my good friend Donald McQuade a weekly call-in radio show on WBAI in midtown Manhattan. We called the show *Thinking Things Over,* and much of the time we riffed, not too pretentiously I hope, on all sorts of topics: books, public manners, American popular culture, advertising trends, New Age banalities, and so on. Occasionally we would interview a guest. We knew we had some listeners because we'd always field a few calls.

On one show we decided to try something different. I pretended to be a psychoanalyst, a Dr. Saul Worriman who had just published a self-help book called *The Now Factor.* I adopted an unconvincing German accent as Don interviewed me about the book's central purpose: how we can make our lives more exciting and meaningful by expanding our sense of the present. I'd years before picked up the idea from William James, who claimed in his classic two-volume *Principles of Psychology* that laboratory experiments showed that most people perceived the "present" to extend for only about twelve seconds. After about a dozen seconds, we feel that something is no longer "now" but has receded into the past, as has, say, writing the opening sentence to this paragraph. Not past in the sense of a year or a week or even an hour ago, but writing that sentence has the feel of "then," not "now." "And what would be some of the advantages of extending our sense of a present, Dr. Worriman?" "Vell, we might feel ve live longer lives. It can increase our ability to focus and concentrate. And, vell, some of my patients tell me their orgasms now seem to last forever." The phones rang off the hook.

If, as many say, living in the present is a sign of a healthy, vital mental attitude, then, it would seem, *expanding* our sense of the present could only enhance our well-being. Dr. Worriman based *The Now Factor* on James's notion that our sense of time can be "sharpened by practice." But as James himself admitted, there's another, simpler way to make twelve seconds feel like an hour: hashish. Under its effects, we "utter a sentence, and ere the end is reached the beginning seems already to date from indefinitely long ago." (Though perhaps he was not thinking here so much about cannabis as about his brother Henry's sentences.) At any event, once we find a way to stretch out the immediate present, to unlock the power of the Now Factor, as Dr. Worriman might say, we can perhaps make ourselves more susceptible to spiritual illumination and artistic creativity. Here is how one of William James's favorite students, Gertrude Stein, put it: "The business of Art as I tried to explain in *Composition as Explanation* is to live in the actual present, that is the complete actual present, and to completely express that complete actual present."

Gertrude Stein has remained one of the most fascinating and remarkable figures in American literary and cultural history. This may be because we have so many Gertrude Steins: the obscure avant-garde novelist before there truly was an avant garde; the modernist prose-poet who not only championed cubism but explored ways to transfer its methods to writing; the legendary Parisian hostess who promoted and befriended Picasso, Matisse, Braque, and countless other distinguished artists; the exile who remained an American patriot and doted on U.S. soldiers during two world wars; the autobiographer and lifelong partner of the enigmatic Alice B. Toklas; the popular lecturer who became a Yogi Berra of quotable literary phrases ("there's no there there"); the celebrated epicenter of a loose international network of artists, writers, thinkers, and socialites, all of whom gathered at 27 rue de Fleurus to pay homage; the mentor of younger contemporary writers like Ernest Hemingway and Sherwood Anderson as well as an inspiration for such literary luminaries to come as William Gass and John Ashbery. And then there's the scientist, the Radcliffe student, professor William James's brilliant protégé, who would go on to the prestigious Johns Hopkins medical school with a special interest in mapping the brain.

At Harvard she studied psychology and philosophy with the academic stars of the time—not just James but his illustrious colleagues Josiah Royce and George Santayana. She was also the "ideal student" of another major figure, though one who quickly faded from intellectual prominence, the German psychologist Hugo Munsterberg. James—who felt an affinity with the younger empirical psychologist—had persuaded Munsterberg to leave the University of Freiburg and come to Harvard, where he quickly became a popular professor who enjoyed entertaining introductory students with clever experiments. Under Munsterberg, Stein would focus on the physiological basis of psychology and learn she had a gift for experimental methods, a gift she would within a few years apply to literature. But first she would perform experiments to understand the basic workings of attention—a topic that fascinated James and Munsterberg—as well as our perception of time, often measured then acoustically. Later in James's seminar she would participate in experiments on automatic writing, another subject that appealed to the always open-minded William James, given his enduring interest in spiritualism and paranormal experiences, an interest many of his fellow psychologists, including Munsterberg himself, believed was unscientific and unprofessional.

Stein's first publications reported on these experiments. "Normal Motor Automatism" (coauthored with a classmate) appeared in Harvard's *Psychological Review* for September 1896, and "Cultivated Motor Automatism: A Study of Character in Its Relation to Attention" came out in the same journal in September 1898. By the second publication she had already begun medical studies at Johns Hopkins. Her keen interests in experimental psychology, automatic writing, the boundaries of attention and distraction and their relation to consciousness, would inform her later work as she left science and began to launch a literary career. Few creative writers at the time would have possessed anything close to her knowledge of psychology, physiology, and medicine, though she never took her medical degree and had begun to spend much of her time with her brother, Leo, in Europe.

By the end of 1903, Stein had settled in Paris as a budding novelist, finding ways to transfer her psychological and philosophical interests to fiction. With some tutelage from Leo, who had moved there to paint and study art, she quickly became acquainted with the contemporary European art scene. She and Leo both enjoyed independent incomes after the death of their wealthy father twelve years earlier; their mother had predeceased him by a year, so they found themselves two affluent, orphaned, bourgeois, Jewish American exiles in the City of Light, both on a quest to reinvent themselves. And it could not have been a better time nor place for reinvention: Paris was bursting with creativity. Frequenting Parisian galleries, they hungrily acquired works by Cézanne, Renoir, Gauguin, Manet, Degas, Toulouse-Lautrec, Delacroix, and within two years or so had added Matisse and Picasso, becoming friends with both. Friendships with the poet Apollinaire and artists like Marcel Duchamp would further introduce her to the cutting edge of contemporary art and letters as she would absorb the emerging cubist movement and eventually dadaism and surrealism.

Although Stein had already been writing rather unconventional fiction (*Three Lives; The Making of Americans*) and nonfiction (portraits of "Matisse" and "Picasso"), it wasn't until 1914 and the publication of *Tender Buttons*—just weeks before the outbreak of World War I—that she achieved a certain fame. I say "certain" because it was as much fame as it was notoriety. Many critics found the work baffling and unintelligible at best; a few extolled its originality; others ridiculed it and its author as deranged. In a piece for *Vanity Fair* in 1923 and later in other essays, Edmund Wilson considered *Tender Buttons* "incomprehensible," although he would not dismiss it with "raucous guffaws" as others had. Based on her earlier work, especially *Three Lives* and the "Portraits," he considered Stein a serious artist and one of the country's truly important writers. He would continue to praise her work, and especially, a decade later, her first best-selling book, *The Autobiography of Alice B. Toklas.*

For all his interest in Stein, Wilson never attempted to interpret or explicate *Tender Buttons*. He concluded, not totally incorrectly, that the work was inspired by her fascination with cubist painting and was an attempt to apply the visual techniques of cubism to literature—"prose still-lifes to correspond to those of such painters as Picasso and Braque." He thought the effort was aesthetically impossible, a dead end, the visual and the verbal arts being so unalike in their methods and media. Yet it was, of course, only the aesthetically impossible that had begun to motivate Stein.

For anyone unfamiliar with the book or who hasn't recently encountered it, *Tender Buttons* is roughly 15,000 words long—my edition runs some 65 pages—and is divided into three parts, "Objects," "Food," "Rooms." It opens:

A CARAFE, THAT IS A BLIND GLASS

A kind in glass and a cousin, a spectacle and nothing strange a single hurt color and an arrangement in a system to pointing. All this and not ordinary, not unordered in not resembling. The difference is spreading.

"Objects" and "Food" consist of similar enigmatic prose "vignettes." Some are a few pages long, others a few words, and all of them, like Montaigne's digressive essays, bear only an oblique relation to their titles. The book's final section, the more essaylike "Rooms," opens:

Act so that there is no use in a center. A wide action is not a width. A preparation is given to the ones preparing. They do not eat who mention silver and sweet. There was an occupation.

And it concludes:

The care with which the rain is wrong and the green is wrong and the white is wrong, the care with which there is a chair and plenty of breathing. The care with which there is incredible justice and likeness, all this makes a magnificent asparagus, and also a fountain.

Wilson's reluctance to translate the "unintelligible" into the "intelligible" would not discourage generations of critics and scholars from making the attempt. Is the work, with its abundance of erotic puns and imagery, a celebration of Stein's newly found sexual relationship with Alice, the "tender buttons" being nipples—or could it be "tend her buttons"? Is it instead a tribute to a newly discovered, blossoming creativity, the *boutons de fleurs* of inspiration? Or

are the tender buttons words themselves, here fastening and un-
fastening the underlying structure of composition and revealing
the work to be sheer *fabrication*? Over the years I have read numerous articles on *Tender Buttons* and have not found a single one fully
satisfactory, that is, in terms of an overall exegesis. Though many
offer piecemeal insights and some, like William Gass's "Gertrude
Stein and the Geography of the Sentence" (1973), may be critical
masterpieces in themselves, I have never come away from any essay
on the work—no matter what the approach—with the feeling of
"Ah, now I get what's going on here." Still, *Tender Buttons* endures,
and quite a few editions remain in print. A newly corrected version appeared in 2014 as a centennial edition promoting "one of
the most important and challenging texts of literary modernism."
Perhaps it gives credibility to Theodor Adorno's comment about
artworks in general: "The more they are understood, the less they
are enjoyed." *Tender Buttons* endures not despite its incomprehen-
sibility but because of it.

Full of puns, repetitions, and internal rhymes, a feast of plurisig-
nification, showing a continuous delight in homonyms (*tender/ten-
der*), heterographs (*read/reed*), and heteronyms (*use/use*), at times
sounding exhortative, at times philosophical and ruminative, with
little that can be identified as a personal voice, with phrases that
start out as aphorisms and then collapse into absurdity, with words
unanchored to syntax or context, with no conventional punctuation, no characters, storyline, or narrative direction, *Tender Buttons*—which Stein began writing in 1912— forcefully and yet play-
fully resists interpretation. Perhaps the clearest part of the work is
its subtitle, "Objects, Food, Rooms," which at least establishes an
interior world of domesticity. I agree with the critic Lucy Daniel
that *Tender Buttons* "is designed not to be 'understood' in the traditional sense." In fact, as Katherine Anne Porter pointed out in an
unfriendly 1947 essay, the relentlessly self-promoting Stein probably knew what she was up to: "She remarked once to her publisher that she was famous in America not for her work that people
understood but for that which they did not understand." As Stein
told a radio interviewer, "If you enjoy it you understand it."

Works like *Tender Buttons* make us aware of the kind of readers
we are. I recall in my junior year of high school finding a copy of
Oscar Williams's *Pocket Book of Modern Poetry* on the circular book
display at Paterson, New Jersey's main Rexall, where I'd often ac-

company my dad, who would pick up his racing sheet and carton of Raleighs and then treat me to whatever inexpensive paperback he'd find me absorbed in. Night after night that anthology would be my bedtime reading as I puzzled over one opaque poem after another. I didn't understand much of what I read, though I enjoyed it all immensely. I could recite "The Hollow Men" (only quietly to myself, of course) and loved the sound of it, but I would have been hard-pressed to supply an interpretation, and that was one of the more lucid poems. Later, in college, I would patiently puzzle over many works—Hopkins, Dickinson, Pound, Stevens, Cummings, and so on—but by then had developed some critical skills that allowed me to accumulate good grades on papers that were essentially my responses to other, more famous critical explications. I can't say which was more satisfying: the state of fascinated puzzlement or the interpretive solution—"The blackbird whistling / Or just after."

Not surprisingly, many readers, especially when it comes to prose, expect clarity and coherence and a more or less summarizable meaning, their criteria for good writing derived, it seems to me, primarily from the standards of current journalism, what we might call "nonliterary nonfiction." Judging from the many essays submitted to this series year after year, this criterion seems true even for those who aspire to literary careers. The prevailing style of nonfiction prose today seems quite the opposite of exploratory or experimental, is less interested in compositional challenges or literary playfulness and much more intent upon sustaining a sincere-sounding, unambiguous, straightforward documentation of largely painful personal narratives. Well and good; but one would hope that *literary* nonfiction would welcome a larger variety of models, a more diverse set of literary standards, an inclusion of more inventive styles. Yet except for a few prose variations —the prose poem (now often termed "lyric essay"), the mosaic or braided meditation, or the numerically segmented piece of nonfiction—it appears that the go-to handbook for most creative nonfiction writers remains Strunk and White's fairly conventional *Elements of Style* and not Gertrude Stein's audacious primer, *How to Write.*

From her earliest fiction, which is wholly "intelligible" (though still innovative and groundbreaking), Stein was aesthetically focused on what she called the "continuous present." As I suggested earlier, I see this aesthetic interest originating in her association with James and his psychological/philosophical studies of time, perception, consciousness, and the "stream of thought." In her earlier works she employed a rhythmic repetition to create sinuous sentences that she felt established a "prolonged present." But as her writing matured—a word many critics would hesitate to use in her case —she grew increasingly fascinated by the act of composition itself. She found *composition* a useful umbrella term because it could encompass creative activity in all the arts (she wrote some wonderful poems on dance). And she also apparently felt, as did her mentor James, that human perception itself depends to some degree upon composition. The world to a baby is "one great blooming, buzzing confusion," as James memorably put it; as we develop we learn to *compose* that "confusion" of perceptions into a world whose material details—this bowl, that table, those plates, these chairs—most of us most of the time agree are physically present.

Yet, as Stein also realized, compositions may require decomposition if they become too stale and lifeless, too familiar. This is what happens to works of art over time. Enter cubism and our perceptions are reformulated and revivified. Writing too goes dead. It requires continuous renewal. Sentences and paragraphs unfold predictably. Stories stop surprising. Syntax and grammar rigidify into formula. Explanations, descriptions, narratives grow tedious. When this happens the author's vision seems not only less vivid but less true. The aesthetic problem as Stein began to articulate it, in her own fashion of course, is tied up with the writer's dependence on two main obstacles to creativity: personal identity and memory. When we overly rely on them, we are then not writing in a "continuous present" but rather copying out prepared thoughts. How can writing be fully alive and creative if the self doing the writing is not also part of what is being created? In a 1936 lecture, "What Are Master-pieces and Why Are There So Few of Them?," Stein claims that at "any moment when you are you you are you without the memory of yourself because if you remember yourself while you are you you are not for the purposes of creating you." And she goes on to say:

Any of you when you write you try to remember what you are about to write and you will see immediately how lifeless the writing becomes that is why expository writing is so dull because it is all remembered, that is why illustration is so dull because you remember what somebody looked like and you make your illustration look like it. The minute your memory functions while you are doing anything it may be very popular but actually it is dull. And that is what a master-piece is not, it may be unwelcome but it is never dull.

As she once told a group of Choate students, "The business of an artist is to be exciting."

A few years before her lecture on masterpieces, Stein discovered a fact about writing that she describes in a long essay, "Henry James." While working on a translation of a friend's poem in 1931 she realized the difference between Shakespeare's plays and Shakespeare's sonnets. The plays, she says, were "written as they were written," but the sonnets "were written as they were going to be written." She maintains that these represent two very different kinds of writing. The plays, unlike the sonnets, were written spontaneously, without a plan and a predetermined form. In Stein's aesthetics, preparation is another serious obstacle to creativity. You don't think before you write, you think *as* you write. And in that way the composition is not an explanation of something else but the composition itself is the explanation, the enactment of a spontaneous and improvisational consciousness intent on capturing the immediate experience. Or, to put it another way, for Stein the literary work is inseparable from its composition.*

Tender Buttons is, in a sense, a compositional event, one that unfolds in multiple directions as we read, unpredictably, continually refreshing itself, never recapitulating, always resisting summary, or a storyline that might establish a time and a place, or a verbal description that might turn into the mere "illustration" she complains about above in "What Are Master-pieces." Without a discernible beginning, middle, or end, without a coherently imagined space, or even an identifiable speaker, the work seems—to some perversely, to others delightfully—to deliberately subvert the tacitly agreed-upon compact of communication between writer and

---

* Perhaps the extraordinarily well read Stein had also in the back of her mind the distinction Coleridge makes between Shakespeare the poet and Shakespeare the dramatist in chapter XV of his *Biographia Literaria* (1817). In fact, I find it instructive to read Stein's experimental works in the context of chapters XII through XV of Coleridge's critical classic, especially his discussion of the Imagination.

audience. It demonstrates an aesthetic that does not value clarity, consistency, and coherence. In other words, it does not rely on traditional modes of rhetoric but instead replaces conventional rhetorical structures with a dynamic poetics that defies normal expository, argumentative, or narrative templates.

Obviously, any piece of writing this strange would also refuse to be categorized generically. What is *Tender Buttons?* It's generally regarded as poetry but it's composed in prose—a repetitive, frequently rhyming prose that relies heavily on such devices as ploce and polyptoton (a staple of seventeenth-century metaphysical poetry), anaphora, assonance, and alliteration. It is prose more grounded in poetics than rhetoric. It is also a prose that plays games with grammar, syntax, parts of speech, tense, mood, punctuation. Stein attempts something remarkable in *Tender Buttons:* as someone who mastered and cherished the rules of English grammar, she demonstrates what might be called grammar's hidden poetry. For readers interested in the literary experimentations of a writer who dislikes nouns but loves verbs and prepositions, I recommend her essay "Poetry and Grammar" (in *Lectures in America,* 1935).

However we want to label it, I prefer to read *Tender Buttons* as an experimental essay. It reminds me that, as Montaigne first shaped it, the modern essay grew out of experiments in prose: "And what are the essays I scribble if not grotesque and far-fetched creatures, lacking save by chance all order, continuity, and proportion?" Montaigne never wrote an essay on the essay, but his thoughts on his genre-in-progress can be found scattered all through *Essais.* And every comment points to the way his innovative prose style reflected the fluctuations of a lively and unbridled consciousness that had no interest in intellectual or narrative closure. And, like Stein, he associated his compositions with art, declaring his prose as "the painting of thought" (*"la peinture de la pensée"*).

Anyone seriously interested in prose experimentation should approach *Tender Buttons* as a writer. Despite its violations of our familiar ways of communicating and making sense, it offers an invigorating alternative to our usual literary formulations. Think of it as an exercise that aspires to do something other than document an identity, defend or oppose a position, reconstruct childhood memories, or tell a troubling life story with its inevitable epiphany waiting to be fired like Chekhov's gun. I'm not recommending that anyone imitate the work—that would be futile and entirely un-Steinien, and as Emerson warns, "Imitation is suicide." But why not seriously consider what Stein is up to as a writer and ask if there is anything to be learned today from her experimental masterpiece? She once said in an interview that she thought "of writing in terms of discovery, which is to say the creation must take place between the pen and the paper, not before in a thought or afterwards in a recasting." That is what she means by writing in a "continuous present." Whether anyone regards the work as successful or not, satisfying or not, it could be refreshing for many writers to engage with her innovative methods and try to imagine how similar experimentation could help keep one's own nonfiction inspired and creative, unpredictably alive. A single creative writing objective that could be learned from *Tender Buttons?* Compose in such a manner that no software application could easily auto-complete every one of your sentences.

In July 1957, a thirty-year-old John Ashbery reviewed for *Poetry* magazine Stein's posthumous *Stanzas in Meditation,* a long poem that for the most part both baffled and delighted him. It reminded him of certain de Kooning paintings and the anfractuous prose of the late Henry James. Ashbery titled his review "The Impossible" and says of the poem something I think applies to a large part of Stein's most ambitious work, that she attempts "what can't be done, to create a counterfeit of reality more real than reality." He concludes by saying that if, upon finishing the book, "we feel that it is still impossible to accomplish the impossible, we are also left with the conviction that it is the only thing worth trying to do." After all, he reminds us, quoting Stein, "If it can be done why do it?"

Note: My reflections on Gertrude Stein were stimulated by Roy Morris Jr.'s recent biography, *Gertrude Stein Has Arrived: The Homecoming of a Literary Legend* (2019), a well-documented and entertaining account of her 1934–35 American lecture tour. For those unfamiliar with Stein and her work, I recommend as an introduction Lucy Daniel's *Gertrude Stein* (2009), a compact and captivating critical biography published as part of Reaktion Books's "Critical Lives" series. Marjorie Perloff's "Poetry as Word-System: The Art of Gertrude Stein" in *The Poetics of Indeterminacy* (1981) offers an indispensable overview of Stein's experiments in form and language.

*

The Best American Essays features a selection of the year's outstanding essays, essays of literary achievement that show an awareness of craft and forcefulness of thought. Hundreds of essays are gathered annually from a wide assortment of national and regional publications. These essays are then screened, and approximately one hundred are turned over to a distinguished guest editor, who may add a few personal discoveries and who makes the final selections. The list of notable essays appearing in the back of the book is drawn from a final comprehensive list that includes not only all of the essays submitted to the guest editor but also many that were not submitted.

To qualify for the volume, the essay must be a work of respectable literary quality, intended as a fully developed, independent essay (not an excerpt) on a subject of general interest (not specialized scholarship), originally written in English (or translated by the author) for publication in an American periodical during the calendar year. Note that abridgments and excerpts taken from longer works and published in magazines do not qualify for the series, but if considered significant they will appear in the Notable list in the back of the volume. Today's essay is a highly flexible and shifting form, however, so these criteria are not carved in stone.

Magazine editors who want to be sure their contributors will be considered each year should submit issues or subscriptions to

The Best American Essays
Houghton Mifflin Harcourt
125 High Street, 5th Floor
Boston, MA 02110

Writers and editors are welcome to submit published essays from any American periodical for consideration; unpublished work does not qualify for the series and cannot be reviewed or evaluated. Also ineligible are essays that have been published in book form—such as a contribution to a collection—but have never appeared in a periodical. All submissions from print magazines must be directly from the publication and not in manuscript or printout format. Editors of online magazines and literary bloggers should not assume that appropriate work will be seen; they are invited to submit clear printed copies of the essays to the address above. Please note: due to the increasing number of submissions from online sources, material that does not include a full citation (name of publication, date, author contact information, etc.) cannot be considered. If submitting multiple essays, please include a separate cover sheet with a full citation for each selection.

The deadline for all submissions is February 1 of the year following the year of publication: thus all submissions of essays published in 2020 must be received by February 1, 2021. Writers should keep in mind that—as with many literary awards—the essays are selected from a large pool of nominations. Unlike many literary awards, however, writers may nominate themselves. A considerable number of prominent literary journals regularly submit issues to the series, but though we continually reach out with invitations to submit and reminders of deadlines, not all periodicals respond or participate, so writers should be sure to check with their editors to see if they routinely submit to the series. There is no fixed reading period, but writers and editors are encouraged to submit appropriate candidates as they are published and not wait until the final deadline. For more detailed information and updates, readers should consult the *Best American Essays* section of the submission guidelines found on the Houghton Mifflin Harcourt website before submitting material: hmhbooks.com/series/best -american.

Much of the work on this annual book occurs during March and April, and so this year it coincided with the earliest stages of the novel coronavirus pandemic. The quarantines and lockdowns naturally made the usual editorial and production processes for this thirty-fifth edition all the more difficult. It's always a pleasure to acknowledge Nicole Angeloro's editorial talents and her ability to coordinate so many moving parts, but this time I especially appreciate all her extra efforts to get the project wrapped up while offices were closed for such a long duration. A heartfelt thanks to others on the Houghton Mifflin Harcourt staff who year after year help make this book possible: Liz Duvall, Mary Dalton-Hoffman, Jenny Freilach, and publicist Megan Wilson. I also thank my son, Gregory Atwan, for his expansive knowledge and support throughout every edition. And this pestilential spring the work would have been exceedingly difficult without the help of my wonderful daughter, Emily, who generously looked after her "high-risk" dad through his weeks of self-imposed isolation.

In addition, I'd like to thank a new friend, Peter Brier, for his inspiring literary conversations and for introducing me to the Huntington Library in San Marino, California, where I now—thanks to him and another good friend, Mimi Schwartz—enjoy the privileges of a reader. I am grateful to the Huntington Library as well; I had planned to rely on its incomparable resources for my comments on Gertrude Stein, but just as I had begun the work government precautions against the Covid-19 outbreak forced the library to close its doors. The Huntington's Reader Services, however, came to the rescue by making their vast network of databases available, enabling me to conduct all the research I required safely online.

It was an enormous pleasure this year to work with André Aciman. Though many now know him as a celebrated novelist, he is also a remarkable essayist who brought to this collection a unique appreciation of the essay's fluctuating and unpredictable character, its perennial connection to the mercurial mind of the first great prose experimentalist, Montaigne. Essays, as Montaigne originally saw them, were literally trials, attempts, ventures—provisional ways of understanding, the artistic products of uncertainty. In that sense, as this collection wonderfully shows, essays can also be thought of as valiant adventures into intellectual and psychological unknowns, into mysteries, public or private, that—despite our best efforts—we may never fully understand.

R.A.

Introduction

"*LO MI STO IN VILLA*," I am living on my farm, writes the exiled Machiavelli to his friend Francesco Vettori. The letter is dated December 10, 1513, and Machiavelli is in Sant'Andrea in Percussina, not far from Florence, where as a disgraced and exiled politician who was put in jail and then tortured, he is now reduced to living a very frugal, beleaguered, and careworn existence. "I have been catching thrushes with my own hands," he writes. "I would get up before daybreak, prepare the birdlime, and go out with a bundle of birdcages on my back . . . and would catch at least two, at most six, thrushes . . . I get up in the morning with the sun and go into one of my woods that I am having cut down . . . Later, with my household I eat what food this poor farm and my tiny property allow. After eating, I return to the inn, where there usually are the innkeeper, a butcher, a miller, and a couple of kilnworkers. I slum around and sink into vulgarity with them for the rest of the day playing *cricca* and backgammon, and these games lead to thousands of squabbles with endless abuses and insults . . . and we are heard yelling as far as San Casciano."*

But after spending all this time on the upkeep of his farm and all the drunken bawling and blustering, Niccolò Machiavelli finally pens one of the most splendid pages ever written by a man of the Renaissance: "*Venuta la sera, mi ritorno a casa ed entro nel mio scrittoio*":

---

* Translations drawn from Allan Gilbert, *The Letters of Machiavelli*, and from J. B. Atkinson and David Sices, *Machiavelli and His Friends*.

When evening comes, I return to my house and enter my study; and at the door I take off the day's clothing, covered with mud and dirt, and put on garments regal and courtly; and fitted out appropriately, I enter the venerable courts of the ancients, where, welcomed with affection, I feed on that food which only is mine and which I was born for, where I am unashamed to speak with them and to ask them the reason for their actions; and they in their kindness answer me; and for four hours I do not feel boredom, I forget every trouble, I do not dread poverty, I am not terrified of death.

Machiavelli will eventually let his friend know that he has been writing an *opuscolo,* a "little work"—not exactly a treatise or a tome of political philosophy, but rather something resembling an extended essay. It is as ruthlessly realistic as nothing the world has seen before, but it could just as easily be an unbridled fantasy dreamed up by an embittered and disenchanted man holed up in the country. The world would soon discover that the title of his *little work* is *De Principatibus,* better known as *The Prince.*

To write his book, Machiavelli needed a very private place. He needed to steer clear of all distraction, all menial gossip and mundane tasks, and find the time to mull over issues that the great historians and thinkers of antiquity had touched on but had never quite formulated and that he was resolved to distill in his skeletal *opuscolo.* I would like to imagine him confabulating with the ancients. I see him hesitate before sitting down to write, already anxious over the numberless times he's had to redraft what he'd written the day before. A side of him wants to reread the classics to glean further insights from their works, while another wants to find a semblance of coherence to his disjointed and failed career as a diplomat and politician. Or he might want to do a bit of both, sharpen his wits against theirs and hear them weigh in whenever he's been led astray. What he is doing is reassembling things he hasn't firmed up yet. What he wants is to let his mind roam as freely as it wishes in his drafts before committing anything to a final version. What he also needs is to be left alone and withdraw from everything bearing on the pointless tumult of his day-to-day life.

In this he cannot but remind me of another Renaissance man, Michel de Montaigne, the father of the modern essay, who merely sixty years after Machiavelli's letter recused himself as best he could from public life and shut himself up in his tower to write and be left with the wisest men of the ancient world. "We must reserve a back shop all our own," writes Montaigne, "entirely free, in which to establish our real liberty and our principal retreat and solitude. Here our ordinary conversation must be between us and ourselves, and so private that no outside association or communication can find a place; here we must talk and laugh as if without wife, without children, without possessions, without retinue and servants."

It took determined escapism for Montaigne to find his *arrière boutique,* as it took banishment and public disgrace for Machiavelli to settle into his *scrittoio;* but solitude is what freed both men to put to paper what couldn't have been more private and more reflective of who they were, what they thought, and how they thought, and ultimately what peculiar and totally unusual mindset had prompted them to write what they did. No one in the modern era had written anything resembling *The Prince* or the *Essays.* These works were born both from public life and from its opposite, solitude.

Solitude is a marvelous refuge, but it can be a scary thing, and all writers struggle with it, particularly when its shadow partner, loneliness, feels imposed or uninvited. The flight from others may be a precondition to any writer's life, yet few are the writers who have embraced solitude without hoping to limit its hold, without begrudging it as addicts begrudge their addiction. Sometimes writing is not so much an escape from society as it is a secret passageway that leads back into the very society they needed to flee, either by bringing them glory from those they've allegedly shunned or by immersing themselves so deeply in what they are writing that they manage to populate on paper a surrogate society that rivals the one they've fled. Writers write because it is their escape from a world in which they may not feel adequate enough, but it is also their way of justifying that escape, of claiming that it was their choice to banish the world, when in reality, as in Machiavelli's case, it was the world that had banished them first.

Machiavelli had a very good reason for writing *The Prince.* It was how he hoped to rehabilitate himself in the eyes of the Medici family, who had imprisoned, tortured, and ousted him from Florence. He was offering Giuliano de' Medici a manual for princes written by a seasoned politician who wanted to show that he held no grudges. All he was going to share with them were some very important ideas on how to acquire power and, once acquired, how to retain it. The irony was lost on no one, least of all on the author himself.

So here he is on his farm, with his thrushes, his firewood, his farmers, the endless squabbling and caterwauling till sundown, finally sitting down with the ancients, biding his time, gathering his thoughts before writing *The Prince*. I have often tried to picture what it was like to sit in what was probably an ill-lit, dingy, cold room, trying to focus while feeling his mind whipsawed so many ways. Machiavelli may already have a vague idea of what he means to write, but it may be more accurate to say that he does *not yet* know what to think on the subject until he begins writing about it. It is the *not yet* that always makes for an arresting piece of writing. Great writing is not the product of an outline, or of ideas that have already been fleshed out and are simply waiting to be transcribed to paper. As I imagine him, Machiavelli, like Montaigne, doesn't write an outline first to then spill his words on paper; he writes because he cannot write an outline. Thinking comes with writing, not before. He doesn't even know what the process of writing will uncover. He writes not only because writing is a better form of thinking but because writing, for all its allowances, is also a form of studied divagation. He strays, he experiments, he improvises, he juggles ideas, and relishes the freedom to think the unthought precisely because writing permits chaos but then redresses that chaos. Besides, the things he thinks he wants to write are literally unthinkable: unthinkable, in the sense that they are too horrifying, too dangerous for thought, but also unthinkable because they haven't been thought before and are difficult to fathom, to think through. They elide and resist thinking—and they could be entirely mistaken, hence in need of correction or erasure. The struggle to write what one hopes is entirely true, and the long incubation every piece of writing requires of a writer who is thinking difficult thoughts, are what ultimately give the writing its depth, its magnitude, its grace.

And this is the very essence of what an essay is. If it knew where it was headed, it would be a report, not an essay; if it had already concluded its argument, it would be an article, not an essay; if it had something to teach or censure, it might be a critique, or an opinion, but not an essay. If it narrated the struggles to recover, say from a terrible childhood, or from poverty, or abuse, loss, grief, addiction, sickness, accidents, and so many other traumatic experiences, it might be an exposé, not an essay. And finally, if, like a clever little ditty, it started somewhere, then meandered elsewhere, and finally, after all manner of agile acrobatics, pirouetted its way back exactly where it started, it would be a piece, but it would not be an essay.

An essay is like a story, only with the difference that the author may have no idea where he is headed. He might know what he feels and wants to say, but he may not know how to get there yet and, frequently, changes his mind midessay or even midsentence. But more importantly, an essay doesn't seek to conclude anything—at least at first—because it is more rudderless than anyone suspects; it does not even want to arrive at knowledge, because its main purpose is to speculate, to explore, to propose, to delay, to reconsider, and always, always to find a pretext to think some more. The last thing an essay seeks is closure; it prefers dilation, errancy, and the need to get lost, as one does when visiting a foreign city only to discover, by sheer happenstance, exactly what one didn't even know one was looking to find. The author of an essay dislikes certitudes and retains the right to change his mind, to cradle not just skepticism but indecision and contradiction as he is writing, even if in the polishing up of an essay he decides to erase all the leads he followed and all the messy footprints left behind on a road he realizes he should not have taken and which he doesn't want his readers ever to suspect he'd once considered. And yet it is the very foray, which he decided to discard and of which no sign exists any longer, that spurred his very best thinking.

An essay, as I said, embraces chaos but ultimately tames it. In the process, however—and herein lies the miracle—an essay may adventitiously uncover an idea, a truth, that only the act of writing could have propelled, because that idea or that truth did not exist before writing uncovered it—because, contrary to a foundational law of physics, something can indeed come from nothing, and the act of writing itself can ultimately generate as persuasive an idea as one that is born from research, from fieldwork, or from a well-formulated thesis. The struggle with the ineffable is what gives birth to the very best that can be thought and said. An idea, or the sense of an idea, has to be stalked, chased, tracked down, smoked out, mistrusted, trapped; and only once tussled with and pinned down can it be burnished and given its luster.

An essayist is someone who examines things in a manner that bears the stamp of his very private, personal, and peculiar manner of reading and interpreting the world around him. You may never know that the essayist is being entirely personal, because most tell-tale signs of a personality have been quietly removed or deftly covered up. But they are there and they are what spurred the writing.

It is this very private, personal source of writing that allows a writer to assume that what is true for him must be true for everyone else as well. It is the ultimate in presumption but also the ultimate in candor. To use Emerson's words, "To believe that what is true for you in your private heart is true for all men—that is genius. Speak your latent conviction, and it shall be the universal sense." An essayist presumes that the more he discloses his own idiosyncrasies and his idiosyncratic way of seeing things, the more he mirrors the readers' own.

This, to repeat, is what Montaigne discovered in 1571 when he finally withdrew to the tower of his castle and began writing things to which he eventually gave the unusual name of *essais,* from the French verb *essayer,* to try, to attempt, to test, to weigh, to assay. An essay is the child of uncertainty. It is not convinced of what others uphold, much less of what it itself upholds, if it catches itself upholding anything. There is never any real proof to what an essayist proposes, nor should there be any if it is, properly speaking, an essay. Yet the more private, the more universal.

Montaigne's essays required free rein to dither and digress; this was his way of looking for what he didn't know he was looking for. It was his foray into a twilight of thinking, probably at a time of day when all intrusions could be avoided, most likely toward sundown. To use the words of Proust about himself—Proust being perhaps the most reclusive writer known to literature—Montaigne's essays, like Machiavelli's *opuscolo,* were "not the children of broad daylight and small-talk but of darkness and silence." Darkness here is probably less a reference to inadequate lighting than a metaphor for what lies buried within oneself and has yet to be brought to light, uncontaminated by either distractions or social chatter or by what Barthes referred to as the *doxa* frequently cuddled by the *bien pensants* of the day. Proust goes further: "That which we have not been forced to decipher, to clarify by our own personal effort, that which was made clear before, is not ours. Only issues from ourselves which we ourselves extract from the darkness within ourselves and which is unknown to others." All an essayist says is, *This is what I see, this is what I know—or think I know. But it comes from me and from how I see.*

It may be false to claim that *The Prince* was written with difficulty or that it was an essay, much less a personal essay. But one could say the same of *Moses and Monotheism,* of *Culture and Anarchy,* and of *The Origins of Totalitarianism.* All these books are private and troubled meditations on something only their authors could have put to paper given their profoundly personal view of the world and their implacably penetrating, disbelieving gaze that questioned all received notions. They disbelieved the world, they disbelieved themselves. How each came to his or her view may be the result of instinct or of the very writing process to which they entrusted their courage, their minds, their trust, their faith. Writing would uncover something, most likely something they did not even know before they sat down to write. Writing allowed them to drift, which is another way of saying to think. The two are seldom very different.

This, in the end, is why an essay is always personal. The way this preface is personal—though I haven't said a thing about me here. And yet you'd have no difficulty picking up inflections of a temperament somewhere, or hints of attitude under allegations of composure and civility. Nor would it be hard to miss the muffled lilt of irony or the undertow of diffidence each time I knew, or thought I knew, what I wanted to say but had no sense of how to get there. I was unsure of myself when I started, didn't know how to grope my way about, or how much I'd have to struggle to lace together clumsy thoughts while burying all traces of my struggle to smooth the jolts between them. I didn't even know what the itinerary of this entire preface would be. I'd start with Machiavelli, because I liked the idea of how he withdrew after an ugly, meaningless day on his farm and found something bordering serenity in his books. I also wanted to bring up Montaigne, quote Proust and then Emerson—that much I knew, because each understood that the only truths worthy of a writer's time are those that end on paper. As for the rest, I kept hoping that one thing or another would eventually turn up to help me along. Something always turns up in an essay, either by chance or by the appearance of chance. It doesn't matter which. An essay always has an unforeseen itinerary, even if the itinerary reveals itself in the writing, after the writing, but never before. And sometimes I just don't want to know what I'm about to write; I want to trust, instead, that something far wiser will step in and just take over.

ANDRÉ ACIMAN

The Best
AMERICAN
ESSAYS
2020

How to Bartend

FROM *Freeman's*

1.

I WAS THE best of bartenders, I was the worst of bartenders. Everyone disagreed, depending on what they were looking for in a bartender. But everyone agreed that I was a mess in those days.

I still find it odd that I bartended. Most of my friends are surprised when I mention it. I never cared much for drinking, rarely spent time in bars, whether gay, straight, or questioning, but for a brief period of time in 1990, tending bar was what I did.

I was thirty, back in school, going for another graduate degree I wouldn't use. You might ask, as any rational person would, why I was trying for a third useless degree. Because I was dying, that's why. That made eminent sense to me at the time. To my mind, it was a most rational decision.

In Lebanon in 1990, the civil war was ending with a mighty crescendo, fifteen years into a regional disaster that tore my country and my family apart. In San Francisco, we were still in the middle of the AIDS epidemic, a disease that killed many of my close friends and within a few years would decimate an entire generation. Oh, and some four years earlier, in 1986, I had tested positive for HIV.

When I was informed of the news—the nice nurse sat me down in an oddly sized chair that made me feel like I was back in elementary school—I did what any rational person would do upon hearing that he had a short time left on this earth: I quit my nine-to-five corporate job, which was the last time I ever held one of those, and went on a six-month shopping spree. I'm sure I don't have to tell you that the most therapeutic sprees are those where you buy nothing of any use. Since I lived in San Francisco, where the weather was moderate for 345 days of the year, I ended up buying stacks of cashmere sweaters. Which, of course, led me to pack those sweaters and move back to Beirut, where the winter was even milder than in San Francisco. I wanted to be with my family because I was frightened and did not wish to die alone. I'd had to sit at the bedside of a friend as he slowly wasted away, alone because his family had disowned him, a vigil that many gay men and lesbians of my generation had to repeat over and over and over, sitting witness to a man's death because his family refused to do so. I did not want that for me.

Off to Beirut I went, my belongings stuffed in my exquisite, recently purchased luggage. I wanted to be with my family even though they were in the midst of a civil war. I sweated mightily as the bombs fell all about me because I was scared shitless. Or was I just too warm in cashmere?

A year later I was back in San Francisco, still not dead but soon to be, I was certain. I sat myself down and told myself that I was almost thirty years old and that I should start behaving like an adult. Sure, I was dying, but I had to decide what I wanted to do with the short period of time left to me. In other words, what I had before me was a terribly shortened version of what did I want to do when I grew up.

So I asked myself, Rabih, I said, what would you do if you had one or two years left to live?

And I said, Get a PhD, of course.

So I asked myself, Rabih, I said, you have an engineering degree and a master's in business and finance, what kind of PhD should you go for?

And I said, Clinical psychology, what else.

So I asked myself, Rabih, I said, how are you going to support yourself in school now that you're not working and you're in credit-card-debt hell because of all the fabulous cashmere sweaters you bought?

And I said, Why, bartend, of course.

See? A most rational decision.

2.

To be completely honest, I did not consider bartending until a friend told me there was an opening for a bartender where he waited tables. I had done nothing comparable in my life, nor had I taken any drink-mixing classes, so I was hired on the spot at that odd establishment. My friend worked in a good old-fashioned diner where every other day the plat du jour was meatloaf (probably the same one). I, on the other hand, was hired to work in the bar upstairs, a faux upscale taproom with an English private club motif: leather fauteuils, pretentiously bound hardcovers in fake bookshelves, and port in the well. In a stroke of genius, the owners had baptized the place the Nineteenth Avenue Diner.

As the newest member of the staff, I was given the day shifts, the slowest. The bar did not have many customers, not at first. I mean, why would patrons of a diner want a spot of sherry or a tumbler of Armagnac after their good old-fashioned burger and fries? Even though I wouldn't make much money, the situation suited me fine, for I'd discovered early on that working was not my forte. It took me less than an hour at the place to realize that I had to change some things in order to make the environment ideal for a person with my temperament. I could not remain standing for ten minutes, let alone an entire shift, so I moved one of the barstools behind the bar, next to the wall on one end, in order to be able to sit comfortably and indulge in my two passions, reading and watching soccer matches.

I don't know why the owners thought an upscale English bar needed four television sets and a satellite system (to show British period dramas?), but I was grateful. I was able to figure out how to find all the soccer games I wanted to watch. For the first month or so, working that almost empty bar was as close to heaven as a job could get.

3.

I'd played soccer all my life. I used to joke when I first moved to San Francisco that I had an easier time coming out as gay to

my straight friends than telling my gay friends that I loved soccer. Soon after I arrived, a friend and I started a gay soccer team,
the San Francisco Spikes. In the beginning, all the team's energy
was directed to playing in what was then called the Gay Olympic
Games, as well as other gay tournaments. By 1986, though, the
Spikes had registered in a regular league, amateur of course, and
by regular I mean that many of the guys on the other teams were
homophobic bastards, or, to use the Linnaean classification, assholes.

Our team was terrible at first. We would lose by scores of 6–0
or 7–0. We were considered a mockery. A player on an oppos-
ing team, a Colombian who went by the nickname Chavo, used
to gleefully celebrate each goal he scored against us by using the
hand signs for fucking. He would go up to every player on our
team, smirking, forefinger penetrating a hole formed by thumb
and forefinger on his other hand. We ignored the taunting.

We began to encounter problems when our team improved. I
believe it was during a game in the second season, against a team
consisting of police officers, that we had our first bust-up. While
the referee had his back turned, a cop sucker-punched one of our
players in the face. A hockey game broke out. For those of us who
had been regularly confronting the police at ACT UP demonstrations, that was our first chance to fight back without getting ar-
rested. No one received a red card. We won the game.

Chavo, however, received a red card the next time we played
his team. Toward the end of the match, we were leading by at least
two goals when he slide-tackled me, taking me out. His cleats dug
into my shin, my heels shot skyward. I thought my leg had been
amputated. As I lay on the turf, Chavo, ever the gentleman, yelled,
"I don't want to get your AIDS, faggot."

Usually I would not have allowed an insult without some sort
of witty comeback. I was a faggot, after all. Even something like
"You're not my type, bitch!" would have made me feel better. But
I was writhing on the dry grass, in such pain that what I really
wanted to scream was "I want my mommy!"

Chavo was kicked out of the match, which set a precedent. He
would get red-carded in every game he played against us after that.

We came in third that season, won our division the next.
Granted, it was not the highest division, but still. The fights lasted
for a season or so before the league clamped down. They even sent

a memo to all the teams stating that any player using the word *faggot* on the field would be automatically ejected.

Bless you, Mayflower Soccer League of Marin!

By 1990, when I began tending bar, the Spikes were one of the stronger teams in our division. We became just another regular team, except we looked better, of course, uniforms pressed and shirts always tucked in.

By 1996, half the players on the team had died of AIDS complications. Half the team, eradicated.

4.

I was leaning against the wall, slouched on my barstool, reading a long novel and minding my own business, when two frumpy-looking guys in color-splattered white overalls walked in. House painters, one presumed correctly. They plopped their hefty behinds at the bar, not at a table, which I hated, since patrons at the bar usually expected to be entertained by the bartender.

I knew I was in trouble when they asked, in a heavy Irish brogue, "Is the Guinness on tap?"

I pointed to the handle, which clearly stated GUINNESS in big white letters.

The answer to their second question was just as obvious. "Is that satellite?"

The third question was the most troubling: "Can we order food here?" No, no, no. These guys expected me to serve them, to actually work. How horrid. I should have kicked them out right there and then. The bar was a classy establishment, but it wouldn't remain so if we allowed Irish guys to drink there. I should have dumped the canister of Guinness. The bar was supposed to be faux English, not Irish.

I had to abandon my stool, present them with a fake smile, and inquire, "What can I get you?" in a disingenuous tone that I hoped would come close to sounding as if I cared. I needed the job.

They ordered their hamburgers, which meant I had to sigh audibly, write the order down, and walk it all the way to the kitchen downstairs. They finished their meal, drank their Guinness, and left me in peace. They didn't know what to make of me, so they didn't engage, not that first day. They just made sure before they

left that I knew how to work the satellite system. They told me
—warned me, really—that they would return the following day to
watch a soccer match. I groaned, they snickered.

Five of them stomped in the following day, loud, violating my
space. When I didn't put my novel down, I heard one of them say
something to the effect of "I told you." I held my finger up, both
to order them to wait while I finished my chapter and to point to
the television, where the soccer game was about to start.

Thus began our tug of war: they would try to get me to work, or
really just do something, anything, and I would try to get them to
leave me alone. It was instant chemistry.

That day one of them ordered something while the others pretended not to know what they wanted, forcing me to put in the order before another of them placed his. Back and forth, down the
stairs and up the stairs, etc. I allowed that shenanigan just once.
I also hated pouring Guinness, which was slower than molasses in
winter, and then I had to wait for the damn thing to settle. The
time it took for a pint of the dark concoction to come to rest was
too long for me to keep standing but not long enough for me to
return to my novel. They ordered their beers at different times,
and boy, could they gulp them down.

By the third or fourth visit, they began a running critique of
my bartending skills or lack thereof, particularly my complete in-
competence at pouring Guinness, which was nothing like pouring
other beers, as anyone with half a brain would know, they kept saying. Of course I had the best pouring technique: I tilted the pint
glass to a mild angle, and with the other hand I flipped the bird at
whoever was criticizing me at that moment. Another technique I
learned quickly was how to say "Fuck off" the Irish way.

You're doing it wrong.

Fockoff.

When one of them told me I should use an inverted spoon to
spread the drip of the beer, I offered him a couple of suggestions
on what to do with said spoon. I declared that there were as many
right ways to pour Guinness as there were Irishmen in the world.
I told them to walk over to an Irish pub, barely a block away, and
harass their countrymen with their orders. No, they did not want
to. They wanted to stay right where they were, and they wanted
their Irish beer. Finally I'd had it. If they wanted their stout poured

their way, they could bloody well come behind the bar and do it themselves. I could not be bothered.

Oh, they loved that. All at once I became the best bartender, and they regulars.

I stopped resenting them for making me work once they started pouring their own beers, a win-win situation if ever there was one. And they were generous with each other. When they went behind the bar, they would always ask if any of the others wanted a top-up, and they'd even wipe up any spillage.

The truth was that I was rude to them because I felt safe from the beginning. I felt at home with them. I had gone to high school in England, and my closest friend at the time was Irish. These men were older than me, but we actually had a lot in common, which was obvious from the first soccer game we watched together. They had a sense of humor that matched mine. They could, and would, make fun of everything. Nothing was sacred, and I couldn't tell you what a relief that was, living in the ever-earnest state of California, which had more sacred cows than all of the Indian subcontinent. They made fun of Americans, the French, the English, you name it. Boy, did they make fun of the English. They mocked Catholics, Protestants, Jews, and Muslims. No joke was out of bounds. They were ever self-deprecating. They tore into each other ruthlessly. And most of all, they made sure to insult me. I dished it right back, of course. I felt as if I were back with my family.

5.

Memory is the mother's womb we float in as we age, what sustains us in our final days. And I seem to be desperately crawling on my hands and knees to get there. Lately I can't remember what I had for lunch yesterday or where I put my reading glasses. I finally sold my car in frustration because I had to look for it whenever I wanted to use it, never knowing where I parked it last. But what happened thirty years ago—that I can remember.

What bothers me to no end is that I can't remember specific details about my Irishmen. I recall what happened, how they sat on the barstools, even some of the precise language used in our conversations. Yet for the life of me I can't remember their faces. I

can't tell you their hair or eye color, how short or tall. I'm unable
to recall any of their names. I remember the name of another bartender who worked the evening shift because my guys could not
stop making fun of it, Riley O'Reilly. They reserved their harshest
mockeries for Irish Americans and their green inanities. I remember the names of my manager, of the waiters who worked at the
diner. But not my Irish guys.

Incidents—incidents I remember clearly. I remember the Irishmen telling me a joke so good that I ended up sliding off my stool
and lying on the perforated rubber mat, laughing my ass off.

I remember this one time, the five were sitting in their usual
spot and another customer was sitting on the other side of the bar.
She was their age, appeared in good health except for a permanent tracheostomy. When I served her a third martini, she asked
me to move closer so she could whisper, "If I faint, please call 911."
I was back to reading my book when I heard an immoderate thud.
She was nowhere to be seen. All five men rushed over to where
she'd been sitting. I leaned over the bar and saw her splayed on
the floor. Luckily, one of the guys ran behind the bar, not to pour
himself a Guinness but to call 911. When the paramedics carted
my customer off, the guys made fun of me for a week, suggesting I
was too short to bartend since I could barely see over the bar.

It kills me that I can't remember what they looked like. All my
teammates who died, I remember. I still have team photos that I
look at every now and then. I have nothing of my Irish guys. They
too might all be dead now. When I walked off my job, it never occurred to me that I would one day wish I had some memento. It
never occurred to me to plan against regret.

6.

I should take that back. I don't remember all my teammates who
died, not all the time. I had lunch yesterday with a friend who had
also been on the Spikes since the beginning. I told him I was writing this essay, and we began to reminisce, about good times and
bad. We began to go over all those who left us. We reminded each
other of quite a few whom we hadn't thought about in so long:
the PhD student whom Thom Gunn wrote a soulful poem about;
the best player we ever had, Phil, who played semiprofessionally in

Australia and could juggle a ball in four-inch heels. I could barely see their faces in my mind's eye.

I reminded my friend of an Ecuadoran who played with us for two or three seasons before succumbing. I don't know why I think of Wilfredo so much, probably because he was such a character, a combination of terribly sweet and utterly strange. No matter what uniform we wore, he'd have the same top as the rest of us, but he declined to wear any shorts except his favorites, a pair of extremely tight red Lycra ones with no underwear. You could see that he was uncircumcised from the other end of the pitch. And he was a damn fine player too, just peculiar, more so than any of us. Most of the team was there at his deathbed to comfort him, his family having refused to have anything to do with him for years.

I told my friend at lunch that I couldn't remember Wilfredo's face, couldn't reconstruct it. How could we, he said, when we spent all our time staring at those shorts?

So many of my friends died while the world remained aggressively apathetic.

7.

To emphasize how odd the diner was, I should tell you this: out of a waitstaff of maybe thirty, only three were gay. Before I worked there, we used to joke that "straight waiter" was an oxymoron, but no, that rare breed did exist.

A flamboyant African American queen joined the staff some four months after I did. Let's just say he tipped the fabulous scale so much that he made me look butch. Of course we hit it off, becoming work-sisters, coining ourselves Butch and Butchette. One day it was Butchette who brought the Irishmen's lunch order from downstairs. As he was leaving, he pulled himself up toward the bar, standing on the lower rung of one of the stools—he too was short—and puckered his lips. I dragged my barstool over, pulled myself up, and we sister-kissed, both lifting our left legs in the air, synchronized swimming without the water. We separated—he returning downstairs, I moving my barstool to its usual position—without saying a single word.

I tried to get back to my book, but couldn't because the Irishmen kept staring at me.

"What?" I asked.

"Why did you do that?" they said.

"We're friends."

"He's a poof," they said.

Slow as I was, I only realized then that these guys had no idea I was gay. I should have noticed. They had been mocking practically everything about me—my looks, my height, my intellect, my going to school, my bartending, my Arabness, my not being Irish —but they had never brought up my homosexuality. They had no idea, which baffled me. I might not have been the most feminine of men, but I always figured that anyone who had seen me walk would recognize from a mile away that I was queer.

"I am as well," I said.

"No, you're not," they said.

"I am too," I said.

"No, no, you're not," they said.

"Oh yes, I am," I said.

"No, you're not," they said.

For them to believe me, I had to use their language.

"I take it up the ass," I said.

"But you play soccer," they said.

I returned to my book. They finished their lunch in silence. I knew they were shaken, or at least quite surprised, but I understood even then that they would not abandon me. It wasn't only that they could pour their own beer (it wasn't free; I trusted that each paid for what he poured). They liked me. They had always found me odd. Now they had to deal with my being odd and queer.

They did come back, and boy, did they deal with it. It took them twenty-four hours, maybe forty-eight, but they returned with a litany of terrible, puerile jokes. Shouldn't I turn my barstool upside down to sit? How many faggots did it take to change a lightbulb? Did I really nickname my goatee "prison pussy"? Was I a pain in the ass because I had a pain in the ass? Their mockery was relentless and relentlessly stupid. I loved it. As I already mentioned, we had quite a bit in common. Our emotional development had peaked in middle school. My jabs back were just as stupid, if not more so. I told them that Bigfoot had a better chance of turning me on than any one of them, that I liked men, not cheap imitations nor works in progress. The jokes would ratchet up in intensity when one of the waiters (not the waitresses) came up to deliver food, since we had over-under bets as to how quickly we could make them blush.

They did not stop making fun of me until I was no longer there.

To this day, whenever I think of them, I begin to giggle all by myself.

We did not have any serious conversations about my gayness. I don't think any of us were capable of it at the time. I remember once, about a month after they found out, one of them asked me if I was afraid of getting AIDS. I told him I was terrified. I was unable to say anything more than that, wasn't sure I could explain such terror. How could I explain that I had night sweats, not from any disease but from the fear of it? How could I tell them that my soul had already been crushed, that dread had shadowed itself unto my heart? I could not tell them I was HIV positive. It was eight years before my first book came out, announcing that fact.

8.

The World Cup was on that summer, and the Irish were in my bar almost every day, watching all the games when I worked. One Sunday there was an important second-round game at lunchtime, and the bar was as full as it had ever been, maybe twenty people, maybe thirty. I actually had to work. I made a rule that everyone had to follow: food orders were allowed before or after the game only. I was not about to leave a match to take an order down to the kitchen. My patience had limits, after all. About ten minutes before the start, I made sure everyone was settled. My Irish guys were in their usual seats on my left, already set with their burgers and Guinness. Some American remarked loudly that the announcers were unsophisticated because they called the game *soccer* and not *football*, as it was supposed to be called. My Irish guys let the poor deluded thing have it. *Football* meant Irish football, as every enlightened person knew, and he should stop trying so hard to be anything other than the provincial Yank that he was. Laughter, uproar, clanking of pint glasses.

And in walked Chavo.

I wasn't sure which of us was more surprised to see the other. His expression changed from stupid at rest, to shocked, to venomous. He hesitated a second or two before reaching the bar, but then he made his decision. He would proceed as his usual nasty self, bless his rancid heart.

"What the fuck are you doing here?" he yelled, loudly enough that the bar quieted.

I did what I always did when faced with a stupid question. What would I be doing standing by myself behind a bar, holding a wiping rag in my hand, surrounded by customers on the other side? Product modeling? My hands Vanna White-ing, *On this upper shelf we have the vodkas and gins?*

No, I replied with a sigh, "I work here."

"Heineken," he ordered.

Why did assholes always drink Heineken? I placed a bottle in front of him, noting that it would not be his first drink of the day. I began to wonder whether he played soccer sober or not. I waited for him to pay, but he went off on a mini-tirade.

"They shouldn't let someone like you work here," he said. "This isn't one of your neighborhoods."

I expected one of my Irish guys to say something. From the corner of my eye, I noticed them drinking their pints.

"What if you give us your disease?" he said.

"Get the fuck out of here," I said. "I'm not serving you."

I took away the beer bottle, turned my back to him, and with a dramatic flourish poured the undrunk Heineken down the sink. He went nuts, high-tirade time. He was going to kill me. I was a lowlife faggot. He was going to jump the bar and break my bones. I was going to regret being born. I was about to order him to leave before I called the police when he quieted, and then I heard a scramble. I turned around and he was already at the door, stumbling out.

Soon after a threat dissipated, the terror always peeked out from behind the patina of bravura and camp. As much as I was loath to admit it, the motherfucker terrified me, on the soccer field or off. I had to control the swell of shaking, steady my breathing.

"What were you doing?" I yelled at my Irishmen when I was finally able to turn around without worrying that anyone would see the panic in my heart. The delicious comfort of rage flooded my veins in hot, resuscitating waves. "How could you allow him to come into our bar and say those things?"

All five were clutching the pint handles the same way, glasses in front of them in the same position, completely dry. They stared at me. I noticed just how menacing they looked, and it took me a minute to understand what had happened.

"We should explain the Irish Hello," one said, holding the empty pint glass and punching the air as if it were a face. "Very popular greeting in Ireland."

"We were going to kill the cunt."

"We were so looking forward to painting his body black and blue."

"The son of a bitch ran out as soon as he looked our way."

"You may be a poof, but you're *our* poof."

"No one but us can call you *faggot*. That fucking faggot."

I told them I had many witty insults to throw at them but I was going to give them a break for twenty-four hours. I would even pour them their Guinness myself, an offer they refused—anything but that.

9.

I stopped working at the bar not long after that. Never saw my Irishmen again. The diner and its taproom would shortly turn into a Chinese furniture store.

I didn't get another degree. Somewhere along the line I would once again perform a one-eighty and reinvent myself again and again.

I did not die. So many friends did. I lost count of how many deaths I witnessed.

These days the San Francisco Spikes have about 150 members. They field four teams in different divisions.

I haven't been able to play soccer in quite a while. These days I run or swim, solo activities.

I did not die and I did not recover.

ELVIS BEGO

Ghost Museum

FROM *Agni*

SOMEWHERE IN THE platonic cloud of ideas a ghost museum
exists, a cave stuffed with works of art that do not cast a shadow
because in a way they *are* shadow. They may once have been stone
or bronze or painted canvas, but they have since been atomized,
disappeared. The Athenians knew even in their own day it could
all disappear. Sophocles told them at the very height of their culture that there was "nothing once known that may not become
unknown." The Greeks may be our fathers who died before we
were even born, but we like to remember that we crawled from underneath their toga. Like the traveler looking at the self-mocking
ruin of Ozymandias, we marvel at the erosive work of time.

If to see is to know, then some of the most famous works in
the history of art are the least known. Myron's wonderfully poised
Disc Thrower, which everyone has seen, hasn't really been seen in
two thousand years. We have Roman copies. Not a single work of
Apelles, the proverbial virtuoso painter, survives. Where is Praxiteles's famed *Aprohodite of Knidos* or his *Eros?* Everywhere and nowhere.

Half a century ago, when archeologists found the workshop of
Phidias at Olympia, they discovered a cup inscribed "I belong to
Phidias"—an astonishingly intimate find, which moves us more because none of his "real" work survives. His *Zeus* and *Athena* were
dead deities long before Nietzsche obituarized them. How much
of Titian, Pontormo, or Fabritius was once made and then un-
made, to say nothing of unknown work by unknown artists from
less-known cultures? How many copies are passed off as originals?

As Walter Benjamin famously observed, works of art have always been reproducible, but the methods and effects of reproduction have vastly multiplied.

This has perhaps intensified our tendency to value precedence, the original, and so we are all in some respect inadvertent Platonists, haters of shadows. Like Borges's heresiarch who takes mirrors and sex to be abominations because they replicate, we instinctively find copies tawdry even as we're inundated with a million reproductions and simulacra every day. But what is the nonphysical content of a copy? What sort of aura does it possess? If Phidias makes two identical bronzes, are they two separate works of art, or two instances of the same, or are they one original and one copy? Does the status of the second suffer for its belatedness?

When we stand in front of a Rembrandt, we feel the artist is present. When that same work is then newly attributed to one of his followers, as has so often happened in the past fifty years, we feel the genius suddenly drain out of it. The artist moves into the next room, though we know the object is every inch the same as it was. We want to be haunted by some sort of primary substance, that embryonic ideal aura.

All this is complicated further by technique, whether the medium is sculpture, print, or photography. For example, an "original" bronze is always a copy of the wax model used to create the mold from which the bronze is cast. In this case, the first original on the market is the copy, a freak of art technique and inverted temporality. That bronze is exactly as much the original as the death mask is the dead person's face. And you could say the mold itself is a copy of its own idea. Yet strangely we would never think of the wax model as anything but the ephemeral means.

If you are perverse enough you can make the argument that the distant copy is in a way a truer carrier of the first idea, the primary substance. Does it not, through the absence of the first body and subsequent reiteration of the primary concept, contain the reduced, thickened ghost, a denser memorial intersection common to both the original and the copy, strengthened, retraced the way a skater might trace and renew a figure in the ice?

All ontologies of art appear to be unstable, yet we cannot shake the feeling that we lose some measure of the aura with each replication.

We call destroyed works of art lost, and materially we recognize this to be obvious, even as we ignore another assumption we hold dear, that the total sum of a work exceeds its plastic elaboration. When we look at a masterpiece, we know that some part of the power of the work is invisible, numinous. In platonic terms, an original work of art is always a copy, a shadow, a contemptible substitute for the first idea, even if the idea was achieved through an accretion of spontaneous gestures, like, say, a de Kooning, or a performance. A destroyed work of art, then, returns the idea to its perfect, primary state. As for fragments, they exist in a limbo, neither here nor there. Fragments, said Cioran, not being alive, can no longer die. This seems to me as true of the lost works.

Among the lost works, we have the known unknowns (works we know we have lost) and the unknown unknowns (works we do not know we have lost). A tiny augury of art's Greek tragedy appears in Pausanias, who tells the story of how the celebrated courtesan Phryne tricked Praxiteles into gifting her his best sculpture and how he then, "lover-like," couldn't decide which was most beautiful. Clever as she was, Phryne had a slave rush in "saying that a fire had broken out in the artist's studio, and the greater number of his works were lost, though not all." Dismayed, Praxiteles runs out, loudly lamenting especially his *Satyr* and his *Eros*. In this way he betrayed himself. Soon enough, the wondrous *Eros* was carted off to Phryne's house. That sculpture has since passed back to its disembodied idea and into myth and memory, into literature, and into a meme that has shaped and reshaped tropes of art. It lives because it once lived.

We deem a destroyed work of art lost because we can no longer hold it in our sight, which seems to say that because we cannot see a painting, it no longer exists. A child's logical fallacy vests the gaze with the power to generate the object. Here it is immaterial whether the work is truly annihilated or merely buried or stolen. The *Laocoön* group was lost for a thousand years till it was discovered in Rome, as a copy of course, which then begs the question if it was *really* discovered at all. We tend to assume a copy cannot be superior to its original. This is the power of the aura of precedence. This is a cultured prejudice. Our culture is all about aura and authenticity, which plainly betrays our anxiety about the state of our own interiority, about the rickety plinth we stand on, whether we are true or simulated, whether we are copies.

This tyranny of precedence appears arbitrary when we look at time's smaller intervals, each now a microterminal. If this now is already gone *now,* and therefore part of the past by the middle of this sentence, you cannot perceive its nature as diminished or essentially distinct against the upcoming, terminal, and soon-to-be-past Now. Does the you of yesterday no longer exist in the you of today because yesterday was taken by the night? Since all things are constantly assaulted by the ineluctable future arrival of their own pastness, the modernist hierarchy of the present vs. the past appears entirely meaningless. This puts into question the claims of every periodization, and every modernism too, the moralistic imperative of every self-declared vanguard of Now. Which now?

Our death-stained literalism about linear time, at the expense of the relative permanence of space, seems to deform our grasp of the reality of things—so that even for the literalist, the world is never rid of its dead. It is permanently haunted by the myriad suspended temporarities.

A work of art is only truly independent when it is destroyed. Only then is it reduced to its essential self, being no longer parasitic on our gaze and consciousness, and no longer cannibalized by the gaze and consciousness of copyists. That is its essential paradox: it is most itself when it isn't, when its aura has been disembodied. Not to sanctify the Bazarovs of the world, armies of iconoclasts, fanatics of the ilk of ISIS or Savonarola, or curators of Entartung, but the disappearance of works of art raises these troubling questions of ontology. One could even go so far as to say that the work is only completed once it is destroyed, the same way that Shakespeare only becomes Shakespeare when he dies, when all his instances have been played out in space, when the list of his works can no longer admit addition, when you can put a terminal date in his biographical parentheses. And so with all of us.

We don't like to look at art's destruction. In art's essence something of our own resides, so that the demise of one suggests the demise of the other. There's a philosophical feebleness in our understanding of the categories of presence and absence—the moment of disappearance unduly wipes out the irreducible span of presence itself. Similar to a fragment, then, a "lost" work of art exists somewhere *between* loss and presence. If ideas are real, and they are, then they are real with or without a body. Yesterday is no less real now than today, precisely because tomorrow the ultra-real today you are inhabiting will be yesterday. If Phidias lived and died, he isn't entirely losable, and neither is his work. As was once said, the past isn't even past.

RACHEL CUSK

Driving as Metaphor

FROM *The New York Times Magazine*

WHERE I LIVE, there is always someone driving slowly on the road ahead. This is by the sea in the English countryside, and the roads are narrow and burrowlike, with high hedges on either side to protect the fields from the coastal winds. The roads are digressive in character, rarely traveling directly to a specific location. They branch across the flat fields like veins. It is hard to see what's coming, and because there aren't many vantage points, it's easy to get lost. Still, it's nothing that requires excessive caution. There's no particular reason for alarm, in fact quite the reverse. Yet people drive at 15, 20, 30 miles an hour. No matter how many of them you get past, there's always another one around the next bend.

A large portion of these drivers are elderly; their cars often are immaculate and new. At certain seasons there are also many tourists, trying to maneuver their caravans and motor homes along the winding narrow lanes. There are farms here, and so it is sometimes tractors that block the road, their big churning wheels flinging clods of mud behind them that spatter across your windshield or land thudding on the hood of your car. There are stretches where the road briefly straightens so that you can see far enough to overtake. People in big, powerful cars do this boldly and calmly and as though insensible to risk. Others hesitate and miss their chance. But no matter how many times you overtake, within a few minutes you will be stuck behind someone else.

This is a rural area, a backwater, and so it could be assumed that people here are rarely in much of a hurry. Alternatively, it could be said that the relative isolation of our lives can make us less aware of others and of the spaces we share. The coast road is the local

thoroughfare: it is usually necessary to take it to get nearly anywhere you might need to go. It passes through numerous villages
whose architecture of narrow bridges and constricted high streets,
though scenic, presents many obstacles to the flow of traffic. Problems are constantly arising, and though it could not be said to be
the fault of these quaint places, they take on something of the
character of an obstacle course when large numbers of vehicles
are trying to pass through them. The houses and cottages here
are old and have remained the same size, while the vehicles that
pass them have become larger: sometimes the cars are no more
than two or three feet from their windows. When the traffic is at
a standstill, some of the smaller cottages look dwarfed by the cars.
It is possible for the people in the cottages and the cars to look at
one another through their respective windows.

Several times a day, the road through a village will be backed
up both ways with stationary traffic, so that it can seem as though
there is some calamity or attraction there. Yet it is only the spectacle of people trying to do what they want where it is impracticable, for the reason that the vehicles are much bigger and more
unwieldy than the humans inside them. At the center of the jam,
you will often find, for instance, a giant motor home and a delivery truck face-to-face, unable to get past each other on the narrow
village street. This situation can sometimes have no solution other
than for one whole line of cars to reverse out of the village to allow the other to pass. If there is no one available to suggest and
oversee this operation, the impasse can last a long time. But usually someone assumes the position of authority. It often becomes
clear that many of the participants trying to unravel these snarls
are unable to fully maneuver and control the cars they are driving.
Others struggle to adapt to the change of circumstance and to the
necessity of acting as a group. Passing such a situation on foot, the
sight of the rows of human faces trapped behind and framed by
their windshields can be especially striking, as though a portrait
painter had drawn them.

On the open road, the slow drivers often fail to effectively communicate their intentions and aims. They will brake for no perceptible reason on a straight and empty stretch, or lose speed until
they come inexplicably to a halt, presumably unaware that there
is anyone behind them. If they signal, they do it too late in the

buildup to an action; often it is a case of working out what they are doing or mean to do by reading their driving behavior. A person who slows down at every junction or side road, for example, can be guessed to be looking for a turn but unsure of where it is. Others will brake suddenly when they pass a pub or a shop, evidently considering going in. The usual autonomy and separation of the car, its hermeticism, is reversed: the responsibility of driving, its visual and mental burden, is passed to those outside it. This area being a backwater, as well as a place for holidaymakers, it may be the case that people feel entitled to shed that burden here. In this remote place, the distinction between private and public worlds is less clear; the contract of the road, its status as a sphere of regulation by agreement, breaks down.

Yet there are others for whom this suggestion of lawlessness is the catalyst for signaling their intentions too zealously. They drive, as it were, sanctimoniously, as though to teach the rest of us a lesson. If they are going to make a right turn, they do it with a great fanfare of long-drawn-out indicating and braking. They obey the rules of the road so deliberately and self-consciously that their behavior becomes distracting, like actors threatening the integrity of a crowd scene by continually drawing attention to themselves and to the role they are being expected to play. It is as though, for them, the road is not a shared reality but a kind of fiction, an opportunity to become visible through disguise.

I have often heard it suggested that elderly citizens should not drive, and that is certainly a consideration where I live. I recall a few years ago, a woman of ninety-four killed a girl of ten at a pedestrian crossing. There have doubtless been a number of such incidents, but this one has stayed in my mind. One reason, I suppose, has to do with narrative, with the fact that the meaning of this woman's life was entirely altered by a single event at its end: this is not how stories generally work. Because she had already lived an unusually long life, I wondered whether the woman wished she had died before killing the girl, but the question of who is responsible in that situation appears to be somewhat opaque. You might see the car as a weapon lawfully placed in the driver's hands, in which case a woman of that age ought perhaps to have decided not to drive it; or you might see the laws that leave the decision to her as murderous. The car itself could be viewed as the murderer, since its capacity for destruction is so tenuously linked to that of the person driving it.

The reason most often given by the elderly for continuing to drive is the wish to retain their independence. Without a car, in other words, they would become subject to and entrapped by the reality of their own lives. There are many others for whom this is also the case, people whose arrangements—whether through force of circumstance or as a result of the choices they've made —would be made untenable by having no car. This is a rural area where few services are reachable on foot, so most of the people who live here fall into that category. To have no car, around here, is to be the victim of circumstance.

Several years ago, as the mother of small children and in a different place, I tried to live without using a car, an undertaking that made every action more effortful in what was already an effortful phase of life. I was not, obviously, trying to make things easier for myself: I was acting as I did out of principle. Something in my circumstances had made cars unappealing to me. Nearly everything I had to do would have been simplified by using a car, and I believe I saw in this fact a kind of death, as though by taking the easy way out I would miss the opportunity to learn the truth about my situation. Other people were often appalled by this decision and treated its consequences with mockery or anger. There were also a small number of parents who had made the same choice. It was not, largely speaking, a choice made for economic reasons; rather, it appeared to be an ethical response to the fact of parenthood, an attempt to take full responsibility for causing new individuals to exist.

These days I often witness the sight of a man or woman on a bicycle with a child and heavy shopping strapped to the back, pedaling furiously through the rain while being overtaken by a stream of cars, or drawn up at a traffic light beside a large clean car with another parent and child sitting calmly inside. The difference between the two is striking without being immediately comprehensible. They might almost be said to represent a mutual criticism; alternatively, they could be seen as demonstrating fundamentally different attitudes to children. If it is true that the cycling parent's behavior signifies at least the willingness to make greater efforts on behalf of his or her child, from the outside it can look like the reverse. The driver could even view the cyclist as irresponsible, for failing to adequately protect his or her child from the dangers of the driver's own vehicle.

Now that my children are grown, I drive again, as though my example no longer counts for anything. I remember, from other phases of life, the feeling of freedom and well-being that came from walking or cycling where I needed to go. But around here, such behavior would be impracticable. It would be the reverse of freedom, or at least it would appear that way. In the past people routinely walked long distances, but now the roads are full of cars. It seems to me that if I walked instead of driving, I would make contact with my younger self and with some truth I have forgotten, but to make that decision would almost be to make the fact of oneself too important.

The village where I live is on the coast road, and there is much talk among the residents about how to control the speed at which people drive through it. The slowness that frustrates and impedes us when we are trying to drive on the roads outside the village becomes immaterial from our perspective as homeowners; from this angle, it appears that people around here drive not too slowly but too fast. This might seem merely a good example of the corrosion of truth by point of view, but for those interested in the facts, one aspect of the mystery is easily resolved: the local council has performed numerous speed-testing exercises on the village road and found that a majority of cars passing through are indeed driving in excess of the speed limit.

We accept that we ourselves are guilty of speeding thoughtlessly through other people's villages but become sensitive in our own. Equally, it might be agreed that a person traveling by bicycle will feel an antipathy toward cars, yet once inside a car can immediately become irritated by cyclists, and as a pedestrian could dislike them both, sometimes all in the course of a single day. What is harder to make sense of is our certainty that everywhere other than our own village people drive at speeds so slow they become dangerous. The speed limit inside the village is 20 miles per hour. A car traveling at 30 would be going too fast, yet on the open road 30 can be considered too slow. Is the explanation, therefore, to be found in the inflexibility of people's speeds, their determination to travel at the same pace no matter where they are?

It is not clear to me whether the residents themselves drive too fast through the village. I have often noticed that people go in for the sermonizing kind of driving when they are in the vicinity of their own house, particularly if that house is troubled by traffic problems: it might be said that they have become disempowered to the degree that their individual example is the only recourse left to them. But equally there can be a feeling of entitlement, of being above the law, on your own terrain. It has been noted that one person often recognized speeding through the village is a member of the parish council, the chief advocate for the imposition of stringent speed restrictions. Where driving is concerned, there seems to be a peculiar difficulty in unifying different points of view: the personal reality of the driver is unassailable, even by his own conscious mind. At the "speed awareness course" that is the penalty for minor speeding offenses, participants are shown a short film in which, asked to concentrate on a particular aspect of the action, they entirely fail to notice a man dressed in a gorilla suit walk across the screen waving his arms and beating his chest. The point we're being asked to accept is that when we drive, what we see is not reality. But what, then, is it?

This is an area of abundant wildlife, and one characteristic of the roads around here is the number and variety of animals that lie crushed everywhere on the pavement. The bloodied heaps of feathers and fur dry out and decay over time, flattened by the traffic until they become pale two-dimensional shapes that are hard to identify any longer as what they once were.

The creatures most commonly killed appear to be the larger game birds—pheasants and quail—that are forever darting out into the road in front of passing cars. The smaller native birds tend to spring away at the sounds of approach, but these big ones seem to exist in a state of strange bewilderment, easily panicked and yet without the slightest idea of how to save themselves. If they are standing beside the road, the noise of a coming car will cause them to run directly in its path. The same is true of the small clumsy deer originally from China—muntjac—that were introduced to the countryside in the 1920s and have steadily multiplied. Rabbits and squirrels, though quick, are ubiquitous and without particular stratagems and are frequently flattened. Hedgehogs, on the other hand, move so slowly that the question of whether they are crushed or not presumably lies entirely in the hands of fate. Occasionally a stoat or weasel will zoom triumphantly across the road like a funny undulating mustache, too cunning to be caught. A roe deer of considerable size once lay by the road outside the village for the many weeks it took it to decay, so that every time you passed, you saw it at a new stage of this process, the sleeping form still there day after day, visible from some way off.

It is doubtless upsetting to hit a bird or animal, and many people swerve to avoid them. Others don't, either because the circumstances would make swerving dangerous or because—whether through indifference or rationality—they don't accept that responsibility for the situation lies in their hands. The driving situation, in other words, does not legislate for the behavior of animals, and so it is not the individual driver's job to avoid them. The car itself, of course, is designed to protect the people inside it, not the objects that cross its path. The airbag that cushions the driver in the event of a collision does not have its exterior equivalent to cushion the thing being collided with. Yet in its weight and hardness, its velocity and power, the car is a more or less invincible aggressor. Nothing soft and living stands a chance against it. When cars were first invented, the number of people and animals they hit was proportionately extremely high: the car was not yet a reality that could be anticipated and avoided, to such an extent that early cars had to have a person walking in front of them waving a red flag. An analogy might be that if rocks suddenly began falling from the sky, many people would be hit by rocks before they developed systems and strategies to protect themselves. Yet around here at least, these systems are rudimentary compared with the cars' own advancements in speed and comfort and passenger safety.

It is often regretted that children can no longer play or move freely outside because of the dangers of traffic; inevitably, many of the people who voice these regrets are also the drivers of cars, as those same restricted children will come to be in their time. What is being mourned, it seems, is not so much the decline of an old world of freedom as the existence of comforts and conveniences the individual feels powerless to resist, and which in any case he or she could not truthfully say they wished would be abolished. There is a feeling, nonetheless, of loss, and it may be that the increasing luxury of the world inside the car is a kind of consolation for the degradation of the world outside it.

*

Because of family circumstances, during the past couple of years I have had to drive frequently to the city and back. Emerging from the countryside, I am often startled by the ceaseless flow of heavy traffic. It seems incredible to me that so many people could be pursuing their private aims in this public way. But are cars people?

The spectacle of mass movement can look like something unstoppable, yet it is the easiest thing in the world to impede the flow of traffic or to bring it to a halt. On my route, there are long stretches of motorway, and the traffic is always thickening or lengthening as it meets and then absorbs an obstruction. It doesn't take much for this thickening to become an actual blockage. The sense of embroilment usually comes without any knowledge of what has caused it: often the first sign of it is an increase in awareness of the individual identity of other drivers. The forward-flying host begins to be differentiated; cars that seemed anonymous and distant become closer and more familiar; a web of recognition begins to form itself. The phase of community that follows—lacking any redeeming narrative or central event—is more or less indistinguishable from mutual entrapment. In this context, the difference between a car and a person is not entirely clear. Moments earlier, the car was the disguise for, and the enlargement of, the driver's will. Shortly, when the traffic stops, it will become his burden and his prison. But during the phase of transition, their mutual relationship seems more biological, a kind of linked separateness.

All sorts of things can cause the traffic to stop: an accident, a scene at the side of the road. It's often surprising how minor these dramas are, compared to the size and extent of their consequences. Their power is cumulative; it arises from the number of people exposed to the incident, however trivial. I once talked to a man who specialized in patterns of traffic flow, and he showed me a set of diagrams illustrating how the merest distraction in one place, something so small that it would cause passersby to briefly glance at it and therefore unconsciously decrease their speed, could over time result in the whole motorway coming to a standstill in another place miles away.

The drama of the road, once you have been observing and participating in it for a number of years, can be seen to change and develop. New themes arise or die out; new narratives emerge and either progress or fade away again; certain behaviors grow widespread and occasionally take hold. In Britain, for instance, the fast lane of the motorway is increasingly full of people driving slowly, while the other two lanes are often more or less empty. On a motorway, it might be said that you ought to know your place: here, increasingly, it is clear that a majority of people—wrongly or otherwise—believe that place to be the fast lane. This belief, and the behavior that attends it, has numerous consequences, one of which is that it is now almost impossible to get quickly where you want to go. Rather than representing an opportunity for passing, the fast lane is dominated by the person going most slowly, who dictates the speed at which everything behind him is traveling.

As a result, despite the fact that the rules of the road forbid it, people here are now deciding to overtake on the inside. There is some confusion in Britain about what this practice should be called: *undertaking* is—it would seem—the logical formulation, despite its funereal associations. It used to be the case that only reckless or seemingly lawless drivers would undertake, but now a wide range of people can be seen doing it, to the extent that when the traffic is heavy, the middle and slow lanes often move faster than the fast one. Undertaking is perceived to be cheating, but the more people do it, the more it becomes justified as a response to the corruption—as it were—of the principle of the fast lane. People decide to take things into their own hands; if there is no longer any fast lane to provide a context for their aims and abilities, they must act for themselves.

On motorways, often a truck will abruptly swerve out into the fast lane to overtake another truck, its size operating as a kind of authority. From a distance, the trucks seem more or less indistinguishable from each other: their differences in speed are minimal; the reasons for one of them to overtake another are not entirely clear. The drama of this act, being slow to accrue, is therefore unexpected when it comes, but its apparent violence is quickly undermined by the bulk and slowness of the perpetrator. A long line of car drivers quickly builds up behind to watch him inching past a vehicle as slow and cumbersome as his own. When he has succeeded, they hurtle by him with contempt. If the difference in speed between the two participants is sufficiently minimal, the contest can take a long time and cover many miles of ground, and when this happens, the overtaking driver becomes, at a certain point, an aggressor again. His lack of power is having serious consequences: angry as they might be, the cars can't get past him. He has rendered them helpless.

It seems possible that people experience more extreme emotions when they drive, and reveal cruder prejudices, than they might otherwise be aware of or admit to. Perhaps the soldiers of the past, in their suits of armor, felt similarly disinhibited and more capable of violence. Road rage is a common occurrence: people can often be seen shouting or gesticulating at one another from their cars, whereas in the street or other public places, such violent outbursts and attacks are rare. Once you're inside a car, it becomes permissible to comment on those outside it, to remark on their appearance or demeanor, with a brazenness absent from most social situations. The occupants of a moving vehicle might even feel licensed to heckle or harass those they see, yet when the car is stripped of its power—by being stopped by traffic lights, for instance, or at a standstill in a traffic jam—and those occupants are exposed, their violence and aggression can rarely be sustained. They may even be frightened of being confronted in the flesh. It has often been observed that people behave in their cars as though they cannot be seen.

Recently, stuck in a traffic jam, I saw an elderly and respectable-looking man leaping wildly and jerkily in his seat, his arms flailing, his face half demented with anger, shouting things at other drivers that could not be heard through the glass.

Occasionally I meet a person who has never learned to drive. Sometimes he or she is a city-dweller for whom the need to learn has never arisen with sufficient force. Sometimes a lack of opportunity is the cause; sometimes privilege is. There are also people who appear to have known from the beginning that driving wasn't for them. Often they are individuals society might label as sensitive or impractical or otherworldly; sometimes they are artists of one kind or another.

I myself never considered not learning to drive. Had I not learned, my life would doubtless have taken a somewhat different course: I would probably not have been able to live here on the coast, for instance. Yet I don't remember it as having been much of a choice at the time; I don't recall having a sense of the alternatives.

I think about it sometimes, the life I would have lived if I hadn't

learned to drive. When I look at my history of driving, I begin to
see in it a brutalizing element. That history, I suppose, has been
analogous to the history of my own will, of all the things I have
made happen that wouldn't have occurred naturally on their own.
Increasingly I find myself wondering at the nature of the story it
has made up: rived with contradictions and inconsistencies and
problems of point of view, its relationship to the truth opaque.
My impatience with the slow drivers on these coastal roads, for
instance, remains at odds with my fear of cycling on those same
roads: perhaps it is myself I am afraid of. Despite my claims to
equality, when my husband and I go somewhere together by car,
I automatically get in the passenger seat. At busy or complicated
junctions, I find myself becoming self-conscious and nervous about
reading the situation: I worry I don't see things the way everyone
else does, a quality that otherwise might be considered a strength.
Sometimes, stuck on the coast road behind the slow drivers while
they decide whether or not they want to turn left, it strikes me that
the true danger of driving might lie in its capacity for subjectivity,
and in the weapons it puts at subjectivity's disposal. But how can
you know when the moment has arrived at which you are no longer capable of being objective?

Recently, renting a car alone on a trip abroad, I realized that
something had changed: the world no longer seemed entirely familiar to me. I struggled to comprehend the strange layout of the
car's controls; navigating out of the parking lot, I couldn't get a
sense of the shape and size of my vehicle, and the interface of
the foreign motorway was at moments unintelligible to me. Other
drivers surged up impatiently behind me, sounding their horns.
I had forgotten, it seemed, how to drive; or rather, the degree of
responsibility that driving entails suddenly seemed unmanageable
to me. Why was everyone else not likewise crippled by this realization?

I moved into the slow lane, but trucks loomed up in the rearview
mirror one after another and then overtook me, their huge forms
seeming about to suck me under as they roared past. I wanted to
pull over, but the inescapable fact was that I had to remain on
the motorway in order to get off it. On that wide, gray, unfamiliar
road, swept along in the anarchic tumult of speeding cars, every
moment all at once seemed to contain the possibility of disaster,
of killing or being killed: it was as if driving were a story I had sud-

denly stopped believing in, and without that belief, I was being
overwhelmed by the horror of reality. The river of cars plummeted
on, relentless and unheeding. But the fact of myself, of my alone-
ness, had somehow been exposed.

Back home, rounding a bend on one of the empty roads where
I live, I came upon an overturned sports car on the roadside. It
was a hot summer's day: the upside-down car had its roof down.
Lying stiffly beside it amid the foaming white cow parsley were its
occupants, a man and a woman, their pale legs sticking straight
out in front of them, their shocked faces as rigid as dolls' faces,
their summer clothes askew. The man still had his sunglasses on;
the woman's broad-brimmed hat lay in the middle of the road.
The accident could only just have happened, but no one had seen
it, and there was no one there.

BARBARA EHRENREICH

The Humanoid Stain

FROM *The Baffler*

IN 1940 FOUR teenage boys stumbled, almost literally, from German-occupied France into the Paleolithic Age. As the story goes, and there are many versions of it, they had been taking a walk in the woods near the town of Montignac when the dog accompanying them suddenly disappeared. A quick search revealed that their animal companion had fallen into a hole in the ground, so —in the spirit of Tintin, with whom they were probably familiar —the boys made the perilous fifty-foot descent down to find it. They found the dog and much more, especially on return visits illuminated with paraffin lamps. The hole led to a cave, the walls and ceilings of which were covered with brightly colored paintings of animals unknown to the twentieth-century Dordogne—bison, aurochs, and lions. One of the boys, an apprentice mechanic, later reported that, stunned and elated, they began to dart around the cave like "a band of savages doing a war dance." Another recalled that the painted animals in the flickering light of the boys' lamps also seemed to be moving. "We were completely crazy," yet another said, although the buildup of carbon dioxide in a poorly ventilated cave may have had something to do with that.

This was the famous and touristically magnetic Lascaux cave, which eventually had to be closed to visitors lest their exhalations spoil the artwork. Today, almost a century later, we know that Lascaux is part of a global phenomenon, originally referred to as "decorated caves." They have been found on every continent except Antarctica—at least 350 of them in Europe alone, thanks to the cave-rich Pyrenees—with the most recent discoveries in Borneo (2018) and the Balkans (April 2019). Uncannily, given the distances that separate them, all these caves are adorned with similar "decorations": handprints or stencils of human hands, abstract designs containing dots and crosshatched lines, and large animals, both carnivores and herbivores, most of them now extinct. Not all of these images appear in each of the decorated caves—some feature only handprints or megafauna. Scholars of paleoarcheology infer that the paintings were made by our distant ancestors, although the caves contain no depictions of humans doing any kind of painting.

There are humanlike creatures, though, or what some archeologists cautiously call "humanoids," referring to the bipedal stick figures that can sometimes be found on the margins of the panels containing animal shapes. The nonhuman animals are painted with almost supernatural attention to facial and muscular detail, but, no doubt to the disappointment of tourists, the humanoids painted on cave walls have no faces.

This struck me with unexpected force, no doubt because of my own particular historical situation almost twenty thousand years after the creation of the cave art in question. In about 2002 we had entered the age of "selfies," in which everyone seemed fascinated by their electronic self-portraits—clothed or unclothed, made up or natural, partying or pensive—and determined to propagate them as widely as possible. Then in 2016 America acquired a president of whom the kindest thing that can be said is that he is a narcissist. This is a sloppily defined psychological condition, I admit, but fitting for a man so infatuated with his own image that he decorated his golf clubs with fake *Time* magazine covers featuring himself. On top of all this, we have been served an eviction notice from our own planet: the polar regions are turning into meltwater. The residents of the Southern Hemisphere are pouring northward toward climates more hospitable to crops. In July the temperature in Paris reached a record-breaking 108.7 degrees Fahrenheit.

You could say that my sudden obsession with cave art was a pallid version of the boys' descent from Nazi-dominated France into the Lascaux cave. Articles in the *New York Times* urged distressed readers to take refuge in "self-care" measures like meditation, nature walks, and massages, but none of that appealed to me. Instead I took intermittent breaks from what we presumed to call "the Resistance" by throwing myself down the rabbit hole of paleoarcheological scholarship. In my case, it was not only a matter of escape. I found myself exhilarated by our comparatively ego-free ancestors who went to great lengths, and depths, to create some of the world's most breathtaking art—and didn't even bother to sign their names.

Auroch Bites Man

Cave art had a profound effect on its twentieth-century viewers, including the young discoverers of Lascaux, at least one of whom camped at the hole leading to the cave over the winter of 1940–41 to protect it from vandals and perhaps Germans. More illustrious visitors had similar reactions. In 1928 the artist and critic Amédée Ozenfant wrote of the art in the cave, "Ah, those hands! Those silhouettes of hands, spread out and stenciled on an ochre ground! Go and see them. I promise you the most intense emotion you have ever experienced." He credited the Paleolithic artists with inspiring modern art, and to a certain degree they did. Jackson Pollock honored them by leaving handprints along the top edge of at least two of his paintings. Pablo Picasso reportedly visited the famous Altamira cave before fleeing Spain in 1934 and emerged saying, "Beyond Altamira, all is decadence."

Of course, cave art also inspired the question raised by all truly arresting artistic productions: "But what does it *mean*?" Who was its intended audience and what were they supposed to derive from it? The boy discoverers of Lascaux took their questions to one of their schoolmasters, who roped in Henri Breuil, a priest familiar enough with all things prehistoric to be known as "the pope of prehistory." Unsurprisingly, he offered a "magico-religious" interpretation, with the prefix *magico* serving as a slur to distinguish Paleolithic beliefs, whatever they may have been, from the reigning monotheism of the modern world. More practically, he proposed that the painted animals were meant to magically attract the actual animals they represented, the better for humans to hunt and eat them.

Unfortunately for this theory, it turns out that the animals on cave walls were not the kinds that the artists usually dined on. The creators of the Lascaux art, for example, ate reindeer, not the much more formidable herbivores pictured in the cave, which would have been difficult for humans armed with flint-tipped

spears to bring down without being trampled. Today many scholars answer the question of meaning with what amounts to a shrug:
"We may never know."

If sheer curiosity, of the kind that drove the Lascaux discoverers, isn't enough to motivate a search for better answers, there
is a moral parable reaching out to us from the cave at Lascaux.
Shortly after its discovery, the one Jewish boy in the group was ap-
prehended and sent, along with his parents, to a detention center
that served as a stop on the way to Buchenwald. Miraculously, he
was rescued by the French Red Cross, emerging from captivity as
perhaps the only person on Earth who had witnessed both the
hellscape of twentieth-century fascism and the artistic remnants
of the Paleolithic age. The latter offered no glimpse of an earthly
paradise such as modern keto-drunk paleophiles like to imagine,
in which our distant ancestors lounged around making up dance
tunes and gnawing on ungulate bones. As we know from the ar-
cheological record, it was a time of relative peace among humans.
No doubt there were homicides and tensions between and within
human bands, but it would be at least another ten thousand years
before the invention of war as an organized collective activity. The
cave art suggests that humans once had better ways to spend their
time.

If they were humans; and the worldwide gallery of known cave
art offers so few stick figures or bipeds of any kind that we cannot be entirely sure. If the Paleolithic cave painters could create
such perfectly naturalistic animals, why not give us a glimpse of
the painters themselves? Almost as strange as the absence of human images in caves is the low level of scientific interest in their
absence. In his book *What Is Paleolithic Art?*, the world-class paleoarcheologist Jean Clottes devotes only a couple of pages to the issue, concluding that "the essential role played by animals evidently
explains the small number of representations of human beings. In
the Paleolithic world, humans were not at the center of the stage."
A paper published, oddly enough, by the Centers for Disease Control and Prevention expresses puzzlement over the omission of
naturalistic depictions of humans, attributing it to Paleolithic people's "inexplicable fascination with wildlife" (not that there were
any nonwild animals around at the time).

The marginality of human figures in cave paintings suggests
that, at least from a human point of view, the central drama of the

Paleolithic went on between the various megafauna—carnivores and large herbivores. So depleted is our own world of megafauna that it is hard to imagine how thick on the ground large mammals once were. Even the herbivores could be dangerous for humans, if mythology offers any clues: think of the buffalo demon killed by the Hindu goddess Durga, or of the Cretan half-man, half-bull Minotaur who could only be subdued by confining him to a labyrinth, which was, incidentally, a kind of cave. Just as potentially edible herbivores like aurochs (giant, now-extinct cattle) could be dangerous, death-dealing carnivores could be inadvertently helpful to humans and their humanlike kin, for example, by leaving their half-devoured prey behind for humans to finish off. The Paleolithic landscape offered a lot of large animals to watch and plenty of reasons to keep a close eye on them. Some could be eaten—after, for example, being corralled into a trap by a band of humans; many others would readily eat humans.

Yet despite the tricky and life-threatening relationship between Paleolithic humans and the megafauna that composed so much of their environment, twentieth-century scholars tended to claim cave art as evidence of an unalloyed triumph for our species. It was a "great spiritual symbol," one famed art historian, himself an escapee from Nazism, proclaimed, of a time when "man had just emerged from a purely zoological existence, when instead of being dominated by animals, he began to dominate them." But the stick figures found in caves like Lascaux and Chauvet do not radiate triumph. By the standards of our own time, they are excessively self-effacing and, compared to the animals portrayed around them, pathetically weak. If these faceless creatures were actually grinning in triumph, we would of course have no way of knowing it.

Meatheads

We are left with one tenuous clue as to the cave artists' sense of their status in the Paleolithic universe. While twentieth-century archeologists tended to solemnize prehistoric art as "magico-religious" or "shamanic," today's more secular viewers sometimes detect a vein of sheer silliness. For example, shifting to another time and painting surface, India's Mesolithic rock art portrays few human stick figures; those that are portrayed have been described

by modern viewers as "comical," "animalized," and "grotesque." Or
consider the famed "birdman" image at Lascaux, in which a stick
figure with a long skinny erection falls backward at the approach
of a bison. As Joseph Campbell described it, operating from within
the magico-religious paradigm,

> A large bison bull, eviscerated by a spear that has transfixed its anus and
> emerged through its sexual organ, stands before a prostrate man. The
> latter (the only crudely drawn figure, and the only human figure in the
> cave) is rapt in a shamanistic trance. He wears a bird mask; his phallus,
> erect, is pointing at the pierced bull; a throwing stick lies on the ground
> at his feet; and beside him stands a wand or staff, bearing on its tip the
> image of a bird. And then, behind this prostrate shaman, is a large rhi-
> noceros, apparently defecating as it walks away.

Take out the words *shaman* and *shamanistic* and you have a description of a crude—very crude—interaction of a humanoid with
two much larger and more powerful animals. Is he, the humanoid, in a trance or just momentarily overcome by the strength and
beauty of the other animals? And what qualifies him as a shaman
anyway—the bird motif, which paleoanthropologists, drawing on
studies of extant Siberian cultures, automatically associated with
shamanism? Similarly, a bipedal figure with a stag's head, found in
the Trois Frères cave in France, is awarded shamanic status, making him or her a kind of priest, although objectively speaking he
might as well be wearing a party hat. As Judith Thurman wrote in
the essay that inspired Werner Herzog's film *The Cave of Forgotten
Dreams,* "Paleolithic artists, despite their penchant for naturalism,
rarely chose to depict human beings, and then did so with a crude-
ness that smacks of mockery."

But who are they mocking, other than themselves and, by ex-
tension, their distant descendants, ourselves? Of course, our reactions to Paleolithic art may bear no connection to the intentions
or feelings of the artists. Yet there are reasons to believe that Paleolithic people had a sense of humor not all that dissimilar from
our own. After all, we do seem to share an aesthetic sensibility
with them, as evidenced by modern reactions to the gorgeous Paleolithic depictions of animals. As for possible jokes, we have a
geologist's 2018 report of a series of fossilized footprints found
in New Mexico. They are the prints of a giant sloth, with much

smaller human footprints *inside* them, suggesting that the humans were deliberately matching the sloth's stride and following it from a close distance. Practice for hunting? Or, as one science writer for *The Atlantic* suggested, is there "something almost playful" about the superimposed footprints, suggesting "a bunch of teenage kids harassing the sloths for kicks"?

Then there is the mystery of the exploding Venuses, where we once again encounter the thin line between the religious ("magico," of course) and the ridiculous. In the 1920s, in what is now the Czech Republic, archeologists discovered the site of a Paleolithic ceramics workshop that seemed to specialize in carefully crafted little figures of animals and, intriguingly, of fat women with huge breasts and buttocks (although, consistent with the fashion of the times, no faces). These were the "Venuses," originally judged to be either "fertility symbols" or examples of Paleolithic pornography. To the consternation of generations of researchers, the carefully crafted female and animal figures consisted almost entirely of fragments. Shoddy craftsmanship, perhaps? An overheated kiln? Then, in 1989, an ingenious team of archeologists figured out that the clay used to make the figurines had been deliberately treated so that it would explode when tossed into a fire, creating what an art historian called a loud—and one would think, dangerous—display of "Paleolithic pyrotechnics." This, the *Washington Post*'s account concluded ominously, is "the earliest evidence that man created imagery only to destroy it."

Or we could look at the behavior of extant Stone Age people, which is by no means a reliable guide to the behavior of our distant ancestors but may contain clues as to their comical abilities. Evolutionary psychiatrists point out that anthropologists contacting previously isolated peoples like nineteenth-century Australian aborigines found them joking in ways comprehensible even to anthropologists. Furthermore, anthropologists report that many of the remaining hunter-gatherers are "fiercely egalitarian," deploying humor to subdue the ego of anyone who gets out of line:

> Yes, when a young man kills much meat he comes to think of himself as a chief or a big man, and he thinks of the rest of us as his servants or inferiors. We can't accept this. We refuse one who boasts, for someday his pride will make him kill somebody. So we always speak of his meat as worthless. This way we cool his heart and make him gentle.

Some lucky hunters don't wait to be ridiculed, choosing instead to disparage the meat they have acquired as soon as they arrive back at base camp. In the context of a close-knit human group, self-mockery can be self-protective.

In the Paleolithic, humans were probably less concerned about the opinions of their conspecifics than with actions and intentions of the far more numerous megafauna around them. Would the herd of bison stop at a certain watering hole? Would lions show up to attack them? Would it be safe for humans to grab at whatever scraps of bison were left over from the lions' meal? The vein of silliness that seems to run through Paleolithic art may grow out of an accurate perception of humans' place in the world. Our ancestors occupied a lowly spot in the food chain, at least compared to the megafauna, but at the same time they were capable of understanding and depicting how lowly it was. They knew they were meat, and they also seemed to *know* that they knew they were meat—meat that could think. And that, if you think about it long enough, is almost funny.

Eyes Without a Face

Paleolithic people were definitely capable of depicting more realistic humans than stick figures—human figures with faces, muscles, and curves formed by pregnancy or fat. Tiles found on the floor of the La Marche cave in France are etched with distinctive faces, some topped with caps, and have been dated to fourteen to fifteen thousand years ago. A solemn, oddly triangular female face carved in ivory was found in late nineteenth-century France and recently dated to about twenty-four thousand years ago. Then there are the abovementioned "Venus" figurines found scattered about Eurasia from about the same time. But all these bits of artwork are small and were apparently meant to be carried around, like amulets perhaps, as cave paintings obviously could not be. Cave paintings stay in their caves.

What is it about caves? The attraction of caves as art studios and galleries does not stem from the fact that they were convenient for the artists. In fact, there is no evidence of continuous human habitation in the decorated caves, and certainly none in the deepest, hardest-to-access crannies reserved for the most spectacular animal paintings. Cave artists are not to be confused with "cavemen."

Nor do we need to posit any special human affinity for caves, since the art they contain came down to us through a simple process of natural selection: outdoor art, such as figurines and painted rocks, is exposed to the elements and unlikely to last for tens of thousands of years. Paleolithic people seem to have painted all kinds of surfaces, including leather derived from animals as well as their own bodies and faces, with the same kinds of ochre they used on cave walls. The difference is that the paintings on cave walls were well enough protected from rain and wind and climate change to survive for tens of millennia. If there was something special about caves, it was that they are ideal storage lockers. "Caves," as paleoarcheologist April Nowell puts it, "are funny little microcosms that protect paint."

If the painters of Lascaux were aware of the preservative properties of caves, did they anticipate future visits to the same site, either by themselves or others? Before the intrusion of civilization into their territories, hunter-gatherers were "nonsedentary" people, meaning perpetual wanderers. They moved to follow seasonal animal migrations and the ripening of fruits, probably even to escape from the human feces that inevitably piled up around their campsites. These smaller migrations, reinforced by intense and oscillating climate change in the Horn of Africa, added up to the prolonged exodus from that continent to the Arabian Peninsula and hence to the rest of the globe. With so much churning and relocating going on, it's possible that Paleolithic people could conceive of returning to a decorated cave or, in an even greater leap of the imagination, foresee visits by others like themselves. If so, the cave art should be thought of as a sort of hard drive and the paintings as information: not just "here are some of the animals you will encounter around here," but *Here we are, creatures like yourselves, and this is what we know.*

Multiple visits by different groups of humans, perhaps over long periods of time, could explain the strange fact that, as the intrepid French boys observed, the animals painted on cave walls seem to be moving. There is nothing supernatural at work here. Look closely, and you see that the animal figures are usually composed of superimposed lines, suggesting that new arrivals in the cave painted over the lines that were already there, more or less like children learning to write the letters of the alphabet. So the cave was not merely a museum. It was an art school where people learned to paint from those who had come before them and went on to apply their skills to the next suitable cave they came across. In the process, and with some help from flickering lights, they created animation. The movement of bands of people across the landscape led to the apparent movement of animals on the cave walls. As humans painted over older artwork, moved on, and painted again, over tens of thousands of years, cave art—or, in the absence of caves, rock art—became a global meme.

There is something else about caves. Not only were they storage spaces for precious artwork, they were also gathering places for humans, possibly up to a hundred at a time in some of the larger chambers. To paleoanthropologists, especially those leaning toward magico-religious explanations, such spaces inevitably suggest *rituals,* making the decorated cave a kind of cathedral within which humans communed with a higher power. Visual art may have been only one part of the uplifting spectacle; recently, much attention has been paid to the acoustical properties of decorated caves and how they may have generated awe-inspiring reverberant sounds. People sang, chanted, or drummed, stared at the lifelike animals around them, and perhaps got high: the cave as an ideal venue for a rave. Or maybe they took, say, "magic mushrooms" they found growing wild, and *then* painted the animals, a possibility suggested by a few modern reports from African San rock artists who dance themselves into a trance state before getting down to work.

Each decoration of a new cave, or redecoration of an old one, required the collective effort of tens or possibly scores of people. Twentieth-century archeologists liked to imagine they were seeing the work of especially talented individuals—artists or shamans. But as Gregory Curtis points out in his book *The Cave Painters,* it took a crowd to decorate a cave—people to inspect the cave walls for cracks and protuberances suggestive of megafauna shapes, people to haul logs into the cave to construct the scaffolding from which the artists worked, people to mix the ochre paint, and still others to provide the workers with food and water. Careful analysis of the handprints found in so many caves reveals that the participants included both women and men, adults and children. If cave art had a function other than preserving information and enhancing ecstatic rituals, it was to teach the value of cooperation, and cooperation—to the point of self-sacrifice—was essential for both communal hunting and collective defense.

In his book *Sapiens,* Yuval Noah Harari emphasizes the importance of collective effort in the evolution of modern humans. Individual skill and courage helped, but so did the willingness to stand with one's band: not to scatter when a dangerous animal approached, not to climb a tree and leave the baby behind. Maybe, in the ever-challenging context of an animal-dominated planet, the demand for human solidarity so far exceeded the need for individual recognition that, at least in artistic representation, humans didn't need faces.

As the Paint Peels

All this cave painting, migrating, and repainting of newly found caves came to an end roughly twelve thousand years ago, with what has been applauded as the "Neolithic Revolution." Lacking pack animals and perhaps tired of walking, humans began to settle down in villages and eventually walled cities; they invented agriculture and domesticated many of the wild animals whose ancestors had figured so prominently in cave art. They learned to weave, brew beer, smelt ore, and craft ever-sharper blades.

But whatever comforts sedentism brought came at a terrible price: property, in the form of stored grain and edible herds, segmented societies into classes—a process anthropologists prudently term "social stratification"—and seduced humans into warfare. War led to the institution of slavery, especially for the women of the defeated side (defeated males were usually slaughtered) and stamped the entire female gender with the stigma attached to concubines and domestic servants. Men did better, at least a few of them, with the most outstanding commanders rising to the status of kings and eventually emperors. Wherever sedentism and agriculture took hold, from China to South and Central America, coercion by the powerful replaced cooperation among equals. In Jared Diamond's blunt assessment, the Neolithic Revolution was "the worst mistake in the history of the human race."

At least it gave us faces. Starting with the implacable "mother goddesses" of the Neolithic Middle East and moving on to the sudden proliferation of kings and heroes in the Bronze Age, the emergence of human faces seems to mark a characterological change—from the solidaristic ethos of small, migrating bands to what we now know as narcissism. Kings and occasionally their consorts were the first to enjoy the new marks of personal superiority —crowns, jewelry, masses of slaves, and the arrogance that went along with these appurtenances. Over the centuries narcissism spread downward to the bourgeoisie, who, in seventeenth-century Europe, were beginning to write memoirs and commission their own portraits. In our own time, anyone who can afford a smartphone can propagate their own image, "publish" their most fleeting thoughts on social media, and burnish their unique "brand." Narcissism has been democratized and is available, at least in crumb-sized morsels, to us all.

So what do we need decorated caves for anymore? One disturbing possible use for them has arisen in just the last decade or so —as shelters to hide out in until the apocalypse blows over. With the seas rising, the weather turning into a series of psycho-storms, and the world's poor becoming ever more restive, the super-rich are buying up abandoned nuclear silos and converting them into "doomsday bunkers" that can house up to a dozen families, plus guards and servants, at a time. These are fake caves, of course, but they are wondrously outfitted—with swimming pools, gyms, shooting ranges, "outdoor" cafés—and decorated with precious artworks and huge LED screens displaying what remains of the outside world.

But it's the Paleolithic caves we need to return to, and not just because they are still capable of inspiring transcendent experiences and connecting us with the long-lost "natural world." We should be drawn back to them for the message they have reliably preserved for over ten thousand generations. All right, it was not intended for us, this message, nor could its authors have imagined such perverse and self-destructive descendants as we have become. But it's in our hands now, still illegible unless we push back hard against the artificial dividing line between history and prehistory, hieroglyphs and petroglyphs, between the "primitive" and the "advanced." This will take all of our skills and knowledge—from art history to uranium-thorium dating techniques to best practices for international cooperation. But it will be worth the effort, because our Paleolithic ancestors, with their faceless humanoids and capacity for silliness, seem to have known something we strain to imagine.

They knew where they stood in the scheme of things, which was not very high, and this seems to have made them laugh. I strongly suspect that we will not survive the mass extinction we have prepared for ourselves unless we too finally get the joke.

GARY FINCKE

After the Three-Moon Era

FROM *Kenyon Review Online*

THE DOZEN FETUSES of the sand shark feed on each other until only one is left to be born.

I

While eating breakfast, I read that some astronomers now believe Earth once had three moons. The scientists have a short list of hypotheses for two moons vanishing: They might have been sucked into the sun. They might have been shattered by the one moon that survived collision. Regardless, those other moons have vanished like glittering charms on a bracelet sliding off a child's wrist, the night sky empty with places where some arrangement of reflected light might have aligned itself against the darkness.

2

As a gift, decades ago, I had photographs of my father, his three brothers, and his sister restored, all of them originally taken when they were twenty-one. My father, beginning in his mideighties, pointed out how they had died in reverse order, beginning with his youngest brother. Each time I visited he made me examine that composite as if I had never seen it. "I'm the only one left," he said as he repeated their names, working backward toward himself. "Who would believe that?"

3

In early spring, when I visit during the year my father turns eighty-
nine, he sings hymns aloud, tells me he wakes each morning expecting to be reborn, repeating it three times as if I'm the genie
for resurrection. He says he hears the brothers I never had softly
talking in the small bedroom where I slept while not one of them
was born. They whisper, he says, about the way he refused them,
saying "never" in the disciplined sign language of the rhythm
method, keeping each of them a jealous spirit.

When he sings "In the Garden," I imagine those brothers, each
day, rising to where my childhood window looks out at the rho-
dodendron roof-high, the peace of its curtain, fragments of light
that testify like character witnesses for weather. They move their
mouths to those hymns that are heavy with sunrise and eternal joy.

The house holds the early darkness and the dry heat of the
furnace, and my father repeats the chorus, raising his voice to be
heard by those unborn boys who wake him each morning like birds.

4

One of my students tells me she devoured her twin in the womb,
a doctor solving that natural crime with the spaced clues of ultrasound. "My mother explained it all to me," she says. "She gave me
a copy of the ultrasound photograph that was taken when there
were two of us."

She confides that she keeps her shadow twin sealed inside a
scrapbook she opens on her birthday, leaving the photo face up
in her bedroom. For when, she says, her family sings around her
cake. For when their voices swell enough to reach her sister.

5

"The face seemed to warm up suddenly, sparkle returned to the
eyes." So wrote a scientist named Robert Cornish in a report to the
University of California in 1933. He was working on a way to revive

the dead by strapping them to a seesaw and rapidly teeter-tottering the corpses in order to circulate their blood.

A long time he and his assistants had spent at this primitive CPR, working the seesaw as if they were attempting to draw water from a long-unprimed pump. At least once, according to Cornish's report, their persistence brought a bit of color to the face of a recent heart-attack victim before it reverted to ashen.

Cornish needed to perfect his technique, but human bodies were hard to come by. He began to work with dogs, personally killing fox terriers, naming each of those freshly dead dogs Lazarus, referencing the optimism of the New Testament story. When some of those dogs breathed again, reviving for an hour or two before dying a second time, he was sure he was on to something.

Better yet, Lazarus IV and V lived for a few months. Newspapers reported the story. There was enough excitement and curiosity about his work that a movie was made that spliced in five minutes of footage of Cornish and his dogs. Lazarus IV and V, however, were blind and brain-damaged, inspiring, according to the newspaper stories, "terror in the ordinary dogs they met."*

6

On my next visit, as an early birthday present, I bring my father a gift, a book that traces the stories behind the composition of more than fifty selected hymns. The words and music for all of the hymns are included, and the book, with its dark, austere cover, has the feel of church about it, as if I should rise from my chair as he opens it, ready to join in singing the processional.

It's been eighteen years since he lost the glasses my mother made him get in order to be able to read any print smaller than headlines. He squints at a few pages, pauses at those which have the hymns printed on them to read the titles that are printed in the large, Old English text font of the Lutheran hymnal he's sung from for more than eighty years. Finally he closes his eyes, one

---

* I originally came upon some of the odd histories in *Elephants on Acid and Other Bizarre Experiments* by Alex Boese.

hand resting across a page, and begins to sing "The Old Rugged Cross."

I take my father to dinner, eating in a restaurant so familiar he can order what he's had three times before without having to read the menu. On the way back to his house he asks me to park on Butler Street for the first time in nearly twenty years. The street is so deserted; there is room for ten cars, but I know to drift up to where a vacant lot sits among the buildings that house bars, a beauty shop, a tattoo parlor, and a long-closed hardware store that still sports its name on the side of the building. He uses his cane to shuffle into the middle of that empty space where the bakery he owned for sixteen years used to stand.

"The bakery's been missing so long, pretty soon no one will know it was here," he says.

"Probably," I say, an easy agreement. It's been almost forty years since the building was torn down a few months after the bakery closed. Shortly afterward, the cement we're standing on was laid over the vacant space to provide parking for people who rented the rooms above those nearby businesses, though now, when I glance up, I can't see any lights in the upstairs rooms on either side of us, and no cars are parked near where we stand.

I half expect him to begin a hymn, but instead he leans on his cane and says, "The house where I was born is gone, and the house where you were born is gone," sounding so mournful I offer to drive him to both sites, one leveled to make room for a widened highway, the other long ago razed and replaced by a church. With the sound of traffic passing, he seems to hear nothing of what I say.

"Right here," he says, and when he spreads his arms, I guess that he's standing at the memory of workbench, that when he pulls his hands back together and lifts them, the cane dangling from his right hand, he is ready to carry something to the bank of ovens in the nearby remembered room.

After a few seconds he lowers his hands, steadies himself, and asks me to stand closer. He tells me my mother is slicing bread, the cash register behind her, the three of us working together because he is icing a wedding cake just before delivery, spiraling sweetness so thick with sugar and lard around the figures of the bride and groom that no one should eat it, trusting me to balance the three white tiers to the car.

7

After my student tells me about her lost twin, I read that before the use of ultrasound, the diagnosis of the death of a twin or multiple was made through an examination of the placenta after delivery. Now, with the availability of early ultrasounds, the presence of twins or multiple fetuses can be detected during the first trimester. A follow-up ultrasound would reveal the "disappearance" of a twin.

8

The year my father turns eighty-nine, a scientist suggested that the new superconductor was capable of creating a cosmological bomb billions of times more powerful than the atomic bomb. He said the odds were as likely as one chance in ten, at least one chance in fifty, speaking like a bookie about the end of Earth when the superconductor began to operate at full power. The rest of his scare was an explanation of how showers of heavy-mass particles might end us with ultradense quark matter, the vocabulary for our vanishing full of unrecognizable nouns.

I wanted to dismiss it, but during the week in which I read that scientist's warning, two friends my age died on successive days, and I woke on the third to a phone call I believed was one more, as if a chain reaction had begun, as likely, it seemed, as the seven billion of us becoming fodder for a brand-new black hole because those superconductor scientists were poised on the brink of Genesis, hurtling back to where nothing is alive but the gods.

9

Because his house becomes so dusty, especially the master bedroom, where I sleep, I have an asthma attack during two consecutive visits. The next time I arrive, I tell him that I have other business the following day, that I have a reservation sixty miles away in order to be closer to my morning appointment.

And that's mostly true. I drive for an hour and stay in a motel along the highway I use to return home. It's a one-hour cut from the four-hour drive, and I've stayed late enough that the trip wouldn't have ended until after 1:00 a.m.

The motel room is clean and free of dust. I watch the late news and sports on the Pittsburgh channel that my father watches each night before he hobbles, bracing himself on furniture and the walls of his hall before lying down in the bed I slept in for thirteen years.

10

In the early nineteenth century there were scientists who demonstrated how electricity seemed to reanimate a dead body. Executed criminals were often used, their faces twitching, an eye opening, an arm or a leg jerking when a powerful battery was connected to particular muscles. There was enough publicity about these demonstrations that's it's nearly certain Mary Shelley was aware of them. So Dr. Frankenstein, with the advantages of her fiction, was able to reanimate the dead, standing over the body like a glorious thunderhead, in love with choice.

11

Once a month, from when I was nine until I was sixteen, my father showed slides, projecting them onto the living room wall. He showed the new ones first: landscapes taken from mountaintops; old buildings shot from such a distance that my sister, my mother, and I were barely recognizable standing in front of them; closeups of flowers he identified, walking up to the image to point out their characteristics with his finger; aging relatives we visited on vacation trips, sleeping in their houses to avoid motel bills. After that he showed old slides, all of them snapped one by one into the metal frames required by the projector. There was never a night when some appeared upside down. Or when a slide jammed, the wall going a brilliant white that made everyone blink.

When I was sixteen, my mother bought him a new carousel projector. In order to use it, he had to unsnap a thousand slides from those metal frames.

12

"I never would have thought," my father frequently said after my mother died, meaning that he would outlive her.

"I thought I'd be with Ruthy by now," he repeated once he passed seventy-five, and he described an afterlife that seemed to be so much a physical continuation I thought he expected to play golf and tend a garden forever, having time to master the sport he'd taken up in his sixties, enjoying fresh vegetables for a billion meals. By the time he was past eighty, I suspected that he worried about finding himself revived as the decrepit man he was becoming.

13

In 1964, when I was a freshman in college, a scientist named James McConnell published the results of his experiments with flatworms. Flatworms were stupid, difficult to teach, but he'd rehearsed them until the brightest reacted to light, learning its link to a simple shock that McConnell supplied. He pulled aside the best of those slow learners and halved those pupils to see whether their heads or tails, both of which survived, could exceed the coin flip of chance. And later, when they were completely regenerated, he doubled those gifted students again into dozens of nervous worms, ones that quivered as soon as the light flashed to prophesize the imminence of pain. They were learning, it seemed, to anticipate the agony of an artificial sunrise and the relief of darkness. Finally, eager to discover whether learning could be physically passed from one generation to another, he fed those that had mastered the simple association of light with pain to those without such training. The success he began to claim was that what one worm had learned could be transferred to another by a regulated cannibalism.

Here, he declared, was the possibility of outrunning the slow meander of evolution. He saw the future of humanity in the precocious curling of worms, memory a matter of gorging to omniscience. There were people, subsequently, who dreamed of their children feeding upon them, how their fear and love and knowledge would be passed on to their children, keeping them, in one sense, alive.

14

"Pretty soon," my father began to say at eighty-five, "I'll be the only one who remembers the old days." He told me his "growing up" stories over and over until it seemed as if he were feeding me his memory. I was a willing listener. I didn't tell him that this was my version of revival, passing through the memories of future generations.

15

The things my mother wore:

Before we drove to church, white gloves that held a tissue to open the car door to keep them from being smudged. The new pair she kept in a box until the next wedding, Easter, or Christmas Eve. The two pairs with three embroidered lines. The one pair with tiny, glittering appliqués.

While I walked into church with her each Sunday, not yet complaining about compulsory attendance, the black veils attached to her hats. The way she could make the veils flutter if she tilted her head and exhaled. How thin the cloth strands were, allowing her space to see the hymnal as she sang each hymn in alto's harmony as if she were in the choir.

In the years before illness took the weight off her body, the girdles she wore with every dress. The sound of elastic being tugged down at the end of each Sunday. How she exhaled behind her closed bedroom door.

16

Vanishing twins may occur in as many as one of every eight multifetus pregnancies and may not even be known in most cases. In one study, only three of twenty-one pairs of twins survived to term, suggesting intense fetal competition for space and nutrition. In some instances, vanishing twins leave no detectable trace at birth. More than one amniotic sac can be seen in early pregnancy. A few weeks later only one.

17

For a few years the headless woman was a staple at the county fair. Justina, she was named one summer, and the pitchman claimed she'd lost her head in a faraway Egyptian train wreck. One year her name was Tiffany, who'd been decapitated when her speeding car ran under a truck. The last one I saw in person was Britt, the bikini girl, beheaded by a shark, so lucky, like the others, to die near a doctor who could save her.

Impossible, I said, by that time in junior high school, but just after I spoke, Britt shuddered, letting me know she was suddenly cold. "What she deserves, dressed like that," my mother observed. Britt's alien silhouette was shadowed on the wall behind us, a threat of flexible tubing twisting up like new plumbing from her sliced, scarf-covered throat.

No matter their names, by then I understood that those women's headless bodies were always going to be young and sexy, preserved for study as if research was driven by lust. The old and the heavy were left headless; nobody repaired boys who were reckless, a thing to consider. "Those women aren't angels," my mother cautioned. "Don't you forget that."

Which was fine with me. By that September, I was an eighth-grader who wouldn't admit that all I wanted was a brainless whore who knew only what touched her—my fingertips and tongue, my lips and warm breath. Right then I was wishing that if there were miracles, I'd rather have my body saved than my soul.

18

Some mornings I want to do CPR on the bodies of the exhausted words. *Nithing. Aboulia. Viduous. Squirk.* Their denotations are so distant someone has published them to make a profit from the obsolete and rare.

Yesterday I saw marbles for sale in a museum gift shop. I plunged my hands into the bin and remembered aggies and oxbloods, cat's eyes, steelies, and glimmers, the names I've heard no one use for decades. I loitered nearby, wanting to see if even one child would choose them for souvenirs instead of a toy he could remote-control. They might as well have been strands of hair plucked from the saints of our least urgent needs.

I watched while the ancient words of *trespasses* and *hallowed* came back, followed by remembering that my mother kept my first-clipped hair and fingernails, that she told me I could have them someday when she was gone, though more than twenty years after her death, those things are as lost as the ancient words for *miserly person, loss of will, empty,* and *embrace.*

19

At eighty-nine my father gives up his cane for a walker. Because he is embarrassed by his weakness, I have to convince him to go to the familiar restaurant. I park by the front door and leave the car running while I help him stand. I unfold the walker and set it up for him, telling him to go inside while I park the car.

When I return, he hasn't moved. During dinner he says, without any prompting, "When you have just one son, there's no room for anything terrible to happen."

20

I mention to the student who absorbed her twin that my daughter sent me ultrasound photos of both of her yet-to-be-born. That I stuck those photos among cards and snapshots and short lists of things-to-do on my refrigerator, not telling her my daughter asked not to know their sex, her two daughters old enough now to study their early selves like scholars of prebirth.

21

Things my mother used:

Two stationary tubs in which she moved the laundry from side to side, rinsing until she lifted each item and guided it into the wringer, the tight space between the rollers squeezing the water from our clothes, preparing them for the light.

The clothesline woven between two steel clothes posts cemented into the backyard. Dozens of wooden clothespins to suspend our laundry above the small lawn through the afternoon from March to November, above the cement cellar floor in winter, where they hung for two or three days like ghosts of ourselves.

Her flatiron. The water she sprinkled to keep its heat from scorching, pressing everything, even our underwear, before she let it retouch our bodies.

22

My daughter has painted a sky of chairs that sparkle like redundant constellations. Her heaven is moonless, the chairs, she says, ascending. The sky bleeds from one side from the wounds she imagines on an adjacent panel, one that waits nearby, brilliant with light. Her two daughters, ages seven and four, dream of painting it blue, a sun shining the chairs invisible.

23

Things my mother did for my father:

Turned on the television. Changed the channel and adjusted the rabbit ears until he could make out the Pittsburgh Pirates or a football game.

Let him read the newspaper at the dinner table, the sports section spread out by his plate while she talked to my sister and me through dinner as if we were a family of three.

Dialed the black rotary phone in the kitchen. Called him when the person he wanted to speak to answered.

24

When my mother died, my father called no one for months, complaining that "everyone has forgotten me."

25

On the way to visit my father, I pass the former site of West View Amusement Park, gone more than thirty years into apartments, a grocery store, the fast foods of familiar franchises. I park where the roller coaster turned sharply before it reached the road and West View's business district. When I close my eyes for a minute to imagine the park restored, one passerby raps on the window to ask if I need help.

26

The science of the three-moon era:

The enormous impact that spawned our moon could have sent other satellites into orbit as well. They likely remained in their orbits for up to a hundred million years. Then gravitational tugs from the planets would have triggered changes in Earth's orbit, ultimately causing the moons to become unmoored and drift away or crash into the moon or Earth. The tugs from the other planets are very, very tiny, but they changed the shape of Earth's orbit, which changed the effect that the sun's gravity has on the moons, which destabilized the lost moons.

27

Things my mother left behind:

Four black veils attached to hats stored in a box under a thick comforter high on the steps to the attic. Five pairs of white gloves, two pairs in boxes, unused.

Deep in a drawer of lingerie, two girdles untouched for a decade.

A washing machine with a wringer attached. A hundred feet of clothesline. Eighty-seven wooden clothespins. A flatiron. The glass bottle with a sprinkler's head on top. The bottle clear, the head light green.

28

There is a haunting poem by W. S. Merwin called "For the Anniversary of My Death." It begins: "Every year without knowing it, I have passed the day / when the last fires will wave to me." Anyone reading those lines surely considers the anniversary of his own extinction.

It's less stressful to research the date and place some species we've never seen died for good—the final great auk on Eldey Island, the last Labrador duck outside New York.

Even more exact, the ones exhibited, like the lone Carolina parakeet that collapsed on February 21, 1918, at the Cincinnati Zoo. The final dusky seaside sparrow dying on display inside Disney World, June 18, 1987, those one-of-a-kinds living for months or years without seeing a body like their own. The rest of us moving on without them, the world made irrefutably new by one more emptiness.

29

Simultaneously, during the three-moon era:

The crescent moon of anticipation,
The half-moon of mercy,
The full moon of joy.

30

When my wife and I are dressed and healthy, her body temperature registers eight-tenths of a degree colder than my ordinary one of 98.6. She shivers in any weather below seventy degrees. Occasionally, in central Pennsylvania, she wears gloves in May and September. It's not much good joking about how she's farther from fever, how sweaters become her, how her jackets are stylish and smart. Or, if I feel the need to use a bit of trivia I picked up from the local PBS station during halftime of a football game, to bring up the Thomsonians, who believed all sickness was caused by a deficiency in body heat, claiming that every disease could be cured by a medicinal steam bath.

It's something to consider, because three months past ninety, my father is wrapped in two late August sweaters, the furnace growling in his delirious house where each plant has wilted like his short-term memory and his stove, for the past year, has been covered by signs that say NO in large letters to lower the probability for fire. My wife and I have driven the two hundred miles to Pittsburgh the day after our own discussion of aging, meeting with a woman who specializes in elder law, the legalese of wills and trusts for the future distribution of whatever assets we have, the talk turning to assisted living, comas, and long-term vegetative states, while air conditioning chilled my wife to putting on the jacket she carries, even in the heart of summer, for overcooled rooms.

Afterward, walking outside to the surprise of warmth, she didn't remove her jacket. "How could you stand it?" she said.

"She made everything seem hypothetical," I said. "It was like we were talking about somebody else who was going to fall apart and die."

My wife hugged herself in the late afternoon sun. "I mean the cold," she said. "It was absolutely freezing in there."

31

Within one of those annotated lists featuring "famous last words" is the final one spoken by Dr. Joseph Green, a nineteenth-century English surgeon. Upon taking his own pulse, he managed, according to *The New Book of Lists,* to say "Stopped" before he died.

My father, by the end of September, has been moved to a facility for the nearly dead. He has a room with a door that doesn't lock, and the first time my wife and I visit he is wrapped in a flannel shirt and one of those sweaters from August, both buttoned to his throat while the heat hums from three baseboards on a warm fall afternoon.

My wife places her jacket on a chair. My father, nearly deaf, guesses at what we say. "That's good," he comments from time to time, imagining, I'm nearly certain, that we're telling him about how well we're doing or what our children have accomplished. "Nothing much going on here," he says at last, but he has begun to take his pulse every ten minutes or so as if he expects to hear, like that dying British doctor, the moment it will stop.

Finally I tell him he's been in this building before, that he and I visited years ago because he had made a significant gift to the foundation that operates this facility. "That's good," he says, reaching for his wrist, and I lean close to say, "Let me show you something special" before I wheel him to the elevator that takes us one floor below, to where I remember the chapel is located.

He doesn't react to the brief journey. My wife helps me navigate his chair between a set of pews in the chapel, and I wheel him to the window he purchased fifteen years ago, a stained-glass mural in memory of my mother, who at that time was already more than five years dead.

He doesn't recognize anything even when I set him inches from the plaque that states his name and hers. I ask him to read, but despite this prompt, he doesn't seem to understand. My wife, who stands nearby, bends down and reads the words aloud, shouting into his ear.

"How about that?" my father says. "It's for Ruthy."

"Yes," I say, "you paid for it."

"How come I've never seen this?" he says, and I wish I'd brought along the photograph of him standing beside the window the day it was unveiled.

My father stares at the window for a minute, and then, without taking his eyes off it, he begins to reminisce about my long-dead mother. He settles on listing old gifts he bought for her—a set of pearl earrings, a Sunday dress, and a piano, all of them things that my sister helped him pick out.

He doesn't mention the one time he asked me to help. In late November, for their fifteenth anniversary, the gift of wax fruit he'd somehow set his heart upon. "Each piece will last and last" is how he put it. I was eleven years old and didn't ask him to reconsider his choice. I thought the fruit looked real, the colors blended to look just short of ripe, as if, when he arranged them in the wooden bowl that sat on our kitchen table the following day, they would be perfect.

My father handled the apples and pears; he hefted the peaches, bananas, and bunched purple grapes. He seemed to be weighing them. Finally he made a small pile of assorted wax fruit on the department store's countertop, estimating, I thought, the size of our kitchen's wooden bowl that was usually full of opened envelopes and advertising circulars that featured store coupons my mother intended to use.

The next afternoon, while my mother was changing clothes after church, he dumped all of the paper out of the bowl and placed the mess on the dining room table. With his right hand, he swept his breakfast sweet-roll crumbs into his left and shook them into the wastebasket. He ran hot water into the stained coffee mug he used for a week between washings, a habit, he'd told me once, that he believed was his gift to my mother, because reusing it reduced the number of dishes she had to scrub every day.

Finally he spread that wax fruit out like a set of trophies. The grapes were the last to go into the arrangement, lying on top, the overhead light reflecting off their surfaces. "Isn't this a pretty picture, Gary?" he said when he'd finished. I heard my mother coming down the hall. Before she entered the kitchen, he added, "Just think. They'll look beautiful forever."

32

The vanished twin can die from a poorly implanted placenta, a developmental anomaly that causes major organs to fail or to be completely missing, or there may be a chromosome abnormality incompatible with life.

33

For a year or two, just after that wax-fruit anniversary, I was fascinated by pretending to be dead. "Soon enough, your time will come," my mother said, catching me holding my breath in front of the sweep hand for seconds on my bedroom clock radio. "Kid stuff," she said. "You should know better."

After that I was more careful about my secret pastime, one that moved past simple breath-holding. In a library book, I studied what the mystics did to appear as if they'd stopped their hearts, shutting down the pulse with a block of wood under the armpit, pressure that worked like a tourniquet. I kept the book in my desk at school, but I mastered that technique well enough to simulate a stilled heart. I laid fingers to my wrist as I died, coming back again and again to briefly muffling one part of my autonomic system, dying in my room, or better, among trees in the game lands near our house, lying down where somebody, someday, might discover me. I stared at the path I'd taken to whatever small clearing I'd chosen, imagining hikers who would turn curious or eager or absolutely afraid, everything so still for seconds that I believed in the power of leaving and returning, the comfort of being sprawled like the nearly drowned, doing CPR on the self, taking that first great gasp and bringing my heart's beat back after someone laid fingertips to my wrist, holding them there in wonder.

34

The second time my wife and I visit the nursing home, I notice that my father has no pictures of my mother in his room, which means I have two more pictures of her in my house than he displays. "Do you want a picture of Mom?" I ask, and he shakes his head.

"It won't bring her back," he says, for once not saying "That's good," and when I show him the wedding announcement I've discovered between the pages of a book about the national parks he had sitting out in his living room, he can recite all four paragraphs from the local weekly newspaper. "Thanksgiving, 1941," he says. "Dorothy Seitz, maid-of-honor. Ruth Lang, given by her brother Karl. Mildred Van Wegan (née Lang) attended from Michigan. The Reverend Blair Claney officiated."

How many times had he read that notice in the twenty years since she'd died? "We had the long weekend for our honeymoon," he says. "And a week after that, the war."

It's nearly Halloween by now, and the children of the nursing home staff wear costumes and go from room to room to do an indoor trick or treat. My father, because he can't hear or he doesn't read the facility's weekly newsletters, doesn't understand, so he has no candy on hand. Regardless, he seems fascinated by the princesses and vampires. "Remember *Frankenstein*?" he says. "I saw it in the theater as a boy. Boris Karloff. That was scary for a boy my age. And then he was in all those movies about trying to raise the dead."

"It's a wish that's always with us," I say, but he doesn't hear.

"Remember *Frankenstein?*" he says again. "I saw it in the theater as a boy. Boris Karloff. That was scary for a boy my age. And then he was in all those movies about trying to raise the dead."

I consider showing him the wedding notice again.

Nearly twenty-one years ago, after my mother died at home, my father told me, "Your mother didn't want a hospital. She'd just seen her sister in misery with the tubes and machines and all that coming to nothing."

This week, when we talked on the phone, my sister has told me that his chart says *Resuscitate* where a choice is asked for. Thirteen years ago, nearly eight years after my mother died, my father's heart was stopped during bypass surgery. For a year, each time I visited, he showed me his scar. "The things they can do," he said. Within the next few years, his brother and sister died of cancer. "There has to be a limit on miracles," he said at the time. "Maybe it's one for each family."

When we get home, I look up Boris Karloff's films. Sure enough, there are some that sound as if they repeat the plot of a doctor trying to raise the dead. *The Man They Could Not Hang* and *The Man with Nine Lives,* for two. The plots feature grave-robbing and secret serums for curing cancer and providing eternal youth. The common denominator is Boris Karloff as the mad scientist, not the reanimated body.

35

During the 1950s, a Soviet surgeon named Vladimir Demikhov sewed the heads of puppies onto full-grown dogs. Both heads were alive. The puppies even lapped milk with their tongues, though it ran from their severed throats. This is how we will be revived one day, he said, meaning with the hearts and lungs of others. Tissue rejection killed those dogs in a month or less.

Those puppies must have wondered why the milk dribbled out behind them. Their heads remind me of old dolls, the way their rubber faces, always with their one expression of breast hunger, could be squeezed loose from their pink, sexless bodies.

Those full-grown dogs, on the other hand, must have been aggravated every moment by the nuisance of a second, useless head.

36

I've made a list of the times I might have died, yet, as my mother always said, "lived to tell about it":

Pneumonia—four bouts, each one relieved by antibiotics.

Being a passenger in a car driven by drunks or speeders—a good many times before the age of twenty-two, surviving each trip unscathed and discovering, months or years later, that several of those drivers eventually killed themselves behind the wheel.

Falling asleep while driving—not me, but the man who'd picked me up as I hitchhiked, a cornfield fortunately level with the high-way at the spot where he left the road.

The list doesn't seem extraordinary except for the time that I braked my Volkswagen hatchback hard when a trailer truck I was passing suddenly veered into my lane. The hatchback locked into a four-wheel drift, lurching sideways across the median strip and through two lanes of oncoming, limited-access speeding traffic, somehow missed by all of them before the tires, just as miracu-lously, caught on the opposite shoulder as I spun and ended up facing sideways.

I took a breath and chose a break in the traffic to cross back to my lanes, swerving into the passing lane where I'd been sec-onds before. Two miles later I exited and found myself behind that same truck at a stoplight. The truck driver climbed down and walked toward me. It was summer. The car wasn't air-conditioned. My window was open. He bent down and said, "Fuck, I'm so sorry. You must be sitting in it."

It didn't take his shaken expression to convince me I'd had something like a last-second pardon.

37

In November I read that another new oldest living person has been certified, beginning her bout with the condensed celebrity of age. As always, the biography opens with the frequencies of cigarettes, beer, and deep-fried dinners. Nobody mentions those faraway vil-lagers who once helped to sell yogurt based on its connection to longevity. The rustic-looking peasants in the television commercials were seen enjoying yogurt while the announcer claimed most of them were over one hundred years old and that some of them were 120 or more.

I think of Joice Heth, the slave who nursed George Washington yet lived to be displayed by P. T. Barnum at 161. Her secret, Barnum explained, was thinness, just forty-six pounds on her ancient frame, as if fasting, not yogurt, was the best defense against death.

My father is approaching half his former weight of 210 pounds. No matter what's served, he cleans his plate; he craves a nightly snack. He hoards the cookies and candy he refused for more than eighty years, making himself sick with overeating in his nursing-home room. "Like a little boy," he says, and then he weeps.

He tells me the woman two rooms away, just turned 101, barely leaves her bed, her bald scalp shimmering pink as a wound. "Ten more years of this," he says, "imagine," the future palpable enough to flop belly-first across his bed, the mattress sighing while the well-fed constellation of inevitability blinks on above the horizon, dragging the dark by its hair, shoulders bent against the weight.

I turn on the television and find a football game, but he slumps forward in his wheelchair, staring at a spot on the carpet between his feet. It's no wonder the shrieks of Earth, as scientists say, can be heard from space, such collective terror slithering along our tongues as we struggle to recall even the wrong answers that blink, strobelike, in the brain until we nearly choke on confusion, our mistaken guesses speeding skyward, humming like the panicked prayers of the dying.

And now, after more than eight decades of devotion to his church, he says nothing about eternal life, not even the back-lot pearly-gates set piece of childhood. He says less and less, his sentences shrinking like cheap trousers, until, during this visit, we share the long conversation of the unsaid, rehearsing the future.

38

Sometimes there are verifiable revivals. It has been confirmed, for example, that a man in Chile woke in his coffin. Sitting up, dressed in his finest suit, he asked for a drink of water before rejoining his family.

Sometimes, however, one revival comes carrying the direct consequence of loss. My student, years ago, was tagged incorrectly after an auto accident, his parents discovering the dead body of his friend when they were asked to verify his identity. Eventually they were escorted to a private room so that the parents of the other young man, just arriving with anxiety and joy, would not cross their path. "Inconceivable" was how a colleague put it when we heard how they had to be told that a mistake had been made, the mother and father guided, at last, to confirm what everyone now understood to be the truth.

And sometimes revival can be extraordinarily terrible. Primo Levi relates that during his days in a Nazi concentration camp, he was assigned to dispose of bodies after a gassing. On one of those occasions, a girl rose from the dead tangle of the gassed, and his work crew was saddened past despair because there was never charity in the camp, all of them knowing she would be returned to the gas, unbearably understanding what was coming, her resurrection so dreadful it would madden the living.

39

Some animals have returned from the dead, resurrected after a century extinct, like the Cebu flowerpecker or Jerdan's courser, both of them sighted and confirmed by the radar of science.

It's the work of Thomas, such confirmations, as close as laying fingertips to wounds. Consider the naturalist on Fiji who searched for Macgillivary's petrel.

His optimism as he set out to lure the lost from extinction's deep privacy. He spent a year sounding its call like a prayer against absence, until one morning the long-missing bird flew into his head as if he were the object of desire.

Consider too how to present that news, breathlessly beginning, "Listen." What's next to say? Each thick history of belief is crammed with illustrations that depict the loneliness of the single sighting, the man, recently, who claimed he had seen the ivory-billed woodpecker sixty years after its case was closed tight by science. Without corroboration, he's become the prophet for improbability, someone with a camera who sits still and loves the silence of expectation while every faint flutter of color turns into the promise that phantoms whisper.

40

My wife and I visit my father a few days before Christmas. He nods off at short intervals, a signal, I'm sure, that something serious is decreasing the amount of oxygen that is reaching his brain. During the four hours we are there, the only thing he responds to is an old album of photos. "Everybody in here is dead," he says, able to name his sister and his three brothers, his two best friends, and three girlfriends, one of whom, near the end of the album, is my mother. His head sinks, one hand resting on her picture. I measure his breathing until he snaps back.

I talk to him by phone on Christmas, calling when I know my sister is there so she will answer and tell him it's me. Twice, as we speak, I am sure he nods off, because there is more than a minute without a response, not even a "That's good." Two days later, while I'm interviewing candidates in San Francisco for a position at my university, he dies.

His minister tells me that my father has fallen back into resurrection's arms, his body surrendering its balance to the trust exam of eternity. He is intent on convincing me that all's well, that the dead are always revived. He doesn't ask me if I share that faith.

41

Some scientists speculate that small, asteroid-sized objects would have lasted the longest as the lost satellites. "They would have looked more like Jupiter or Venus in the sky than a satellite," one scientist has said. "They would have resembled very bright stars."

42

After all the post-funeral things are settled, I make two last visits to my father's house, keeping them as short as possible, the asthma-attack–inducing dust an issue, now, in every room. What I want most are photographs, especially those that help to deny the *never* of what is irretrievable.

I spend half of that time in my old room rummaging in boxes

from department stores that closed decades ago. Inside one from Horne's are photos so unfamiliar that I barely recognize myself from ages six to eleven. After I look at others in the box I can tell that the photographs were taken by an uncle, that they were stored in my bedroom closet after both he and my aunt had died. My father, about ten years earlier, had claimed all of them from another empty house.

My sister, a church choir director, keeps the book of hymns.

43

The moon, recently, was a celebrity, full and a few miles closer than usual, enough to bring two neighbors outside near midnight. A perigee moon, science calls it, the tides heaving up higher as well.

Looking at his watch, one of my neighbors suggested "Auld Lang Syne," but I was alone with remembering the approach of planet Melancholia in a film I had seen the year before, how, for one perfect night, it was sized exactly like the moon, the sky brilliant with the fascination of malevolence and the approach of oblivion.

44

Today I woke with the coffeemaker set to 6 a.m., its cough driving me out of sleep like a smoke alarm. Within an hour three birds flew into the living room windows, one of them dead in the iris, the other two missing. A neighbor says it's three flights of the same bird, but I remember the music of those thumps, the variation of size and speed, and I see the colors of the vanished above the trees, shades necessary as water as I stand beneath them, my face upturned to spaces they have left in the sky.

RON HUETT

Cosmic Latte

FROM *The Normal School*

Paper Planes

I AM SIX years old. It is Father's Day, and my mother and I are visiting my father at the minimum-security federal prison camp in Boron, California. I don't know why he's here, only that he has been taken away from us and that we moved out to this sparse desert area to be closer to him. Boron FPC had been an air force base until a few years ago, and the large plaster-white radar dome on top of a tower in the middle of the facility makes it easy for me to pretend that we are visiting Epcot at Disney World. We meet my father in the cafeteria, which is slowly filling with women like my mother and children like me. The kindergartners and first graders among us exult at the sight of our fathers and burst forward to hug their huge crouching bodies. The middle school kids and teenagers hang back and get pushed by their mothers to acknowledge their fathers.

The vending machines sell microwavable soup cups and browning bananas and tasteless prepackaged sandwich triangles, so this is what we all eat for lunch. Robin Leach wishes us champagne wishes and caviar dreams from a television mounted behind a thick sheet of clear acrylic in a box high on the wall while our mothers sip from cans of RC Cola and Tab and ask our fathers how they are holding up before launching into detailed updates of our families' financial problems and court cases. Our fathers respond by telling our mothers to call in a favor with So-and-so, to make sure to tell the lawyer such and such, and to remember to put money on his books—yeah, things are tight, but he gotta eat too, damn.

My father surprises me with a present that he made in the wood-working shop—a large blue wooden toy chest painted with Looney Tunes characters—and my mother asks him how she's supposed to get it into our apartment by herself. *You're not by yourself, Diana,* says my father. *You got Ronny to help you. Ain't that right, Ronny? You're the man of the house while I'm away, aren't you, Ronny?*

Yes, I am! I say.

As our parents' conversations grow more whispered and more of their words become s p e l l e d   o u t to protect the youngest of us from overhearing, we begin slipping away from our lunch tables. Some of us whip around the room playing tag. A group of teenagers sit adjacent to each other by the window without inter-acting much. Toddlers squirm and kick and fuss in their mother's laps, demanding to be set down. Several of the kids my age are at a table with cups of crayons and a few coloring books, making last-minute somethings to present to their fathers before they leave.

An inmate sees me trying to decide what I want to do and mo-tions me over to his table. He is a white man with a gray, bristly beard. When he coughs, black tar comes up, and he spits it into a wad of paper towels gripped in his hand. He offers to teach me how to origami paper into an airplane that loops when you throw it, and I have a lot of fun learning this from him. The trick is to make a plane with a flat, heavy nose and upturned flaps in the back, and to throw it with just the right amount of force. While we crease plain white sheets into crisp aerodynamic shapes together, the man leans in and says, *Hey, do you know what your daddy is? He's a——!* He's real friendly and encourages me to go tell my father what he said, so I get excited. I fold another airplane into being, a perfect one that loops three, four, five times and glides onto its belly when it lands, and run back toward my parents, flying it in my hand stretched out high above my head.

Daddy! I say, and I throw the plane to him, releasing it like a dart. It performs two large curlicues in the air before reaching him, and he catches it in the crook of his arm like a football, laughing. *Say!* he says. *That's pretty good, Ronny! Did you make this?* I plop my little body next to his on the plastic yellow bench of the cafeteria table and say, *Yeah!*

Then I say, *Daddy, guess what, I know what you are!*

Oh, yeah? What's that, Ronny?

You're a——! I say. *The man told me.*

My mother's eyes treble in size, and she shouts, *No! Never say that word again! Do you know what that means?* I do not know what the word means. My father says nothing. He puts the knuckles of both hands onto the table and pushes himself up. He stands like that for a long while, leaning onto both fists, staring with all the tiny muscles in his jaw flexed at the smirking man who taught the word to me. My mother is standing now too, looking worried, rubbing small soft circles into my father's back and speaking something soothing into his ear. The guard standing by the door to the cafeteria takes a few steps toward us and shouts demands that my father sit down. He eventually does so, slowly lowering himself onto the table bench with my airplane crumpled in his left hand.

This is my introduction to the word and the last time I will ever speak it against another black person.

Time to Eat

My mother and younger sisters and I are at Mom Mom's apartment in Redondo Beach. When I was a toddler, my speech impediment turned the words *grandma* and *grandmother* into a mishmash of unintelligible syllables that fumbled off my lips, so I tried to call her "Mom's mom" and in the process coined an affectionate nickname, one that she has forbidden me from abandoning regardless of the embarrassment it causes me.

Mom Mom's apartment is filled with the familiar Thanksgiving smells of turkey cooking in the oven, huge platters of mac and cheese, potatoes au gratin, and green bean casserole cooling on the kitchen counter. But there are also her peculiar additions to the holiday—beef goulash, *nudli* dumplings, and sour cherry soup made from recipes my great-grandmother brought with her from Hungary. My mother has learned these recipes too, but something's always missing when she makes them, some secret something that only Mom Mom seems to possess.

Mom Mom's a crafter. We never leave her apartment without new handmade MC Hammer pants and button-up shirts, or dolls and cheaply framed needlepoint mallards made from the stacks of patterns in her sewing room. She is very productive, and every time we visit her apartment it's more cluttered with her work. Today a new set of knitted dolls catches my eye in her living room.

They are resting on the huge, sweet-smelling cedar chest in which she keeps her collection of VHS tapes recorded from HBO and Showtime broadcasts. There are three dolls, all dressed in formal, old-timey clothes that remind me of the way the actors dressed in *Mary Poppins*. One is a white man with brown-button eyes, brown hair, and a smile denoted by a thin upturned curve of thread. The next is a blue-eyed white woman with long yellow hair made of yarn, wearing a wide-hemmed dress over a frilly lace petticoat. These two dolls have identical thin noses. The last doll is of a dark, brown-skinned man with black eyes, a wide nose shaped like an upside-down poblano pepper, and large red lips made from felt stretched over a gap-toothed grin.

I start playing with the dolls and realize that their clothes are held together in the back with small white strips of Velcro, and thus removable. While my mother's helping Mom Mom in the kitchen and my sisters are watching a Care Bears movie on the living room TV, I'm busy exploring these dolls. I rip the hooks and loops of their clothing fasteners apart and learn that the dolls are anatomically complete underneath their clothes. The woman has small cotton-filled breasts on her chest and a triangle of pubic hair crafted from loops of black yarn between her legs. The white man features a normal-looking penis, unremarkable save for the fact that it exists. But the black doll, I discover, possesses a member whose size makes no sense to me. As I puzzle over this purposeful and baffling difference between the male dolls, Mom Mom and my mother begin bringing huge platters of food out from the kitchen.

Ronny, come help set the table, says Mom Mom. *It's time to eat.*

Tupperware

Jilynn is darker than Vanessa and me, the deep golden brown of her skin the color of the crust on our whole wheat peanut butter and jelly sandwiches. Vanessa is the color of the wheat that crust surrounds, not even any darker than I am, really. But both are recognizably black in a way that I am not, and it changes the way people treat them. The first time I take them to the corner store, I notice that the white man who owns the store calls his wife out from the back room and points them out to her with his eyes. She hovers around them in the candy aisle and watches them, straightening candy boxes that don't need straightening, while I stand a few feet away, trying to decide which comic book I want to buy.

When I rejoin my sisters and ask them if they have decided what they want, the woman says, *Oh, they're with you?* I tell her *Yes,* that these are my sisters, and she nods and returns to the back room. She has never hovered over my shoulder the way she did my sisters, and I know they weren't doing anything to bring on this extra scrutiny. They always behave in public. So I'm beginning to understand that the skin I wear has been bleached of something that my sisters still have, made somehow more palatable. I don't get watched in the candy aisle—I just buy what I want. There's an inexplicable advantage in being white, and my skin is received as though it's shrink-wrapped tight around the body of a white person, even though it's infused with the vestigial flavors of my ancestors, like dollar-store Tupperware that has been left in the microwave for too long.

Translucence

It is a few days before Christmas. My name is still Ronny Valentine, I still live with my mother, and she's taking my sisters and me to meet a stranger for the first time. The man's name, I'm told, is also Ronnie—spelled with an *ie* appended at the end, the grown man spelling—but most everyone calls him Red or Red-Top, on account of his hair. He lives a long drive away, in Los Angeles. After we descend from the freeway into his neighborhood, my mother pulls our borrowed Cadillac over to the curb and twists her body around to face me and my sisters in the backseat. She explains that this old friend of hers whom we are visiting shared a special bond with me when I was a baby, that he is my godfather, that I was named after him.

So if he says anything weird to you, that's what he's talking about, she says.

'K, I say.

Ronnie isn't there when we arrive at his mother's house. She is a frail, old brown woman named Mary, which I think is interesting, because the wet, big-eyed way she looks at me somehow reminds me of the way Mom Mom does sometimes, and her first name is Mary too. This Mary's hands have a consistent tremor to them that makes me wonder how her hair got pressed so perfectly. Maybe it's a wig. She maintains the cleanest, quietest little house I've ever seen. Her couch is encased in a clear thick plastic cover, and every bare part of my body sticks to it when I sit down. She asks me how I'm doing in school, what I like to do, who my friends are. She has a strange sick smell on her breath that I notice when she gets a little too close to me, which is often.

Ronnie's brother Harry arrives soon after we do. He's somewhat lighter-skinned than Mary, with conked-out hair and a smile that shows a lot of gum. He is gregarious and flashy and wrapped in a too-tight polyester leisure suit and wide-lapel shirt. When he enters the house he holds Mary's hands in his in the doorway and kisses her on the forehead, sharing a sweet moment that is a mystery to me.

Hi, Harry, says my mother over Mary's shoulder. *How's Barbara?*

Oh, she's good, says Harry without looking at her. *She wanted to come too, but we didn't have anyone to cover for her in the office today.*

Harry comes all the way into the house and claps his hands together when he finds me watching the adults from the couch.

There he is! he says. *Wow, Ronny! I haven't seen you since you were a baby, knee-high to a grasshopper, man, look at you—you're damn near grown.*

Hi, Mr. Huett, I say.

Call me Harry, he insists.

I notice that no one's paying my sisters the same level of attention that I'm receiving.

Then Ronnie arrives, and the mood in the house shifts in a tiny, confusing, almost imperceptible way. Like Harry, he greets his mother on the doorstep, but more anxiously. He's eager to get inside. I wonder what he's running from. He has the most familiar face I have ever seen. He kneels down and shakes my hand, and when I look into his eyes I get uncomfortable and recoil. He peers into me with an intense, too-familiar friendliness. I can tell that the way he sees through me makes my mother nervous, so I decide he's making me nervous too. Like my father Youless, he is a black man, but a high-yellow one who wears his hair in a short puff of reddish brown Afro. His biscuit-colored hands have precious manicured fingernails but are also callused, possessing a patina of black grease that has taken root in the whorls of his knuckles. He works with his hands, a mechanic, something to do with buses.

He possesses an arsenal of gestures and behaviors that I know I've seen somewhere before.

Before we leave, Ronnie waits for my mother to be occupied with putting my sisters' coats on, takes me into the dining room, and says, *Hey, kid, hold on a second. I have something for you.* Then he gives me a perfect, uncreased hundred-dollar bill. I try to decline it, but he insists that I take it and makes me promise to spend it on myself. When Harry sees this he comes over and slips me another twenty dollars. I have never seen this much money in my life, let alone possessed it. Then Mary asks me if I like chocolate and strawberry milkshakes, and when I say that I do, gives me a case of Ensure meal replacement drinks, which taste much more like chalky thick medicine liquid than milkshakes.

On the long drive home it occurs to me that my sisters didn't get anything from the generous family we visited. I have my mother stop at a Thrifty's drugstore, where I buy a Scrabble board game as my Christmas gift to her and a couple of cheap stuffed animals for Jilynn and Vanessa. I keep Harry's twenty for myself and surprise my mother with the rest of the money, because I know she's worried about our finances. I'm delighted to be able to do this but also confused by the fact that Ronnie and Harry gave me so much money. I don't know a lot about money, but what I *am* sure of is that nobody just gives it to you unsolicited, in large amounts, for no reason. It makes no sense to me that they would do this.

There is a thought percolating within my brain folds, or perhaps it is a memory insisting itself on my consciousness.

Clipboard

I am sitting in the front office of my new elementary school. This is the second time I've transferred schools—that my family has abruptly had to carry trash-bag luggage to a new apartment—so far this year. My mother hands the lady behind the counter a clipboarded enrollment form. The lady flits confused glances from the form to me, to my mother, back to the form. She's puzzling over a discrepancy. *Oh, ma'am, you've made a mistake,* she says. *You checked off your son's race as "other" and wrote, "child is biracial black-slash-white."*

Yes, says my mother, and I start shaking my head behind her

—not because she's wrong, but because I'm clearing my head of a premonition.

But your son is white—

Bitch, don't you think I know what race my son is! shouts my mother, fist hammering down, pen on a chain jumping off countertop, office lady realizing she done fucked up . . .

Wobbly Spirals

It is another too-hot afternoon in summer, 1985.

My mother and I have been sitting together on the front porch of our house for hours, while she struggles to say something to me; I don't know what. I'm not really paying attention.

I have a golden cocker spaniel with big flappy ears. Her name is Tuffy, because when she came to live with us I didn't know she was a girl, and I desired for her to be tough, like I imagine I am. She's running around our threadbare yard, snapping her little jaws at the air, plotting an escape. The last time she got out I had to chase her barefoot down the street. The baking black asphalt blistered my soles, and now I'm sitting here on this decaying wooden bench, with clear liquid weeping from the bottom of my feet into my socks.

I do know, though, what she isn't saying.

My sisters are somewhere behind us in the house, arguing and wrestling over who gets to play with what doll. They've been bickering all summer, their little voices producing a constant, irritating background din. *Just take turns!* I shout into the dusty window screen.

What's so complicated?

Ritchie has ridden by on his bike several times. The first time, he paused at our gate and asked if I could come play T&C Surf Designs on his Nintendo, was told: *later.* Now when he passes by, he slows down, reads our faces, keeps coasting.

I caught a fat, iridescent June bug this morning and tied it by a leg to the porch banister with a piece of string, and now I'm watching it fly in a buzzing, never-ending, increasingly unstable loop. It chooses not to land, to remain a shimmery purple-green streak, condemned to zip exhausted, wobbly spirals in the air. My mother, likewise, continues to talk in circles that never quite settle on what she's trying to get at.

Finally I just say it for her: *That guy Ronnie is my dad, isn't he?*

She nods her head, says, *Yes,* and now what I know and what I have believed for the past several months are the same thing.

Ritchie's turning the corner back onto our block. My Mongoose bike is lying on its side on our driveway. I pick it up, call out to him, start pedaling.

Ice Cream

My name is Ronny Huett now. My father took me with him to the Social Security office several months back, where we sat on hard, plastic chairs connected in a row for hours with my birth certificate, until he was allowed to approach a window and have the indifferent woman on the other side of the Plexiglas barrier disentangle whatever it was that my mother and Youless did to falsify my name. I live with Ronnie in an apartment in Mom Mom's building in Redondo Beach. I call him Dad or Pop, and he mostly calls me "hey kid." His friends, the ones that made it back from the Vietnam War with him, call me Lil Red after him.

The day Pop asked me if I wanted to stay and live with him, I had to call my mother and tell her I wasn't going to be coming back home, and it was hard. She accused me of abandoning her and my sisters and was not wrong. They still live in Ontario, California, and Youless lives somewhere else with the new family he has started with a woman named Anne.

Redondo Beach is a mostly white city, or at least we live in the whitest area of this mostly white city, and I haven't figured out how I'm supposed to behave here yet. I haven't made any friends at my new school, and my grades have continued the slide they started the year before. I'm embarrassed by this but can't seem to make myself do the things a person would do to get better grades. Pop's gone for work a lot, and Mom Mom's supposed to watch me when he isn't around, but this arrangement has, in practice, been a failure. I've started to ditch school and go to the huge library on Pacific Coast Highway instead, where I can read whatever I want. Sometimes I sit at the microfiche machines and spend hours reading newspapers from the previous year, or the year I was born, or random dates from decades ago. I know that if I were to go to the arcade at the Del Amo Mall in Torrance, my truant ass would get caught, but somehow none of the adults I interact with here notice or care that I'm at the library during school hours. I am invisible here.

I go to the beach nearly every day and alternate between getting sunburned and tanned. As my skin peels off and sheds, my body turns three colors at once: brown, red, and white, like Neapolitan ice cream. The too-bright, soft new baby skin that replaces the brown that sloughs off is always the wrong color.

But sometimes black people I don't know approach me on the street and ask, *Excuse me, but are you part black?* And when I say, *Actually, yeah, my dad is black,* they nod and say, *Yeah, I thought so. I got a cousin, he look just like you.* And we connect with each other briefly in a way that reminds me that I have family out there, that I am part of a proud diaspora, that I am not actually all alone in the world.

Random white strangers have started approaching me too. Only they demand to know, *What are you?* and refuse to accept any answer that evades their need to categorize me. They feel entitled to a complete, satisfactory answer. I knit my brow in mock confusion and look at my arms and say, *I think I'm a person.* Or I say, *I'm an American,* or *I'm a boy,* or, *I read recently that we're all made up of about 60 percent water.* I give any answer I can think of that isn't the one I know they want.

No, but what are you, really? they say.

My name's Ronny Huett, I answer, as though that's what they asked me. *Nice to meet you.*

Hypertension

I am nineteen years old, applying for a job as a mail clerk in the hypertension and nephrology division of Harbor-UCLA Medical Center. During the course of my interview with the head of the department, I mention that I've been diagnosed with high blood pressure. He wants to know what I'm doing to treat this condition, and I answer, *Nothing.* Suddenly his complexion changes, and he confronts me. *Excuse me, but you're black, right?* he spits. I begin to stammer, because this seems irrelevant to whether or not he should hire me as a mail clerk. He grows more agitated: *You are in fact a black man, are you not?* he demands. I say, *Yes—yes, I am. I'm black.* I wonder how he knows to ask me this; white people so rarely perceive it. He calms down and explains that African Americans with high blood pressure are predisposed to develop kidney disease. He hires me and makes me spend my first day at work in the dialysis unit, watching what he insists will happen to me if I don't take medicine to bring my blood pressure under control.

Storytime

I work at the Borders Books and Music at the World Trade Center in New York City. Two of my coworkers and I have been given the privilege of performing storytime in the kids' section on Tuesday mornings. The children gather around us in an amorphous and chaotic semicircle next to the big brown trunk of the fiberglass tree on the second floor of the store. Dina reads the stories and helps Lisa sing the songs, and I accompany them on my guitar. The children perform adorable, clunky, arrhythmic dance moves when I play. Their Haitian and Dominican nannies gossip and laugh a little too loudly, while Lisa and I attempt to corral the children back onto the bright, primary-colored rug, and Dina reads *Goodnight Moon* or *Love You Forever* or my favorite: *No, David!*

Dina's Greek, with a huge tangle of black hair and a mouth that is always twisted into a smirk. She possesses a husky, satisfying laugh that reverberates against the walls of every room in which it's summoned, so I'm always scheming to make her laugh. I mostly succeed. Lisa has sandy yellowish-brown skin, hair that coils into tight blond kinks, and green eyes. She has a tattoo on her shoulder of the same goofy cat-face sticker that I happen to have on my guitar.

She is, like me, half black and half white. My first week working in the store, she hung around the stockroom for a while, watching me break down pallets of books before approaching me when we were alone, talking about, *Hey, Ron, you know we got something in common, right?*

I leaned onto my forearms against the large cube of boxes I was unpacking, lifted my chin toward her in recognition, and said, *Yeah . . . damn half-breeds!* and she laughed.

Today I am tuning my guitar and practicing "Mulberry Bush" (which I've transformed into an indie-rock toddler-dance hit) in the break room. Two of my coworkers, both black, are taking their break at the same time as me.

Willie asks, *Do you know any Bob?*

Dylan? I say, and they both roll their eyes at each other.

I knew you were gonna say that shit! says Jamila, and I realize that I have failed a test.

Naw, man, naw, says Willie. *I meant Marley.*

And the annoying thing is, I know lots of Marley songs. I perform "Three Little Birds" for five-year-olds every Tuesday.

But no Dylan.

Stars and Bars

I have been waiting over an hour for a Saturday bus. I'm keeping a wary eye on an agitated white man who keeps pacing around the bus stop and in and out of traffic, talking angrily to himself about something. When he passes especially close by, I see that he has the stars and bars of the battle flag of the Army of Northern Virginia tattooed on the meat of his hand above his thumb. So I watch him a little more closely, but surreptitiously, out of the corner of my eye, while acting like I'm looking forward. When the bus finally comes, I get one foot onto its stairwell when the man comes up to me from behind.

He whispers it into my ear: *I know what really you are, ——.* As though I had been hiding it. As if I'm disguising myself under a mask that is my own face.

It's shocking—not just that a man could be so bold and so intent on being hurtful to me that he would invade my space and put those words into my head, but also because he has revealed himself to be a racial savant, capable of seeing in me what is imperceptible to most. And now I have to decide if I want to most likely lose a fight with this man right here in the street and then walk a few miles home, or step all the way into the bus.

I choose to get on the bus and lose a fight right there on that street anyway.

Saltwater

I am twenty-seven years old, hanging out in a car by the beach, breathing in fresh saltwater air with a woman I'm interested in and her friend. They've made a bet. The friend turns to me and asks, *Hey, you're part black, right?* and I tell her that I am. She gloats and taunts her friend with I-told-you-sos. The woman I'm interested in thought I was white. It turns out that she is half black too, was born in Liberia, actually. Her father's white, and her mother's Ghanaian.

I thought she was Hispanic, which shows how much I know.

Not in Carson

I am walking across the street, holding hands with my girlfriend, Jackee. We live together with a few of my friends in a rented house. I'm still very interested in her. A car full of young Hispanic men pulls up and starts yelling at us, because they think that I am white, that she's Mexican, and that we are in an interracial relationship. *Not in Carson!* one yells. *You can't do that shit here!* But she's the only woman I have ever been with who's the same exact race as me. I've dated women of various races, but Jackee is the only one who is like me, both black and white at once, while also a little bit more of one than the other.

Water and Power

Fifteen feet. I am climbing a pole. With each step I stab a spike into its soft creosote-soaked wood and run a caress up its back with my gloved hands. Twenty feet. My body adopts an efficient sloth-like rhythm. My leather pole strap dangles in a long loop from my belt, swinging. Thirty feet. I let go of the pole with my right hand and reach down to my hip. I unclasp one of my strap's snap hooks and throw it over the crossarm and around the pole. Then I clasp it to my left hip and lean back, no hands, connected to the pole only by my heel gaffs and this belt.

I'm an apprentice lineman for the Los Angeles Department of Water and Power. Today I've been given the opportunity to deconstruct this pole from the top down. I hook one foot around the pole and lean at a severe angle, Supermanning my body out so that I can reach the far end of the crossarm.

Come on, Caveman! Mike is shouting up at me. He's a fifth-step apprentice, a white man a few years younger than me who comes from a family of linemen. It's his job to begin the process of infusing me with the skills and swagger required of a bona fide electrical distribution mechanic, or else to haze me out of the industry. His approach relies heavily on demands that I buy him breakfast, which I flatly refuse to do, threats of poor evaluations, and insults regarding my abilities and appearance. I have a prominent brow and a beard, so he didn't have much trouble nicknaming me.

Now he's watching me struggle up here. Whoever put the nut on this insulator bolt must have been pissed off at his wife or something. Why take it out on the next guy, though? Jesus fucking Christ, why ratchet it down so tight? What's the point? I thumb the worm screw between the jaws of my wrench forward until they have clamped down as tightly as possible against the stubborn nut, and I push its handle away from me as hard as I can with both hands. I strain and exert, pushing with all of my body into the wrench handle, with my lips pursed tight, feeling Mike pacing below me, getting nowhere.

What's the problem up there? he calls.

Fucking nut won't move, I say. *What's it look like?*

Later we are eating lunch together in the cab of our truck. Mike is irritated with me because it's taking me too long to strip the pole, and at this pace we are going to be working in this backyard all day. I'm pissed at myself too, because he's right. I drip sweat and eat my turkey sandwich with my gaze fixed into the future, plotting how I'm going to work when we get back. I'm fixing to disassemble the shit out of this pole when we get back—

All right, Caveman, we're gonna switch off after lunch, says Mike. *I'm gonna do the rest of the pole, and you'll take over on the ground.*

I'm disappointed, and I hate this paternal, hair-tousling mode I see Mike sliding into.

You'll get it next time, Caveman, he says. *I just gotta get the fuck out of this neighborhood, eesh.*

My body tightens, because I know he's about to say it. I can smell the word on his breath. He has probably been chewing on it all day, turning it over on his tongue, savoring its mouthfeel. He recognizes some Neanderthal quality to my appearance that makes me not quite like him, but he doesn't see my blackness. He is too comfortable around white people, something I can never be. I put my sandwich down and wait.

I hate working downtown, he says. *Hanging out all day in these damn —— alleys and—*

Don't say that shit around me, I say, and he screws his face up like *I'm* offending *him.*

What's up, Caveman? he says. *You got something you want to say to me?*

Yeah, shut the fuck up with your —— alleys, I say. *Keep that shit to yourself, Mike.*

Gas and Electric

I am thirty-five-years old, listening to voicemails at work. One is from the United States Department of Labor. They've called me several times already, but I had assumed their messages were some kind of identity-theft scam and ignored them. This message is more urgent. I learn the reason that I never got a response to the job application I submitted a few years back to be an apprentice lineman for that company in Maryland: they discriminated against me because I had outed myself as black on the application. It didn't matter that I had spent two years going to trade school earning certificates and commendations after work to qualify myself for the position. They just tossed my application in the trash with those of fifty other black applicants. The fact that my blackness is translucent was irrelevant. The terms of their settlement with the Department of Labor means that they now owe me thirteen thousand dollars, but I seriously consider not accepting the settlement check. I need this money. But I'm also afraid that I will have to collect it in person for some reason, and I don't think I can handle another inevitable racial interrogation.

Cardboard

My sons, Henry and Ben, are four and three years old. Both of them are the same color beige as me. *Cardboard babies,* my wife and I call them. But their skins, like mine, are closer to the color of the roll of Kraft art paper that cascades down over the top of the Ikea drawing easel in their bedroom. It used to be that personal computers and other office machines only came in either this same tawny shade of beige or else a drab light gray. When I was a young man I was the color of every stifling workplace I wanted to escape. And like mine, the skins of my children are tissue-paper thin, such that you can see our blue veins tracing proof of life across the soft insides of our forearms.

But today Henry tells me that he and Benny are yellow, that Ma is brown, and that I am orange. Orange is darker than yellow, is it not? But thanks to their maternal grandmother, these children are closer to Africa than I am. And I can't see the orange in me that Henry perceives. Maybe he senses that I'm a Lil Red too: after all, yellow mixed with a little red is orange. Alternately, he could be smelling that red-hot angry me that I hide from him, safely wrapped tight inside the folds of the comforting blanket of my light-colored skin. Maybe some of that leaches out onto him sometimes, even though I don't want it to.

Dusty Cowboy

I am thirty-eight years old, visiting my old friend Jeff at his new home in New Mexico. We are making music with a new buddy of his. His new friend is an actual cowboy, perennially covered in a soft layer of dust and horse stink. I'm noodling little guitar licks over the song he's playing, only halfway listening to the lyrics. I'm thinking: *Okay, his wife left him, he's been drinking, lost his dog, some shit like that. This is a country song.* Then I stop playing and slowly put my guitar down, because I've realized that he's singing about how there's nothing more useless than a white girl with a ——. He sees my discomfort and explains to me that this is a song by David Allen Coe, that it's a very funny song actually. I don't see the humor in it, and I'm damn sure not going to play along to it. So he shrugs and plays it without me while I just sit there in a daze, knowing that this smiling white cowboy with his huge tombstone teeth hates my mother and my father and my wife and my children and me. He has no idea what I am.

And what I am is a white-looking, blue-eyed black man, the undercoverest brother you are ever likely to meet. I'm the consequence of the love that this dusty cowboy finds so unnatural, the horrible miscegenated thing that results from white women like my mother being made "useless" by black men like my father. So is my wife, a medium-brown black woman. And so are my children, two beautiful light-skinned boys who are black on both sides.

Gremlins

When I found out that I was going to become a father, I suddenly became obsessed with going to college. I promised myself that my children would know that the world is a huge place filled with opportunity and that I'd model this fact by getting a degree myself. So I began attending classes at Santa Monica Community College at night and on the weekends, and after a few semesters I got a letter inviting me to apply to Columbia University. When I was a young man the idea of going to college struck me as a ridiculous and unattainable fantasy. I don't think either of my parents graduated from high school, and I only barely did. Now I find myself taking advantage of an opportunity to attend an Ivy League university and to keep the promise I made to myself and my sons before they were even born.

Today a young white undergrad I befriended during my first semester here texts me to announce that she has decided she wants to have a black baby. Now she wants my advice on how to raise one. *There are three rules,* I tell her: *No bright light, don't get them wet, and never feed them after midnight, no matter how much they beg.* She's too young to get the reference, but it doesn't matter.

What are you even asking me? I say. *You love them a lot, and you take care of them, what do you think?*

No, I mean . . . how do you raise them to be black? she asks.

You can't, though, I say. *Because you don't know what that is. Let their father handle it.*

Cosmic Latte

I am procrastinating on the Internet. Somewhere amid my friends' status updates and the listicles and the news articles I learn that a team from Johns Hopkins University has determined that the average color of the universe is *Cosmic Latte,* which is to say beige. If you were to stand outside the cosmos and look back down and into it from a sufficient distance, the beautiful multitude of colors that differentiate all of the objects and gases and light and radiation contained within it would melt together into one light-beige whole.

So: my children are the color of everything.

LESLIE JAMISON

A Street Full of Splendid Strangers

FROM *The Atlantic*

WHEN I WAS young, the beauty of church always belonged to other people: the believers. They saw the same stained glass I saw, but when its jeweled light cut their skin into kaleidoscopic colors, they somehow belonged in that light in a way I never would. They could feel the lilt and soar of the hymns as truth, as collective yearning, as a tin-can telephone connecting them to God. That's what I told myself. I told myself I was alien to that beauty—I'd never be anything but an interloper lurking just outside its grace.

Some version of that girl I'd been in church—with legs too long for her denim overalls, and palms covered with half-moon crescents where she'd dug her nails into her skin—was summoned for a different rapture, years later, by the photography of Garry Winogrand. Some version of that girl was told, *This is beauty you belong in.* The first time I entered the Brooklyn Museum's 2019 exhibit of his color photography, part of its force was this immediate sense of invitation, as if a door had been carved in a wall, leading to some new world, and now I could cross into it—or perhaps simply see more clearly that I'd been living in that miraculous world all along. It had only disguised itself as something familiar, or banal.

Even the physical structure of the exhibit contributed to this sense of invitation—induction into some holy ordinary realm, hidden in plain sight. At the entrance you had to part a thick black velvet curtain to step into a long gallery that was as cool and dark as a cinema, with huge color slides projected on the walls: A dark-haired teenage girl in a white bathing suit silhouetted against a bright blue sky. A little boy in tiny shorts putting his coins into a vending machine to buy a Coke. Old ladies in folding chairs on the sand, playing cards. A woman propped on her elbows on her beach towel, a messy MICKEY stick-and-poke tattoo on her arm, cat's-eye sunglasses hiding her mood. A man lying on his back, with his blue canvas sneakers tucked beside him and the sunlight pouring across his body, the cigar in his mouth pointed straight up toward the sky. These photographs seemed born of a gaze that regarded strangers with faith—in their beauty, in their humanity, in their radiance—and suggested a radical innocence, almost transgressive, in an era when the country has often felt divided past the point of repair, certainly past the point of goodwill.

Winogrand was deeply drawn to public spaces—sidewalks, bus stops, airports, beaches, motels, campgrounds, highways, boardwalks, carnivals, zoos, parking lots, pools—and his photographs opened onto these restless, gritty infinitudes, often landing on a single wistful or bewildered or determined individual amid the larger crowd. The exhibit, steeped in the moods and fashions of the 1950s and '60s, felt like time travel: women in chiffon scarves, men washing their Mustangs, people dressed in their Sunday finest for the airport or their bathing caps for the beach. It was easy to follow these accents of the era into nostalgia for another time—a time when daily attention to the glorious undertones of the mundane had been possible, and justifiable. But of course this unremarkable glory is still everywhere, all around us. It still lives in precisely those in-between moments the photos captured, in all their incandescent immediacy: people smoking alone on the sidewalk, or leaning their head against another's shoulder. People showing off, goofing off, getting off flights. People reaching for each other on threadbare towels laid across the scorching sand.

Years prior, during my early attempts to get sober—when I was spending many evenings each week in church basements—I'd fallen in love with a quote from the writer and theologian G. K. Chesterton:

> How much larger your life would be if your self could become smaller in it; if you could really look at other men with common curiosity and pleasure . . . You would break out of this tiny and tawdry theatre in which your own little plot is always being played, and you would find yourself under a freer sky, in a street full of splendid strangers.

Now here it was, this dark gallery with its windows of light: a freer sky, a larger theater, a street full of splendid strangers. These slides were a tutorial in the proximity of the sacred, how it was never far from us: a family having a picnic against a backdrop of rolling white sand dunes; street clowns at a parade beneath a sign advertising DALLAS' FINEST HAMBURGERS; flight attendants in their powder-blue suits, clustered on an asphalt divider, shadowed by palm trees and boxy off-white airport hotels. These ordinary strangers literally gave off light. It glowed across the faces of the ordinary strangers watching them. The exhibit felt like a recovery meeting. It felt like going to church. I couldn't get enough of it.

After my first visit, I kept coming back. I must have visited that exhibit at least thirty times. Mostly I went with my baby; it was, among other things, a useful way to pass the hours of our days. But I brought everyone I could. I wanted to be there with my friends, my friends' babies, my mother, my aunt, the ex I hadn't spoken with in years. I wanted to bring my grandmothers back from the dead so I could be there with them. It was a secular cathedral, a church of regular life, this dark room lit by luminous slides. They lined the walls like stained-glass windows, but instead of showing saints or biblical scenes or the stations of the cross, they showed daily existence: two kids flipped upside-down on a handrail above a storm drain; a man in a striped shirt licking a cone of vanilla soft-serve, that moment of pleasure like a whittled point of stillness inside the frenetic circus of Winogrand's hustle and bustle.

These were stunning scenes not because they were extraordinary but because they weren't. They were full of ordinary people seen so clearly that they became extraordinary in their beauty. "How do you make a photograph that's more beautiful than what was photographed?" Winogrand once asked. But I didn't see his photos that way. I didn't think he was making the world more beautiful; I thought he was excavating beauty that was already there. His alchemy didn't turn the world holy so much as it revealed that the world had been holy all along—outside the doors of the museum, and inside them too, *we* were holy. That was part of the grace of his work, how it suggested that anyone could be art, that the people standing in that darkened room were no less radiant than the people glowing on the walls in front of them.

*

Born in the Bronx in 1928, Winogrand was a New Yorker at his core, though he also described himself as a "student of America," and often crisscrossed the country on road trips, taking photographs of gas stations and rest stops and motel pools and highways. He disliked the terms *street photography* and *snapshot aesthetic,* but it's not hard to see why people use these terms to characterize his photos, which suggest immediacy and spontaneity, capturing fleeting moments of the present tense in their frames. Winogrand initially studied painting at Columbia University, but "found painting a slow, deliberate process that demanded lots of patience," as his friend Tod Papageorge put it. "He preferred to work in a way [that] could convulsively seize what it described . . . Photography answered his agitated sense of self."

Looking at Winogrand's photographs of the open roads and beaches of America, its motels and airports, and especially the crowded sidewalks of its most populous city, I found myself thinking of Walt Whitman, who had roamed the streets of his beloved island of Mannahatta a century earlier. Maybe Whitman found his own answer to an "agitated sense of self" in his peculiarly radical vision of expansiveness—his feeling of effusing into others, and feeling them effuse into him, a faith both ecstatic and arrogant. Whitman certainly felt composed of strangers. His 1860 poem "To a Stranger" addresses itself to them:

> Passing stranger! you do not know how longingly I look upon you,
> You must be he I was seeking, or she I was seeking, (it comes to me as
> of a dream,)
> I have somewhere surely lived a life of joy with you . . .
> You give me the pleasure of your eyes, face, flesh, as we pass.

Winogrand's photos are saturated by this fascination with strangers—this faith in the strange rub of molecules between anonymous bodies, and the fantasies we spin from the faces of others. If Winogrand considered himself a student of America, then that Brooklyn gallery was a rhapsodic articulation of the curriculum he'd been studying. It was organized into eight themed clusters, like textbook lessons: "Coney Island," "Early Color," "In the Streets," "Portraits and Still Lifes," "On the Road," "Travel," and, in the back, facing each other: "Women" and "White Masculinity." Though he was mainly known for his black-and-white photographs, Winogrand produced more than 45,000 color slides during the '50s and '60s—making slides was less expensive than making prints—and it feels essential and deeply moving that the photos weren't turned into prints for the exhibit. As slides in rotation, more than 450 in total, they felt warmer and more alive, more in motion.

"Sometimes I feel like . . . the world is a place I bought a ticket to," Winogrand once said. "It's a big show for me, as if it wouldn't happen if I wasn't there with a camera." Many of his photographs document the rapt or wary faces of people absorbed by some pageantry or performance that is unseen, out of frame: a crowd gathered in a bruised-blue dusk around a garbage can labeled CLEAR LAKE, LET'S BE NEAT, all pointing at something in the sky —fireworks? shooting star?—or four women standing in front of a carnival lemonade stand, looking fascinated and perhaps a little repulsed. We cannot see what they are looking at, only their faces doing the looking. Winogrand was less interested in the spectacle itself and more interested in what happened to us when we beheld it. How it gathered us. That gathering—in the shadows of the carnival booth, the asphalt parking lot beneath the fireworks —was what he'd bought a ticket to: the show of our wonder and discomfort, our yearning for enchantment.

When I first stepped onto Winogrand's street of splendid strangers, I'd been separated from my husband for four months. I was fond of saying that I lived on Planet Women. It felt as if all the men had been banished from my life, or at least from my days. Perhaps that was part of why I often found myself sitting at the far end of the Winogrand exhibit, my back turned on the section called "White Masculinity," hopelessly entranced instead by the women across from it, as if these women were a refuge, a solace, a womb: a woman with a bouffant on a barstool, sitting between a slot machine and what appears to be a Jack and Coke; another one solo at a grimy diner table, hunched over a plate of eggs and toast. Something in me reached toward the woman smoking alone in her convertible, with the sun setting behind her and the wind whipping her hair. She made solitude look liberating, while others made it look like a grind; I knew the truth everyone knows, which is that it's both.

Looking at those women, I kept thinking of something my friend Jake had written about walking up and down First Avenue in the weeks after his best friend's death: "On the streets of New York the trances of strangers' lives were written on their faces. I felt like I was everyone's mother, and that everyone was mine." I kept thinking, *These women are all my mothers.* Maybe that sounds absurd or melodramatic, but something about the cool, dark room stirred these wild surges of emotion. Its luminous panels opened my nerves to the unknowable inner lives of people I would never meet, and its shadows obscured the embarrassing sentiment displayed across my features whenever I projected too much onto the projections of their fleeing bodies.

If Winogrand was a devoted chronicler of public spaces, then during the many hours I spent in that shadowy hall—close to the sweat of strangers, to their morning breath, to their invisible daydreams, their untold anguish, their ordinary restlessness—I felt the exhibit itself becoming another kind of public space, our bodies assembled in that room, giving one another our eyes, our faces, our flesh. We were an iteration of the gatherings illuminated on the slides around us: the cluster of folks sunbathing by the pool of the Tally Ho Motel, or the ad hoc community pooling in the shadows under the Coney Island boardwalk—a mom with her toddler sleeping on her lap; a shirtless man doing pull-ups on the wooden rafters, someone else's laundry hanging behind him. Or the three women in bathing caps and bloomers standing in the surf, facing away from the camera, gazing at the swimmers farther out, beholding that revelry and yet not fully immersed in it. Those of us in the gallery found ourselves in some version of that purgatory as well—at once drawn in and kept on the fringes. As Whitman once wrote, "Both in and out of the game and watching and wondering at it."

Since my separation, I'd been seeking solace in public places—had spent pockets of that aching winter in the Russian baths tucked behind Coney Island high-rises and the ones in an old tenement basement on Tenth Street. Placing my body in those unbearably hot rooms alongside the bodies of other people whose names I'd never know was a way to remember heat during that long, frigid season. In the spring I took my baby on long walks around Prospect Park, past the smoking charcoal bricks and sizzling hamburgers of strangers, as she rode like royalty in her stained and fraying baby carrier, close to my heart. When we got home and I lifted her back onto the floor—where she could actually stand, breaking my heart and remaking it—the dampness of her back and the dampness of my chest were matching continents of sweat. The residue of our bodies in proximity was a faint echo of the months when there had been no skin between us at all.

On the subway that summer, I found myself leaking tenderness toward the unknowable strangers sitting across from me, playing Candy Crush on their cell phones and picking up their kids' dropped Popsicles. Someone in a church basement quoted Plato: "Be kind, for everyone you meet is fighting a hard battle," which was not actually something Plato said. It was something a nineteenth-century Scottish minister said, but the urge to make the sentiment ancient or immutable made me love it even more. In any case, it seemed suddenly clear to me that everyone on the Q train during rush hour was fighting a hard battle, and so was everyone in the unbearable heat of underground saunas, and I wanted to tell each and every one of them, *I know you are fighting! And you! And you!* Instead I took myself to Winogrand, over and over again. His photographs were daydreams. Or rather, they were a technology for daydreaming. They were spurs to spin stories about the lives of the people he'd preserved in their frames: three men carrying a rolled-up rug into an apartment building; a hand with pink nail polish reaching for a glazed cruller.

"There is nothing as mysterious as a fact clearly described," Winogrand said, and his photographs perform some version of this seduction by way of plain exposure. "That's all there is, light on surface," he also said, which made me think of a deceptively simple statement Edward Hopper had made about his own art: "What I wanted to do was paint sunlight on the side of a house." John Szarkowski, a former director of photography at the Museum of Modern Art and one of Winogrand's great champions, once said that his photos were "not illustrations of what he had known, but were new knowledge." It's true that his photos gaze not toward the legible but toward what's still being discovered, though I have always experienced them less as knowledge than as frames placed around unknowing. They do the work James Baldwin called for when he said, "The purpose of art is to lay bare the questions that have been hidden by the answers."

That pink-nailed hand reaching for the glazed cruller—who did that hand belong to? What joy was her indulgence celebrating? Or else what consolation was she seeking, for what pain? Or perhaps the pain in that photograph was not hers but mine. Perhaps Winogrand's photos invite us not only to imagine the lives of strangers but to respect the ways these imagined lives are also, always, projections of our own. We are perpetually finding in the face of another person whatever jigsaw piece—foil or mirror—fits our needs in that moment. When his photos capture crowds, they always mind the gap: they recognize what we can't know about the people around us, and the ways in which crowds are just collections of discrete solitudes.

Winogrand is often understood as a photographer of crowds rather than of isolation. "Winogrand seems so contrary in spirit and style to Edward Hopper," the critic Geoff Dyer writes in *The Street Philosophy of Garry Winogrand*. "Hopper is the painter of loneliness, emptiness and isolation, motionlessness; Winogrand is busy, manic." Yet Dyer keeps mentioning Hopper when he writes about Winogrand, and I think he's onto something. Part of the brilliance of Winogrand's photos—part of what they understand about what it means to be alive, among other lives—is that the line between being lonely and being surrounded is porous, and the states are often simultaneous. In one photo, an elegant woman stands on a sidewalk full of men—in her black dress, with her black gloves, a circle of white pearls around her neck, her solitude like a bubble on that crowded street. Winogrand's Coney Island photographs are particularly deft in their evocation of the ways we are alone in crowds: the man smoking in the dappled shade and sunlight beneath the boardwalk, surrounded by the blurred bodies of others; a boy's face close-up, his cheeks and jawline caked with sand, someone else's feet disembodied behind him. Solitude is not the opposite of public gathering but one of its constituent threads. A public space is nothing more than a collection of opaque faces, each one a mystery of loss and longing, like a silent disco—strangers listening to different songs, all their bodies dancing together.

On Winogrand's street full of splendid strangers, people kept disappearing. This was part of the exhibit's design—every horizontal slide clicked to a new one after eight seconds, every vertical slide after thirteen seconds—and there was excitement and frustration and pathos in their rotation. It replicated the flux and flow of the public spaces Winogrand documented, the way strangers rise like visions and then flee from our sight; the way someone might get off the subway just as we've started to build a story to explain her puffy eyes: her secret affair, her broken heart, her sick child. "The woman in the yellow swimsuit looks like you!" my friend whispered in my ear, but by the time I looked up, she was gone. When I raised my cell phone to capture two people wearing foil sunbathing collars—looking like flowers in a kid's play, their faces framed by golden petals—they'd already disappeared before I could pin them in place, trap them for good, make them my own.

If Winogrand's strangers kept fleeing, perhaps that's why I kept returning—so I could keep finding them again. More than any other museum exhibit I've ever seen, it was one I was hungry to come back to. The photos kept revealing new layers: How many times had I seen that couple embracing on a towel before I noticed the rough layer of stubble lining the inner curve of her armpit—that sudden intimate shadow? And how many times did I see the bronzed man doing a handstand at the beach—balanced on the supine body of another man lying across the sand—before I noticed how their hands were clasped together, their fingers interlaced?

The exhibit, on display from May to December, held—like a long exposure—the ways my life changed in that time. On our first visit, my daughter sat quietly in her stroller, still a baby sucking her two fingers. By early fall she'd become a busy toddler, full of plans—she wanted to run around the exhibit, to grab the pen I was using to take notes. She no longer wanted to observe the energy of these photographs; she wanted to embody it, channel it, claim it for herself. The exhibit took me from early separation to the horizon of divorce—as if marking the time I spent crossing the long hillside of that pain. Winogrand had taken many of the photographs I was looking at in the midst of his own divorce, bringing his children on outings to the New York Aquarium and the Central Park Zoo. I felt I could see the ghost of this backstory in his zoo photographs—in particular, how they held pain and wonder side by side. Szarkowski saw in these zoo photos proof that Winogrand could find beauty even in cloistered or sorrowful places: "His appetite and affection for life is so great that even this scarred and crippled version of it is capable of moving him to sympathy."

On days when I found myself simmering with resentment, locked in endless internal arguments—the kind you keep litigating, even if you know you can't win them—I'd take my daughter to Winogrand and let the world get large around my anger. That felt more possible than "letting go" of it, and certainly more possible than resolving it. I could just show up in the hallway of strangers and let them surround it. In recovery, people like to say, "Sometimes the solution has nothing to do with the problem," and Winogrand's photographs had nothing to do with my problems. They just reminded me of the ordinary, infinite world—how it was still there, waiting. *How do you make a photograph that's more beautiful than what was photographed?* This spring, his photos asked me to believe there was a more beautiful version of everything, even the ugliest, messiest struggles—if you could just regard them from the right angles, crop them the right way, capture them at the right moments, recognize the core pulse of their humanity.

Though for many months I kept my back to the men in the "White Masculinity" section, I eventually turned to look at them too, in all their pathos and fallibility, their bruised and blustering egos: men in suits, men at football games, men smoking and taking photos of flowers and gazing at naked mannequins in a store window. An elderly man with his head thrown back, laughing. Ha! And I was actually happy for him, for whatever he was laughing about.

Once, I was kneeling beside my daughter's stroller, feeding her Cheerios to keep her quiet for a few more moments, and it felt so *right* to be on my knees in that darkened room—as if I were praying to the sunlight glowing on the skin of all these ordinary human animals. Every one of them was fighting a great battle.

The first time I came to Winogrand without my daughter was on Mother's Day. Sunday was the afternoon each week that she spent with her father. Missing her was a primal sensation: I could feel my heart beating toward hers, across town, toward her seashell toes, the wispy brown curls at the back of her neck, her Cheerio breath. Her absent stroller felt like a phantom limb. At the museum entrance, I reflexively went to the special stroller door. The lobby was full of mothers with their children. The world was full of babies whenever mine was somewhere else.

The Winogrand exhibit was full of babies that day too: a tattooed hand holding a baby in a sky-blue coat; twins in a double pram, in matching white hats and matching white blankets, their matching blue eyes staring wide—staring at me. A toddler in the park held a baby doll of her own. Everybody wanted her baby close! Other photos held the girl my daughter might someday be-

come: a girl hoisted up to see a city parade, with long, coltish legs
and double-buckled Mary Janes; a girl drinking a Coke in the shallow end of a swimming pool.

Missing my daughter was a bottomless feeling. I'd never *needed*
art so badly as I needed it that day. I needed to be delivered from
myself, back into the richness of the world; needed to be reminded
that beauty could surprise you, that it was lurking in the strangest ruts and crevices—a tray of relish dishes gleaming in the sun,
a huge parking lot skirting the base of snowcapped mountains.
The faces on those walls were faces I would never know—faces
that were no longer themselves, that were fifty years older, or else
dead—but they'd be part of me forever, in their sublimity and anonymity, preserved in the amber of the spring and summer's ache.
Sometimes the solution has nothing to do with the problem, and
missing my daughter was not something to be solved. It was something to be met with stunning, unspeakable, regular beauty, and
then left intact—pain living behind the radiance, its shadow and
also its spine.

JAMAICA KINCAID

A Letter to Robinson Crusoe

FROM *Book Post*

The true symbol of the British conquest is Robinson Crusoe, who, cast away on a desert island, in his pocket a knife and a pipe, becomes an architect, a carpenter, a knife grinder, an astronomer, a baker, a shipwright, a potter, a saddler, a farmer, a tailor, an umbrella-maker, and a clergyman. He is the true prototype of the British colonist, as Friday (the trusty savage, who arrives on an unlucky day) is the symbol of the subject races. The whole Anglo-Saxon spirit is in Crusoe: the manly independence; the unconscious cruelty; the persistence; the slow yet efficient intelligence; the sexual apathy; the practical, well-balanced religiousness; the calculating taciturnity.

—James Joyce

Dear Mr. Crusoe,

Please stay home. There's no need for this ruse of going on a trading journey, in which more often than not the goods you are trading are people like me, Friday. There's no need at all to leave your nice bed and your nice wife and your nice children (everything with you is always nice, except you yourself are not) and hop on a ship that is going to be wrecked in a storm at night (storms like the dark) and everyone (not the cat, not the dog) gets lost at sea except lucky and not-nice-at-all you, and you are near an island that you see in the first light of day and then your life, your real life, begins. That life in Europe was nice, just nice; this life you first see at the crack of dawn is the beginning of your new birth, your new beginning, the way in which you will come to know yourself —not the conniving, delusional thief that you really are, but who you believe you really are, a virtuous man who can survive all alone in the world of a little godforsaken island. All well and good, but why did you not just live out your life in this place, why did you feel the need to introduce me, Friday, into this phony account of your virtues and your survival instincts? Keep telling yourself geography is history and that it makes history, not that geography is the nightmare that history recounts.

Perhaps it is a mistake to ask someone like me, a Friday if there ever was one, a Friday in all but name, to consider this much-loved and admired classic, this book that seems to offer each generation encountering it, sometimes when a child and sometimes as an adult who becomes a child when reading it, the thrill of the adventure of a man being lost at sea, then finding safety on an island that seems to be occupied by nobody, and then making a world that is very nourishing to him physically and spiritually.

I was a ravenous reader as a child. I read the King James version of the Bible so many times that I even came to have opinions early on about certain parts of it (I thought of the Apostle Paul as a tyrant and the New Testament as too much about individuals and not enough about the people); I read everything I could find in the children's section of the Antigua Public Library, situated on a whole floor just above the Government Treasury. If there was something diabolical or cynical in that arrangement, I never found it, but if it does turn out to be so, I will not be at all surprised. Among the many things that would haunt me were these three books: *Treasure Island* by Robert Louis Stevenson, *The Water-Babies* by Charles Kingsley, and *Robinson Crusoe* by Daniel Defoe. Yes, yes, my early education consisted largely of ignoring that native Europeans were an immoral, repulsive people who were ignorant of most of the other people inhabiting this wonderful earth. Also, they were very good writers, that was true enough.

What made a native of Europe, less than two hundred years after Christopher Columbus wandered into the mid-Atlantic Ocean (where he found a paradise and proceeded to undo it), imagine himself alone on an island far away from his home? Had his world, the world of Europe, become so burdensome to him, and the presence of all those new people and the things to be done to them in their "New World" become so overwhelmingly burdensome, that "all alone" became a heaven and a haven, a metaphor for becoming a new person, a perfect person? What makes such a person imagine himself (for it would be a him) the only survivor of a catastrophe at sea, and finding himself alone on an unknown island (unknown to him) construct a self that is confident, complete, and reasonable (within such boundaries), assured of his place in the order of things, in command of the order of things? For there are no real moments of doubt in this narrative that all will be well, or that he will emerge from this catastrophe enhanced in all the ways his enhancement requires.

Alone is always accompanied by loneliness, at least if you are an English person of a certain time. There doesn't seem to be a single one of them who does not need a companion. Somebody has to polish his shoes or make her tea or at least listen to tales of things the listener will never know. An English person of a certain time must have a Friday. Christopher Columbus ambled into the Caribbean archipelago on a Thursday in October 1492. He met people who seemed to look remarkably like Friday. Columbus immediately began to make a detailed list of their physical characteristics and their ways (they were so amiable, even their dogs didn't bark) and immediately judged them beneath him: Columbus gave a man a sword; the man, having never seen a sword before, held it by the blade.

So just how did Daniel Defoe conceive of a parable for the 1492 adventure? What if Christopher Columbus and his gang of hardened criminals and coldhearted adventurers had arrived in the Antilles and found themselves stranded with no way of going back whence they came? Would Columbus then have been a refugee dependent on the kindness of these strangers? Crusoe though is that rare kind of refugee: the refugee who is not suffering from hardship of the usual kind attached to a refugee: economic hardship, political persecution; he is having an existential crisis, a crisis seemingly known only to the privileged person from Europe, having come along with their Enlightenment. You know who doesn't have such a crisis? A person living quite comfortably in a climate that is called paradisiacal and who has no need for much clothing, with, not far away in the background, a jungle, not a forest.

Ennui, a domesticated, localized version of an existential crisis, is not for the Fridays of this world. We are vulnerable to the insane needs and greed of our own Other, that native of Europe; we have our flaws, but at this point we Fridays, when we are spoken of, are not regarded as part of the vast array of human experience, we are regarded as wanting, as illegitimate forms of the human family, as forms of Being meant to tend sugarcane and reap cotton, mastering the role of performing in perpetuity the Other, the Other that is always lacking in the full form and dignity that is the human condition.

The vivid, vibrant, subtle, important role that the tale of Robinson Crusoe, with his triumph of individual resilience and ingenuity wrapped up in his European, which is to say white, identity, has played in the long, uninterrupted literature of European conquest of the rest of the world must not be dismissed or ignored or silenced. Quite the opposite: it is evidence of the ignorance, the absence of moral knowledge and feeling, the realization once again that the people who lay claim to the "Enlightenment" needed enlightenment and that the rest of us were perfectly okay and that because of them we are in search of something that some of us already knew: when confronted with a sword, accept it by the blade, for the handle only leads to more blades, and the more blades and better blades that await in the long run—and life is the long run—are of no use at all.

So Dear Mr. Crusoe,

Please don't come. Stay home and work things out; your soul, a property you value very much, will be better off for it.

Sincerely,

Jamaica Kincaid

JOSEPH LEO KOERNER

Maly Trostinets

FROM *Granta*

THE TRIP WAS my son's idea. Leo's spring break no longer overlapped with his younger sister's, and she would be going to Colonial Williamsburg, to fit her grade's focus on early America, then on to Barbados. He wanted something equal but opposite. At school there had been debates about affinity groups, about who qualified for one and whose identity needed support now, in the Trump era. Leo got caught up in a dispute about whether the internment of Japanese Americans in the Second World War was worse than the Nazis' treatment of the Jews. Perhaps because Holocaust history wasn't on the curriculum, or maybe just because of who joined the debate, the consensus seemed to him to lean toward Japanese American internment as the greater injustice. Arguments around victimhood, reading *Man Is Wolf to Man*—Janusz Bardach's memoir of the gulag—and a sibling's impulse to counter Caribbean travel with something cold and rainy, all steered him toward a journey I had several times planned but never undertaken, to Minsk in Belarus.

For five years I had been making a documentary about Vienna. Half the film chronicled the Viennese invention of the modern architecture of home. I explored dreams of homemaking dreamed by the city's leading architects, artists, and thinkers—Klimt, Adolf Loos, Freud, Wittgenstein, etc.—as they tried to make the expanding capital of the Habsburg Empire livable for ethnically diverse and mutually antagonistic immigrants. The other half was personal. It revolved around a painting by my father depicting the living room of his childhood home in Vienna, with his parents, Leo and Fanny Körner, safe inside. My father had escaped Austria in 1938, leaving his parents behind. He created the painting from memory in 1944 in Washington, D.C., while waiting to be shipped to Europe as an officer in the information branch of the U.S. Army. It came to hang above my childhood bed in Pittsburgh, Pennsylvania, where my father met my mother and settled in 1952. What fascinated me about the work was less its meticulous inventory of my grandparents' vanished home than a strange coincidence that occurred in it. Through a window in the depicted living room, at the far end of a vertiginous street view my father managed almost photographically to recollect, there appeared, tiny but recognizable through their distinctive semicircular entablatures, the two windows of our own top-floor apartment in Vienna, where we spent our summers. Back in 1944, when my father reimagined them, our apartment's windows belonged to a kind of pictorial shorthand for other people's homes. One long block of anonymous apartment buildings, each facade featuring scores of nearly but never quite identical windows, ours happen to occur in the painting almost at its perspectival vanishing point—what in German is called the *Fluchtpunkt,* which means, literally, the point of flight or escape. By 1968, when we began to lease our two-room flat on the Volkertplatz, at the end of the street leading back to my father's old home, no one realized that he had perfectly but inadvertently captured our telltale windows in his painting. To me, who first noticed the detail, the imaginary bridge spanning the two homes seemed uncanny.

In the film, my father's painting starts as just one expression of the dream of the Viennese interior. It illustrates how ordinary people turned their small rented flats (everyone rents in Vienna) into beautiful enclaves. But exploring the later history of the apartment —how my grandparents were evicted to make room for "Aryan" tenants, and how their neighbor in the apartment right next door, a fervent Nazi who claimed to have personally founded the Hitler movement in Austria, seized the whole apartment building from its Jewish owners—the story veers to nightmare. Overnight, after Hitler's March 12, 1938, annexation of Austria, Vienna's two hundred thousand Jews effectively lost their right to live in the city. In the film the story of the Körners and their apartment is told by an archivist from the Israelitische Kultusgemeinde Wien (Vienna Israelite Community). The Kultusgemeinde is where, since 1849, births and deaths of Vienna's Jews are recorded. After 1938 the institution was forced to organize the emigration and deportation of Jews. For Fanny and Leo the paper trail turned out to be chillingly complete. Not only their forced "deregistration" to Minsk but also the precise facts of their transport there by train were fully documented. Commanded to report to a "collection point" in the Sperlgasse for "resettlement" in the German-occupied east, they departed in the early hours of June 9, 1942, from Vienna's Aspang railway station aboard a special train with the designation Da 206 (the *Da* stood for David, as in Star of David). At Vawkavysk, formerly Wołkowysk, the track gauge changed and passengers were forced from third-class cars into cattle cars—police reports record deaths already here.

Even with his excellent Czech, Polish, Belarus, and Russian, our archivist struggled to read aloud the stations listed on the twisting route from Vienna to Minsk, since some of the towns had disappeared, their names forgotten or changed. Caught on film, his halting reading of these names from the original train report helped conjure the distance traversed. Further documentation revealed that in Minsk the 1,006 passengers of Da 206 were herded into trucks and driven twelve kilometers southeast to a place called Maly Trostinets. There, on the afternoon of June 15, within a stand of young pine trees deep in the Blagovshchina Forest, they were shot, their bodies then thrown into long ditches and covered with quicklime. Later transports arrived at Maly Trostinets by train along tracks that had been previously abandoned, and gas vans replaced murder by shooting, but the protocol—execution immediately upon arrival in the early afternoon—and the place in the forest remained the same.

My son had helped with sound in an early interview for the film, and he had heard talk of a reconnaissance trip to Minsk and Maly Trostinets. In the end we decided to confine the filming to Vienna, letting the archivist's voice gesture toward the unimaginable. But our failure to follow through on our plans bothered Leo. Reading up on the twentieth-century history of Belarus, where, after starvation and mass killings already under Stalin's rule, the Nazi occupiers killed about a third of the total population, including some 250,000 Jews, and where, since 1994, people still live under Soviet-style dictator Alexander Lukashenko, Leo proposed a journey by train from Vienna via Warsaw and Vawkavysk to Minsk.

There we would stay in the gigantic Hotel Belarus, with its panoramic views of the city and an enormous swimming pool decorated with social-realist mosaics of athletes, Red Army liberators, and muscular Viking Rus'. To orient ourselves we would visit the Museum of Architectural Miniatures, where most of Belarus's monuments and castles can be visually explored in tiny scale models. Using Yandex.Taxi, the app which Leo promised to obtain, we would be driven out to the Mound of Glory, a pair of soaring bayonet-shaped obelisks atop a huge hill formed of scorched soil from the country's "heroic" destroyed cities, much of the soil carried by hand by schoolchildren. Time permitting, we would spend an afternoon at the Stalin Line Museum. There a segment of the fortifications that ran along the erstwhile western border of the Soviet Union (built to withstand a Polish invasion but useless against the Germans in 1941) has been carefully restored, and vintage mortars and Kalashnikov rifles can be fired for a modest fee. Maly Trostinets itself, online comments report, could be reached only with difficulty by bus, and taxi drivers could not be expected to have heard of the place. The sprawling Memorial Complex was also said to be confusing, with monuments and plaques containing inaccurate or contradictory information. But Leo downloaded a whole library of maps and made certain that Minsk was a safe place even for tourists who had lost their way. His proposal was hard to turn down, since I had a week free in March, and his half-siblings, Ben and Sigi, were eager to join us from England. I also secretly regretted my own peculiar inertia, which had paralyzed me as far back as I can remember.

The fate of my father's parents had always been the great family mystery. The Nazis had murdered almost all his relatives: this was all we knew and all we thought could be known. Two younger cousins managed to escape via child transports to England and Palestine, and they learned nothing more than that all the ones unknown to us, the ones living in Vienna as well as the oil-mining relatives in Boryslav and Stryi, in Galicia, now western Ukraine, had vanished without a trace. In the absence of facts, rumors flourished. In 1941 my father's brother Kurt had been deported with his wife, Olga, to Kielce, in occupied Poland, and a letter to my father from his parents in Vienna seemed to suggest that they contemplated joining Kurt. This would have meant that they, together with Kurt and Olga, would have probably died in Treblinka after the liquidation of the Kielce ghetto in August 1942. Other concentration camps were sometimes named. A college course on the anthropology of kinship required from each student a family tree. I listed eighteen of the disappeared relatives on my father's side as having died in Auschwitz, followed by a question mark. On the other hand, I dimly remembered having once been shown a note with the words *"abgemeldet nach Minsk"* written on it in my mother's hand. *Abgemeldet* (deregistered) was correctly spelled, so I assumed that my mother, who barely spoke German, must have transcribed the word from somewhere, or had it spelled out to her, but her recollection of where she got this information was cloudy, and her theory about it—that her parents-in-law might have fled eastward into Russia—caused me to ignore the clue.

The idea that Leo and Fanny somehow survived obsessed my mother. For years she read nothing but Holocaust literature and collected newspaper stories about lost relatives turning up out of nowhere. She disliked her own parents up in Escanaba, especially her father, whose Catholic piety concealed a violent temperament. And she had little in common with her sister's family in Iowa —all incurious Lutherans who never once left the U.S. An aspiring concert violinist on a scholarship to a music conservatory in Pittsburgh, she met and married my father. Divorced, exotic, and seventeen years her senior, my father was partly an escape from her own family. She identified with my father's family and contemplated converting to Judaism even though my father's parents had abandoned that faith. She felt closest to his mother, Fanny, who was supposed to have been independent, sensible, and strong—as opposed to the supposedly passive, emotionally frozen Leo. She imagined Fanny still alive, alone and trapped in Siberia or China. My father did little to counter this fantasy. He would just shake his head in annoyance and mutter to my sister and me that this was "a bunch of shit," while my mother held up her theory as yet more proof of his callousness. "Your father only thinks about himself."

What exactly he knew remains to me a mystery, but that he knew that they were murdered was obvious. Reading through old letters, I found that already in 1946 my father had inquired at the Red Cross in Vienna and confirmed that his parents were dead. Furloughed from the army, he had also visited a close Christian family friend, an unmarried secretary at the national railway, who passed on to him some vital papers concerning his two surviving cousins. By the time I met her, Stefanie Lukas had become a deeply unpleasant old lady who forced us to call her Aunt Steffi and whose apartment was crammed full of valuables originally belonging to my grandparents—we would have coffee and cakes with her seated around a table covered with a beautiful lace doily made by my grandmother's hand. These things were probably given to her for temporary safekeeping, but she never admitted it, and at her death, out of spite, she left everything to her cleaning lady, who (we think) kept the good things and threw everything else away. Having boarded for a time in my father's family home, Aunt Steffi knew all about Leo and Fanny's eviction, their reduced accommodation in two successive Jewish "collective apartments," and their deportation to the east. She could have given a full account of their final days in Vienna, but she chose not to. Instead she spoke to us endlessly about her own plight during the war, and how, dressed in her office uniform, she stayed for days in one of the huge bunkers in the Augarten as the bombs destroyed the buildings all around.

In the army my father had served in the OSS, the Office of Strategic Services, the wartime predecessor of the CIA. He designed posters and brochures that publicized information on the enemy, including Nazi atrocities. After his discharge in April 1946, he reenlisted in the U.S. military government in Germany, so throughout the war and afterward he had early access to facts about the Holocaust. The paintings he made in Berlin at the time, which established his international reputation, were explicit acknowledgments of, and monuments to, the murder of his parents. It was obvious to us as children that our yearly four-month stays in Vienna, made ostensibly so that my father could paint from life views of the city and its environs, were in fact a protracted form of mourning. Why else would we, each year, leave our happy life in Pittsburgh to travel to what seemed to us a ghost town in order to trail after my father while he looked for things to paint? And why else would we end up of all places there, on the Volkertplatz, in an apartment whose only selling point was its view? For me the painting of my grandparents in their living room came to symbolize this unquiet past. It must have been painted when my father had some hope that they were still alive. On the table between them, he shows the esoteric board game—an invention by his hobbyist father—still in play, with the blues and yellows almost tied. And he lets the string from his mother's knitting rise up over the blown-glass arms of the chandelier and down to the little dancing ball of thread as if to connect himself and us viewers back to home, to the mother who, Penelope-like, weaves as she awaits the exiled hero's return. And in fact, on forms filled out for his military service in 1944, when he painted that looping thread, he still listed his mother as his closest living relative. Via the painting's glimpse of the Volkertplatz, then, the painting also managed continually to project this tiny but real glimmer of hope forward into the future, into our home that we therefore restlessly inhabited.

It wasn't until 1997 that I discovered the facts. I was in Vienna writing the catalogue for a retrospective of my father's work at the Belvedere. Knowing how reluctant the Viennese audience was about confronting its Nazi past, I felt queasy about my incurious vagueness concerning my grandparents' deaths. *"Auschwitz"* with a question mark felt woefully inadequate in such a context. Through a friend visiting from Oxford I chanced to meet Simon Wiesenthal, who told me to go to the Bevölkerungsamt—he spoke the word slowly so I could write it down—but no institution by that name was to be found. Then, in the process of paying my German translator, I visited the offices of *Illustrierte Neue Welt,* a Jewish journal founded in 1897 by Theodor Herzl and still published in Vienna. There the editor in chief (my translator's mother) told me what to do. You simply went to the Israelitische Kultusgemeinde and they would tell you everything there was to know. Later that day I found myself across the desk from the duty archivist in her windowless office adjacent to Vienna's main synagogue. Before I could finish describing my mission, Frau Weiss reached for a big book of birth records and brusquely opened it to the right page: "Heinrich Sieghart Körner, born Vienna, August 28, 1915, died St. Pölten July 4, 1991." It was less my father's name, with its original, long-abandoned Wagnerian "Sieghart," that took me by surprise than the precision concerning his recent death, because the archive felt so much like a time capsule, with old records preserved but no longer updated. While I mumbled something appreciative, Frau Weiss—on the basis of my father's birth record —had swiftly located a slip of yellowed paper in a big cardboard box, which she laid neatly before me. There, written in ink in one script, was the name Leo Körner and the words *"mit Gattin nach Minsk."* A note had been added in another script in pencil: "(*deportiert*)." Remembering my mother's mysterious note, I believed I stood again before the same impasse. But Frau Weiss, assuming a practiced bedside manner, explained that all of the more than nine thousand Viennese Jews officially deregistered to Minsk had in fact been forcibly deported—the word *deported* on the yellowed slip had been added after 1945, probably by an archivist like Frau Weiss. And all these many thousands had only passed through Minsk, through back tracks in its freight train station, sent secretly on their way to a terrible place called Maly Trostinets. There they were all shot or gassed upon arrival. We know this, she explained, because of train records, war trials testimony, and a single survivor's report—only seventeen people were known to have survived transports from the German Reich "to Minsk."

Frau Weiss then showed me an old handmade poster on her office wall diagramming the bureaucratic maze devised to make leaving Austria first difficult and expensive for the Jews and then impossible, as emigration turned into forced transport to death camps in the east. Created by someone employed in the Israelitische Kultusgemeinde Wien, the poster resembled Otto Neurath's utopian isotypes, but put to murderous use—its creator was probably killed in 1942.

Frau Weiss also gave me pamphlets to read. I learned that the use of Maly Trostinets as a killing site marked an important turning point in the Nazi genocide. Hitler intended his invasion of the Soviet Union to be a swift war of extinction. Not only was the Bolshevik enemy to be destroyed, entire populations were to be killed or starved to death to create *Lebensraum* for Germany. German and "Germanic" colonizers would farm what would become the vast new breadbasket of his Thousand-Year Reich. By late 1941, Hitler steered these murderous plans more urgently toward the Jews. The masses of Jewish people in the conquered territories, together with the remaining Jews of Germany and Austria, would be transported by train to purpose-built killing factories. Unlike concentration camps, which killed some prisoners and worked others to death, these camps would exterminate new arrivals immediately, using poison gas, and their remains would be incinerated in huge crematoria. The few prisoners forced to do the gassing and burning would also be killed in efficient rotation, leaving no witnesses or evidence behind. Such operations would be undertaken in territories far to the east of the German Reich. Shrouded in the fog of war and soaked with the blood of Stalin's atrocities, the lands around Minsk seemed optimum for this purpose. A railway hub, Minsk had long-distance tracks in all directions, as well as spur lines to obscure enclaves close by. One of these was the abandoned Soviet kolkhoz Karl Marx beside the village of Maly Trostinets—the name means "Little Trostinets" and has many alternative spellings: Trostenets, Trostinez, Trascianiec, Trostenec, Trastsianiets, Tras'tsanyets. With tracks leading into it, buildings sufficient to house guards and slave workers, and two secluded forests at its edge, this tiny settlement—emptied of its inhabitants and fenced as an off-limits *Wehrdorf*—became an improvised forerunner of the huge extermination camps under construction in occupied Poland, something between a killing site like Babi Yar and the industrial death facilities of Treblinka, Sobibor, and Belzec.

The Jews of Vienna were the first in the German Reich to be deported for "resettlement" in the east. This little-known distinction was the direct consequence of another forgotten Austrian first, the eviction of Jews from their homes in 1938. It was Vienna's grassroots anti-Semitism that invented, suddenly and to the surprise of the Nazi authorities, the idea of rendering Jewish citizens homeless and at the mercy of the police. It was also mainly Viennese Jews who, between May 6 and October 10, 1942, were murdered in Maly Trostinets. Tens of thousands of Jews from elsewhere died there too, together with Soviet soldiers, Belarusian citizens, both Jewish and Christian, and partisans. The total estimated death count ranges from 80,000 to more than 300,000; the signage at the Memorial Complex claims 206,000, on the basis of an early Soviet report. After the Nazi defeat at Smolensk in October 1943, a massive secret exhumation action was launched to hide the killings from the approaching Red Army. Soviet prisoners were forced to reopen the ditches in the Blagovshchina Forest and carry the decomposed corpses—called *figuren* (figures) by the Nazi commander Arthur Harder—to a colossal bonfire, fueled by wood gathered forcibly from neighboring farmers. The unearthed remains were sifted for dental gold and burned in five-meter-high piles on a grill constructed of train rails.

Maly Trostinets's existence was uncovered when the Red Army

retook Minsk in July 1944 and found at its outskirts thirty-four huge smoldering pits filled with ashes, twisted tracks, and human remains. After 1945 the area was forgotten, a fenced-off no-man's-land. Parts became landfill—mushroom-shaped methane vents still stud the fields around the memorials, and in the 1990s fragments of toppled Soviet-era monuments were dumped on the wasteland while new apartment blocks rose up all around. The history of Maly Trostinets was further obscured by the sheer number of killing sites in Belarus. During their three-year occupation, the Nazis destroyed, by some estimates, as many as five thousand villages and six hundred towns, killing most or all of the inhabitants, and operated at least seventy death camps. The Soviet authorities sealed the archives, since vast numbers of Belarusians had been murdered by Stalin's secret police between 1938 and 1941, and in 1989 a Belarus commission indicated that at least thirty thousand people perished in the woods of Kurapaty, just a few kilometers from Blagovshchina Forest. The place name Maly Trostinets itself disappeared from maps when the area became incorporated into greater Minsk. Until the 1990s, when the archives were opened up to historians, the enigma of my grandparents' disappearance was a collective mystery shared by thousands of families with Viennese relatives.

We arrived in Minsk at an auspicious moment. In five days' time, just after our departure, President Alexander Lukashenko together with Chancellor Sebastian Kurz of Austria and a host of dignitaries would inaugurate the first monument at Maly Trostinets to openly acknowledge the murder of Viennese Jews. Vladimir, our guide and a filmmaker who had just completed a documentary about the Minsk ghetto, had announced our visit to the Austrian ambassador to Belarus, as well as to Belarus state television, turning our visit into a minor public event. Vladimir's daughter, an aspiring documentarian herself, filmed us together with the TV crew, as if to create a "making of" film of the network coverage. In reality, she just hoped to put together a film for our family, while the television crew itself was just shooting B-roll for their coverage of the official ceremony. Rain was predicted for that day, and interviews with survivors' families would be harder to organize.

As a child I was troubled by having two persons in my head. One was an "I" that lurked in silence deep inside me. The other was a voice, loud and vociferous, that narrated, usually mockingly, whatever it saw me doing. This "announcer," as I called it, couldn't be shut up, and if ever the inaudible "I" managed to conjure a third person to speak on its behalf, the "announcer" would only shout louder his rude commentary. Over time these struggles ebbed, perhaps because the "announcer" finally became me. But Maly Trostinets somehow brought the two inner persons back to mind as I tried to edit out from my experience the various people documenting it, myself included. On the way to the Blagovshchina killing site, walking through five stylized train carriages intended to symbolize the last journey taken by victims before their death, Vladimir invited me to imagine my grandparents there. Speaking softly into my ear, he recalled what is known about those final moments, how the arrivals had to leave their labeled suitcases in a neat pile for later delivery, how they were fooled into thinking they had reached their promised new homes, and how, in groups small enough to control, they were forced to undress and kneel at the edge of the pit. I knew these details, all of them extracted from war trials testimony and a single witness report, and I would have wanted to walk the choreographed path by myself, or hand in hand with my children. But of course I could have done that as well, instead, and I was grateful to Vladimir for his effort, as I knew from long before that such imaginings were completely beyond me, and it now seemed indecent to my grandparents' memory for me to picture them doing that here, in this real place where I walked.

On scores of trees in the forest, people had hung yellow laminated memorial plaques with the first names and death dates of murdered relatives. My children wandered under the tall pine trees looking for the names Fanny and Leo, to no avail. In the forest the TV crew turned their camera away; Vladimir stood quietly in the wings. I had the feeling of being, literally, too close to the trees to see the forest. The only past that came back to me was the one my father recollected most vividly: his parents, strolling in their beloved Vienna Woods.

The common German word for monument is *denkmal*, from *denken* (to think) and *mal* (to mark or to sign). Monuments are marks, sheer presences of one kind or another, that cause one to think, perhaps in a state of reproof—a German synonym for *denkmal* is *mahnmal,* from *mahnen* (to warn or to admonish). The word *mal* has a temporal charge and can also mean a point in time or an event, as in *diesmal* (this time) or *es war einmal* (once upon a time), and indeed most monuments are there to make us think about the past. The more historically conscious a culture, the more monuments it builds. In the nineteenth century, Germany was the veritable homeland of historical consciousness. There history came to be understood as the principal force and secret "cunning" of human life. By a strange twist of irony, what the Germans did in the twentieth century precipitated the greatest dilemma in the history of monument-making: how to commemorate the Holocaust. Not only was there the problem that victors tend to erect monuments and Germany was a defeated perpetrator; the cruelty and the scale of what had to be commemorated defied thought, while all traditional statements of warning, even the simple admonishment "to remember," sound pedantic, as if made with the obscene presumption that such atrocities can ever be morally or historically understood.

In 2015 two tall bronze slabs formed of expressionistically rendered prisoners, fences, and barbed wire, and representing prison camp gates set ajar, were erected at the newly landscaped Memorial Complex at Maly Trostinets. Called the Gates of Memory, the monument came with a text that spoke only of the "Minsk residents" and "civilians deported from Europe" who were murdered here. The familiar (and politically charged) omission of Jews as victims troubled many visitors to the site. One such visitor was Waltraud Barton. Born Protestant in Vienna, she had discovered that her paternal grandfather had divorced his first wife (a convert from Judaism) in 1938, and that after serving as maid and nurse in the household of her now-remarried husband, she was sent to her death at Maly Trostinets. When Barton went to Maly Trostinets in 2010 to pay her respects to this forgotten family member, she was appalled to find no mention of Austrian Jewish victims, and so she resolved to commemorate them, first unofficially through those yellow plaques, which she had organized, and then in the form of a permanent memorial, which eventually the Austrian government funded.

This was the monument about to be inaugurated when we made our visit, and our reactions to it were what Belarus television wanted to capture on film. Designed by the Viennese architect Daniel Sanwald and fabricated by the same Minsk sculptor who created the Gates of Memory, the new Massif of Names consists of ten closely packed columns cast from a clay model in dark gray fiber-reinforced concrete. Each pillar represents one of the train transports from Vienna, but the whole massif reads as a single fissured block, suggesting the compacted burial of bodies underneath. Its shape, dimensions, medium, and avoidance of figuration recall Rachel Whiteread's Holocaust memorial on the Judenplatz in Vienna, though Sanwald's underlying idea is simpler than Whiteread's. About halfway up all the pillars, in what looks from afar like erosion or damage, runs a concave frieze of first names. When we arrived at the monument, the film crew trained its cameras on the four of us circling the massif in search of the names of my grandparents. They turned out to be widely separated, but then, as we knew without saying, theirs were common Viennese names and could stand for any number of victims of that name. Vladimir encouraged us to put pebbles on the little platforms created by their names, according to Jewish graveyard custom. His daughter had two candles at hand, which my children lit in Leo and Fanny Körner's honor.

But there was a nagging question. Since nearly all of the Viennese Jews killed at Maly Trostinets are known quite precisely by their full names and addresses, because the transport lists recorded these, why represent only first names? Why this insistence on anonymity when one powerful feature about this site is the fact that it contains such documented individuals? Austrians targeted their own meticulously registered and deregistered Jewish neighbors, and Austrians—railroad engineers, boilermen, train conductors, brakemen, stationmasters, and policemen—participated knowingly in the killing, even vying with one another in their zeal, although one report survives of Viennese guards aboard the transport trains complaining of not having enough provisions for themselves, and of having to work on Sundays. An early transport was placed on a siding, with the Jews locked inside, while the Austrian train crew took Sunday off.

It turns out that it was the Belarus government that would not accept last names on the new monument. It was argued that such elaborate naming would dishonor the tens of thousands of Christian Belarusians murdered at Maly Trostinets, whose names have disappeared. An old saying comes to mind: some people will never forgive the Jews for Auschwitz. Or as Thomas Hobbes put it, harm so grievous that it cannot be expiated "inclines the doer to hate the sufferer." What made the Nazis so punctilious as murderers was that their final solution demanded every Jew be eradicated, as one stamps out every last virus of a deadly disease. Yet even though it was this distinctive murderous hatred that preserved for posterity the names of exterminated Jews, such distinction has bred a paradoxical second-order enmity. In the minds of some in Belarus, both the Nazi perpetrators and their special enemy belong to the long list of intruders. From this perspective, the first-names-only compromise is perhaps an effort to "decolonize" the nation's history. Rendering the Jewish dead anonymous equalizes historical representation that — so the thinking goes — has been monopolized by Jews.

I had been back in the States for about a week when I received from Vladimir a link to the official news report on the dedication ceremony. Broadcast on the All National Television, it began with an anchorman explaining that while Austria refused to remember a certain "page of its history," President Lukashenko bravely called on all nations to create a monument "to the Austrian citizens of Jewish origin" who died in Maly Trostinets. And suddenly there we were on film, searching the Massif of Names for Fanny and Leo. The camera had captured us artfully. Peeking around the monument's edge, or finding us through its fissures, it made our movements look candid and private: a hand placing a pebble between the *L* and *E* of *Leo,* Leo my son lighting a candle for his namesake, the four of us huddled in silence in the cold March wind. And then, intercut with these shots, there was me speaking into the microphone about family history. That interview had made Leo uneasy. He worried about how things caught on other people's cameras can come back to haunt you, although when his friends started forwarding the link he didn't seem worried.

On the deeper question of whether it would have been better to have visited Minsk on our own, he was of two minds. The television crew had been distracting, and Vladimir had turned my attention away from the family and hijacked what Leo had intended as an intimate adventure. But he and his half-brother Ben had managed to sneak off to the GUM department store, torpedoing Vladimir's "special bus tour" of Minsk, and we avoided a curatorial tour of a School of Paris exhibition and instead walked the length of the city by ourselves to one of Leo's planned destinations: a graveyard of Soviet-era statues, with huge heads of Stalin in plaster, stone, and bronze balanced on cheap storage racks. But these outings felt like stolen moments. Sigi had arrived from the airport in the middle of a dinner at a gallery restaurant with no explanation of why we were there, and because our time was so densely scheduled, it wasn't until the third day of our visit that she fully understood who Vladimir was and why he was in control. But she, Ben, and Leo agreed that on balance, our visit had been much richer thanks to our Belarus guides.

For me privacy had never really been an option. I contacted Waltraud Barton ostensibly to put us in safe hands, which she did, through Vladimir, but I did so also to manage my encounter with Maly Trostinets through the buffer of outsiders. The trip felt to me like the coda to a film and not like the end of a journey, which is why it came as no surprise to find cameras on our arrival. My own film had been designed to avoid closure, since closure was impossible to achieve. Everything headed in the direction of my father's childhood home, the place pictured in his painting, yet that home, indeed the whole apartment building, had been destroyed by a firebomb—in 1946 my father took a snapshot of its ruins and labeled the photo "My House." Everyone working on the film agreed that the building that rose up from the rubble should not be shown, just as we, when we lived in that neighborhood, never looked up to those modern third-story windows that seemed like cruel impostors. Unable to bring closure, the film—or was it me, under the film's control?—tried nightmarishly to repeat. It took its loving shots of "beautiful Vienna" directly from paintings by my father, and it staged the interviews with archivists and historians as curious vignettes, like the ones my father painted in the city, with me and my sister posing as models.

I hated to pose for my father. Interrupting our free movement through the city, forcing me to stand still in strange positions for hours at a time, posing exposed me to my condition as an actor in someone else's plot. And it confirmed the sense I had of myself as being always already narrated by that infernal "announcer" to a silent audience of one. If I made peace with that inner demon, it was only by putting myself in his position and telling the story of his story. The terms of that truce came back to me in Maly Trostinets. Approaching the pine forest with Vladimir's voice in my ear, I found no one at home inside me to feel what I ought to have felt. Perhaps my children, who walked before me into the woods, were able to put the past to rest, but I cannot and will not speak for them.

ALEX MARZANO-LESNEVICH

Body Language

FROM *Harper's Magazine*

I AM EIGHT years old, sitting in my childhood kitchen, ready to watch one of the home videos my father has made. The videotape still exists somewhere, so somewhere she still is, that girl on the screen: hair that tangles, freckles across her nose that in time will spread across one side of her forehead. A body that can throw a baseball the way her father has shown her. A body in which bones and hormones lie in wait, ready to bloom into the wide hips her mother has given her. A body that has scars: the scars over her lungs and heart from the scalpel that saved her when she was a baby, the invisible scars left by a man who touched her when she was young. A body is a record or a body is freedom or a body is a battleground. Already, at eight, she knows it to be all three.

But somebody has slipped. The school is putting on the musical *South Pacific,* and there are not enough roles for the girls, and she is as tall as or taller than the boys, and so they have done what is unthinkable in this striving 1980s town, in this place where the men do the driving and the women make their mouths into perfect *O*'s to apply lipstick in the rearview. For the musical, they have made her a boy.

No, she thinks. They have *allowed* her to be a boy.

What I remember is the flush I feel as my father loads the tape into the player. Usually I hate watching videos of myself. Usually there is this stranger on the screen, this girl with her pastel clothing, and I am supposed to pretend that she is me. And she is, I know she is, but also she isn't. In the third grade I'll be asked to draw a self-portrait in art class, and for years into the future, when I try to understand when this feeling began—this feeling of not

having words to explain what my body is, to explain who I am
—I'll remember my shock as I placed my drawing next to my classmates'. They'd drawn stick figures with round heads and blond
curls or crew cuts; they'd drawn their families and their dogs and
the bright yellow spikes of a sun. One had drawn long hair and the
triangle shape of a dress, and another short hair and jeans. How
had they so easily known what they looked like?

I had drawn a swirl.

Now, in the kitchen, what I notice is that my siblings are squirm-
ing in their seats, asking if they can leave—and that I, somehow,
am not. I am sitting perfectly still. Is it possible that I want to see
this video? The feeling is peculiar. I have not yet known the pleasure of taking something intimately mine and watching the world
respond. Someday I will be a writer. Someday I will love this feeling. But at eight years old, my private world both pains and sustains me, and sharing it is new.

My mother hushes my siblings and passes popcorn around the
table. My father takes his spot at the head. Onscreen, the audito-
rium of an elementary school appears. At the corner of the stage,
there are painted plywood palm trees.

Then the curtains part, and there I am. My hair slicked back,
my ponytail pinned away, a white sailor's cap perched on my head.
Without the hair, my face looks different: angular, fine-boned. I
am wearing a plain white T-shirt tucked into blue jeans, all the frill
and fluff of my normal clothing stripped away—and with it, somehow, so much else. All my life I have felt ungainly—wrong-sized
and wrong-shaped.

But look. On the screen. There is only ease.

I don't know whether the hush I remember spread through the
kitchen or only through me. My mother is the first to speak. "You
make a good-looking boy!" she says.

I feel the words I'm not brave enough to say. *I know.*

Soon after, I began to ignore the long hair that marked me so
firmly as a girl, leaving it in the same ponytail for days on end, until it knotted into a solid, dark mass. All my friends were boys, and
my dearest hours were spent playing Teenage Mutant Ninja Turtles
on the lawn with my twin brother and the neighbor boy. My room
was blue, and my teddy bear was blue, and the turtle I wanted to
be was Leonardo, not only because he was smart but because his

color was blue. When my twin brother got something I didn't—to go to the baseball game, though we were all fans; to camp with the Boy Scouts while my sisters and I were shuttled off to the ballet; to keep the porn mags I discovered in his bedroom—and the reason given was that he was a boy, rage choked me with tears. That was grief, I think now, the grief of being misunderstood.

One afternoon, when my brother yet again went shirtless for a game of catch and I wasn't allowed to, I announced to my father that I didn't want to be a girl, not if being a girl meant I had to wear a shirt. My father went to get my mother. They whispered together, then my mother explained that I should be happy to be a girl—there were so many good things about it. I knew there were; that wasn't the problem. The problem was that people kept calling *me* one. I remember realizing I couldn't explain this to her.

Back then, in 1985, the word *genderqueer*—how I now identify, the language that would eventually help me see myself—hadn't yet been invented. The term wouldn't come into existence for another decade, nor would *nonbinary*, which first appeared in an online forum: "Do you ever really feel as if you've moved from that nonbinary existence as a transsexual into a real man or woman?" Note the way *nonbinary* was positioned from its inception as transitory, as a passing through. It could not itself be a destination, the end to a story. As the scholar Jay Prosser has written, "Transsexuality is always narrative work, a transformation of the body that requires the remolding of the life into a particular narrative shape." It is the narrative constructed in retrospect—perhaps even more than the body—that makes the self recognizable, even cognizable. But narrative requires language. What word was there for me then that could have conveyed the wrongness of everything?

So I said nothing. In middle school I looked up and realized that everyone had chosen sides. The girls suddenly wore makeup and sparkles. The boys no longer played with them. Not choosing sides meant everyone would see that you were other. By then I already felt so other I couldn't bear it. And so the years of frosted pink and purple eye shadow began, and the earrings I bought in packs at Kmart, my favorite a pair of tiny turquoise dangling airplanes. In girl or boy or neither form, I have always been a fan of excess.

At eighteen I admitted to myself that it was the girls who caught my eye, not the boys. Terrified, I kept this too a secret, and kept dating boys until, at twenty-eight, I met a woman who pursued me. In her, I chose—as I would keep choosing—the sort of woman who made me feel safe. They wore long earrings like I did; sometimes we traded glitter eye shadow, and when we went to bars together we were at once highly visible and utterly invisible. Men asked if we were sisters. They bought us drinks.

All of this felt like fakery even as I lived it, my life arranged into a role like those in the plays I did throughout high school. To live that way—to make your life suit a prearranged story, a gender —was possible.

Until abruptly it wasn't. I was in graduate school when this changed, dating a woman who identified as butch and looked so much like a boy that the first time I went to meet her at a bar, I walked right by her on the street. When I stood with her I was always read as the feminine one; I was always safe; nobody knew my secret. I told my graduate school I was taking a leave of absence, moving to New Orleans to research a murder that I would eventually write a book about. I told no one that this was a lie; I already had the research I needed. I moved to figure out something I could not articulate even to myself, but that on some quiet level I had been wondering about since I was eight. My body did not feel like mine. My life did not feel like mine. Was there a self that wouldn't feel like a costume?

I don't know when I first learned of Christine Jorgensen, only that even decades after her gender-confirmation surgery, she was still my first image of what transgenderism, and transition, looked like. In the footage of her returning home to the United States from Denmark after her operation, in 1953, she steps off the plane in a thick, high-necked coat, her hair pinned up and curled just so beneath her hat, her heels smart and her stride strong. Once, she was a GI, but now she stands flanked by uniformed officers, and no one would ever mistake her for one of them. She is a lady.

In front of a tall microphone, cameras flash. Her eyes are wide, searching. "I'm very impressed by everyone coming," she says. But she doesn't quite look impressed. She looks stunned. She turns her head left to right. Presumably it's the cameras she's looking at, the size of the crowd that has come to see her. But she also seems like she's taking in the strength of the gender line she's just crossed. Will there be a movie deal? a reporter wants to know.

Perhaps the theater? What will Jorgensen do with her new body, her new notoriety?

"I thank you all for coming," she says. "But I think it's too much."

Some fifty thousand words from the major wire services followed. The size of the hunger that greeted her showed how shocking her trespass was. "How does a child tell its parents such a story as this?" she mused in a letter from the time. To be born and considered one sex. To return home another.

After her, children *did* tell their parents stories like this, and slowly, painfully, a narrative spread, one that situated the transgender person as "trapped" in the wrong body—a confinement that could only be relieved by transforming into the other sex, the true self. By the sixties, what was then called transsexuality was widely recognized. On November 21, 1966, a front-page article in the *New York Times* announced that Johns Hopkins was now performing sex-change surgeries at its new Gender Identity Clinic. By 1975 a nationally syndicated advice columnist was writing that a transsexual person "has the soma (body) of one sex and the psyche (mind) of another." The goal of a sex-change operation was to make the two align, thus making possible the "ultimate goal" of the transsexual person—which, the columnist reassured his readers, "is to marry. This provides psychic confirmation that the change to the new sex has been complete." In 2011 Janet Mock told *Marie Claire* that when she had had to live as a man, she "had lived with the sheer torment of inhabiting a body that never matched who I was inside, the one devastated by the quirk of fate that consigned me to a life of masked misery." It was only once she'd crossed over fully—when she could finally live openly as a woman—that she could imagine a future. "No more dress-up," she said. "No more pretending."

In New Orleans I stop pretending. The Boston girl who looks like a boy comes to visit me in the small apartment I have taken in the Irish Channel. I love the pink light over the streets each evening, the night-blooming jasmine scenting the air, even the splashed beer of the revelers from the bars on the corner. When I sit on my stoop reading at sunset a man rides by on a bicycle wearing a silver tin-man suit, a red felt heart pinned over his chest. As he passes, he doffs his oilcan hat. I raise my glass of wine. In the French Quarter I have seen trapeze artists in bars; I have seen goths dressed in their vampire black. In this city you can be anything you want to be.

Maybe this is what makes me brave. One night she and I are dressing to go out, her in men's jeans and a long-sleeved T-shirt and me in a short black dress with puffy sleeves that I pair with cowboy boots. I have fixed my hair into pigtails even though I am thirty, going for some image of girlhood, emphasizing the difference between us. Flirting. I lift a silver flask to my lips for a swig of whiskey, and she snaps a photo of me right then. Looking at that photo now is like looking at the moment before.

"Can I try on your jeans?" I ask. The jeans with the button fly and the loose fit. Jeans like I have never before put on my body, afraid of how I might feel in them.

Does she flinch? I am too nervous to notice. She looks at me, long and steady, and says, "Sure."

Then she snaps what is still the happiest photo of myself I have ever seen.

My memory is that when she lowers the camera this time, her face is grim. "We're going to break up."

I hardly hear her; I am peacocking around the apartment. Grinning giddily, turning this way and that in front of the mirror I usually avoid. This rightness, my God. It's possible to feel this way?

"We're going to break up," she says again.

I tuck my smile away like folding up an outfit. "Why?"

She gestures from the jeans—her jeans—to my face. "Look at you. You're not going to be happy as a femme anymore."

"So?"

"I'm butch. I need to be with a femme. Besides." I remember her sighing. "You're going to start dating femmes, I know it. Two butches together wouldn't be right. It would be like two femmes. That doesn't make sense. The masculine and the feminine together, that's how it should be."

Soon I am alone again with my dog in the New Orleans apartment, and a pair of jeans I bought from the men's department of Target without even trying them on. The fly comes up well past my belly button, the crotch sags, they fit atrociously—they are instantly my favorite thing I have ever owned. I buy a pack of men's white ribbed tank tops and a pair of Converse with skulls on them, and

I start dating a girl who wears flared skirts in all kinds of weather. I open all the doors and order all the beer and when we fuck I am only ever on top and I am only ever inside of her.

And I'm happy, sort of, except for the way that playing a butch role feels like performance too.

So it is in New Orleans that I first type *ftm,* female to male, into Google, late one sleepless night, comforted by the blue light of my laptop and my dog snoring at my feet. Once I begin, the words I have never dared think before come in a torrent. I still can't say them aloud, but I can type them at night when no one is looking. *Transgender. Testosterone. Transition.*

Lying on my back, a steady pour of whiskey at my side, I study the photographs that follow. The chests rendered flat with the scars from top surgery. The biceps and traps swollen with new hormones. The constructed dicks of bottom surgery—not a choice all, or even most, FTM people make, but an option, the remolding of a body. The remolding of a life. I watch the footage of Christine Jorgensen over and over. Is this rebirth what I want? Is this what will finally make my life, and my body, my own?

In the years that followed, I argued with myself over whether I felt trapped enough to truly be trans. Some days I would decide yes, and that I'd make the necessary changes to be recognized as a man as soon as I felt brave enough. Other days I would decide no—never because I didn't feel trapped, but because I wasn't sure being seen as a man was what would save me. It wasn't that *man* felt right; it was that *woman* felt wrong, and what could be the alternative?

Four years of late-night Googling passed before I could say any of this aloud. When I finally did, it was to a lover, a woman I'd fallen for the instant I'd seen her sitting in a crowd at a reading, her hair long and curly (like mine), her jacket black leather (like mine), her shoulders broad and tough as mine had never been. She was unabashedly *she:* hips that swung from side to side when she walked, lips plump and swollen, a lilting accent in her voice that drove me mad. On our first date she showed up in a tie, and I was so flustered and surprised I could scarcely speak all night. Wasn't I supposed to wear the tie? I don't think I said that. I hope I didn't say that. But she must have sensed something, because for the years we were together, she never again wore one.

Instead she donned the stilettos, the fishnet stockings, once a dress so tight, that rode so high under the curve of her ass, that I nearly followed her around the family party we were attending with a jacket. After we fought so badly we broke up, I found I could not stop thinking about her ass, her lips, the way when she straddled me in bed her hair swung in my face. The visions lasted for months, a haunting. Finally I sent a note unsigned in the mail—no name, just words of want. We met at a motel and still we didn't speak. Just the white sheets, her breasts I'd missed so much, the black confection of string, knotted into the shape of a flower, that revealed itself when I pulled off her clothes. We fucked until we were sweaty and the sheets were sweaty and everything smelled like I was home again.

Maybe that's what made me brave again. "I'm not . . . ," I whispered, my fingers curled in her hair, my lips to the sweat of her neck. "I don't feel like . . . I've never felt like . . . ," and then finally, "I don't think I'm a woman."

And her, bless her, what did she do? She told me she knew, from the way she felt me swell under her tongue. She told me she could tell from how hard I got and how much I swelled. I didn't have the body of a woman, she said. She'd known it all along.

Perhaps her response now sounds reductive, essentialist in the way she read identity in the contours of my body. But that's not how her words felt. They liberated me. She was saying that biology need not be assumed as cold, incontrovertible fact that had nothing to do with behavior or want. Rather it too could be conceptually constructed, seen as reflective proof of who a person was. The body rewritten with the pen of identity. As the cultural historian Thomas Laqueur points out, the body is always interpreted. "The body itself does not produce two sexes," he writes, let alone two genders. We created these categories. We named them. We drew —we draw—the lines that define them.

Until the late eighteenth century, only men were conceived of as a full gender. Women were understood as not-men rather than a category unto themselves—defined through difference, through lack. This extended even to the body: the ovaries understood as not-quite testes, with no name of their own; the vaginal canal understood as the inverted and undescended sheath of the penis. Laqueur argues that the telling of sex in Genesis—Adam creating Eve from his rib—need not have led to an understanding of a different category in the cultural imagination, only a difference of degree. What wasn't quite a man was a woman.

If someone with female-looking genitalia behaved in a way that was more like a man—if she had the assurance understood to be the domain of men, if she wished to have a profession, like the writer George Sand or the artist Rosa Bonheur, if she wore trousers and seduced women—she was thought to be an androgyne or hermaphrodite. Her genitalia might look the same when examined by a doctor (as they often were and, one imagines, horribly), but the explanation then was that medicine itself just couldn't yet see the difference. Her behavior was an amalgamation; her body therefore must be as well. Behavior, how one wished to live—the story began from this origin. Desire mapped itself onto the body.

I don't ever want to deny the oppression and policing of that period. Yet the privileging of desire, of behavior, reminds me of the freedom I felt from that past lover's response. After that night in the motel, we invented language of our own, stories spun from our bodies in bed. Neither of us had yet heard the term *nonbinary,* nor the term *genderqueer.* Our understanding of what *trans* meant was still beholden to the binary, and so neither of us could say, then, whether I was trans. Only that I didn't feel like a woman. So I wasn't one. She said my body was different, and I believe that to her, under her touch, it was. In time, hormones would do the work of her tongue. In time, hair clippers and binders would do the work of her gaze. But back then it was her.

What she saw helped me see myself.

Three years ago I went to get my headshot taken. I chose the photographer carefully. She takes conservative photos. When she asked whether I wanted makeup and hair, I said yes. I brought two ties to the photoshoot but then agreed to only a single photo in which I was wearing one. My hair was long then, and the stylist straightened it with a blow dryer and a brush and then individually recurled each curl with a wand. The makeup artist applied lip pencil as close to my lip color as he could find. I became a facsimile of myself. I looked older. I looked harder. I looked for all the world like a true-crime writer from New Jersey, which is, I suppose, one version I could tell of my life.

The photograph that resulted appears on the jacket of my first book, which is a memoir. The name on that book is a name I don't use anymore. The portrait is of me; it is deeply not me. The French psychologist and philosopher Jacques Lacan posited that it is in a child's infancy that, upon encountering a reflection of themselves in a mirror or window, they are introduced to apperception, the idea that they themselves are not only a self but an object that is viewed and interpreted by others. In a way the moment of recognition in the mirror is also a moment of splintering: from the private self to the self that is apprehensible to the other. This moment of alienation never resolves. There instead develops a state of subjectivity, a mediation by the outside world, an awareness of being perceived.

"Even in my own mind, I have erased myself," the writer La-Tanya McQueen muses, thinking of the times she has picked up a piece of fiction and begun to read it and assumed all the while that the characters are white, when she herself identifies as mixed race. What does it mean not to exist in your own imagination? And what does it mean to live like that for so long that you assume it is the only way?

The headshot is a very expensive thing I will never use again. A very expensive monument to my last attempt to conform to a binary that never suited me. A monument to a change that took a long time to come and then arrived very swiftly and that I do not think will ever change back. When a dear friend who has known me only in the after—the way I look now—first saw the picture, they were silent a long time, so long that I thought they must be half asleep or stoned or something. What was going on? The moment became awkward.

Then, finally, they laughed. "I'm sorry," they said. "It's just that I can see you're in there somewhere, in that person, but . . ." Then they laughed again.

What the photograph really is is a portrait of limited risk. I was trusting you, reader, with one story of my life. I was not ready to be open about another.

Last March I finally cut off my hair. I was in Sydney, on the other side of the world, and I made an appointment with a stylist whose cuts I'd seen on Instagram. I walked in and asked her to shear the curly hair that was well past my shoulders. Use the clippers, I said. For the first time in my life, I felt the buzz against my scalp. Afterward I suppose I was in shock. I nearly cried. As I walked the streets, unsure where I was going or where I should go—unsure, it felt like, of this body I had found myself in—I passed a men's clothing store whose window displays I'd admired days before. I went in. I left several hours later, holding two bags that contained nearly a month's salary's worth of clothing, neatly folded, suddenly loving the way everything looked on me. I wore some of that clothing on the plane home, twenty-two hours in a button-down shirt and stiff blazer. On two different continents, airport security called me "sir," and then, seeing something in me on a second glance, "I'm sorry, ma'am." I did not correct them either way. At home I introduced myself to new people as Alex and asked them to use the gender-neutral pronouns *they/them*. I did not mention this to people who had known me for years, nor correct them when they called me Alexandria. My driver's license had expired, so I went to the DMV. Waiting for my ticket number to be called, I snapped a photograph of my expired license, of the woman of ten years ago with her long, curly hair and her wide grin, her shirt falling off one shoulder to expose a bra strap, her dangling earrings. That woman would move to New Orleans one week later. Sitting in the DMV, I took a selfie: the skin of my scalp under the fade, my shirt buttoned to the collar, unsmiling. I posted it to Instagram together with the license. "Gender is a social construct," the caption read.

At some point I realized that I didn't and don't believe in narrow rules of what counts as trans, and I don't want to transition to a binary place where I would be perceived as male. For so long I thought that was the only other option, and then I was stuck, because that idea didn't feel right either. The only time I am ever emotionally attached to my breasts is when I imagine someone taking a knife to them. Yet binders leave me headachy, unable to breathe. I would love to change the countless small facial signifiers that lead people to sort me as female, yet doctors caution that it's impossible to predict how the body will respond to even low doses of testosterone. It took me eleven years to decide to take that risk. Now I watch as my body slowly changes, monitoring, looking for the right point. I don't want to pass as a man any more than I want to pass as a woman. I don't want to be perceived as either. Because I am not either. I want to be seen.

I am far from the only queer person to have been liberated by a loosening of the binary. Janet Mock later disavowed the 2011 *Marie Claire* piece that described her as trapped, saying that she now understands her experience as more fluid than that. In March the singer Sam Smith came out as nonbinary and cited a string of other celebrities whose visible examples had allowed Smith to envision a narrative for themself. Mattel recently released its first gender-neutral doll, citing the need for gender-nonconforming children to see themselves represented. Queer identities are a daisy chain of becoming, a passing-on of possibility.

I have come to think of the questions that followed my own becoming in terms of the number of drinks required for people to ask them. There are the one-drink questions, like "So, do you prefer 'Alex' now? For everything?" or even, "Are you trans? Is this the beginning of a transition?" And then there are the questions that arrive only after a friend has embraced me, has sat across from me in a warm-wooded bar, has ordered one drink and then another. "I feel comfortable with you," they sometimes begin, and smile at me or reach a hand across the table for a squeeze, affirming our intimacy. The words that come next never feel spontaneous, somehow, but mannered, as though they have been sitting just beneath the surface and are not for me, or not only for me, but for the changing times and language we live in.

"Because I feel comfortable with you, I trust I can ask you this. I haven't had anyone to ask." They sip. "I know I'm supposed to use gender-neutral pronouns for you now. But I've known you as a woman for such a long time. Am I really supposed to think of you differently now?" And then a moment later, after, perhaps, more steadying alcohol, "I mean, what am I supposed to think of you *as*?"

This is a risky political moment to identify as trans while questioning the universality of the narratives that have dominated the public imagination of transgenderism. In many parts of the country—more than ever before—binary trans people are finally recognized, able to tell a story of who they are, able to be seen. But under what the National Center for Transgender Equality rightly calls "the discrimination administration," trans people are under unprecedented and terrifying attack: re-banned from serving in the armed forces and no longer necessarily eligible for health-care coverage, mental-health counseling groups, or admission to homeless shelters. Soon the Supreme Court will decide whether people can be fired from their jobs just for being trans. This isn't merely a rollback of civil rights protections. It's a war, an attempt to legislate a group of people out of existence by making it too precarious for them to live. Trans people, particularly trans women of color, already face high rates of violence: Hali Marlowe, shot to death on September 20 in Houston, Texas, was at least the nineteenth trans woman murdered just this year.

Under these circumstances, it's difficult to say that the categories that have helped so many people be seen and see themselves —categories that are now threatened, that must be defended as legitimate—might still be too restrictive for some, like me. To ask for protections not just for those for whom the gender binary feels true but also for those of us who have had to find language that transcends it. To ask for, and claim, language of our own.

That language takes time. Recently a new acquaintance stopped me in a stairwell. "You had more hair when we met," he said. His tone was friendly, but I was immediately wary. I didn't just have less hair. I dressed differently. I went by a different first name. I used different pronouns and had asked my workplace, my insurance, and my landlord to recognize that. Soon, I knew, I would start to look subtly different, the hormones doing their work. I understood the subtext, what he might really be asking. "When did you decide to cut it?"

How could I answer? What few words would convey the complexity of a life? I had decided with every step away from the binary, every step toward being comfortable with myself. We've never had a narrative for who I am, but I am trying now, trying with language, trying to tell this story in a way I and others can understand, a way that figures the middle as the destination. I thought back to the child I was, the one who knew that *girl* didn't quite fit, who liked the look of *boy* and couldn't yet know that that wouldn't quite fit either, the child who didn't have the language and would need to write and live and feel a way into it, wait for society to invent the very words that would allow them to be seen.

All I said was, "When I was eight."

CLINTON CROCKETT PETERS

A Thing About Cancer

FROM *Boulevard*

EVERY YEAR, NINE thousand feet above the sea on the plateau
of Antarctica, fifty people wave goodbye as the last plane takes off
and winks out over the horizon. The women and men settle in
for a gloomy winter, isolated February to October. Temperatures
plummet to minus seventy Celsius, concreting cameras and mor-
phing jet fuel into a solid. The scientists, galley workers, and unlucky endure at the Amundsen-Scott South Pole Station in near-
hibernation inside a building on stilts, riding above the windblown
snow. They will not see another human face for eight months.

On that first night of winter, the polar residents congregate in a
gymnasium where they otherwise smash volleyballs, learn salsa, or
duel at kung fu. When the supply plane has flown, the crew dim
the gym lights and unfurl a movie screen. They sit and eat popcorn. Some, perhaps, cuddle. The words *The Thing* burn across the
gym, a phosphorescence like an Antarctic whiteout.

They settle in and watch movies featuring a polar station isolated and attacked by a shape-shifting alien during the first week of
dark. The South Pole residents screen all three *Thing* films (from
1951, 1982, and 2011), each based on the novella *Who Goes There?*
by John Campbell, about an alien that survives frozen winds, consumes human flesh, and secrets in shadow.

Of the three *Thing* movies, John Carpenter's is the clockwork
of terror. The story is "cyclical, mythical," according to film critic
Anne Billson, happening long ago and yesterday. It has birthed a
prequel, novelization, video game, fan site, graphic novels, and a
very fun board game. It is Carpenter's favorite creation, as well as

one of Quentin Tarantino's, who twice filmed self-described *Thing* homages, *Reservoir Dogs* and *The Hateful Eight.*

It is one of my favorite movies, yet it reminds me of my father's cancer. I first watched this movie as a teenager when my dad was disintegrating from a tumor that had invaded his skull and clawed its way around his brain. Dad's outer appearance morphed from weight-lifting six-footer to a cornhusk who could barely talk.

I'm curious about the tentacles of *The Thing* and other body horrors, how they slither into our imaginations, how they squeeze us into panic yet earn fans' ardor. Why do I watch a movie yearly that recalls my father's demise just as those polar astronauts do when winter closes in?

One half of men and one third of women will discover monsters inside their bodies. By this time next year, seven million people will have died from cancer. Soon it will rise past heart disease as the most common way to wink out in the world. They say some horrors are universal.

Cancer is known as a "clonal" disease. It stems from an ancestral cell that duplicates and radiates, ad infinitum. A life form arises, a misbegotten child—a Frankenstein monster rampaging against its creator.

Imhotep, a proto-neurosurgeon, described cancer in Egypt in 2635 BCE, finding a mass, a slithering crop of aliens bulging from a patient. "A ball of wrappings," he called it. Incurable, ravenous. He noted how cancer swelled and spread and hardened, how there was nothing to be done.

Hippocrates, in 400 BCE, coined *cancer* from *karkinos,* which of course means "crab." Some Greeks thought cancers moved around flesh like sea creatures. Hippocrates saw tumors entering swollen organs, pinchers radiating around, and he thought of a beach crab dug into sand. He believed tumors burrowed into bodies as if to hide inside.

Another Greek word migrated to mean cancer, *onkos,* or "burden," from which *oncology* comes. Cancer, along with culture, is what we have carried from our ancestors across seven continents. What we will perhaps one day bear with us to the stars.

Archeologists have uncovered ancient skeletons that show clear signs of cancer. Some of the world's oldest digs, dating 1.8 million years ago, reveal tumor scars volcanoing from bone. Cancer is not a new monster. Like a Hollywood screen killer, it has been inside the house all along.

The Thing opens with stars. A spinning saucer burning toward Earth, a reference to Carpenter's much-loved *It Came from Outer Space* (1953). A friendly Alaskan malamute arrives at America's South Pole Outpost 31. He is chased by grenade-tossing Norwegians in a helicopter. Later the Americans fly to Norway's burned-out camp. They discover an iced coffin, a block housing a monster-sized hole. A doctor thinks it might be a fossil chopped out of Antarctica, an alien separated not by cosmos but by time. A Thing gets into the American station; the residents aren't sure what or when or if it could be one of them. There's a revving of paranoia, joint-twisting effects, a downcast, perfect ending.

What sits with viewers who watch *The Thing* most, I think, is the creature, the muck of existence erupting from bodies. Twenty-two-year-old special effects coordinator Rob Bottin spent a year on *Thing*, doubling its effects budget. He led a crew of forty designers, illustrators, engineers, sculptors, and food artists. He worked seven days a week for a year. At one point he had to be hospitalized for exhaustion, pneumonia, and a bleeding ulcer.

Bottin threw everything at his creations: stop-motion, hydraulics, remote-controlled robotics, puppeteering, latex, fiberglass, rubber, KY Jelly, mayonnaise, gelatin, jam, and bubble gum. The Thing is a kaleidoscopic display of biology. It is "a writhing anatomical stew," according to Anne Billson. Phenomenologist Dylan Trigg writes that the Thing is "a synthesis of . . . evolution, a formless and grotesque realization of matter."

The film displays destabilizing sequences of men falling apart, melted by unseen conquerors. In one scene two Americans find charred bodies bleeding into each other like an aborted human mitosis. During another sequence an angry flower erupts from a blood-lathered dog.

The monster becomes an intergalactic mongrel, an ecological nightmare, complicating the boundaries of bodies and environments. Trigg writes, "The creature . . . serves as an expression of the origin of life itself."

*

When the Thing absorbs and becomes a human character—Bennings—he is stripped and coated in an algaelike ooze. The Bennings-creature sports the same red hair and beard, puts on Bennings's coat, and crashes through a window outside. Like a toddler, it loses its legs and collapses as other men circle, flares casting phosphorescent halos. The Thing's face is Bennings's (American actor Peter Maloney), but his humanity disappears into his hands, snaking in cardinal directions, bent as with rheumatism. The Bennings-Thing lifts these hands as if to implore the circling men to help him with a body that won't cooperate, to help figure itself out.

This was the moment the film teleported me to my dad's bedside, his hands curled to nubs, fingers unresponsive. The hands that once zipped across a keyboard at eighty words per minute as a sports writer, that threw footballs at me with quarterback precision. His limbs resembled burn-victim hands, melted together. Sometimes his fingers sprouted black nails. The hands would scratch against and tear my dad's skin. His hands betrayed him.

Once I entered his shared room at an elderly care center and found him with his hands held up to the light. His milky blue eyes tried to examine them. His skin was so translucent that you could see through it into the deeper reaches of flesh where sight was not meant to go.

At age sixty-one, my dad lost his hands, his sight, and his voice. Words and sense escaped him, and at times he would just cough the indecipherable. Sometimes he'd yell. When Bennings becomes a Thing, he stares at the camera, lifts his mangled hands, and cracks his mouth open for a howl that hybridizes a wounded dog's growl with a rusted gate's groan. The Bennings-Thing utters this ghostly rumble, and I see my dad in the snow, hands raised to the flares, unable to make sense of who he is, how he came to be kneeling before these men, and why his misshapen hands could no longer help him.

There are several theories about why audiences crave the system-shock of body horror. Filmmaker Philip Brophy coined the term in reference to Carpenter's monster. He writes, "The essential horror of *The Thing* was in the Thing's total disregard for and ignorance of the human body." It doesn't abide borders of identity written in flesh.

Many critics connect body horror's 1980s heyday with the AIDS crisis. Other theories on the genre's workings stem from viewers who witness *The Fly* and other skin-freezers during MRI scans. Adrenaline levels jump, hearts beat like hummingbirds. It's the quick-fix, roller-coaster hypothesis. Gross-outs give viewers a bump. There is also the common theory of any horror as taboo-breaker. Horror lets us let our inner caveperson loose. For Carol Clover, author of *Men, Women, and Chainsaws*, horror is "the form that most obviously trades in the repressed." It holds up a mirror that peers into our guts.

John Campbell had a mother who was an identical twin. Her sister frequented the Campbell household, and it was impossible for young John to tell mother and aunt apart, which terrorized him. For Jack Halberstam, gothic monster critic, the most successful monstrosities possess "a remarkably mobile, permeable, and infinitely interpretable body." When a novel or film includes eclectic creatures, "meaning itself runs riot," he writes. The horror of unreason.

The quaking at body erasure goes back to Medusa, the wendigo, *Gilgamesh*'s Humbaba—spanning human history and the globe. Japan's Baku is one such chimera, mythologically created from the spare parts of other animals and feasting on human dreams. These beasts bleed past species borders, incorporating reptiles, plants, insects, birds, and nightmares. Humans grow less human, less individual. The Thing is not just a parasite but something that *becomes* a part of us, threatening our identities as people.

The Thing's early tagline was "Man is the warmest place to hide." When I learned this, I recalled that each person secrets 100 trillion microbes, many of which a human cannot live without because these tiny beings compost our food. We have entire zoos in our mouths and perched upon each eyelid. The average person walks around with a quart of more-than-human life. Our every mitochondrion has DNA separate from our own.

Stephen King writes in *Dance Macabre* that horror reaches us "where you, the viewer or the reader, live at your most primitive." Horror reunites consciousness with animality, science with dreams. Body horror will not let us forget that we are a grubby animal, from and returning to soil. It brings us to an ancestral, biological soup.

Film critic Robert C. Cumbow writes that *The Thing* is "an image of what we *are* rather than what we might become." We are not just individuals but ecosystems.

In John Campbell's time, Antarctica remained uncharted. Even today it sweeps like a well of mystery undergirding Earth, a repost for fantasies and madness. The setting evokes the unknown, un-plumbed, an "out there."

The Amundsen-Scott South Pole Station is named for two men: early twentieth-century Norwegian explorer Roald Amundsen and British naval officer Robert Scott. Amundsen was the first man to complete an expedition to Earth's basement, in 1911. He and his Norwegian crew utilized skis, sleds, and fifty-two dogs, butchering many of the canines for meat en route. Robert Scott died trying. He made it to the pole five weeks after the Norwegians, but he and his men froze returning.

When Scott's and his companions' corpses were located, they carried the first ever discovered Antarctic fossil, *Glossopteris*: woody seed-bearing ancients, once stretching one hundred feet tall. *Glossopteris* are hard to classify because they are a giant shrub and kind of a tree and related to everything. At first taxonomists called them ferns. Then gymnosperms. Their name extends from Greek's *glossa*, meaning "tongue." Their leaves resemble the fleshy organs with which we speak.

Glossopteris proved that Antarctica was forested and joined to other landmasses. Gondwana, the ancient collection, linked con-tinents floating on a magmic tide. *Glossopteris* sprouted in all the lands of Gondwana and shriveled up into ice. They grew and died and evolved into many things, including proof that our lands were once one, that plant life, like humans, and even terra firma, is mutable, coming together and then exploding apart at the bottom of the globe.

In *The Thing*'s tensest scenes, characters appear possessed or as-saulted by disease. One character seems to have a heart attack, and the doctor grabs the defibrillator. Concluding the film is another character, white-bearded, limping, clutching a bottle of Scotch like an elderly man making his way down a wintry street.

Cancer, in its weird way, is an apex predator *and* a demon pos-
sessor, "a blind fate, a vast pitiless mechanism," as H. G. Wells once
called it. It inhabits and reigns over. It tears bodies apart, feasts on
our organs, *becomes us.*

Oncologist Siddhartha Mukherjee writes in *The Emperor of Mala-
dies,* "If we, as a species, are the ultimate product of Darwinian selection, then so, too, is this incredible disease that lurks inside us."

I think I watch *The Thing* because it reminds me that the dangers I sometimes imagine lurking outside my body are already inside. It humbles me that identity, like the giant mass of Gondwana,
is explodable, that my flesh will crumble. I don't want this to happen, as I know my dad didn't. But it's supposed to, and in a way,
like the function of clergy or last rites, *The Thing* prepares me for
an afterlife.

Whatever thoughts I have in my brain and whatever love in my
heart, at the end of my consciousness I am a shrub-tree about to be
frozen in the Antarctic. I am, in a sense, that ancient arbor life, an
amalgamation of parts destined toward a new order. Body horror
reconnects me to my malleable, animal manifestation of matter. It
creates space for me to contemplate my demise, as indeed watching my dad decompose while living did. There are no good deaths,
just bodies frozen for a time before their elements are unleashed.

Perhaps explorers will one day discover me.

There once lived a well-postured Minnesotan, Arthur Aufderheide, tall, perpetual wearer of bolo ties. He worked at the International Mummy Registry in Duluth, Minnesota, and was known as
the "Mummy Doctor."

Every workday, Aufderheide dissected samples from over six
thousand body parts in various stages of disintegration, harvested
from hundreds of mummies. Even in a museum, the desiccated
monsters are devoured by mold and time. So Aufderheide tooled
quickly to extract what information he could from the long-dead.
He had trained as a paleopathologist, microscoping for disease
within ancient skeletons and fossils. He wanted to see what took
our ancestors, the secrets in their bones.

Aufderheide literally wrote the book on monster care, *The Scientific Study of Mummies,* which includes a nineteen-step recipe for
shrinking a head. He once called his work "salvage pathology." It's
like finding a wreck on the bottom of the sea or an outpost in

the South Pole and searching for clues. "Often," Aufderheide said, "you're working with an alphabet soup of broken-down proteins where there used to be organs."

Much like the Thing breaks down its victims, death breaks down bodies. Within minutes a dead human begins eating itself, a process called autolysis. Cells rupture, their own enzymes devouring them. Once-friendly bacteria turn on our stomachs, climbing the bloodstream and digestive tract to devour livers, lungs, hearts, and brains. This is what body horror is: things that were us now feeding on what's left.

Ancient Egyptians knew enough to remove the intestines of the dead so they could mummify. But what are we without the organs and millions of species of bacteria that break down our food? What are we without guts? The Egyptians would also salt the bodies, coat them in pitch, and pickle them. Creepily, eyes are one of the last organs to decompose.

Looking at what killed mummies—medieval influenza, tuberculosis, spiderwebbed craniums—helped Aufderheide reveal the sources of our plagues and the progenitors of our deaths. But only 10 to 15 percent of mummies divulge their cause of death. The rest tantalize, suffocate with mystery. Some mummies are indecipherable.

After he died, my sister and I called around to medical facilities because Dad had willed his body to science. Yet none would take him, because his organs were so wrecked from cancer, so changed by disease and the efforts to contain it, that he was deemed unfit for scrutiny. My dad was cremated, which is what Carpenter's characters do to Thing-torn bodies.

A dead body, given time, embraces itself. Lungs collapse back into the rib cage. Browning livers migrate up into the chest. Tongues shrink like browning leaves curl. Limbs contort inward. Aufderheide routinely found ears rolled like cigarettes.

But in 1990 he found another thing altogether. Aufderheide inspected the left arm of a one-thousand-year-old mummy taken from Egypt. It was a woman in her midthirties at death. Her skin wax paper, torso a melted and reconstituted candle.

Aufderheide held her left arm as one takes the hand of the elderly, just as I walked my dad across the carpets of the care center with his skin like sewn-together snowflakes, liver spots streaking into scars.

Aufderheide held the old woman's arm and found a mass. Something had erupted from her bone, hot lava in the form of a crab. It had broken her skin, a Thing tearing its way out.

It was cancer, preserved. Mummified. That ancient monster that is also human, cells exploding from their frozen form. An instigator of autolysis, murderer of fathers. Civilization's alien conqueror. A being not torn from space but waiting inside our bodies throughout time, ready to bring us into another world.

The Other Leopold

FROM *Michigan Quarterly Review*

"HE LOVED BIRDS. Leopold."

"Aldo? He was a tree man. Not a bird man."

"No, not Aldo. The other Leopold."

For me there is only one Leopold: Aldo, the midwestern environmentalist who wrote *Sand County Almanac.*

"Nathan."

"Nathan Leopold?" This does not make sense.

"He loved birds."

"Leopold and Loeb? The murderer?"

"Yes, the murderer."

In this way, on a quiet spring evening, I learned that Nathan Leopold, famous for teaming up with Richard Loeb to commit the crime of the century by murdering fourteen-year-old Bobby Franks, was a birder.

The voice on the other end of the phone was the president of the small college where I teach. Leon, as we all call him, knows nothing about birds.

"Why do you know this?"

Leon had just had dinner with the Nobel Prize–winning scientist James Watson, who codiscovered the double helix structure of DNA. Now eighty-seven years old, Watson had just published his memoir, which is really a tribute to his father. His father was a birder. Who birded with Leopold.

"Read Watson's memoir," Leon urged. "You'll find it interesting."

These bits of birdy information float toward me, spicing the day like the birds themselves. They add to the gifts of bird mugs and caps, owl-faced refrigerator magnets to make me feel like I've slipped on, like a perfect coat, a new identity: I am the bird woman. Fifty years old and for the first time in my life I have the sense that who I am, who I think I am, and how people see me align. Like a juggler, I'm able to catch all three balls and send them back in a perfect arc into the air.

The transformation to bird woman happened so quickly in the past three years. Having my binoculars with me everywhere I go is surely the first clue that I'm always on the hunt. So on my morning walk, a neighbor stops me to ask what bird is killing the birds at her feeder (most likely a Cooper's hawk, I say), and a student sends me an email gushing about a bird sighting ("It was so shiny, speckled"; I refer her to the European starling). But beyond the birds themselves, I get regular gifts by email or phone: Have you read Robert Frost's poem "Ovenbird"? Or Theodore Roethke's "The Far Field" ("For to come upon warblers in early May / Was to forget time and death")? At a divisional party, a colleague is surprised I don't know the Mel Brooks movie *The Producers*. "I'll send you the link," she says. "You'll love it." In the film, Max Bialystock is looking for the "Kraut" Franz Liebkind. "He's up on the roof with his boids. He keeps boids. Dirty . . . disgusting . . . filthy . . . lice-ridden boids."

And then a golden birdy tidbit: Leon calling to tell me that Leopold, whose story I know of mostly through films like Hitchcock's *Rope* and the more recent *Swoon*, loved disgusting, filthy, lice-ridden boids.

James Watson Sr., just back from the front in World War I, was birding in Jackson Park in Chicago when he ran into Nathan Leopold. When birders meet in the field, we stop and share sightings, talk bird talk, beginning with *See anything good?* Maybe Leopold bragged about his collection of birds — three thousand by the age of fifteen. From that first encounter, the two young men became regular birding partners.

Unless your birding partner is your spouse or your loved one, a birding partner is a particular relationship. You spend hours together, often in silence; you know what they eat, how often they pee; you know how they respond to luck, both bad and good, in finding a bird. You see their ability to focus, watch their memory in action as they identify a bird. You are witness to their kindness to-

ward the birds or their selfishness. You know your birding partner
well and also not at all. Often you don't know what they do when
they go home, how they make a living, how they vote, or whom
they love. Did Watson, in those fresh days of scouring the ponds
and woods of Chicago, ever have a hint that bright and charming
Leopold, half in love with his beautiful friend Richard Loeb, was
capable of kidnapping Bobby Franks and bludgeoning the boy to
death—arrogantly believing they could commit the perfect crime,
were so smart that they were superior to the law?

Leopold was smart by many measures of smartness: he spoke nine
languages, had an IQ of 200, graduated from the University of
Chicago at age eighteen. I thought of birders as smart, as people
with sharp minds who savored small details. Birders are not all articulate or well-read and are often socially awkward, but all birders
share one characteristic that I associate with intelligence: curiosity.
Without curiosity there are no birds. In an endless loop, curiosity
lures the birder out, and the birding in turn builds an even greater
curiosity. Curiosity is a tonic, one that makes a person buoyant,
light-headed, happy.
    I also saw that many (often the best) birders shared another
characteristic with Leopold: a confidence that bordered on arrogance.

Leopold was not a casual birder but someone headed toward a
life as an ornithologist. In 1920 Watson and Leopold, along with
obsessive birder George Porter Lewis, published an eighteen-page
pamphlet titled *Spring Migration Notes of the Chicago Area*. Leopold
kept a keen eye on migration around Chicago. In 1922, at the age
of eighteen, he published his first paper, "Reason and Instinct in
Bird Migration," in the ornithological journal *The Auk*. In this article he looks at a few instances of accidental birds, like the Harris's
sparrow, that then appear more frequently. If migration is controlled by generations of instinct, these changes in a bird's range
come about through reason or learning, he concludes. Here was
the brilliant young man arriving at conclusions that saw the birds
as smart as well.
    Leopold spent a brief stint of his college years at the University
of Michigan, where he studied birds under Norman Asa Wood,
famous for finding the first nest of a Kirtland's warbler. The Kirt-

land's is one of North America's rarest songbirds, with a very narrow range, breeding in the jack pine region in just a few counties in Michigan, so that locals call them jack pine birds. It is a larger warbler, with a yellow chest adorned with a black-striped breast band. Wood describes the birds as quick and restless, with a direct, slightly undulating flight. It is named for a renowned Ohio naturalist, Jared Kirtland, on whose farm the first specimen was shot in 1851.

Under Wood's guidance and with Watson at his side, Leopold embarked on a trip to find a Kirtland's nest. His first year, they traveled "well-nigh impassable roads" to the banks of the Au Sable River. In 1922 they found not one Kirtland's, probably because the trees in the region they searched were too tall; the Kirtland's is a bit fussy, preferring trees between five to twelve feet in height. In the spring of 1923 the young ornithologists journeyed out again. After fighting through several hundred yards of dense jack pine, they heard a bird sing. There it was, "every muscle in his body tense" as it let "out a burst of clear, bubbling song" that they could hear a quarter of a mile away. This was the fourth nest found of this secretive warbler.

The next day Leopold returned to observe the nest from 9:50 to 11:30, noting activity every few minutes, including the number of times the bird sang in a minute, how often it flew to the nest, and how agitated it was by his presence. His notes reveal his mind: careful, thorough, attentive to details.

To document this find, they wanted to photograph and film the birds. In order to have better light, they decided to cut down some of the surrounding jack pines. It's hard to believe any of them thought this a good idea, and it wasn't. Though the birds were "surprisingly tame," once the trees were down, the female became timid, hesitant to feed the young. When she did come in, a brown-headed cowbird baby, dwarfing the Kirtland's, snatched the food. So Leopold took things in hand, removing the brown-headed cowbird baby. Without knowing it, Leopold was initiating a conservation measure still used today to help the fragile Kirtland's warbler population: protecting the young from being victims of parasitism.

After a lunch break (this seems so civilized—food matters!) the young men returned for further observation of the nest. Alarmed by the fact that the parents were not attentive to the young, they decided to feed the birds themselves. Lying near the nest, Leopold was able to feed the nestlings two horseflies. Soon the adult Kirt-land's warblers grasped the pleasure of being hand-fed and landed on Leopold's thigh and shoe. It was fed a total of seventeen flies. A black-and-white photo, taken from a moving film, shows Leopold on his belly, his hand enormous as he pinches a fly between index finger and thumb in offering to the warbler.

Why am I so mesmerized by this image of a man who is capable of murdering another person gently feeding a bird? Why am I— the word I want to use is *thrilled*—to find this famous murderer in my birdy midst? Perhaps it is because it offers such stark evidence that we all hold within ourselves contradictions. Though most of us dawdle toward kindness, then inch in the direction of cruelty, Leopold vaults. Anyone with such conviction, I admire, even envy. *Commit!* Leopold did: to the birds, to this awful murder.

Leopold arrives at a few general notes on the bird, including that the nests are often found near roads, suggesting renaming the bird the roadside warbler; that the bird doesn't walk, as previously reported, but hops; and that its diet consists mostly of centipedes, worms, and caterpillars. This seems scant information given the hours of observation. Leopold's small contribution makes me marvel over the volumes of birdy detail available on eating, breed-ing, nesting, and flight. All of this must have taken lifetimes of observation by people capable of watching birds like monks in meditation.

According to Watson, Leopold collected a few of the Kirtland's warblers, one sent to the Field Museum in Chicago and another to the Cranbrook Institute in Detroit. Watson was uncomfortable with the collecting, "fearing that the loss of only a few birds might tip this species toward total extinction." Leopold does not include information about collecting the birds in the article he published in 1924, "The Kirtland's Warbler in Its Summer Home," which he first delivered in person at the annual meeting of the American Ornithological Union.

What becomes clear in reading this article is that the qualities of a good birder or young ornithologist—keen, careful observa-tion and a steely patience—are the same qualities needed to plot a murder. Leopold and Loeb spent months working out the details of their almost perfect crime.

*

I calculated that it would take a well-timed spring trip to Michigan to see a Kirtland's warbler, the bird both rare and geographically limited. Unless, of course, a Kirtland's were to make a rare and unexpected appearance in Central Park, which it did in the spring of 2018. I happened to be in New York City visiting a friend in the hospital. Sunday morning, I ventured to the park with little hope of seeing the bird. Still, I knew that I would enjoy the morning air, and the search would give me courage to shoulder the weight of hospital air.

The minute I entered the park, a dizzying number of glorious warblers—bay-breasted and Cape May—greeted me. Soon a slight man, nondescript except for his binoculars, approached me and asked if I wanted to see the Kirtland's. I grinned like we had just made a drug deal.

"It just showed up," he said as he walked me back to a tree. There he pointed at a bird hopping from branch to branch.

Really? I thought as I put up my binoculars.

There it was, like a small yellow miracle, happily living where it didn't belong. Near me stood a gaggle of birders who had formed like a paramecium, tentacles of scopes and cameras all pointed toward the bird.

I would like to say that I lingered for hours, appreciating every feather, how the bird wore an elegant gray headscarf, wore white spectacles, and had black dashes like it had been scratched on its yellow breast. I would like to say that I savored this once-in-a-life-time event, this bird that connected me to Nathan Leopold. But I was cold and hungry and anxious about my friend, who two weeks later would be dead. And what of the bird? Did it survive its detour through the East Coast?

In 1967 the Endangered Species Conservation Act listed the Kirtland's when evidence showed their populations had crashed from one thousand to four hundred birds. Later, with the Endangered Species Act of 1973, the Kirtland's Warbler Recovery Team formed to protect the jack pine habitat and to guard the nests from cowbirds. Their efforts have worked. In 2012 there were an estimated four thousand Kirtland's warblers. Still, it is not a bird that will ever soar off of the endangered species list. It will forge forward only with the help of watchful scientists and environmentalists.

In his article, Leopold offers thoughts on why the Kirtland's is so extremely scarce, sounding an early warning that this was a fragile species. His observations are credited as leading to future conservation measures used to help save this rare warbler. What if we remembered Leopold as an early crusader for this special warbler and not for his sensationalized crime? Would it be possible to reverse the narrative of his life? Is this possible with anyone's life? Making such a shift would be like saying *Nixon* and thinking first of the Clean Water Act and Clean Air Act rather than Watergate. Or maybe the point isn't to define a person's life by one part, but to allow the person to be the range of talents and failures that they are.

On May 17, 1924, Leopold with his friend George Lewis tried to bag some Wilson's phalaropes, which flew out of Wolf Lake, adjacent to Eggers Woods in Chicago. A Wilson's phalarope is a sandpiper-looking bird with a needlelike black bill. Like other phalaropes, it moves about in a nervous way, often spinning on a pond to stir food to the surface with its lobed toes.

Four days later, Eggers Wood would become famous not for phalaropes but for the body of Bobby Franks, found in a culvert by a man making a shortcut through the park. Leopold and Loeb had taken Bobby, who was a distant cousin of Loeb, into their car, killed him, then transported the body to the woods.

Leopold and Loeb were scrupulous, yet all it takes is one small slip. The central piece of evidence that led the police to Leopold's door was a pair of reading glasses found near the body in the woods. Only three such frames had been sold in the Chicago area: one to a woman, one to a man who was overseas at the time of the murder, and one to Nathan Leopold. "I told Captain Wolfe I'd been out there [Eggers Woods] recently. I had even tripped that day, not twenty feet from the place the body was found, when I tried to run in my rubber boots to get a shot at a Wilson's phalarope . . . A Wilson's phalarope is rare enough in the Chicago area so you don't forget about it when you collect one." In his memoir, Leopold describes tripping in the police station to show how the glasses could have spilled out of his pocket. As I read that scene I found myself perversely rooting for Leopold to walk away, to get away with murder so that he could continue his bird-finding ways.

None other than Clarence Darrow, the best lawyer that money could buy—both families were splendidly wealthy—defended the two boys, who pleaded guilty to both kidnapping and murder. Both crimes carried the death penalty. Leopold's father asked Watson to testify for his son. Watson refused, fearing for his job and worried about the repercussions if it became public knowledge that he was a longtime friend of the perpetrator of this brutal crime that had become a media sensation. And really, what could he have added to the testimony? That Leopold was a good, sharp birder, that he had tenderly fed Kirtland's warbler babies by hand? Would that have swayed the jury?

Darrow's stunning, twelve-hour-long closing defense convinced the jury not to hang Leopold, who was only nineteen, or Loeb, who was twenty. His defense altered the course of capital punishment in this country. Leopold and Loeb were sentenced to life plus ninety-nine years.

Life plus ninety-nine years without birds?

Luckily, birds are never far away, not even in a prison. Open fields surrounded Stateville Prison, located near Joliet, Illinois. Horned larks and vesper sparrows nested in the field behind the prison, and in a marshy area, killdeer darted about, emitting their hysterical cry. From a back window of his prison cell, Leopold could hear the birds. He gazed out over the wall, watching the "gradual onset of the soft spring twilight. A robin perched on the wall and greeted the coming night with his joyous carol. To me the song of the robin has always been one of the most beautiful sounds in the world—and one of the most nostalgic. It brought back vividly many memories of long ago."

I am grateful for Leopold that he had these birdsongs. Part of my sympathy lies in the fact that I have taught in the prison program started at Bard College, once a week driving out in the evening to a maximum-security prison to teach men who are incarcerated for much of their lives. In our short breaks and after class, they would approach me and ask for things: an article or book to help them write a paper, more supplies. They weren't asking for me to bring in contraband or a file to chisel their way out of prison, but the ask always had that desperate edge to it. I hesitated until I finally understood that, so deprived of books or birds, family or freedom, they wanted whatever they could get, finding perhaps some solace in these small items. I have no doubt that the birdsong brought Leopold that solace.

But really my sympathy for Leopold, in jail forever, emerges because I think of him as a fellow birder, feeding those Kirtland's babies. And birders, whatever our many failings, are generous in one particular way: we want others to see and hear what we have seen and heard. We want to share the beauty and wonders of the world.

In learning that Leopold was not just a cold-blooded, arrogant murderer, the sort of beautiful, slimy guy in *Rope,* but a fellow birder, I had to expand who I imagined birders to be. And I sure wasn't arriving at a simple birder profile. I had met or read about birder scientists and poets, musicians with their sharp ears, older women and young skinny men, artists who note color and eye rings, egomaniacs and social misfits, presidents, environmentalists, photographers, and murderers. This range appealed to me just as the range of the birds themselves did.

Leopold doesn't just listen to the birds. Another inmate, described as a "Mexican working in the Fiber Shop," picked up a fledgling horned lark and tamed it. It was grown and "looked like a regular bird instead of a powder puff on legs, the way the youngsters do. It was quite tame." Leopold buys this bird for ten sacks of tobacco. The bird would fly to him when he whistled and had the freedom of Leopold's cell in the evenings (though I admit that it's odd to read of a prison cell as freedom). In a prison no bird is going to come to a good end, was my first thought. And sure enough, the bird, left in the stockroom, lets curiosity get the better of him; he pecks a piece of cheese on a mousetrap.

After this horned lark, Leopold acquired a few others as pets, one as a fledgling. He shows great determination with this baby bird, as for the first few feedings he had to pry open the bird's beak. He also shows great tenderness: "When full of worms, he'll fluff out his feathers and cuddle up hard against your shoe. It's pretty easy to lose your heart to one of the soft little things." So Leopold did have a soft heart, giving it to the soft little birds.

His favorite bird was a robin he named Bum, who flies about visiting the men, whom he refers to as "cons," in their cells. Bum came when Leopold whistled and loved his raisins. Then one day the bird was found in a brown paper sack with its neck broken. "If the fellows in E House could have got hold of the man who killed him, I think they might have wrung his neck." That seems about right in a prison.

Clarence Darrow was aware that Leopold might do more with

his love of birds. On September 20, 1924, he writes to Leopold, "I am ambitious for you to write your bird book." Again, on March 9, 1928, "I am still anxious that you should have a chance to write a book about birds." Leopold claims in his memoir that he never wrote a book on birds. In fact he did.

In 1958, after spending thirty-three years in prison, Leopold was paroled (Loeb was brutally killed in prison). This unexpected parole was granted because Leopold had volunteered for wartime malaria experiments. He was also a model prisoner, offering language classes and developing the prison library.

One condition of his parole was that he live in a rural region of Puerto Rico where no one had heard of his crime of the century. At age fifty-seven, he found work as a medical X-ray technician, married Trudi Feldman Garcia de Quevedo, and wrote his bird book, the *Checklist of the Birds of Puerto Rico*.

MATTHEW SALESSES

To Grieve Is to Carry Another Time

FROM *Longreads*

1.

I HAVE BEEN reading books about time: theoretical physics, evolution, parallel universes. Recently I realized that I was reading them because I wanted one to tell me how to go back in time—to before my wife died of cancer.

In *The Order of Time,* physicist Carlo Rovelli challenges our concept of time. Time passes more quickly the closer one is to a gravitational mass (like a planet or a star or a black hole). This fact is popular in science fiction. A space traveler might return to Earth to find that her friends and family have aged more than she has. Even at different altitudes on Earth, time is different. Rovelli writes that if identical twins separate early in life and live one in the mountains and one below sea level, then they will find in old age that the one below sea level has aged more, being closer to the center of the planet.

Time, Rovelli claims, is not linear. It is a gravitational field. If he is right, time is like everything else in the universe and must be made up of extremely tiny particles. There is no past or future; we only experience it this way.

So why, my grief asks, can't we change times simply by changing our perceptions? Rovelli suggests that our linear experience of time is due to thermodynamics. The second law of thermodynamics dictates that the total amount of entropy in the universe can never decrease, only increase. For us, or at least in our section of the universe, time operates in only one direction.

As consolation, Rovelli offers the *mind* as a time machine—we travel via memory. This is a disappointing compromise. In mourning, memory is only another cause for mourning. It does not change time, only reminds one that time has passed.

2.

I was adopted from Korea when I was two. As an adoptee I grew up with a constant awareness of two times: one in which I lived and another in which I would have lived if not for my adoption. The latter time was always with me—people often reminded me that I was living a borrowed life. Either they told me to "go back to my country" or they demanded my gratitude for sharing theirs.

I had been told that my birth mother was likely a prostitute, and that in my nonadopted life I would be poor and hungry and likely a prostitute too. As a child I tried to imagine myself in this second scenario, not because it seemed better, but because I wanted to belong. I imagined a me the same age as I was, whose birth mother had kept him even if it made her life more difficult. I doubt I knew what a prostitute was—I knew only how people looked at me when they said the word, like I should be afraid of myself.

In the worst fights with my parents, I would threaten to return to Korea to my "real" family. I was really asking for reassurance that I had one. My parents would tell me to try it, to go back if I wanted to. They knew I could not. It wasn't like going to a friend's house—I didn't know where my birth parents were in Korea, or even who they were, or how to speak to them.

3.

This summer, when my wife died in her Korean hometown, I held her lifeless hand and thought, *Let me go back just one minute.* I thought, *Don't leave me yet. Stay here.* To touch her still body, completely different and yet barely changed, was to be aware that a *moment* is all that stands between life and death. Time was the only distance; life felt *close by*. It seemed as if the only reason I couldn't go back in time was that I didn't know where time was.

After the funeral I would play with our kids in the apartment we'd rented and feel her presence in the other room. I would be about to call out to her when I would remember who I was now. What I mean is, I didn't remember that she was dead, I remembered that I was alone.

In a way, a marriage is two people living in a single time. You learn each other's schedules, when to call, when to eat together, who picks up the kids on which day, who has an appointment when. Strangers constantly ask you to tell the story of how you met, so that *the past* becomes *the time in which you didn't know each other.*

When my wife died, my life was thrown out of time. My past didn't seem to connect to my present. How had the last thirteen years turned me into an only parent of two young children, owner of a house in the suburbs of a midwestern city with a job that paid too little to send the kids to child care? It didn't seem possible that I'd made those choices. I would never have made them alone. My life only made sense if my wife was alive.

4.

Memory is essential to storytelling because stories exist *in time*. If one were to read a novel random page by random page, the novel would not have its intended effect. The effect comes from the order in which you read its words: a reader must remember what she has read before and make connections to what she reads next.

Without memory the sentence you are reading now would not make sense. By the time you got to the word *sense,* if you did not remember the words before it, you wouldn't know what *sense* referred to.

Our linear experience of time, combined with our selective memory, means that as we live, humans construct ongoing stories about who we are. That is, our memories influence our present actions (you don't stick your hand in the fire twice) and likewise our present actions influence our memories (sticking my hand in the fire was not in vain: it taught me something).

Each recollection of a memory—a process called *reconstruction* or sometimes *reconsolidation*—changes that memory. In her book *Reconsolidation,* Janice Lee writes about the risks of remembering her deceased mother: "The emotional or psychological state you are in when you recall [a] memory will inevitably influence the reconsolidated memory. Recalling a memory during these stages of inadequacy, repentance, sought-after impossibilities . . . may be dangerous."

When your beloved dies, your memory is at risk. Your past no longer fits your story of who you are. In order to change your story, you must change either time or memory.

At first, when my wife died, I couldn't stop thinking about all of the ways I had failed her. Failure was a logical story that led from my married past straight to my widowed present. How did I get here? I asked my wife to move to America, where we don't screen for stomach cancer. I taught her that hospital visits are expensive and to go only in clear emergencies. I mistook her cancer symptoms for morning sickness. I caused stress that exacerbated her illness.

Freud's idea of healthy grief (mourning, as opposed to melancholy) is the process of removing your desire from a lost object and reinvesting that desire in something/someone else. This definition suggests that to grieve your beloved healthily is to change your love for her. Grief often causes survivors to forget the face of the dead. That face belongs to a shared time that is lost when the beloved is lost.

To remember is not to time-travel; it is to alter how time *feels.*

5.

The feeling that your life is not your life is the premise of many stories—*Total Recall, Atmospheric Disturbances, ME, The Doppelgänger.* Why does this feeling occur?

In *Atmospheric Disturbances* the narrator is convinced that the woman who claims to be his wife is not really his wife, that his real wife has gone missing. The belief that a loved one has been replaced by an impostor is called Capgras delusion. It was first identified in 1923, when a psychiatric patient claimed her husband and children were "the object of substitutions." In *Atmospheric Distur-*

bances the narrator's search for his wife results in his entanglement (or his belief in his entanglement) in a secret society that fights wars in parallel universes.

In our quantum world, the multiverse is a natural leap from Capgras delusion. To think you have entered a parallel universe is a tidy solution to the problem of your missing reality. One of the most interesting aspects of Capgras delusion is the element of love. Usually it is not a stranger who has been replaced but a beloved. In the 1990s psychologist Haydn Ellis and others theorized that Capgras delusion is the result of your mind recognizing a face without feeling the love that you normally associate with that face.

Love is how we know we are in the right time.

6.

Capgras delusion is like an extreme mirror to impostor syndrome, which is the feeling that everyone else sees you as an impostor. (They don't believe you're a physical replacement, only that you do not belong where they are.) In impostor syndrome, the subject himself is the one in question. The subject himself does not feel loved.

This kind of perceived inadequacy often comes up in my Asian American studies course, especially when my students of color talk about their mostly white school. I understand impostor syndrome as a professor of color—and as an adoptee. The more you feel that you are an impostor, the more that feeling affects your behavior. As a child I became good at math because I was told that real Asians were supposed to be good at math.

In Asian American studies, my students talk about impostor syndrome as dangerous to their sense of self. If an Asian American kid is supposed to get perfect grades, for example, it becomes a failure of self to get a B. You build your story of who you are around the story of who you are supposed to be.

As a kid, the boy I saw each day in the mirror was white, not Korean—I couldn't have described my actual facial features. I wasn't looking in the mirror for something I recognized. I was looking for something that belonged in my life. I knew that I was supposed to look like my parents and friends.

An image, like a memory, is not about accuracy; it is about

value. We fill up an image with what we believe is important about it. If that image appears without its value, as in Capgras delusion, we can't recognize it. It doesn't fit our story: it is out of time.

An adoptee like me can look in the mirror and see not the image he sees but the image he wants other people to see when they look at him. Viewing himself as an impostor, he can fill up his image with impostor values. He might be able to love himself only by replacing his image of himself with the image of other people's love.

But, as my Asian American studies students say, it is dangerous to think of yourself as someone you are not. When the cops show up, you have to remember what you look like.

7.

The stress of multiple stories is the stress of living in two times at once. A psychologist friend does her research in a "time lab," studying how bilingual people experience time differently from monolinguals. Bilinguals, she says, are often late. It takes a bilingual person more time to process information. "You can't turn off language," she tells me, and the language(s) you speak impacts your internal "clock."

In order to understand any symbol you have to recall its associated value. In order to understand a word you have to recall what the word means. The example my friend gives me is the word *peacock*. When you read *peacock*, it takes longer to process than when you read *man,* since you have fewer episodic experiences with the word *peacock*. For a bilingual person, those episodic experiences are split between two languages.

Each and every word, each and every symbol and image, has to be processed through memory and so has a small effect on your sense of time. Why are bilinguals often late? Their time ticks away little by little. When they live and work among monolinguals, bilingual people also have to keep track of other people's time, which means more processing. It sounds exhausting.

Our memories are supposed to fade. We are supposed to forget. There are some people whose memories never seem to weaken —like Jill Price, who describes the condition as "maddening." In 2017 Price told the *Guardian* it was "like living with a split screen:

on the left side is the present, on the right is a constantly rolling reel of memories." For sufferers of perfect memory, the past is not recalled—it seems to play out alongside the present. The cost, for Price, is that painful events from the past continue to torment her. In some interviews she says she wishes to be normal and in others she says she wouldn't trade her memory for anything.

8.

Once in a novel I wrote that my twenty-two-year-old protagonist wanted more than anything to be old, to look back at his life and know everything had worked out. When you are young the future stretches endlessly before you, full of possibilities. Now I am thirty-seven, with two kids, and the thought of the future exhausts me. Every day I want to quit the time I am in and join my wife. Every day I want to rest.

Maybe if I were older, or younger, my body could accept the situation more easily. At night, thinking about everything I should have done, I can barely sleep. In the morning my body aches as if it held someone all night.

The first thing I bought after my wife's funeral was a massage chair.

When I was twenty-three, I went back to Korea for the first time since my adoption. I took a job teaching English. I flew in before a major holiday (I didn't know this at the time) and everything was closed for days. The school housed me in a love motel, where the TV got two channels, both soft-core porn. I wanted to give up, I wanted to go back to knowing what to eat and how to communicate: I wanted to return to America. It seemed clear, at last, that I belonged fourteen hours to the west.

And then I showed up for my first day of work and met the woman I would eventually marry.

Marriage is what allowed me to live in one time, rather than one time in which I was never adopted and one time in which I was. I married a Korean woman, as I might have done had I never left Korea. Yet I met her while teaching English, which I could do because I had grown up in America. We made a shared life, a Korean American life, and now that shared life is the time I carry.

In my dreams I go to that other time. I dream that my wife is still in the middle of cancer treatments, that it is still conceivable she will come out of them okay. I don't dream of a time that has never existed—I don't dream of her recovery. I dream of taking care of her. I dream that our shared time has simply gone on.

Then I open my eyes, and the present is pain. I keep my other time close for as long as I can before I forget my dreams.

PETER SCHJELDAHL

77 *Sunset Me*

FROM *The New Yorker*

LUNG CANCER, RAMPANT. No surprise. I've smoked since I was sixteen, behind the high school football bleachers in Northfield, Minnesota. I used to fear the embarrassment of dying youngish, letting people natter sagely, "He smoked, you know." But at seventy-seven I'm into the actuarial zone.

I know about ending a dependency. I'm an alcoholic twenty-seven years sober. Drink was destroying my life. Tobacco only shortens it, with the best parts over anyway.

I got the preliminary word from my doctor by phone while driving alone upstate from the city to join my wife, Brooke, at our country place. After the call I found myself overwhelmed by the beauty of the passing late August land. At mile eighty-one of the New York State Thruway, the gray silhouettes of the Catskills come into view, perfectly framed and proportioned. How many times had I seen and loved the sight? How many more times would I? I thought of Thomas Cole's paintings, from another angle, of those very old, worn mountains, brooding on something until the extinction of matter.

Patsy Cline was playing on the car radio: "Walkin' After Midnight." Not a great song, but performed in Cline's way of attending selflessly to the sounds and the senses of the words. Showing how art should be done. She was thirty when she died in a plane crash, consummate.

I was at the wheel of my first brand-new car since 1962, a blue Subaru Forester that I dote on. I wanted for nothing. I want for nothing. The other night I dreamed that I fetched the car from a parking lot only to find that it was another Subaru Forester, with two hundred thousand miles on it, dirty and falling apart. (That's diseased me now, I suppose.) But the real one sits gleaming on East Seventh Street today.

Twenty-some years ago I got a Guggenheim grant to write a memoir. I ended up using most of the money to buy a garden tractor. I failed for a number of reasons.

I don't feel interesting.

I don't trust my memories (or anyone's memories) as reliable records of anything—and I have a fear of lying. Nor do I have much documentary material. I've never kept a diary or a journal, because I get spooked by addressing no one. When I write, it's to connect.

I am beset too by obsessively remembered thudding guilts and scalding shames. Small potatoes, as traumas go, but intensified by my aversion to facing them.

Susan Sontag observed that when you have a disease people identify you with it. Fine by me! I could never sustain an expedient "I" for more than a paragraph. (Do you imagine that writers speak "as themselves"? No such selves exist.) Playing the Dying Man *(Enter left. Exit trapdoor)* gives me a persona. It's a handy mask.

I've lost the scraps of my aborted Guggenheim memoir, but I remember that it started something like this:

> On September 9, 1956, in the very small Minnesota town of Farmington, my family of seven settled in, as we did every week, to watch *The Ed Sullivan Show*. We had the living-room lights off because we were still confusing TV with film. Elvis Presley came on. My grandmother said, "Disgusting!" My parents made discontented sounds. When Presley finished, I left the house and started walking over to my friend Richie Sievers's house. Autumn leaves covered the sidewalks and ground. I met Richie coming the other way. One of us said, "Did you see that?" "Yeah, what do you think?" "I don't know. What do you think?" "I don't know." We stood silent, kicking at leaves. Something had happened.

I thought I'd braid my life into cultural history. That went nowhere.

*

Death is like painting rather than like sculpture, because it's seen from only one side. Monochrome—like the mausoleum-gray former Berlin Wall, which kids in West Berlin glamorized with graffiti. What I'm trying to do here.

Swatted a fly the other day and thought, *Outlived* you.

I grew up in small-town Minnesota being regarded as the rich kid, because my father's firms (first manufacturing plastic bags, then engineering inventions including the NASA Echo 1 and Echo 2 Mylar-balloon satellites) were the biggest businesses around. I had no sense of this, thinking that the kids who sucked up to me and the others who bullied me were reacting to my true self. This left me deeply confused. Years later I asked my mother if she had been aware of the pattern. She said yes. I asked why she hadn't said anything to me about it. She said, "Because people shouldn't be like that."

The Midwest!

My mother was a prairie princess, the only child of a school superintendent who doubled as a postmaster, from a tiny town in North Dakota. My father was a railroad worker's son from another. I was born in Fargo. In the summer of 1945, when I was three and a half, alone in the kitchen of my great-uncle Martin's farmhouse—water by hand pump; chamber pots and an outhouse—a grizzled man came in and tried to grab me. I ran screaming. It was Dad, home from the war.

My mother maintained a peaceful home, and neither she nor my father was ever physically abusive. But they were wrapped up in themselves and each other to the extreme of being jealous of their five kids, of whom I'm the oldest. From my father's point of view, God forbid my mother should waste affection on me that could go to him. Zero sum. Everything that he had went into his work, and everything that she had went into him. The one and only way I could attain his attention was to be insolent, to make my mother cry. Then he'd rage but at least make eye contact.

I grew up with a craving for and a resentment of authority. This bedevils me still.

In love letters my mother addressed him as the President, and he called her the Student Body.

What my parents were doing having children mystifies, beyond the given, during the Depression and the war eras, that marriage required it. My father was a self-made extraordinary inventor and engineer and a successful but credulous—i.e., exploitable—entrepreneur. He may have suffered lifelong post-traumatic stress from his ordeals as a grunt in the Battle of the Bulge. He wouldn't talk about it except in bursts now and then. But he had nightmares.

My father's fragmentary stories from the war left big gaps in time. Here's what I can piece together. He was a private in a division, the 84th, that helped to roll back the German advance. He was hunkered down in snow on the day that my sister Ann was born, two days before Christmas, 1944. His infantry units would creep to the edge of villages to suppress any antitank fire ahead of armored advances. Once, one of our own tanks churned across a foxhole he was in, burying him and killing the man, a close friend, next to him. My father was a radio operator until, ordered to take a radio to a cutoff platoon, he and another soldier came under mortar fire. They dived into a shell hole. The mortars zeroed in, "like someone bouncing a basketball around the hole," he said. A near-hit wounded his partner. Making a break for it, my father helped the man and lugged the radio, which, when they reached the platoon, was found to be wrecked by shrapnel. He was awarded a Bronze Star and spent the rest of the war as a rifleman.

I have a photograph of him with some of his comrades outside a battered church. He grins rather maniacally and holds a lectern —inexplicable loot from the church. He brought home a German helmet and uniform, a German rifle-cleaning kit, a piece of transparent plastic from the cockpit canopy of a downed Messerschmitt, an artillery-shell casing, a large fragment of an exploded grenade, and a steel ammunition box on which he had painted, in his elegant engineer's hand, his division logo and the names of the places where he had fought. I played continually with those objects as a boy, fantasizing about military glory.

Once, he spoke of being under artillery bombardment in a forest. It frightened me. His tone hinted at still-unrelieved, helpless terror.

Late in life, going dotty (or dottier than usual), my father contemplated returning to the battle zone of the Ardennes and seeking out German privates who had fought on the other side. He wanted to test his theory that they had hated their officers as much as he had hated his—whose sole aim, from his perspective, was to squander the lives of their men.

I recounted this plan to the German painter Anselm Kiefer, who was born in 1945. As I recall, though he doesn't, he said, "Don't tell your father. Our men loved their officers."

I was friends with Kiefer for a while, as I was with many artists over the years, until about twenty years ago. The friendships fell apart. Closeness is impossible between an artist and a critic. Each wants from the other something—the artist's mojo, the critic's sagacity—that belongs strictly to the audiences for their respective work. It's like two vacuum cleaners sucking at each other.

My father was on a cutting edge—quite literally, as one of the first to discover how to simultaneously cut and seal polyethylene with a hot knife, experimenting in the basement of our modest house. He invented the plastic-lined paper sickness bag for airplanes, for which he received a dollar. (The patent belonged to the company he was working for.) What remained of the family fortune when he died has all but gone to the care of my mother, who is chipper at the age of a hundred and two.

Too much about my dad? Exactly! His charisma bleached the identities of his five children. I spent years of my childhood trying to win his approval and years of my adolescence trying to provoke his disapproval, until I had to accept that he didn't care either way. When I told him on the phone, in 1998, that I'd been hired by *The New Yorker*, there was a long silence. Then he said, "Oh, you kids!"

Too little about my mother? Exactly again. My memories of her from my childhood amount to a uniform haze of bland niceness punctuated with flares of incomprehensible anger or tears and almost no sense of emotional connection. She was, and remains, a constant reader without a trace of intellectual curiosity. She tells everybody that she's proud of me. I'm a credit to her.

I was set up to be the tower-of-strength big brother, a surrogate parent, and my three younger sisters and my younger brother bought into it. But my heart was a loveless void. I broke free at the cost of hating myself for letting my siblings down. Estrangements ensued that now, one by one, are healing. Ann, Don, Peggy, Mary, and me: an accountant, a geographer, a massage therapist, a chef, and an art critic. We've done all right.

Still, people I know will roll their eyes—same old Peter!—at how little of their deserved shrift they're receiving from me here as, alone, I linger again with my lifelong lover: you, reader.

I was a kid crazy about language and an omnivorous reader. At breakfast I'd pore over every word on a cereal box as if it were holy writ. The first poem I remember writing was at a class picnic on the last day of sixth grade. I lay back on the grass, looking up. A hawk soared overhead. This wasn't unusual, but it gave me an odd feeling. I rolled over and wrote what I knew was a poem because it looked like one. All I recall of it is a chorus: "Winged avenger from the skies!" I'm not sure that I even knew what an avenger was. I took the poem to my teacher, who said, "Peter, this is very unpleasant." That smothered my literary drive for some years.

In a car with high school classmates after a picnic party somewhere in rural Minnesota—a bottle had been passed, and I would have proof that Cheetos were on the bill of fare—I said to stop. I tumbled out and barfed beside the road. The vomit was bright orange. It puddled on bright-green grass. The summer sky was bright blue. I thought I had never seen anything so beautiful.

My rags-to-riches-to-fewer-riches father decided that his children should make their own way in the world, as he had. So no financial support beyond college and such emergency aid as was required to pay a fine, say, rather than have me spend a year in jail (pot bust in Maine) and, oh, yes, the funds for the little yellow Austin-Healey Sprite in which, dropping out of college in Minnesota, I drove east on a slim chance. That was in 1962. I was twenty.

I had wanted out of school and, after a landlocked upbringing, yearned to see an ocean. In those days cities of any size had dailies. I sent letters to papers in small cities near big ones, three on the East Coast and three on the West. Only the *Jersey Journal*, in Jersey City, replied, offering an interview. I drove through a day and a night, my tiny car drafting behind barreling trucks, to Journal Square, which glistened in the sun after a night rain. An editor asked where I was staying. I think I mumbled something. He said, "You don't have a place to stay, do you?" Then he said, "Oh, hell, take a desk."

*

Hudson County, New Jersey, was epically corrupt. Several Jersey City mayors have gone to jail. One day in 1963, a reporter hung up the phone and announced, "Tony Pro is having another press conference." Mysteriously, everybody laughed. "Let's send the kid," someone said.

At the Teamsters headquarters in Union City, Tony (Pro) Provenzano sat behind an immense desk, flanked by central-casting bodyguards. Other reporters lounged and smoked. Only I had a notebook ready. Tony Pro told a series of obscene jokes about Attorney General Robert Kennedy, who was crusading against the Mob. And that was that. Tony Pro stood at the door shaking hands with us. *Crinkle.* In my palm was the first fifty-dollar bill I had ever seen. I said thanks, but I really couldn't. I set the bill down when he wouldn't take it back.

Staring eyes greeted my return to the paper, and the editor in chief called me into his office and shut the door. He said, "I don't know what you did or what you said, and I don't want to know. Never do it or say it again."

Later that year, when Provenzano was on trial in Newark for extortion, he sat down beside me during a break and chatted amiably about something, maybe baseball.

I acquired the most useful writing discipline of my life from fat, cigar-chewing *Jersey Journal* copy editors—burned-out reporters —at desks in a half-circle facing the city editor. With No. 1 pencils, like black crayons, they'd eviscerate my copy. I'd rewrite, and they'd do it again. Finally they sent it down to the Linotype—the old racketing, reeking contraption for setting type from molten lead. Those men still sit by as I write, pencils in their itching paws.

"Sleeping the big sleep." Raymond Chandler proved that the American form of Montaigne-grade aphorism is the wisecrack.

Wisecracks in Chandler are existential rescues of imperiled self-possession. Worth the risk to the detective of a punch in the gut. And conserving calm for noticing the world.

"A slanting gray rain like a swung curtain of crystal beads."

"A few windows were lit and radios were bleating at the dusk."

I lost my interminably heavy-petting virginity with the recently graduated fiancée of a college friend who was still at school, a senior. I had been invited to my friend's parents' penthouse on Sutton Place South, an apartment that was deluxe beyond my dreaming. A spotlighted Willem de Kooning painting stunned me: wild but somehow purposeful, clinching an unstated argument. The woman and I left together and fell to making out in the elevator, then proceeded to a cheap hotel on Lexington Avenue. We had a frenzied affair, only about sex. It was what's now termed empowering.

I went back to college in Minnesota for a year, dropped out for good, returned to the Jersey City job for three months, unwisely married, spent an impoverished and largely useless year in Paris, had a life-changing encounter with a painting by Piero della Francesca in Italy, another with works by Andy Warhol in Paris, returned to New York, freelanced, stumbled into the art world, got a divorce, which, while uncontested, entailed a solo trip to a dusty courthouse in Juárez, Mexico, past a kid saying, "Hey, hippie, wanna screw my sister?," to receive a spectacular document with a gold seal and a red ribbon from a judge as rotund and taciturn as an Olmec idol.

When I started writing criticism, in 1965, in almost pristine ignorance, I discovered that I was the world's leading expert in one thing: my experience. Most of what I know in a scholarly way about art I learned on deadlines, to sound as if I knew what I was talking about—as, little by little, I did. Educating yourself in public is painful, but the lessons stick.

In 1966, after a few months of writing mostly one-sentence reviews for the *Art News,* I was hired as the art critic of the *Village Voice,* for the first of three stints with the often marvelous weekly. (The others spanned 1980–81 and 1991–98.) I had a problem besides inexperience: a question of priorities, between meeting deadlines and doing lots of drugs—a no-brainer in more than one way. I lasted in that job for only a few weeks. Meanwhile the poetry scene, centered on St. Mark's Church, was both expanding and unraveling, as rock songs displaced poems as soul food for young hearts and minds. But the art scene boomed. Art parties were immeasurably more fun than poetry parties.

Starting in 1967, I began writing regularly for the *Times'*s Sunday Arts & Leisure section. The section's editor, Seymour Peck, a flinty New Yorker, had me write columns on movies, theater, rock music, and television as well as on art, extending my capacities while cracking down on my flakiness. He practically invented me as a functioning professional.

My uptown feats didn't impress people whom I looked up to in the downtown art scene, where antibourgeois hardheadedness and minimalist disdain for the "literary" reigned. They were contemptuous of the *Times*. I was Peter the poet, a relative nobody. Advice to aspiring youth: in New York, the years that you spend as a nobody are painful but golden, because no one bothers to lie to you. The moment you're a somebody, you have heard your last truth. Everyone will try to spin you—as they should, with careers to think of. For about a dozen years I hung out, drank, and slept with artists who didn't take me seriously. I observed, heard, overheard, and absorbed a great deal.

One drunken night a superb painter let me take a brush to a canvas that she said she was abandoning. I tried to continue a simple black stroke that she had started. The contrast between the controlled pressure of her touch and my flaccid smear shocked me, physically. It was like shaking hands with a small person who flips you across a room.

At a time, in the early seventies, when I slept a lot, I kept track of my dreams, writing a book distilling some of them. For example, "Conceptual Art":

> I am in Cleveland on a sort of official art junket. With the head of the local museum — a handsome, dapper black man — I visit a young artist in his new loft. The loft is large and sunny; facing its dozens of windows are dozens of old, uncomfortable-looking armchairs.
>
> Jokingly, I suggest that the artist could create "a terrific Conceptual art-work entitled 'Golf'" by placing a golfball on each of the chairs, then, with a golf club, hitting it through a closed window.
>
> To my surprise, I am taken seriously. The artist agrees to perform the work the very next day.
>
> As for the police, who will obviously be called when the street below is showered with golfballs and broken glass, the museum director has a plan. There is a secret passage from the loft to a building next door, he says, and in that building a large sum of money is hidden that we can use to finance our escape from Cleveland.
>
> We all agree that "Golf" will be an event of tremendous artistic importance.

That prose-poetic experiment ended when I entered Jungian therapy and presented my dreams for interpretation. They all made abundant sense, which was entertaining but not terribly helpful. My problem was not a lack of connection with the collective unconscious. I was a fucking poet. My problem was getting out of bed in the morning.

The birth of Brooke's and my daughter, Ada, on St. Patrick's Day, 1976, saw to that. When your baby cries, you're out of bed before being fully awake.

Ada was present when my oncologist, at Memorial Sloan Kettering, gave me six months or so to live. Ada asked me what I wanted to do. Revisit Rome? Paris? I would forget that I said, "Nah. Maybe a ballgame." She arranged it, with family and friends: Mets versus Braves, at Citi Field. Glorious. Grandson Oliver caught a T-shirt from the midgame T-shirt cannon. Odds of that: several thousand to one.

Writing consumes writers. No end of ones better than I am have said as much. The passion hurts relationships. I think off and on about people I love, but I think about writing all the time.

Writing is hard, or everyone would do it.

You're reading an exception, which is pouring out of me. It's the first writing "for myself" that I've done in about thirty years, since I gave up on poetry (or poetry gave up on me) because I didn't know what a poem was any longer and had severed or sabotaged all my connections to the poetry world. An impermeable block has crumbled, my muse being, I guess, the grim reaper.

I'm given pause here by my unreconstructed reverence for extreme states of mind and feeling. Think William Blake and Edgar Allan Poe. Huysmans. I've often quoted Baudelaire: "I cultivated my hysteria with terror and delight." But I also thrilled to the august sanities of Paul Valéry ("Stupidity is not my strong suit") and Auden ("Poetry makes nothing happen"). Another extreme.

Extremity was the spirit of my drug-using, which I never really enjoyed: pot, acid, DMT, and downers taken pragmatically, in service to "systematic derangement of the senses" (Rimbaud). Did the drugs help? I don't know. The acid taught me things about the mind by making all of its workings simultaneously perceptible, though to no one—ego dissolving like Alka-Seltzer in warm water.

*

I dodged the Vietnam draft by staying awake for three days and nights on speed, taking any other drugs that came to hand, rolling in dirt, presenting myself at the induction center on Whitehall Street, and trying to cooperate. The draft officials discarded me like a used condom. I felt guilty. I brooded that some guy would have to go in my place. I had faked psychosis so well that my sanity teetered for months afterward.

Baudelaire wrote of having been "brushed by the wind of the wing of madness." I have felt that breeze at times, though not in a great many years now. I still have the occasional thought that what is commonly deemed sanity is absurd; but I let that slide.

I met Susan Sontag once, at a party. She came up and praised something that I had written. Thrilled, I began chattering about I don't remember what. Sontag froze. She retreated, taking backward steps before turning away. It dawned on me that receiving her blessing was supposed to have been enough: a solemn initiation. I had presumed on it.

At the end of my multidrug sixties, I figuratively put all the chemicals in a funnel, and they came out bourbon. Jack Daniel's on the rocks, with a splash, except when scarce funds reduced me to Heaven Hill. Alcohol was liberating for me at first. A standard progression: great, good, fair, poor, bad, very bad, and then a phase for which any word but *hell* fails. Halfway through the second drink, there may be a flicker of the old euphoria, quickly snuffed. You chase it in vain for the rest of a wretched night. It's over for you. A line has been crossed. Yet you cannot imagine yourself not drinking. The obsession is at one with your core sense of self.

Brooke drinks. We keep a full liquor cabinet. I mix drinks for guests without a qualm. The booze is a different chemical in their bodies from what it would be in mine. Pleasant for them, poison for me.

Free. Sort of free. Who's free? I can see the paragraphs I'm writing as little jail cells, penning me into perspectives, conceits, ideas, jokes, and memories—stories! Not an original type of anxiety, for a writer.

Writers can be only so conscientious about truth before becoming paralyzed.

I remember thinking in the sixties that becoming emotionally paralyzed could be cool if one were in an interesting enough position. Coolness was the holy grail then. I was hopeless at it. Sincerity is my accursed default.

I had a rage of ambition and an acrid dissatisfaction that, along with a love of the world, were bound to come out somehow. The self-centered motives have waned. It's harder to pitch into writing with less to prove or avenge. To start a critical essay, I must prod myself until the old mesmerized flow resumes.

When I finish something and it seems good, I'm dazed. It must have been fun to write. I wish I'd been there.

In my drinking years I took to saying, for a laugh, "The only thing I want in life is a written apology from everyone I've ever met." Arrogant! But, truth to tell, arrogance—as a placeholder for confidence, of which I had none—enabled me to brave the world when I was young.

The same goes for snobbery, a necessary stage for the insecure until we acquire taste that admits and reflects the variety of experience. To limber your sensibility, stalk the aesthetic everywhere: cracks in a sidewalk, people's ways of walking. The aesthetic isn't bounded by art, which merely concentrates it for efficient consumption. If you can't put a mental frame around, and relish, the accidental aspect of a street or a person, or really of anything, you will respond to art only sluggishly.

I like to say that contemporary art consists of all artworks, five thousand years or five minutes old, that physically exist in the present. We look at them with contemporary eyes, the only kinds of eyes that there ever are.

I retain, but suspend, my personal taste to deal with the panoply of the art I see. I have a trick for doing justice to an uncongenial work: "What would I like about this if I liked it?" I may come around; I may not. Failing that, I wonder: "What must the people who like this be like?" Anthropology.

I assess art by quality and significance. The latter is most decisive for my choice of subjects, because I'm a journalist. There's art I adore that I won't write about, because I can't imagine it mattering enough to general readers. It pertains to my private experience as a person, without which my activity as a critic would wither but which falls outside my critical mandate.

I write for readers and not for artists, who can buy the magazine and read me like anyone else if they're interested. I didn't always. When I was young, I had personal and coterie loyalties. Then I decided to see how responsible a critic I could be, open to ideas but never prescriptive or proscriptive. By academic measure, this makes me not a true critic at all. I can live with that.

Family and friends are being wonderful to me in my sickness. I've toiled all my life, in vain, to like myself. Now the task has been outsourced. I can't go around telling everybody they're idiots.

I always said that when my time came I'd want to go fast. But where's the fun in that?

True story: a friend received a preliminary diagnosis suggesting advanced breast cancer. Normally shy, she took this as license to tell or show everyone in her circle how little she liked or respected them. False alarm. It was cat-scratch fever. She moved overseas.

"When a man knows he is to be hanged in a fortnight, it concentrates his mind wonderfully," per Samuel Johnson.

"Why isn't Schjeldahl's copy in?" "He's dead." "Uh, okay, then." The best excuse.

The most delicious poem about someone dying is Auden's "In Memory of W. B. Yeats" (1939), with these lines:

> But for him it was his last afternoon as himself,
> An afternoon of nurses and rumours;
> The provinces of his body revolted,
> The squares of his mind were empty,
> Silence invaded the suburbs,
> The current of his feeling failed; he became his admirers.

The poet Ron Padgett pointed out to me the technical shrewdness of the compound last line: the all-time best use of a semicolon in place of a line break. Then there's the sterling *became:* nothing is left of Yeats but others' thoughts of him, and the thoughts of him enhance the others, like badges.

We wear as many such badges as there are dead people we admire. The Shakespeare badge. The Jesus one, though he cheated on Easter morning. At what hour did the Savior reopen his eyes? At dawn? Before it, with time to kill?

Seeing Hans Holbein's *Dead Christ* (1520–22) shook Dostoyevsky's Christian belief: a two-days-gone corpse in a warm climate, a *thing*.

Simone Weil said that the transcendent meaning of Christianity is complete with Jesus's death, sans the cherry on top that is the Resurrection. I think so.

"I believe in God" is a false statement for me because it is voiced by my ego, which is compulsively skeptical. But the rest of me tends otherwise. Staying on an as-if basis with "God," for short, hugely improves my life. I regret my lack of the church and its gift of community. My ego is too fat to squeeze through the door.

Disbelieving is toilsome. It can be a pleasure for adolescent brains with energy to spare, but hanging on to it later saps and rigidifies. After a Lutheran upbringing, I became an atheist at the onset of puberty. That wore off gradually and then, with sobriety, speedily.

I had a moment, while anticipating my diagnosis, of feeling special. But what's as commonplace as dying? Everybody does it. I also had an instant of fancying that I could drink again. That evanesced in a flash. Fellow alcoholics know that the beast, though out of mind, survives. My thought was a foul little burp from a cave.

Life doesn't go on. It goes nowhere except away. Death goes on. Going on is what death does for a living. The secret to surviving in the universe is to be dead.

Self-knowledge! Almost better never than this late. (I don't mean that at all. But I enjoy the sound of it.) I am endeavoring to practice self-forgiveness. I believe it's recommended.

As for folks out there in resentful and envious circles who will be glad to have me out of the way, they, by their pleasure, afford me a bonus credit for increasing human happiness.

"Everyone, it seems, loves Peter Schjeldahl," an art website opined recently. I know for dead sure that's not so. To the extent that it's plausible hyperbole and because I believe in a balanced universe, the people who hate me do so with enough intensity to square up the sums.

I think of righteous nonsmokers "in the hospital dying of noth-ing." That's a line for a role that Brooke played, as a chain-smoking coroner, in a not-great movie, *Just Cause* (1995), with the great Sean Connery, who may or may not have had a say in cutting the line from the released film because it stole the scene. Soon after that she proved her ability, which I've lacked, to break habits by quitting both smoking and acting. Her subsequent enterprises have ranged from an antiques-and-whatnot store, Brooke's Variety, to a spectacularly unusual minigolf course on land that we own in the Catskills.

Nicotine stimulates *and* relaxes. Beat that. I understand that it teaches the brain to prefer it to a natural neurotransmitter, acetylcholine, which, among other boons, promotes mental agility. Nicotine does the same, better. How many quitters never miss smoking? (Liars line up on the left.) The times I tried to stop, I wondered what writers do.

L., who is no longer alive, became pregnant on our second date, in 1963. A backstreet abortion in Chicago left her sterile. I married her out of guilt mixed with infatuation. (She was wild and adored me while sleeping around, as I did too, but I couldn't keep up.) We lasted for most of five years, possibly because a man I disliked had said that he gave us three months.

Lee Crabtree. Jairus Lincoln. Jeff Giles. You don't know about them. They were friends of mine who died young. I'll get over Lee's suicide, in 1973, only when I've joined him. I was harsh the last time I saw him, hiding my love.

Lee was the pianist and musical arranger for the Fugs. One night after an awful fight with L., in which for emphasis I punched out a window, I showed up at Lee's, bleeding. He bandaged and calmed me. He had a big plastic toy horn that I started to toot on. Lee sat at his electric keyboard, and we jammed. Later he showed me sheet music that he had printed of our improvised creation: "The Red Horn Polka." We collaborated on a song, "Police State," that became the Fugs' first-act closer but isn't on any album, perhaps because it was too dirty, even for them.

Lee was the gentlest, most generous person amid a prevalence of shitheads, who, at the worst possible moment, included me. I knew that he was struggling with his repressed homosexuality. Having been so good a friend, he sorely needed friendship.

At a temporary job on the twelfth floor of a building in midtown, he was seen, at a window, to wave affably to a random person in another building. Then he climbed out the window and stepped into space.

Bury me. Nix to cremation. I want an address that people know they can visit even if they never do. Phooey to dust on a random sea breeze or strewn on a field of unoffending vegetation. Or in a jar? Think about it.

Though cemeteries waste real estate. Better a Walmart parking lot?

Really, do as you please with the corpse—not me, not mine. I believe in earnestly agreeing to deathbed wishes and then forgetting about them, unless it's to satisfy those among the living.

Between bulletins from my body that say this isn't so, I still feel like a kid inside. Four and a half years ago, while rushing to catch a bus ("Don't run for a bus" was a rule for longevity in Mel Brooks's *2000 Year Old Man*), I tripped trying to leap, gazellelike, over a chunk of broken asphalt and must have caught a toe. When I came to on the street, surrounded by strangers, I had no memory of falling or of much else (who I was, where I was). There was blood. My glasses were smashed. I said, "I'm okay." The strangers strenuously disagreed. An ambulance had arrived.

I was mostly conscious when wheeled on a gurney into an emergency room in Greenwich Village. A scrawny old-time Village-hipster type was driving the nurses crazy about something, likely trying to wheedle drugs. Strolling past and glancing down at me, he said tenderly, "Die, baby." That didn't seem like a terrible idea, right then, and it struck me in a remote sort of way as the funniest thing I'd ever heard.

A CAT scan to check out a suspicion that my neck was broken (weird story short: my neck was found to have broken and healed sometime in the past, unbeknownst to me) incidentally discovered a spot in my left lung. This later led to hospital visits for scans and tests, including a needle biopsy (ouch), all of them inconclusive. Fed up with the rigmarole, I refused further investigation. Shouldn't have? Live and learn.

Shakespeare wrote of "desiring this man's art and that man's scope." I find this comforting. But who was he thinking of? Marlowe? Someone forgotten although evidently fucking incredible?

Originality is overrated, except by people who have it. It's like an untamed, ungrateful beast you're trapped with. If people praising you knew the half of it, they'd think twice.

I think of Lee Crabtree and of all suicides. What happens? One night in the early seventies I perched on a tenement-roof edge despite my fear of heights, legs dangling, and ordered myself to let go. It was amid a love disaster. I truly thought I'd jump. But something inside me laughed derisively. Who was I kidding? Humiliated, I went downstairs. Some, in a crisis, must lack the laugh or muffle it for long enough.

Twice I've been to Oaxaca during the Day of the Dead, when the departed members of families have their favorite food, drinks, and perhaps cigarettes set out for them at meals. It's understood that at the table, the dead consume the immaterial goodness of these things. The families visit them overnight in graveyards. I was deeply moved by the implication that death may be a major life event, such as birth, confirmation, and marriage, but that it doesn't mean you're *gone*. We spare the dead a bit of the life in us. I shuddered suddenly during my second walk among placid, candlelit groups. It hit me that the dead were reciprocating: a bit of the death in them for us. Never fully dead, never fully alive.

I may have this wrong, but I'm savoring the idea. Today the little bit of death in me has sat up in bed and is pulling on its socks.

I remember arriving in an Italian village by train after midnight and walking past a cemetery where candles burned at every grave, with no one around. Or I think I remember it.

We have lousy memories. Proust had a lousy memory. (There is no "little patch of yellow wall" in Vermeer's *View of Delft*.) Memory is a liar. It's a heap of dog-eared, smudged, incessantly revised fictions. The stories make cumulative lies—or, give us a break, conjectures—of our lives. This is okay because it had darn well better be.

Who's "we"? You know.

Meaning is a scrap among other scraps, though stickier. Meaning is so much better than nothing, in that it defines *nothing* as everything that meaning is not. Meaning prevents nothing from being only nothing. The "nothing that is not there and the noth-ing that is," Wallace Stevens noticed. The same nothing, but a dif-ference of attitude.

A random shame: I was visited in New York by P., a soft-souled, brilliant friend from high school and college, a concert pianist. High on speed, I was arrogant and callous, watching the effects on P. with cold-blooded detachment. Finally he said in a hurt tone, "I always thought you had a modesty about you. But not so." I could have said something, admitted my drugged state, made amends the next day. But a devil in me exulted.

Years later a scene occurred that might work well in a novel set in the early seventies, in case you're writing one. I was seeing a terrific artist, H., at least as prone to defiance as I was. I saw that P. was giving a concert. I asked H., my not-really, because she was so independent, girlfriend, to attend with me. She got the message, which was not fully conscious but true: besides wanting to make up with P., I relished the prospect of showing her off. Usually down-town casual, she showed up in heels, a stunning dress, diamonds or what looked like them, and a mink coat.

After the terrific music, especially Liszt, we joined P. and some other people in champagne toasts. P. facilitated introductions by asking the men—only the men—to say what they did. H. let that develop for about half a minute and detonated, "Let's start this over! Let's play *What do the women do?*" The company gawked. She was magnificent! With a flourish, she left the theater. I tagged along moments later, stricken. Out on the street, she was gone. I limped home. I saw her only in passing after that. I didn't try again to reconcile with P.

The shock of feminism came none too soon for guys, including me, who had lorded in a sixties bohemia that mandated women be doting helpmeets to their entitled—because genius—men. Those domesticities went down like a row of dominoes at the first breath of female revolt. With no new model for relationships, libertinage reigned. I guess it was fun for some people, but it piled up emo-tional wreckage left and right.

The art scene was always a third or more gay—often the best third. My chief poet heroes were Frank O'Hara and John Ashbery. John complained to me that he had thought that with success he'd have his pick from a meat rack of young poets. "How come you're all *straight*?"—stretching out the last word to sound like something nasty going through a mangle.

How straight was I? I'd always been nervous about homosexuality. Didn't that mean I was repressing it? Given that everybody seemed to be having sex with everybody, not to mention being soused or stoned nightly, I decided to face the facts. A gay friend I approached would have nothing to do with me in that way. Well! I hooked up with a bisexual friend, but too much to drink made whatever happened a blur. So I seduced a straight friend. It was interesting. Nice, but obvious. I didn't rule out doing it again, but I never have.

There were brief affairs that I think neither the woman nor I really wanted; but this wasn't an adequate excuse then. An entropy of the heart grew in me, as did, which I didn't suspect, a yen for monogamy.

My last bachelor fling was semi-scandalous, in the art world, and volcanically erotic. I like to say that it burned the carbon out of my cylinders. She broke up with me on a street corner, denouncing me and storming off. I stood there for a spell grinning from ear to ear. I figured that I had mastered swinging singledom. Then I met Brooke.

I remember, in rehab, on the Upper East Side in 1992, an alum of the place, a tough guy from Queens, addressing the nightly AA meeting. He told us of once showing up at some clinic, drunk and filthy and soiled with his own diarrhea, and throwing a fit because the doctor was ten minutes late. "If you're a real alcoholic," the guy said to us, "no matter how low you go, you *will* have an attitude." He added, "If you're a real alcoholic, you will never feel quite right. Whatever you want will be a little bit out of reach. Can't handle that? Get the fuck out of here and get drunk." I went up to him afterward, in tears, to thank him. He said, "You heard me?" I said yes. "Good," he said, turning and walking away as if from some crap on a sidewalk. Saved my life.

The rehab was crowded with crack addicts, some of them felons. I was the rare middle-aged, middle-class white man in the joint. It was loud at all hours. Scared, I couldn't sleep. I told Brooke, on the building's pay phone, that I had to get out. She said, "Cope," and hung up. Saved my life.

See, Brooke is a child of alcoholics, as I'm not. I grew up and became one. She grew up and married one. She knew I was a mess but thought the drinking part was normal, until she got wise and kicked me out of the house. (Note to anyone who knows an active alcoholic: never, ever sympathize. If you suspect you're going to, shut your eyes, plug your ears, and hum.)

I bottomed out in the rehab, where I had gone as a condition for being allowed back home. I thought I was serious. I always had been when, previously, I was dry for periods of up to thirteen months: going to meetings at first, dewy with pity for people who plainly had been far worse off than I was. I wouldn't admit that we shared the identical fate, wherever we ranked along its descending scale.

On the third or fourth of my twenty-eight days there, I was climbing stairs and paused, too exhausted for another step. I harbored a nebulous conviction that I could tolerate only so much pain, short of a red zone in which I would go mad or die or something terrible would happen. And that anyone should see as much and want me to do anything—have a drink or a drug, for starters —to make it stop.

I thought, *They say one day at a time. How about one second?* I stared at my ticking watch. A black abyss opened. I was numbly aware that I wasn't insane. I wasn't dying. Reality was droning on as usual, with impartial sunlight streaming through a nearby window and picking out swirls of dust motes.

A perfectly demented thought blazed up. Roughly: *What if they find out I'm not really an alcoholic and throw me out of here? I need this place!* I believe it was the last, deepest rootlet of my denial, expelled. Not an alcoholic?

My daughter, Ada, has told me that in her childhood she spent years trying to interest me. I hadn't noticed. She was sixteen when I got sober. She said, "Let's see if I get this straight. *Now* you want to be my dad?" It took a lot of time and change and is still underway. I don't know if it's a consolation prize for Ada, or what it is, that she turned out to be fantastically interesting.

Meeting Brooke, having Ada, and getting sober are my life's top three red-letter days.

Cigarette brands I remember smoking for at least a few months running: Alpine, Salem, Newport, Camel, Lucky Strike, Parliament, Kent, Gauloises, Benson & Hedges, Nat Sherman. Finally (and I do mean finally), Marlboro Gold (formerly Lights), the crack cocaine of tobacco products, containing all sorts of cunning chemicals and a somewhat insulting whisper of sugar.

Doing the math, I reckon that I have smoked about a million cigarettes—and enjoyed every one of them, not that you care.

Tried gum, patches, and e-cigarettes. Not the same. I use nicotine lozenges to not be twitchy on airplanes, while driving with family, and indoors anywhere except in my offices in our city apartment and country house, with exhaust fans in opened windows—challenging during summer heat and winter cold. Smoking today requires grit.

Quit now? Sure, and have the rest of my life be a tragicomedy of nicotine withdrawal.

Mishaps. I had polio when I was eleven, in one of the last big epidemics before the Salk vaccine. I remember riding my bike home from school, every bump like a knife through my brain. Rushed to the local hospital for a spinal tap—every bit as horrible as you may imagine, but the one sure means of diagnosis then—and throwing up in the back of the family station wagon on the way to the polio-specializing Sister Kenny Institute, in Minneapolis.

I had a bed, but there were too many kids, so some were laid out in halls. Screaming all night. Dying. And always the mechanical sucking noise of iron lungs. I had no paralysis, but I was much weakened, spending seven weeks in the hospital and subject to physical therapy for months. Meanwhile my family was quarantined at home. Food was left at the doorstep.

For a summer just out of high school, I worked at a resort in Glacier National Park, in the Montana Rockies. I hitchhiked on days off with a copy of *On the Road* in my back pocket and a big jackknife that I practiced opening in a flash in preparation for the lethal fights that I fantasized about. I told one truck driver, in what I imagined to be the right accent, that I was from Lexington, Kentucky. He said, "Lexington, Kentucky, boy, my hometown!" I feigned sleep.

Another time I climbed a manageable-looking mountain, setting out at dawn with pockets full of candy bars. It became steep, then close to vertical. As I clung to a rockface, an eagle launched, shrieking, from a ledge just above me and sailed into the blue

distance. Higher up there was snow, and there were bear tracks in
the snow. I thought the mountaintop was a sloping ridge. I crawled
up it and found a sheer drop facing the inaccessible summit. Had
I had acrophobia before, or did my subsequently lifelong case of it
begin then and there? I hugged rock and sobbed. The next thing
I remember is striding and tumbling down a side of the mountain
covered in deep gravel, grabbing bushes to slow myself. I alighted
in brambled woods, disoriented. I had the sense to follow a trick-
ling stream, and I was kept on course by the feel of the water as
night fell. I emerged, a tattered scarecrow, on the park's one highway. Cars sped up at the sight of me in their headlights until one
stopped.

I'm not in physical pain as I write, though I tire quickly and nap often. I have been receiving, every three weeks, an immunotherapy
infusion—not chemo, and not a cure—which, at the outset, the
doctor said had a 35 percent chance of slowing the disease. (At
those odds in Vegas, you're broke within an hour, but in baseball
you're a cinch for the Hall of Fame.) A recent scan shows marked
improvement, likely extending my prospect of survival. But I have
to wonder if, whatever betides, I can stay upbeat in spirit. A thing
about dying is that you can't consult anyone who has done it. No
rehearsals. No mulligans.

At a bar when I was first in New York, I smirked dandyishly at my
reflection in the mirror behind the bottles. I looked handsome! I
was stirring my drink, Scotch on the rocks, with my right index finger, which in the mirror became my left one. The moment seemed
ineffably cool. Clown!
    I ordered coffee at a diner. The guy said, "Regular?" I said,
"Well, sure." Surprise: milk and sugar. In the Midwest coffee was
black, no sugar. Brooke remembers being a Texan newbie in New
York and seeing a store sign that read COFFEE RICE & BEANS. Fascinated, she asked for a pound of coffee rice. You get to be clueless
in a new place only briefly. Don't waste the chance to have truths,
great and small, burst upon you.

Brooke was an actress and standup comic from Dallas. Introduced
at a Whitney Museum opening by A., a woman connected to both
the art and the entertainment worlds, we despised each other im-

mediately. I deemed Brooke a bubblehead, and she noticed that I
was a jerk. Then she attended a poetry reading I gave, which, whatever its quality, turned out to be the best of my life, because she
liked it. Next, A. invited me out to dinner and then, perhaps getting cold feet at what it implied, asked if she could bring Brooke.
I said something like "Sure, why not?"

It's forty-six years later. Brooke is in bed rereading *Pride and
Prejudice,* as she does two or three times a year, with a Mets game
muttering on the radio. I have no doubt that our two cats cuddle
beside her. It's night at our place in the Catskills, moonless and
clear. I could turn off my office light and look out a window at the
sky choked with stars.

Brooke has Texas grit: respecting everyone and taking no shit
from anybody, least of all her spouse. When she's mad it's scary,
tapping a rage that once fueled her escape from an awful family.
There's no recourse but to duck and wait for it to pass, which it
does. The sun began to shine on my life when I gave up arguing
with Brooke. She is also very funny and brings out the fun in others, her spouse not excluded.

Ada asked her mother how to stay married. Brooke said, "Don't
get divorced." If you don't divorce, you are 100 percent married
no matter what's going on. I am so glad we stayed together that,
for once in my verbose life, words to express it fail me.

Oddly, or not, I find myself thinking about death less than I used
to. I thought that I might be kidding myself in my explorations
of the subject while my life stretched ahead of me to an invisible
horizon. But no. The thinking cut channels in which I now slip
along. They involve acceptance. Why me? Why not me? In point
of fact, me. Dying is my turn to survey life from its far—now near
—shore. These extra months are a luxury that I hope to have put
to good use. "To have put." See? While here, not here. Like a camera situated nowhere and taking in every last detail of the pulsat-
ing world.

God creeps in. Human minds are the universe's only instruments for reflecting on itself. The fact of our existence suggests
a cosmic approval of it. (Do we behave badly? We are gifted with
the capacity to think so.) We may be accidents of matter and
energy, but we can't help circling back to the sense of a mean-

ing that is unaccountable by the application of what we know. If God is a human invention, good for us! We had to come up with something.

Take death for a walk in your minds, folks. Either you'll be glad you did or, keeling over suddenly, you won't be out anything.

A. O. SCOTT

Under the Sign of Susan

FROM *The New York Times Magazine*

1. I spent my adolescence in a terrible hurry to read all the books, see all the movies, listen to all the music, look at everything in all the museums. That pursuit required more effort back then, when nothing was streaming and everything had to be hunted down, bought, or borrowed. But those changes aren't what this essay is about. Culturally ravenous young people have always been insufferable and never unusual, even though they tend to invest a lot in being different—in aspiring (or pretending) to something deeper, higher than the common run. Viewed with the chastened hindsight of adulthood, their seriousness shows its ridiculous side, but the longing that drives it is no joke. It's a hunger not so much for knowledge as for experience of a particular kind. Two kinds, really: the specific experience of encountering a book or work of art and also the future experience, the state of perfectly cultivated being, that awaits you at the end of the search. Once you've read everything, then at last you can begin.

2. Furious consumption is often described as indiscriminate, but the point of it is always discrimination. It was on my parents' bookshelves, amid other emblems of midcentury, middle-class American literary taste and intellectual curiosity, that I found a book with a title that seemed to offer something I desperately needed, even if (or precisely because) it went completely over my head. *Against Interpretation.* No subtitle, no how-to promise or self-help come-on. A ninety-five-cent Dell paperback with a front-cover photograph of the author, Susan Sontag.

There is no doubt that the picture was part of the book's allure—the angled, dark-eyed gaze, the knowing smile, the bobbed hair and buttoned-up coat—but the charisma of the title shouldn't be underestimated. It was a statement of opposition, though I couldn't say what exactly was being opposed. Whatever "interpretation" turned out to be, I was ready to enlist in the fight against it. I still am, even if interpretation, in one form or another, has been the main way I've made my living as an adult. It's not fair to blame Susan Sontag for that, though I do.

3. *Against Interpretation,* a collection of articles from the 1960s reprinted from various journals and magazines, mainly devoted to of-the-moment texts and artifacts (Jean-Paul Sartre's *Saint Genet,* Jean-Luc Godard's *Vivre Sa Vie,* Jack Smith's *Flaming Creatures*), modestly presents itself as "case studies for an aesthetic," a theory of Sontag's "own sensibility." Really, though, it is the episodic chronicle of a mind in passionate struggle with the world and itself.

Sontag's signature is ambivalence. "Against Interpretation" (the essay), which declares that "to interpret is to impoverish, to deplete the world—in order to set up a shadow world of 'meanings,'" is clearly the work of a relentlessly analytical, meaning-driven intelligence. In a little more than ten pages, she advances an appeal to the ecstasy of surrender rather than the protocols of exegesis, made in unstintingly cerebral terms. Her final, mic-drop declaration—"In place of a hermeneutics we need an erotics of art"—deploys abstraction in the service of carnality.

4. It's hard for me, after so many years, to account for the impact *Against Interpretation* had on me. It was first published in 1966, the year of my birth, which struck me as terribly portentous. It brought news about books I hadn't—hadn't yet!—read and movies I hadn't heard about and challenged pieties I had only begun to comprehend. It breathed the air of the '60s, a momentous time I had unforgivably missed.

But I kept reading *Against Interpretation*—following it with *Styles of Radical Will, On Photography,* and *Under the Sign of Saturn,* books Sontag would later deprecate as "juvenilia"—for something else. For the style, you could say (she wrote an essay called "On Style").

For the voice, I guess, but that's a tame, trite word. It was because I craved the drama of her ambivalence, the tenacity of her enthusiasm, the sting of her doubt. I read those books because I needed to be with her. Is it too much to say that I was in love with her? Who was she, anyway?

5. Years after I plucked *Against Interpretation* from the living room shelf, I came across a short story of Sontag's called "Pilgrimage." One of the very few overtly autobiographical pieces Sontag ever wrote, this lightly fictionalized memoir, set in Southern California in 1947, recalls an adolescence that I somehow suspect myself of having plagiarized a third of a century later. "I felt I was slumming in my own life," Sontag writes, gently mocking and also proudly affirming the serious, voracious girl she used to be. The "pilgrimage" in question, undertaken with a friend named Merrill, was to Thomas Mann's house in Pacific Palisades, where that venerable giant of German *Kultur* had been incongruously living while in exile from Nazi Germany.

The funniest and truest part of the story is young Susan's "shame and dread" at the prospect of paying the call. "Oh, Merrill, how could you?" she melodramatically exclaims when she learns he has arranged for a teatime visit to the Mann residence. The second-funniest and truest part of the story is the disappointment Susan tries to fight off in the presence of a literary idol who talks "like a book review." The encounter makes a charming anecdote with forty years of hindsight, but it also proves that the youthful instincts were correct. "Why would I want to meet him?" she wondered. "I had his books."

6. I never met Susan Sontag. Once when I was working late answering phones and manning the fax machine in the offices of *The New York Review of Books,* I took a message for Robert Silvers, one of the magazine's editors. "Tell him Susan Sontag called. He'll know why." (Because it was his birthday.) Another time I caught a glimpse of her sweeping, swanning, promenading—or maybe just walking—through the galleries of the Frick.

Much later I was commissioned by this magazine to write a profile of her. She was about to publish *Regarding the Pain of Others,* a sequel and corrective to her 1977 book *On Photography.* The furor she sparked with a few paragraphs written for *The New Yorker* after

the September 11 attacks—words that seemed obnoxiously rational at a time of horror and grief—had not yet died down. I felt I
had a lot to say to her, but the one thing I could not bring myself
to do was pick up the phone. Mostly I was terrified of disappointment, mine and hers. I didn't want to fail to impress her; I didn't
want to have to try. The terror of seeking her approval, and the
certainty that in spite of my journalistic pose I would be doing
just that, were paralyzing. Instead of a profile, I wrote a short text
that accompanied a portrait by Chuck Close. I didn't want to risk
knowing her in any way that might undermine or complicate the
relationship we already had, which was plenty fraught. I had her
books.

7. After Sontag died, in 2004, the focus of attention began to drift
away from her work and toward her person. Not her life so much
as her self, her photographic image, her way of being at home
and at parties—anywhere but on the page. Her son, David Rieff,
wrote a piercing memoir about his mother's illness and death. Annie Leibovitz, Sontag's partner, off and on, from 1989 until her
death, released a portfolio of photographs unsparing in their de-
piction of her cancer-ravaged, seventy-year-old body. There were
ruminations by Wayne Koestenbaum, Phillip Lopate, and Terry
Castle about her daunting reputation and the awe, envy, and inadequacy she inspired in them. *Sempre Susan,* a short memoir by
Sigrid Nunez, who lived with Sontag and Rieff for a while in the
1970s, is the masterpiece of the "I knew Susan" minigenre and a
funhouse-mirror companion to Sontag's own *Pilgrimage.* It's about
what can happen when you really get to know a writer, which is
that you lose all sense of what or who it is you really know, including yourself.

8. In 2008 Farrar, Straus & Giroux, Sontag's longtime publisher, is-
sued *Reborn,* the first of two volumes so far culled from nearly one
hundred notebooks Sontag filled from early adolescence into late
middle age. Because of their fragmentary nature, these journal
entries aren't intimidating in the way her more formal nonfiction
prose could be, or abstruse in the manner of most of her pre-
1990s fiction. They seem to offer an unobstructed window into
her mind, documenting her intellectual anxieties, existential wor-
ries, and emotional upheavals, along with everyday ephemera that

proves to be almost as captivating. Lists of books to be read and films to be seen sit alongside quotations, aphorisms, observations, and story ideas. Lovers are tantalizingly represented by a single letter ("I."; "H"; "C."). You wonder if Sontag hoped, if she knew, that you would be reading this someday—the intimate journal as a literary form is a recurring theme in her essays—and you wonder whether that possibility undermines the guilty intimacy of reading these pages or, on the contrary, accounts for it.

9. A new biography by Benjamin Moser—*Sontag: Her Life and Work,* published last month—shrinks Sontag down to life size, even as it also insists on her significance. "What mattered about Susan Sontag was what she symbolized," he concludes, having studiously documented her love affairs, her petty cruelties, and her lapses in personal hygiene.

I must say I find the notion horrifying. A woman whose great accomplishments were writing millions of words and reading who knows how many millions more—no exercise in Sontagiana can fail to mention the fifteen-thousand-book library in her Chelsea apartment—has at last been decisively captured by what she called "the image-world," the counterfeit reality that threatens to destroy our apprehension of the actual world.

You can argue about the philosophical coherence, the political implications, or the present-day relevance of this idea (one of the central claims of *On Photography*), but it's hard to deny that Sontag currently belongs more to images than to words. Maybe it's inevitable that after Sontag's death, the literary persona she spent a lifetime constructing—that rigorous, serious, impersonal self—has been peeled away, revealing the person hiding behind the words. The unhappy daughter. The mercurial mother. The variously needy and domineering lover. The loyal, sometimes impossible friend. In the era of prestige TV, we may have lost our appetite for difficult books, but we relish difficult characters, and the biographical Sontag—brave and imperious, insecure and unpredictable—surely fits the bill.

10. "Interpretation," according to Sontag, "is the revenge of the intellect upon art. Even more. It is the revenge of the intellect upon the world." And biography, by the same measure, is the revenge of research upon the intellect. The life of the mind is turned into

"the life," a coffin full of rattling facts and spectral suppositions, less an invitation to read or reread than a handy, bulky excuse not to.

The point of this essay, which turns out not to be as simple as I thought it would be, is to resist that tendency. I can't deny the reality of the image or the symbolic cachet of the name. I don't want to devalue the ways Sontag serves as a talisman and a culture hero. All I really want to say is that Susan Sontag mattered because of what she wrote.

11. Or maybe I should just say that's why she matters to me. In *Sempre Susan,* Sigrid Nunez describes Sontag as

> the opposite of Thomas Bernhard's comic "possessive thinker," who feeds on the fantasy that every book or painting or piece of music he loves has been created solely for and belongs solely to him, and whose "art selfishness" makes the thought of anyone else enjoying or appreciating the works of genius he reveres intolerable. She wanted her passions to be shared by all, and to respond with equal intensity to any work she loved was to give her one of her biggest pleasures.

I'm the opposite of that. I don't like to share my passions, even if the job of movie critic forces me to do it. I cling to an immature (and maybe also a typically male), proprietary investment in the work I care about most. My devotion to Sontag has often felt like a secret. She was never assigned in any course I took in college, and if her name ever came up while I was in graduate school, it was with a certain condescension. She wasn't a theorist or a scholar but an essayist and a popularizer, and as such a bad fit with the desperate careerism that dominated the academy at the time. In the world of cultural journalism, she's often dismissed as an egghead and a snob. Not really worth talking about, and so I mostly didn't talk about her.

12. Nonetheless, I kept reading, with an ambivalence that mirrored hers. Perhaps her most famous essay—certainly among the most controversial—is "Notes on 'Camp,'" which scrutinizes a phenomenon defined by "the spirit of extravagance" with scrupulous sobriety. The inquiry proceeds from mixed feelings—"I am strongly drawn to Camp, and almost as strongly offended by it" —that are heightened rather than resolved, and that curl through

the fifty-eight numbered sections of the "Notes" like tendrils in an Art Nouveau print. In writing about a mode of expression that is overwrought, artificial, frivolous, and theatrical, Sontag adopts a style that is the antithesis of all those things.

If some kinds of camp represent "a seriousness that fails," then "Notes on 'Camp'" enacts a seriousness that succeeds. The essay is dedicated to Oscar Wilde, whose most tongue-in-cheek utterances gave voice to his deepest thoughts. Sontag reverses that Wildean current, so that her grave pronouncements sparkle with an almost invisible mischief. The essay is delightful because it seems to betray no sense of fun at all, because its jokes are buried so deep that they are, in effect, secrets.

13. In the chapter of *Against Interpretation* called "Camus' Note-books"—originally published in *The New York Review of Books*—Sontag divides great writers into "husbands" and "lovers," a sly, sexy updating of older dichotomies (e.g., between Apollonian and Dionysian, Classical and Romantic, paleface and redskin). Albert Camus, at the time beginning his posthumous descent from Nobel laureate and existentialist martyr into the high school curriculum (which is where I found him), is named the "ideal husband of contemporary letters." It isn't really a compliment:

> Some writers supply the solid virtues of a husband: reliability, intelligi-bility, generosity, decency. There are other writers in whom one prizes the gifts of a lover, gifts of temperament rather than of moral goodness. Notoriously, women tolerate qualities in a lover—moodiness, selfish-ness, unreliability, brutality—that they would never countenance in a husband, in return for excitement, an infusion of intense feeling. In the same way, readers put up with unintelligibility, obsessiveness, pain-ful truths, lies, bad grammar—if, in compensation, the writer allows them to savor rare emotions and dangerous sensations.

The sexual politics of this formulation are quite something. Reading is female, writing male. The lady reader exists to be se-duced or provided for, ravished or served, by a man who is either a scamp or a solid citizen. Camus, in spite of his movie-star good looks (like Sontag, he photographed well), is condemned to hus-band status. He's the guy the reader will settle for, who won't ask too many questions when she returns from her flings with Kafka,

Céline, or Gide. He's also the one who, more than any of them, inspires love.

14. After her marriage to the sociologist Philip Rieff ended in 1959, most of Sontag's serious romantic relationships were with women. The writers whose company she kept on the page were overwhelmingly male (and almost exclusively European). Except for a short piece about Simone Weil and another about Nathalie Sarraute in *Against Interpretation* and an extensive takedown of Leni Riefenstahl in *Under the Sign of Saturn,* Sontag's major criticism is all about men.

She herself was kind of a husband. Her writing is conscientious, thorough, patient, and useful. Authoritative but not scolding. Rigorous, orderly, and lucid even when venturing into landscapes of wildness, disruption, and revolt. She begins her inquiry into "The Pornographic Imagination" with the warning that "no one should undertake a discussion of pornography before acknowledging the pornograph*ies*—there are at least three—and before pledging to take them on one at a time."

The extravagant, self-subverting seriousness of this sentence makes it a perfect camp gesture. There is also something kinky about the setting of rules and procedures, an implied scenario of transgression and punishment that is unmistakably erotic. Should I be ashamed of myself for thinking that? Of course! Humiliation is one of the most intense and pleasurable effects of Sontag's masterful prose. She's the one in charge.

15. But the rules of the game don't simply dictate silence or obedience on the reader's part. What sustains the bond—the bondage, if you'll allow it—is its volatility. The dominant party is always vulnerable, the submissive party always capable of rebellion, resistance, or outright refusal.

I often read her work in a spirit of defiance, of disobedience, as if hoping to provoke a reaction. For a while I thought she was wrong about everything. *Against Interpretation* was a sentimental and self-defeating polemic against criticism, the very thing she had taught me to believe in. *On Photography* was a sentimental defense of a shopworn aesthetic ideology wrapped around a superstitious horror at technology. And who cared about Elias Canetti and Wal-

ter Benjamin anyway? Or about E. M. Cioran or Antonin Artaud or
any of the other Euro-weirdos in her pantheon?

Not me! And yet . . . Over the years I've purchased at least three
copies of *Under the Sign of Saturn*—if pressed to choose a favorite Sontag volume, I'd pick that one—and in each the essay on
Canetti, "Mind as Passion," is the most dog-eared. Why? Not so I
could recommend it to someone eager to learn about the first native Bulgarian to win the Nobel Prize for Literature, because I've
never met such a person. "Mind as Passion" is the best thing I've
ever read about the emotional dynamics of literary admiration,
about the way a great writer "teaches us how to breathe," about
how readerly surrender is a form of self-creation.

16. In a very few cases, the people Sontag wrote about were people
she knew: Roland Barthes and Paul Goodman, for example, whose
deaths inspired brief appreciations reprinted in *Under the Sign of
Saturn*. Even in those elegies, the primary intimacy recorded is
the one between writer and reader, and the reader—who is also,
of course, a writer—is commemorating and pursuing a form of
knowledge that lies somewhere between the cerebral and the biblical.

Because the intimacy is extended to Sontag's reader, the love
story becomes an implicit ménage à trois. Each essay enacts the
effort—the dialectic of struggle, doubt, ecstasy, and letdown—to
know another writer, and to make you know him too. And, more
deeply though also more discreetly, to know her.

17. The version of this essay that I least want to write—the one
that keeps pushing against my resistance to it—is the one that
uses Sontag as a cudgel against the intellectual deficiencies and
the deficient intellectuals of the present. It's almost comically easy
to plot a vector of decline from then to now. Why aren't the kids
reading Canetti? Why don't trade publishers print collections of
essays about European writers and avant-garde filmmakers? Sontag
herself was not immune to such laments. In 1995 she mourned
the death of cinema. In 1996 she worried that "the very idea of the
serious (and the honorable) seems quaint, 'unrealistic' to most
people."

Worse, there are ideas and assumptions abroad in the digital land that look like debased, parodic versions of positions she staked out half a century ago. The "new sensibility" she heralded in the '60s, "dedicated both to an excruciating seriousness and to fun and wit and nostalgia," survives in the form of a frantic, algorithm-fueled eclecticism. The popular meme admonishing critics and other designated haters to shut up and "let people enjoy things" looks like an emoji-friendly update of *Against Interpretation,* with "enjoy things" a safer formulation than Sontag's "erotics of art."

That isn't what she meant, any more than her prickly, nuanced "Notes on 'Camp'" had much to do with the Instagram-ready insouciance of this year's Met Gala, which borrowed the title for its theme. And speaking of the 'Gram, its ascendance seems to confirm the direst prophecies of *On Photography,* which saw the unchecked spread of visual media as a kind of ecological catastrophe for human consciousness.

18. In other ways, the Sontag of the '60s and '70s can strike current sensibilities as problematic or outlandish. She wrote almost exclusively about white men. She believed in fixed hierarchies and absolute standards. She wrote at daunting length with the kind of unapologetic erudition that makes people feel bad. Even at her most polemical, she never trafficked in contrarian hot takes. Her name will never be the answer to the standard, time-killing social-media query "What classic writer would be awesome on Twitter?" The tl;dr of any Sontag essay could only be every word of it.

Sontag was a queer Jewish woman writer who disdained the rhetoric of identity. She was diffident about disclosing her sexuality. Moser criticizes her for not coming out in the worst years of the AIDS epidemic, when doing so might have been a powerful political statement. The political statements that she did make tended to get her into trouble. In 1966 she wrote that "the white race *is* the cancer of human history." In 1982, in a speech at Town Hall in Manhattan, she called communism "fascism with a human face." After September 11, she cautioned against letting emotion cloud political judgment. "Let's by all means grieve together, but let's not be stupid together."

That doesn't sound so unreasonable now, but the bulk of Sontag's writing served no overt or implicit ideological agenda. Her agenda—a list of problems to be tackled rather than a roster of positions to be taken—was stubbornly aesthetic. And that may be the most unfashionable, the most shocking, the most infuriating thing about her.

19. Right now, at what can feel like a time of moral and political emergency, we cling to sentimental bromides about the importance of art. We treat it as an escape, a balm, a vague set of values that exist beyond the ugliness and venality of the market and the state. Or we look to art for affirmation of our pieties and prejudices. It splits the difference between resistance and complicity.

Sontag was also aware of living in emergency conditions, in a world menaced by violence, environmental disaster, political polarization, and corruption. But the art she valued most didn't soothe the anguish of modern life so much as refract and magnify its agonies. She didn't read—or go to movies, plays, museums, or dance performances—to retreat from that world but to bring herself closer to it. What art does, she says again and again, is confront the nature of human consciousness at a time of historical crisis, to unmake and redefine its own terms and procedures. It confers a solemn obligation: "From now to the end of consciousness, we are stuck with the task of defending art."

20. *Consciousness* is one of her keywords, and she uses it in a way that may have an odd ring to twenty-first-century ears. It's sometimes invoked now, in a weak sense, as a synonym for the moral awareness of injustice. Its status as a philosophical problem, meanwhile, has been diminished by the rise of cognitive science, which subordinates the mysteries of the human mind to the chemical and physical operations of the brain.

But consciousness as Sontag understands it has hardly vanished, because it names a phenomenon that belongs—in ways that escape scientific analysis—to both the individual and the species. Consciousness inheres in a single person's private, incommunicable experience, but it also lives in groups, in cultures and populations and historical epochs. Its closest synonym is thought, which similarly dwells both within the walls of a solitary skull and out in the collective sphere.

If Sontag's great theme was consciousness, her great achievement was as a thinker. Usually that label is reserved for theorists and system-builders—Hannah Arendt, Jean-Paul Sartre, Sigmund Freud—but Sontag doesn't quite belong in that company. Instead she wrote in a way that dramatized how thinking happens. The essays are exciting not just because of the ideas they impart but because you feel within them the rhythms and pulsations of a living intelligence; they bring you as close to another person as it is possible to be.

21. *Under the Sign of Saturn* opens in a "tiny room in Paris" where she has been living for the previous year—"small bare quarters" that answer "some need to strip down, to close off for a while, to make a new start with as little as possible to fall back on." Even though, according to Sigrid Nunez, Sontag preferred to have other people around her when she was working, I tend to picture her in the solitude of that Paris room, which I suppose is a kind of physical manifestation, a symbol, of her solitary consciousness. A consciousness that was animated by the products of other minds, just as mine is activated by hers. If she's alone in there, I can claim the privilege of being her only company.

Which is a fantasy, of course. She has had better readers, and I have loved other writers. The metaphors of marriage and possession, of pleasure and power, can be carried only so far. There is no real harm in reading casually, promiscuously, abusively, or selfishly. The page is a safe space; every word is a safe word. Your lover might be my husband.

It's only reading. By which I mean: It's everything.

LIONEL SHRIVER

Semantic Drift

FROM *Harper's Magazine*

REGARDING THE PURPORTED rules of English syntax, we tend to divide into mutually hostile camps. Hip, open-minded types relish the never-ending transformations of the way we speak and write. They care about the integrity of our language only insofar as to ensure that we can still roughly understand one another. In the opposite corner glower the curmudgeons. These joyless, uptight authoritarians are forever muttering about clunky concepts such as "the unreal conditional" that nobody's ever heard of.

I've thrown in my lot with the pedants. Yes, language is a living tree, eternally sprouting new shoots as other branches wither . . . blah, blah, blah. But a poorly cultivated plant can readily gnarl from lush foliage to unsightly sticks. The Internet has turbocharged lexical fads (such as *turbocharge*) and grammatical decay. Rather than infuse English with a new vitality, this degeneration spreads the blight of sheer ignorance. So this month we address a set of developments in the prevailing conventions of the English language whose only commonality is that they drive me crazy.

I long ago developed the habit of mentally correcting other people's grammatical errors, and sometimes these chiding reproofs escape my lips ("You mean 'Ask *us* Democrats'"). Marking up casual conversation with a red pencil doesn't make me popular, and I should learn to control myself. Yet fellow philological conservatives will recognize the impulse to immediately regroove one's neural pathways, the better to preserve one's fragile ear for proper English. That ear is constantly under assault by widespread misusage that threatens by repetition to be—another on-trend verb—*normalized*.

For even we rigid, grumpy anachronisms are vulnerable (a blobby political catchall I now encounter dozens of times a day). I recently received what I pleasantly mistook for a fan letter, only to unfold the very sort of mortifying reprimand that I myself hurl at grammatical slackers. My last column in Britain's *Spectator* had employed *laid* as the past tense of *lie.* The stern correspondent was understandably disappointed in me. Granted, I don't envy second-language speakers obliged to memorize the perverse tense pairings *lie/lay* and *lay/laid,* but for me those conjugations were once second nature. My instincts have been contaminated. Proofreading that column, I'd sailed right past the mistake. Those prissy mental corrections my only protection from descent to barbarism, I resolved forthwith to be more of an asshole, if only in my head.

I had the good fortune to be raised by articulate parents who spoke in complete sentences. They didn't talk down to their children; we imbibed vocabulary like *echelon* along with our strained peas. I had no idea at the time what a favor they were doing me. I owe my parents that ear.

Consequently, when my seventh-grade English teacher spent the whole year on grammar, punctuation, and sentence diagrams, I was contemptuous. I wanted to write stories. I didn't need to learn the rules. I could hear when a usage was incorrect without resort to *Fowler's.* Yet I later felt I owed that teacher an apology.

When I taught freshman composition as an adjunct in my twenties, knowing the rules facilitated passing them on to my charges. I hammered it home to hundreds of eighteen-year-olds that, aside from rare instances of extremely short sentences that effectively function as a list ("I came, I saw, I conquered"), you absolutely *must not* join complete sentences with a comma, which may constitute the only true altruism of my otherwise selfish life. Put it on my tombstone: "She battled comma splice."

As far as I can tell, most schools today downplay grammar and punctuation if they teach these subjects at all. (Last year in Iowa authorities banished S. Keyron McDermott as a high school substitute teacher for criticizing "second-grade" grammatical errors in students' prose.) The neglect shows. I resist teaching creative writing if only because, on the few occasions that I've done so, the students have proved too creative. Young aspirant writers are working on novels but can't produce comprehensible, error-free sentences. Whether they know it or not, today's MFA candidates are crying out for primitive instruction on the accusative case, which would readily clear up any confusion about *who* versus *whom* (a perfectly civilized distinction that the animals are now clamoring to revoke). Though what they want is tips on character development, what they need (and in my classes got) is a five-minute lowdown on the semicolon.

Absent such instruction, this endangered punctuation mark has slid willy-nilly to the em dash, a crude demarcation that cannot imply relatedness or contrast, much less clearly separate list elements that contain commas. Capable of being inserted whimsically just about anywhere, the em dash effectively has no rules, and is therefore horribly suited to an era of semantic anarchy.

Education's having turned its back on teaching the technical aspects of composition is partially responsible for deteriorating standards in prose and speech. Lacking any familiarity with the structure of their language, people find linguistic rubrics arbitrary and unreasonable. Utter grammatical dereliction in English departments conveys that knowing the rudiments of one's language is unimportant, in which case "correct" English is unimportant too; it feeds the lazy, convenient, and therefore wildly popular view that there is no such thing as correct English.

Thus we witness the precipitous demise of the adverb, now that the very word *adverb* is lost on most people; mainstream newspapers now use *quicker* rather than *more quickly* to modify a verb. Many a subeditor suffers under the misguided impression that when the subject comprises a fair number of words, it is not only acceptable but mandatory to put a single comma between the subject and the verb (e.g., "The Jack and Jill who went up the hill to fetch a pail of water, fell down." Anathema!). Comparative and superlative forms are no longer prescribed but a matter of mood; one of my favorite movies might be titled today *Dumb and More Dumb. Literally* now means *really,* or, worse, *figuratively.* (Anyone claiming that "my head literally exploded" would not have lived to tell the tale.) *Notorious* is employed with such abandon as a synonym for *famous* that when using it correctly one can never be certain that one's pejorative intensions have been understood. The differentiation between quantity and number having been deep-sixed, *less* and *fewer* now are interchangeable. Thus on the rare occasions these adjectives are actually deployed accurately on TV, my husband and I will interject mischievously, "He means *fewer* water" or "She means *less* bottles."

Just try explaining that *as* is used with clauses while *like* takes a direct object when your audience hasn't the haziest idea what a clause or a direct object is, and don't expect your average American to infer that a direct object will hence take the accusative case. In the absence of any structural grasp, even examples (*as I do* versus *like me*) won't make a lasting impression, and meantime you've merely identified yourself as a pain in the butt. So forget the even more tortuous explanation of the restrictive and nonrestrictive uses of *that* and *which*, even though this distinction can have huge implications for the meaning of a sentence.

So when writing dialogue in fiction I often feel guilty. I'm supposed to make my characters speak as (not *like*) they would in real life. Yet rhetorical verisimilitude propagates the very errors that I revile. Now that the predicate nominative is dead and buried, I can't have a character announce "It is I!" without also conveying that this person is unbearable, perhaps outright insane, or imported from a previous century through time travel.

Therefore I too contribute to semantic drift. In our digital age, online dictionaries are revised almost continually, whereas the issuance of a new print edition of *Webster's* or the *Oxford English Dictionary* is the expensive labor of many years. In the analog world, then, official changes to meaning and usage were subject to considerable scrutiny, discouraging the institutionalization of commonplace mistakes. These days, what were once authoritative and inherently conservative reference sources easily acquiesce to mob rule. Misconceptions transform lickety-split into new conventions. We consolidate ignorance.

Although well-spoken, my parents nevertheless embraced two errors of usage, both of which my brother and I have struggled to rectify in our own speech, because misunderstandings instilled in childhood are tough to override. Hence when the copy editor on my first novel claimed that there was no such word as *jerry-rig*, I was incensed. Determined to prove her wrong, I went to my trusty, dusty-blue *Webster's Seventh* (based on the august *Webster's Third*), only to find she was right: *jerry-rig* wasn't listed. Apparently I'd grown up with a garbled portmanteau of *gerrymander, jerry-build,* and the word I really wanted: *jury-rig*. The scales fell from my eyes.

A convert, I explained to my mother her lifelong mistake, but she was having none of it. "Oh, no," she said gravely. "*Jury-rig* refers to rigging a jury, which is very serious." Explaining the allusion to a jury mast, a makeshift sail, with no etymological relationship to a judicial jury, got me nowhere. It's fascinating how ferociously people will cling to their abiding linguistic assumptions, however wrongheaded.

Although this is an argument I should have won in 1986, I'd lose it today. Dictionary.com informs us, "*Jerry-rigged* is a relatively new word. Many people consider it to be an incorrect version of *jury-rigged,* but it's widely used in everyday speech." With no such embarrassment, *Merriam-Webster*'s online dictionary now proudly lists *jerry-rigged* as meaning "organized or constructed in a crude or improvised manner." The mob—and my mother—have won. So much for my precious filial condescension.

Or take *nonplussed,* which I was taught meant "blasé." When another copy editor forced me to look this one up, it turned out to mean almost the opposite: "at a loss as to what to say, think, or do." What I thought meant "unruffled" pretty much meant "ruffled." But after laboriously internalizing the correct meaning of *nonplussed,* I find I needn't have bothered. Enough other people have made my parents' mistake that at the top of a Google search *nonplussed* is defined as "surprised and confused so much that they are unsure how to react," and "Informal, North American: not disconcerted; unperturbed." Great.

I ask you: What good is a word that now means both "perturbed" and "unperturbed"? This democratic inclusiveness of delusion effectively knocks *nonplussed* out of the language's functional vocabulary. If it means two opposite things, it ceases to communicate. If I say I'm nonplussed, what do you know? I'm either dumbfounded or indifferent. I might as well have said nothing.

So, given the pervasive misunderstanding of *enervated,* any day now online dictionaries are bound to start listing an accepted meaning of the word as "excited and keyed up," and that will be the end of *enervated.* If the adjective ever formally means either "energized" or "without energy," we'll have to chuck it on the trash heap.

We also find semantic drift in pronunciation, one instance of which has ruined a favorite party trick. I used to love submitting that *flaccid* is actually pronounced "flak-sid," challenging my incredulous audience to look it up and sitting back to watch the consternation. (That un-onomatopoeic hard *c* in a word for "floppy" is counter-instinctual.) My defiant company always vowed to keep mispronouncing the word anyway. At last mass cluelessness has prevailed. According to *Business Insider,* "The standard pronunciation is 'flak-sed,' not 'flas-sid' . . . Until recently, most dictionaries listed only the first pronunciation." That "until recently" pours cold water on all my fun. The accepted pronunciation "flas-sid" has even slithered into the modern *OED.*

Within the past couple of years, one misappropriation has spread like knotweed. In linguistics, *performative* has an interesting and specific definition. It describes a verb whose usage enacts its action, as in "I *promise,*" "I *curse* you," "I *apologize,*" "*bless* you": these are performative verbs. "I now pronounce you husband and wife" is a classic "performative utterance." In my old print dictionaries, the word meaning "relating to performance" is *performatory*—an adjective that has failed to catch on—and the linguistic meaning of the now-fetishized word has been lost. For *performative* in the sense of "posturing and insincere" is everywhere, now that *virtue signaling* appears to have exhausted itself. As we went through *virtue signaling* like single-ply toilet paper—the term only took off after a *Spectator* piece in 2015—there must be a brisk market for descriptions of left-wingers vaunting their ethical credentials with self-serving theatricality. (Search *performative* and Google suggests "performative wokeness.") Given such a hunger for words to capture it, moral flamboyance is clearly a mark of the age.

The steady decay of English syntax is a first-world problem par excellence, and tsk-tsking over sloppy grammar amounts to a haughty and rather geriatric form of entertainment. Besides, my own generation probably instigated this decline in the first place. For my erudite father, *decimate* can only mean "destroy a tenth of"; hypocritically, some semantic drift strikes me as sensible, and I happily employ the verb's broader sense. My father decried Captain Kirk's "to boldly go where no man has gone before!" though split infinitives leave me, if you will, nonplussed.

We let-it-all-hang-out boomers may have celebrated lingual creativity, but the dangling dependent clauses and modifiers that have grown rife, even in books, hardly qualify as inventive. Neither can "between you and I" pass for a form of self-expression. Honestly,

English requires so little declension in comparison with most languages that expecting the declension of pronouns in compound objects isn't asking for the moon.

However picayune and pitifully old-fashioned the bereavement may seem to most people, for me the erosion of style, clarity, and precision in everyday speech and prose is a loss. Call it a quality-of-life issue. A century ago, in diaries or letters to the editor, ordinary people wrote with astonishing elegance and correctness. Elegance is related to correctness.

In the fiction biz, of course, syntax is a matter of craft. Early in my career I still had a blind, unjustified confidence in my semantic inner ear, often railing against the edicts of officious, nitpicking copy editors. I was always wrong. If nowadays I also wrangle with copy editors, that's because the more recent crop's acquaintance with English syntax is abysmal. Their poor grasp of the discretionary and nondiscretionary comma is not their fault. Never having been taught the rules in seventh grade, they don't even have the vocabulary to cogently discuss our differences, because they don't know a predicate nominative from a hole in the ground. But I want to be saved from myself, because I suffer from the same misconceptions as anyone else. (I'm still shaky on *may* versus *might*.) I want an expert, a stickler, a real whip-wielding dominatrix. Yet all the terrifying taskmasters bashing me over the head with Strunk and White appear to have died off.

It's always dangerous to display hubris about one's proper English, since pedants like nothing more than to catch out other pedants. Fellow curmudgeons will also recognize all of my bugbears as losing battles. Ultimately, the evolution of language is a story of mob rule. But surely there's a tattered nobility to valiantly fighting wars that we know we can't win.

MARK SULLIVAN

Ode al Vento Occidentale

FROM *The Gettysburg Review*

> But when composition begins, inspiration is already on the de-
> cline, and the most glorious poetry that has ever been commu-
> nicated to the world is probably a feeble shadow of the original
> conception of the poet.
>
> —Percy Bysshe Shelley, *A Defence of Poetry*

HALF PAST SIX in the morning, early in May, and the city of Florence is uncharacteristically quiet in the presummer heat, its domes
and towers gauzed in humid stillness. As always, this is a place so
extravagantly beautiful and bedecked with masterpieces of Western civilization that walking its streets or entering its churches and
museums is like being able to move bodily through the pages of an
art history textbook. It's also a place loud with literary echoes—of
Dante, of course, but also of the English-speaking Italophiles who
spent time here: George Eliot, Henry James, E. M. Forster, and,
especially on my mind at the moment, Percy Bysshe Shelley. Yet for
all this cultural opulence, Florence remains a city and has all the
noise and dirt and traffic and ramshackle construction that make
cities nearly unlivable and irresistible at once; it seems we have
an attraction to exuberance in even its most chaotic form—here
with the added, dubious enticement of being one of thousands of
tourists from every part of the world, crammed into the clown car
of a relatively small urban space. Hence the earliness of the hour,
the only time it's really possible to move through the streets with
the fluidity necessary for running, before the hotels have begun to
serve their guests the *colazione* included with the price of a room,

and before the late-rising Italians would think it reasonable to face the bracing splash of another day.

I'm also up early because we arrived from New York only a day ago, and my circadian rhythms are as bumpy as the old paving stones in the narrow lanes, refusing to accept that the fall of darkness signals sleep or that a heavy gloom through the hotel curtains means morning hasn't arrived. The French poet Francis Ponge refers to the "peculiar state of traveling" where the spirit finds "a repose that is the exact opposite of sleep." Though I don't think he exactly had jet lag in mind, I can understand the notion that this hypersensitive state, where every impression causes a jagged alertness, has an almost hypnotic effect.

I cross the empty Piazza Santa Maria Novella, amazed at the contained explosion of the church facade's green-and-white-marble patterning, then walk the alleylike Via de' Fossi to the base of the Ponte alla Carraia on the north bank of the Arno. From there I turn east on the Lungarno Amerigo Vespucci and begin my run, the river on my left and a few other joggers and cyclists providing the only company on this normally jammed road.

The previous day I scouted all this out, knowing from a visit a couple of years ago Florence's inhospitality to runners and realizing I would need to find an early route along the peripheries if I was to get any exercise during our weeklong stay. My wife is here to teach watercolor painting to adult students, and since my role is limited to helping a bit with logistics and taking advantage of the free accommodations, there should be plenty of time to maintain my running routine, if the city itself cooperates. On the map, this course along the Arno looked promising. It led out of the city to the Parco delle Cascine, a long stretch of green that seemed ideal for recreation but wasn't featured in the guidebooks. The Internet wasn't much more informative, with scant descriptions on various travel sites making Florence's largest park seem a bit shabby, though busy with strollers and markets on weekends, along with comments by some runners that it might not be the safest place. And also this odd fact: somewhere in this park is the site where, in 1819, Shelley had the inspiration for and began to write the "Ode to the West Wind," long one of my favorite poems.

So some reconnoitering seemed wise, and the day before, while my wife greeted her students, I walked past the elegant hotels lining the river, by the grand mansion of the American consulate

—its machine-gun-bearing guards a jolting reminder that the city was *not* just a pearly vision—through a parking lot, and up some stairs to a wide, pavemented piazza leading into the park. Now, entering the Cascine by this route, I find, as yesterday, that the advance notices were not wrong, that despite a certain romantic luxuriance of vegetation and exotic spread of umbrella pines, like some enormous nonaqueous form of lily pad, the park is somewhat overgrown and undermaintained, its broken, claw-footed lamps strangely out of keeping with the image of Florence as a fanatic preserver of its past. And yet, also strangely, this slight seediness feels welcoming rather than off-putting, a sign that ordinary people—like the few I see walking dogs, dribbling soccer balls, or also running—are living their lives here rather than tidying it up for visitors.

I'm soon on a central path shaded by large elms and oaks. The air steaming in and out of me feels almost tropical, given the occasional palm tree in the distance and the mist eddying around the hills north of the valley. I pass some kind of racetrack with bleachers behind fencing, low brick buildings that seem to be botanical labs, the occasional playground, a tram crossing, and a broad piazza named for John F. Kennedy, with fountains, terraces, and another parking lot. I'm paying particular attention to the surroundings, not only because of the excitement of unfamiliarity and my Ponge-like state of lucid dreaming, but in the hope of finding the locus of Shelley's inspiration.

According to the information I stumbled across, there should be a pyramid-shaped fountain at the site—called Fonte di Narciso because it bears an image of Narcissus—along with a commemorative plaque. I have no idea where in this rambling park that fountain might be, but I'm guessing that it would be on the main path and am keeping watch for anything conspicuously triangular. The only object that seems to fit the description, however, is a distinctly unfountainlike, imposing stone structure looming at the side of the path. This building does indeed have the shape of a pyramid, so initially I think this must be it, some mausoleum-styled folly whose waterworks, in keeping with the park's neglected state, no longer function. But on drawing closer I notice a door with grilles and decide the whole thing must be an elaborate maintenance shed.

As I turn around at about the two-and-a-half-mile mark, I feel pleased that the Cascine has proved to be such a picturesque and nearly ideal place to run, but I'm disappointed at not being able to commune with the spirit of Shelley. But what, after all, would I hope to gain from standing on the spot where certain rhythms and words began to combine in Shelley's subconscious, eventually welling up to take the concrete form of stanzas scribbled in a notebook? Why this desire to approach the source of inspiration when Shelley's words themselves, like the wild spirit of the wind that the poem invokes, continue to live and move through memory and literary tradition? As Shelley himself wrote in the *Defence of Poetry*, inspiration is so vanishing and ungraspable, it is akin to the leaves skittering away at the beginning of the ode, the ghosts from an enchanter fleeing.

What can be said about inspiration? It's a famously difficult state to define, and the whole topic is a bit of an embarrassment in our post-postmodern age, to the point where many people, artists among them, would consider the very notion hopelessly Romantic and unhelpful, a remnant from an earlier set of beliefs before the world became disenchanted. When I was learning to write, manuals and craft essays emphasized effort over serendipity—you can't teach someone how to be inspired, after all—the virtue of diligence rather than the divine spark. The idea, exemplified by some of William Stafford's advice to poets, was that getting started trumped waiting around, that work came from work. The rallying cry was Rodin's injunction to Rilke: *"Toujours travailler!"*

All true, but this emphasis on work seems to leave out the most important part—that moment when effort becomes gliding and the slog turns into song. As a practical matter, this approach helped writers move beyond self-consciousness and inhibitions by focusing on problems of form and language and removing the burden of having something significant to say, but it also meant that questions of quality and meaningfulness tended to remain at a frustrating remove, at best relegated to some vaguely Freudian notion of openness to deep psychic promptings and at worst left to the judgment of outside authorities. (Stafford once said that it was the job of editors to keep poets from publishing their bad work.) Meanwhile, in the everyday world of trying to get that work done, writers and artists continued to experience moments where ideas

and images poured out of them with unwonted insistence and flu-
ency, and these moments of flow and integration seemed to be
largely the point, the clarity that all the grinding effort somehow
prepared the way for but didn't explain.

So perhaps the first thing to say about inspiration is precisely
that it is intermittent, flickering, and that a great deal of the work
of the artist seems to involve tending the flame to keep it from
going out. These spikes of lucidity are what Virginia Woolf calls
"moments of being," distinguished from all the "nonbeing" that
usually permeates our lives—the unconscious drifting through
the days and months and years without discerning the depths and
patterns, without achieving perspective. These moments, Woolf
says, can be overpowering and have to be managed, but they reveal "that the whole world is a work of art; that we are parts of
the work of art . . . We are the words; we are the music; we are
the thing itself." Emerson says something similar in his essay "The
Transcendentalist" when he describes the "double consciousness"
of living most of the time in dull routine but being shot through
with intimations of something greater. He describes the "faith" of
the transcendentalist as the belief that a time will come "when the
moments will characterize the days."

Shelley, for his part, addresses this intermittency in a famous
passage of the *Defence*—beloved by James Joyce's alter ego Stephen
Dedalus—when he compares the inspired mind to "a fading coal,
which some invisible influence, like an inconstant wind, wakens
to transitory brightness." What's interesting in Shelley's account is
that the spirit, when wakened by inspiration, already seems to be
suffering a diminution, a fading from some original conflagration
—perhaps from the fire of experiences that cannot be assimilated
as they occur. Thus, in keeping with his Platonic tendencies, Shelley's image of inspiration combines a flash of insight with nostalgia, involves remembering as well as heightened awareness. Woolf
herself singles out three memories from childhood when she first
became aware of these "moments of being," and many artists have
connected inspiration with preserving some of the wonderment
and freshness of a child's perceptions in adulthood. Rilke, for one,
advised his correspondent in *Letters to a Young Poet* that, in order
to write, he should "turn [his] attention" to childhood and "try to
raise the submerged sensations of that ample past." It may be that

one reason for the inconstancy of inspiration is the near impossibility of recovering and maintaining this receptivity when functioning in responsible adult life.

Shelley's account of inspiration seems almost written with the
"Ode to the West Wind" in mind, though he composed the essay in
1821, two years after the poem. The wind that wakens the fading
coal could be the wind addressed throughout the ode, and indeed
Shelley's poem is one long invocation and beseeching of the wind
to use its power to lift his spirit from "a heavy weight of hours"
to its former heights—specifically, to those of boyhood, "When
to outstrip thy skiey speed / Scarce seemed a vision." Moreover,
each of the first three sections of the poem ends with the plaintive
plea to the wind, "O hear!," as though some part of the poet *were*
still a child striving for the attention of a distracted or indifferent parent. Seen in this way, "Ode to the West Wind" becomes an
extended inspired performance about an absence of inspiration,
a prayer that to some extent answers itself. When, at the poem's
climax, the speaker petitions the wind, "Be thou, Spirit fierce, /
My spirit! Be thou me!," he enacts a kind of grammatical and lexical fusion—subject eliding with object, uppercase "Spirit," in the
sense of divine force, becoming its lowercase human equivalent
—an act all the more moving for its feeling of being accomplished
in the poem but perhaps not in actual life. For the poet continues
to make requests of the wind, with the imperatives *drive* and *scatter* and "Be through my lips . . . / The trumpet of a prophecy,"
as if not aware that its request has, in some sense, already been
granted. And in the famous, proverbial final lines of the poem—
"O wind / If Winter comes, can Spring be far behind?"—the use of
a question for a conclusion rather than a direct statement (or than
the exclamatory mode of most of the rest of the poem) seems to
indicate skepticism on the poet's part that his invocation has been
successful. It's as though he doubts that his sacrifice to the gods
will ensure the consistent renewal of longed-for light and life, and
indeed, isn't one of the characteristics of such sacrifices that they
are rituals and must be forever repeated?

Two days later, keeping to my usual every-other-day running routine, I'm again awake early, walking through the deserted corri-
dors of the Grand Hotel Baglioni, a little less exhausted now that
the time change and my body have begun to synchronize. The

piazza in front of Santa Maria Novella is again empty, except that an organization promoting cross-cultural study within the EU has begun to set up tents and a stage for a youth festival (its slogan on a banner, in English: "Here begins your movement"). I follow the same route down Via de' Fossi to the Lungarno, then right toward the Cascine.

Florence has been unusually hot for the beginning of May, and the morning is gray and vague as moisture rising from the river stalls in the just-warming air. I've been avoiding the heat and crowds by dodging the tourist magnets of the Duomo and Accademia, trying to skirt the city center altogether if I can, and finding refuge in the coolness of the lesser-known churches (lesser-known but still packed with frescoes and altarpieces by Botticelli, Ghirlandaio, Orcagna) and in the company of the relatively unvisited Donatellos and Michaelangelos in the Bargello. And this strategy of staying on the margins has made me feel oddly at home here, since it resembles the New Yorker's studied avoidance of Times Square and most of the rest of what constitutes the tour-guide version of that city. Florence turns out to be a very different place when seen this way, its loveliness taken for granted by university students hanging out around the Piazza della Santissima Annunziata, by families shopping at farmers' markets in the Oltrarno, by parents stopping for gelato as they walk their kids home from school.

When I enter the park again, I try to be as aware of every landmark as possible. A little more searching on the Web at the hotel has told me that the Narcissus fountain should be near the pyramidal building (which, it turns out, was originally an eighteenth-century icehouse used to store cheese when the park was still a dairy farm; *cascine* means "dairy maids") but not right next to it. So, still hoping for some contact with the fierce spirit of nearly two hundred years ago, I'm again on the lookout for anything with a pointed shape and a catch basin. And finally I see what I'm looking for off to the side of the main path, a dark wedge more like an obelisk than a pyramid, with a rectangular base and water flowing at the bottom.

As I approach the fountain, it's not hard to see how I missed it the first time. The word *fountain* had conjured in my mind something like Central Park's Bethesda Fountain, a large pool surmounted by a life-sized statue, whereas this *fonte,* though taller than head height, is on a much more modest scale and lies perpendicular to the main path, backed into a fence rather than set off in open space. The *fonte*'s greenish stone almost merges with the agate atmosphere, which deepens around the fountain under the mass of overhanging trees. Its structure consists of the obelisk-like top and the blocky base, from which a sculpted face, presumably that of Narcissus, stares into the shallow pool below. Rather than shooting into the air, as I had imagined, water trickles from Narcissus's open mouth into the pool; two semicircular steps lead up to the basin, looking whimsically like water that has overflowed the rim and is spreading below in solid waves.

At first I'm still not sure I've found the right fountain, because, despite the approximately triangular shape and spouting mask, the reality is so far from my expectations. But then I notice a plaque mounted on the obelisk that, even with my weak Italian, I understand contains a dedication to Narcissus. What I don't see, however, is any sign that mentions Shelley or "Ode to the West Wind," not beneath the plaque or on the base or on some separate post nearby. I walk around the area for a few minutes, but there is no indication that the twenty-seven-year-old Shelley stood on this spot, listened to the leaves rustling on the pathways and swirling through the air like damned souls in Dante, and called to the force that moved them as "Destroyer and Preserver." As I begin to move away to finish the rest of my run, I can't help feeling disappointment even in the face of apparent success—perhaps not so much because the spirit of Shelley has eluded me again, but because this entire urge to pin down the source of a great poem has begun to seem like folly.

If one prominent characteristic of inspiration is its inconstancy, like an old analog radio signal that strengthens and weakens according to topography and the vagaries of the weather, the other classic marker for the inspired state is that it comes from outside the self. "Sing, Muse," Homer says at almost the beginning of Western poetry, implying that his voice will merely be the vehicle for the divine agency, and ever since poets have spoken of being taken out of themselves, raised to new heights, dictated to by an unknown power. "Yours are the powers," Horace declares to his muse, "by which my verse gives fame," and even though this and later invocations to the muse might seem more a matter of convention than conviction, the notion that the artist becomes other to herself when most caught up in creation speaks through the durability of this tradition. Indeed, the difficulties attendant on such self-displacement seem to be inextricably connected with the impossibility of extending and living in an inspired state. I think of Rimbaud—who declared, *"Je est un autre"*—and his attempt at a systematic derangement of the senses, which ended in his abandoning poetry altogether. Or Rilke again, whose calling upon the muselike angels in the first of the *Duino Elegies* leads to the realization that "even if one of them pressed me / suddenly to his heart: I'd be consumed." So the creative act seems to involve the artist in a paradox: a loss of self when one is most fluent and singing, a feeling of irresponsibility for what one brings into the world.

These feelings undoubtedly implicate deep ambivalences and taboos, not only superstitions about the lastingness of a creative gift over which one seems to exercise little control, but also a certain fear of presuming and overreaching. In ancient Hebrew the only possible subject for the verb *to create* was "God," a linguistic embodiment of the reverence and mystery surrounding the making of something out of nothing. Of course, artistic creation is partly a matter of traditions and established practices, of working in and against forms and subjects that have been handed down —witness the conscious use of classical models like Horace in Shelley's ode. But however much we inherit and refashion, there is still the inexplicable moment of spontaneity when we fuse these elements with our own experience and imagination into something new. It's very much the way Noam Chomsky describes speech as constantly generating new sentences out of the genetic and cultural legacies of language. And both of these aspects of creation— the spontaneity that by definition arises unbidden; the inheritance we have not ourselves made—exist beyond us so that inspiration, the in-spiriting of a power outside oneself, seems both an essential human act and a Promethean usurpation of the prerogatives of divinity.

The French philosopher and mystic Simone Weil took the ancient Hebrews' belief that only God could create a step further, stating that God alone had the right to use the first-person singular. In Weil's theology, God is a thought that thinks himself, and the content of that thought is synonymous with his name, "I am."

According to Weil, because God is at the center of all things, "it must be recognized that nothing in the world is the center of the world, that the center of the world is outside the world, that no one here below has the right to say I." Weil's view of an inspired drawing-closer to God is an emptying of the self, an impoverishment and renunciation, what she terms *decreation*. This may seem an extreme view of what it means to seek inspiration, to call for the aid of the gods in seeking a kind of self-annihilation, but is it really so different from the traditional self-abandonment implied by summoning the muse to take possession of one's voice? In Shelley's poem, as we have already seen, such a transformation lies at the very heart of inspiration.

The "Ode to the West Wind" begins with the invocatory *O*, the speaker calling on the wind to hear his prayer for renewal. It's an odd invocation, though, with its emphasis on the "leaves dead" driven "like ghosts" and "pestilence-stricken multitudes"; its description of seeds blown into furrows, "each like a corpse within its grave"; and its apostrophizing of the wind as "Destroyer and Preserver." This hardly seems the language with which to propitiate, and the second section, which details the wind's massing of clouds before a storm, continues in the same vein:

> Thou Dirge
>
> Of the dying year, to which this closing night
> Will be the dome of a vast sepulchre,
> Vaulted with all the congregated might
>
> Of vapours from whose solid atmosphere
> Black rain and fire and hail will burst, O hear!

This is nearly apocalyptic. And while the third section, concerning the wind's stirring of the seas, is less dark and more painterly, it too speaks of imagining aquatic plants that "grow grey with fear / And tremble and despoil themselves," like their terrestrial counterparts at the approach of the "Destroyer and Preserver." At one level Shelley is bringing together the earth, air, and water as elemental witnesses to the dramatic and traumatic change of seasons, but at another his speaker is figuring his own distraught and despairing mind, a situation that becomes even clearer in the fourth section, when he wishes he could be as passive as a natural phenomenon taken up by the wind's activity. If, he says, such were the case,

> I would ne'er have striven
>
> As thus with thee in prayer in my sore need.
> Oh! lift me as a wave, a leaf, a cloud!
> I fall upon the thorns of life! I bleed!

According to his biographer Richard Holmes, Shelley had ample reason at this moment in his life to feel in sore need: a vicious personal attack upon him in a prestigious journal, "his apparent impotence to help the downtrodden people of England" after the Peterloo Massacre, "the disasters of his private life," which included the death of his young son and a sense that the vitality of his youth was slipping away. But none of these specific troubles are mentioned in the poem, and even Shelley's evidently political desire for the wind to use him as "the trumpet of a prophecy" of reform and liberty can be read as a more general call for renewal. What strikes the reader, what makes the poem an enduring masterpiece, is not its relation to Shelley's own state of mind but its articulation of a universal predicament: the loss of power and enthusiasm, the decline from the heights of youth, the falling upon the thorns of life, the sense of winter coming on.

Shelley captures this predicament by contrasting what Hannah Arendt describes as the "rectilinear course" of individual life with the "circular movements" of natural cycles. As Arendt succinctly puts it, "This is mortality: moving along a rectilinear line in the universe where everything, if it moves at all, moves in a cyclic order." From the beginning of the poem Shelley's speaker evokes a universe with whose circular motions he is out of step: the "winged seeds" that the wind hastens to "their dark wintry bed" will "lie cold and low / . . . until / Thine azure sister of the Spring shall blow / Her clarion" and fill them with new life — new life and inspiration that the speaker also longs for. This speaker is undergoing, as it were, a tragedy of geometry. He yearns to bend his linear course into a round that will take him back to his beginning, to be as much a part of the cycle as the leaf and cloud and wave, but the only way human beings can merge with this cycle is through the ultimate loss of self: death and being absorbed into the organic process. And this is why, through art, he seeks another kind of self-dissolution, an identification with the wind that will both destroy and preserve him, that will shatter the ordinary Euclidean bounds and show the line curving to meet itself in infinity.

The very form of Shelley's poem exhibits the drama of individual life pushing against the limitations of its designated shape. The poem is arranged in five sections or cantos, each fourteen lines long and comprising four tercets in terza rima and a concluding rhyming couplet. The length of each section, of course, indicates a sonnet, though the cantos do not fall into traditional sonnet movements, while the terza rima—so appropriate for a poem written in the city of Dante—creates a verse that moves forward by turning back on itself. Shelley thus plays a form, the sonnet, that proceeds toward closure in the final couplet against one that is open and expansive but circular. Even individual lines and moments in the poem take up this theme of enduring while falling away, as in the cry "I fall upon the thorns of life! I bleed!," which may seem at first an assertion of ego until we notice that the first-person pronoun is unaccented both times it appears in the line, as if experiencing its own immolation. And the poet's beseeching of the wind to break the boundaries between them and "be thou me" desires a kind of linguistic sublation of subject and object, first person and second, nominative and accusative. It's a wish for an extinguishment that is also an intensification, an othering that is equivalent to identity, and (Weil again) identity is infinite proximity.

Another two days and I'm back early in the park for my final run of the trip. Tonight my wife will finish her teaching duties with a celebratory dinner, and tomorrow we'll take the train to Arezzo for a few days of pure vacation, following the Piero della Francesca trail. The Cascine is again smeared with mist and somnolent as I pursue my own trajectory within circularity, running a straight course, past the landmarks of fountains and buildings and lawns that have begun to be familiar, before looping back on my tracks.

The visit to this ancient city—so caught up in the ambivalences of contemporary tourism and global commerce, with migrants' stalls in cinquecento arcades selling scarves and leather goods produced in China or in Mafia-connected sweatshops, and people from everywhere taking endless selfies next to Renaissance monuments that are some of the very first embodiments of this modern sense of self—has been both disconcerting and deeply moving, though I have to admit to envying those earlier grand tourists, like Shelley, with their months-long opportunities to educate their tastes in such places. Approaching and missing the spirit of Shelley during this week has continued to nag at me. It seems a significant omission somehow, and I'm still thinking about it as I pass the Narcissus fountain again and head toward the further reaches of the park.

This disappointment probably has something to do with my own stage in life. No longer young, I've come to that point where discouragements and losses begin to accumulate and outweigh, at times, the moments of elation and integration Emerson talks about, where the inspired instances that once would wipe away several weeks of frustration have become even more infrequent. This ebbing of enthusiasm seems to be a hazard of middle age, especially when, as in my case, the more tangible signs of success, like publications and recognitions, thin out or become so sparing at times as to seem desultory and disconnected. When you add to this the difficulties that accompany almost anyone's moving past the middle of life—the sudden or gradual loss of loved ones, the physical ailments that are managed rather than healed, the coming to terms with limitations only to make further adjustments downward—it's not surprising that I would be attracted to Shelley's crisis and breakthrough, his yearning for inspiration that became its own fulfillment. I wouldn't be so melodramatic as to say I've fallen upon the thorns of life (though isn't one of the things we love about poems that they allow us to say things we would be embarrassed to say in our own voices?), but I can certainly appreciate Shelley's metaphor of the "heavy weight of hours" that makes time itself into a kind of gravity. Time too is said to bend and slow down around massive objects; the object in this case is the fact of our rectilinear course, and the differences between my circumstances and Shelley's, the almost two hundred years and age discrepancy that separate us, seem unimportant next to this common lot.

I'm thinking about all this as I approach the fountain for the last time on the way back and decide to stop for a final look. As before, the area is tranquil—bucolic but not exactly arcadian with all the modern park accoutrements of chain-link and asphalt—the city just beginning to make its sound of an orchestra perpetually tuning. The fountain looks slightly disheveled in the way that old, neglected monuments do, wearing time like a once magnificent and now patched robe. I take a valedictory walk around, and then I see it: low down on the right side of the obelisk, almost at the base, a dingy stone plaque half grimed with city soot and blighted by weather. Nondescript as it is, I still can't believe I managed to miss it before. Was I so preoccupied with getting back to running, or so blinded by the preconception of some bold commemoration, that I couldn't see the plain reality right in front of me? (Well, admittedly, not right in front but off to one side and mounted pretty low.) In all capitals it reads:

NEI PRESSI DI QUESTA FONTE
DETTA DI NARCISO IL POETA SHELLEY
COMPOSE NELL AUTONO 1819
L'ODE AL VENTO OCCIDENTALE

In truth, the plaque is so unobtrusive that I would guess many people pass the fountain without noticing it. And somehow, after my initial disbelief that I could have been so unobservant, I find it endearing that this remembrance of *il poeta* Shelley seems almost familial on the part of the people of Florence, like an heirloom kept on a shelf so long it's no longer seen. So this is the spot, or at least "around" here. I take a moment to inhale the ambience of this spring day, with its thick air and verdigris tones, so different from the autumn one when Shelley wrote his poem, and then begin to run back to the hotel again.

Does the place where an inspiration occurred matter? Shelley evidently thought it did and appended a note to the first publication of "Ode to the West Wind," specifically siting the poem in this park on the banks of the Arno. "The poem," he wrote, "was conceived and chiefly written in a wood that skirts the Arno, near Florence." This was not the only time he identified a poem with a place; his comment on "Mont Blanc" also equates a location with the feelings it evokes, and his works contain a number of "Lines Written" poems titled after their place of composition. Clearly this association mattered to him, as it mattered to the person who proposed the plaque and the civic committee that approved it. And as it matters to me, though it's difficult to say just why. I've made other literary pilgrimages, to Keats's and Shelley's graves in Rome, for instance, and felt stirred by the pathos of their lives and my fondness for their work. But this is something different. How many plaques in the world commemorate the writing of an individual lyric poem? I would wager that this is close to the only one.

Running back along the Lungarno, I focus on the Italian word *compose*. It suggests the combining of often disparate materials into a structure, as well as designating a state of calm or rest. In a way it unites the two verbs from Shelley's note—*conceived* and *written* —into a single act, giving definite form to an initial impulse. The truth about art is that it takes more than a moment's illumination; it is also the proverbial ten thousand hours of work that let an artist know what to do with that moment, the composition and revision, the failure and trying again. (Richard Holmes, as I would later recall, records that Shelley had made two false starts on the poem in the days leading up to his final attempt with "Ode to the West Wind"; writing, it turns out, *does* come from writing.) It is the patience that Emerson counsels between the episodes of transformation. Perhaps this plaque is particularly moving because its very unobtrusiveness seems to speak to this third quality of inspiration: its inextricable dependence on our mundane lives.

Shelley asks the wind to become, through his lips, "the trumpet of a prophecy" that will announce a new era and a rebirth in Shelley's own life. In so doing he circles back to the beginning of the poem where he imagined the west wind's "azure sister," the spring wind, blowing "her clarion o'er the dreaming earth" to awaken new life. This image of the trumpet, so redolent of the Last Judgment, manages to unite the entire cycle of the seasons— from birth to fullness to decay and death and back again—within the ring of the poem, and by identifying himself with this image, Shelley is allowed to escape his rectilinear course and embody that cycle. More: this circle keeps expanding—as the universe is said to do—into space that it is itself creating as new readers come to the poem and absorb its message, while the rhetorical question that concludes the poem seems to keep the figure from entirely closing and permits its circumference to move continually outward. This is all certainly an emblem for inspiration, like Weil's radically uncentered version of the self, but it is also a demonstration of what art can achieve through masterful composition.

This expansion had to begin somewhere, and in this case that spot can actually be located, near a fountain in a wood by the banks of the Arno. Shelley may have thought that the result of his inspiration was, like the images in Plato's cave, a mere shadow of a greater reality, but without that shadow, his inspiration could not spread and vivify in a way that his poem so clearly declares as its aim. *Inspiration* is the name we give to that paradoxical experience where a lightning flash seems as though it could last forever and a loss of self becomes the discovery of identity; any product of this transformation is bound to feel both touched with mystery and hopelessly embedded in a less ethereal medium. But Shelley also seemed to realize the consequence of that diminished, sensual world for whatever reality we may at times perceive as higher. His poem, after all, asks the wind to scatter his words wide like the leaves it is sweeping from the forest, and, in a full rhyme, to extend his verse to the universe.

MARK SUNDEEN

Holiday Review

FROM *Virginia Quarterly Review*

Entire House
Beautiful Village Life in Andalusia
Jimena de la Frontera, Spain
3 guests • 1 bedroom • 1 bed • 1 bath

Mark, June 2018

WE STAYED ONE night at Karl's place in Jimena de la Frontera in southern Spain. Let me begin with the PROs. As advertised the house was beautifully situated in a whitewashed medieval village and from the sunny roof terrace we could see miles to the Rock of Gibraltar and the Mediterranean. The cobblestone lanes were so steep I had to goose the Fiat. The pleather lazyboy didn't exactly capture the gypsy soul of Andalusia, but that's fine because the sheets and towels smelled of fresh detergent.

The main PRO was price. At $53 USD a night it was the cheapest in town. We planned this trip on short notice and could barely afford three weeks in Spain. Our summer had freed up unexpectedly and we needed to leave home. Hospital bills piled up. As I told Karl in my first email, my wife had spent four months in Jimena de la Frontera as a teenager and wanted to return. He didn't reply but that's okay we're all busy and besides, instructions for letting ourselves in were clear and I wasn't seeking a friendship during our four nights especially since Karl lives in South Africa. Point is I knew this wasn't going to be a palace.

CONs

It was already 8 p.m. when we arrived and C took me walking up to
the old castle ruins on the hill where she used to hang out as a kid,
purple sun lingering, so it wasn't until late that I saw the place was a
bit dirty. I'm not a fussy person. I'm not even very clean. I've spent
hundreds of nights just throwing a sleeping bag down in the dirt,
and C and I lived in the back of a car for two months in Mexico.
But the shower was stained with mildew and paint flaked off. Same
thing behind the toilet, a black array of mold. It wasn't a matter of
not having been scrubbed, rather a general sense of disrepair. The
shower curtain was torn, patched with masking tape. The old white
plaster walls were smudged with fingerprints and dotted with nail
holes. I suppose we could have bailed right away, but by the time
we got a whiff of the musty mattress it was midnight.

Still I felt like a jerk canceling the remaining three nights.
Since Karl's place lacks Wi-Fi I had to compose my complaint the
next day from the terrace of the hotel down the block, all shaded
by palms and lime trees, succulents blooming in clay pots. I've
never canceled an Airbnb. You can read my other reviews; I'm
no complainer. Look at Maria's place in Madrid—five stars across
the board. Maria was waiting there when we arrived bedraggled
from the airport after the overnight flight from California and she
gifted us a bottle of Spanish wine and a tortilla. You can see that
my review was 100% positive even though I didn't sleep well, but
that's because I was awakened in the night by C's sobbing, obviously not Maria's fault.

Karl's response was swift and polite. He offered a partial refund,
saying the system was forcing him to charge a cancelation fee of
fifty-five dollars. Fine. He added:

> some times an occasional guest creates the perception of problems
> that stems from another reason that later emerges because after all it's
> not a hotel and people often project that need for that type of environ-
> ment.

I was irked that Karl implied that the mildew was not a problem
but merely my perception of a problem, and that the peeling paint
was just my projection of inner turmoil, and that I didn't know

what a hotel was, but really I just wanted my money back. By now we'd had coffee and toast at the hotel. C used to drink beer on this very terrace and was pleased to see it unchanged.

Karl wrote to say he had a second house we could move into. We trudged up the steep lane upon which C's knees ached and we met Karl's housekeeper who showed us around. It was a step up, clearly where Karl himself stayed. His surfboard hung in the entry, his videocassette collection lined the wall. But as we walked back down the hill, C and I felt a coldness. "Moving into Karl's other house is just moving closer to Karl," she said. "Here's where Karl sleeps. Here's where Karl brushes his teeth." Even the kind woman who showed us around: "Here's the person who cleans up after Karl." We moved to the hotel where I clicked to cancel, sure that Airbnb would remove the fee.

By then we were hungry so we traversed the cobblestone to Bar España where we sat on the terrace with a wide view of the cork forests and cattle range of Andalusia and I drank a beer with a ration of prawns in butter and garlic while C had mineral water and a mixed salad with tuna and egg. Save for the old men watching soccer, we had the place to ourselves.

"How long was his spirit in the world?" C said.

"Where is it now?" I said.

"I want him so bad."

Any relief we felt being extricated from Karl's gloomy little homes was premature. Upon returning to our new room with its sparkling bathtub we splashed into the pool on the roof, where C found an avocado fallen from a tree and I discovered Karl's latest note.

Hi Mark it appears that C is looking for something other than the style of place you booked and as such a normal cancelation should apply because 2 places can't be that wrong. As I said before, normally the real reason comes out later. It appears that C desires a more refined hotel like establishment.

Typically I wouldn't use this venue to emote but Karl's note hurt my feelings. It was chauvinistic to assume it was my wife, and not me, who could not appreciate the grime on the lid of the trashcan. Actually it was me who objected to the single nonstick fry pan dangling above the stove, Teflon flaking in ribbons; me who was saddened by the table made of particleboard and held together with Scotch tape.

But what really wounded me was the way Karl casually referred to C by first name as if he knew her. He had no right.

Karl, may I address you directly? We had other plans for this summer. I had planted and watered a patch of grass under the mulberry tree where we would hang a swing. We bought the stroller and the crib and the Bjorn thing. Instead we came to Jimena. When my wife came here as a girl, it was not on some lark, but because her house burned down and her parents were caught without insurance or savings, and a family friend offered to take her to Spain as a nanny for their son. Same thing now: this was not our first choice.

After your note refused our refund we took a long walk along the lazy river, the Rio Hozgarganta, with its stone aqueduct and Roman mills with shady pools. Thousands of pink oleanders blossomed along its banks and we peeled off our clothes and plunged into the green water. My wife told me a story about walking this river alone when she was fifteen. A shepherd had approached and invited her to see a cave. This sounded like a bad idea, but she'd never met a shepherd before, didn't even know they still existed, and, most importantly, hell yes she wanted to see a cave. Once they arrived he asked for a little kiss, and she bolted past him and sprinted to freedom. Most of the traits I love about her are depicted here. First, she has the courage and wanderlust to be roaming the woods by herself. Next, she gives people the benefit of the doubt. She also has the sense when things go bad to run like hell. But what I love most of all is her curiosity, her insistence on knowing all the world, especially its oddities like shepherds and caves.

We swam and swam, floating in flowers. Karl, we named our son Silver and swaddled his flawless body in a hand-knit shawl and when I pushed C's wheelchair out of the hospital elevator, she said, "Put the sunglasses on my face," and the people smiled at us like the bundle in her lap was filled with joy. As for the car seat, I left it with the nurses because I couldn't bear to bring it home empty. A Mormon friend sent me a note. "You and your wife will raise your son in the spirit world. I testify this to be true." We drifted in those oleanders. Where was our son? Where was that spirit world?

Karl, you're right that a real reason comes out later. For me it was the tear in the bedsheet. My wife pointed it out to me in the morning. I guess that's the other reason we are in Spain, to make another baby, to start again our family. We held each other with soaring tenderness and neither of us cried.

I thought my suffering was boundless, but that morning it reached its bottom limit. I was not willing to launch our new life from your stale mattress with its torn sheet. I was not going to nourish my wife with a meal fried in your cracked skillet. And your other home—even though it was nicer—it too reeked of a sort of aging-man-loneliness and I suspected that in the closets and cabinets I'd discover small grenades of despair.

I wanted to forget you, Karl, but as the days passed you dwelled in my chest with a deep ache. Someone in Jimena told me that you have two grown daughters who live here, that they used to look after the house, but there was a falling-out, and since then the place has sunk into disrepair. I was not surprised. I felt estranged from you after just two days.

Karl, my bones are pierced! I am afraid of all my sorrows. My patch of grass sprouted up green and tender just in time to place folding chairs upon it. My brother drove across Albuquerque to Home Depot and bought wooden boards and a six-pack and built a tiny crate. We had to put him in there, Karl. C's parents drove our son up to Montana and in a grove of birch behind their house I dug a hole with my brother and dad and nephew and niece through the duff and the rocks and clay to where the spring water seeped. His little fingernails kept growing and I wanted to clip them but couldn't bring myself to do it. I laid my son in a box lined with cedar boughs and we sprinkled his body with water from the sea and water from the river.

Karl, my soul is weary of my life. Why did you take my son, my only child? And why not me instead? I will never be able to call my son on a Saturday afternoon and ask him to run down to the rental and scrub the mildew in the shower.

But I will call to him anyway. When I'm old I will call out to my son: When you're done painting will you replace the fry pan. Spare no expense—get a heavy one cast in iron with a handcrafted oak spatula. Maybe our guests will be lovers and he'll cook breakfast and carry it to the terrace where they will kiss and nap in the warm sun. And, son, buy a new set of sheets, take my credit card, the softest cotton the color of cream. Gather buckets of the pink oleanders that line the Rio Hozgarganta that flows through Jimena de la Frontera, arrange them about the bed. Make it nice. Son, those lovers might just be your mother and father conjuring you by miracle back into this world. We may never know a stranger's sorrow until we know our own. Their hearts are fragile, so be kind. Make the bed, boy! Make it lovely.

ALISON TOWNSEND

My Pink Lake and Other Digressions

FROM *Cimarron Review*

AH, THE SWEET relief of digression. You slip into it with a sense of recognition and release, as if entering the pond where you first learned to swim, or putting on your frayed purple velour bathrobe at the end of the longest workweek in the world. This is how your mind always works best, sliding sideways from one subject to another, moving associatively, like a butterfly flitting from one flower to the next, dipping and sipping deeply, an invisible trail of scent stretched behind you. One minute you hear your husband's voice in the kitchen, cajoling the collie, who is grieving, like you, for his sister dog, Annabelle, buried on the back hill two days ago. "Eat something, Togo," he says. "Please eat." And the next minute you hear your father's voice, fifty years ago, offering the family dog half a buttered bagel and saying, "That's my boy, that's my boy."

Your father and his red wool work shirt. The kitchen with his watercolor paintings of Revolutionary War soldiers, old copper pans from France shining on the wall beside the brick oven, and the battered round table where you and your sister drank endless ironstone china cups of Tetley tea after school, gossiping about the day. Her eyes were so much like your mother's—dead when you were only little girls—you sometimes told her so. But when you did she'd turn snotty, scathing, mean, saying "You're so *sensitive*." As if sensitivity were a crime. And meanwhile, Daylily Creek babbled along outside through the lower meadow, its surface catching the light, reflecting it in rippling panels like moiré silk on the ceiling.

You follow the long, looping lassos of thought that is not

thought exactly, but something looser, something liquid that rises and falls, like waves or currents of air. "Everything is connected to everything else," your mentor and creative mother, Holly Prado, said once, explaining what she thought you were trying to do in the wild, breath-driven rushes of words you read shyly from your journal each week in her writing workshop. "Have you seen the film Jeanne Moreau directed called *Lumière*?" she asked. "Moreau does visually what you're trying to do with words. You've got to go see *Lumière*." You never did see the movie, but felt obscurely pleased, as if you'd been seen, which you had. Around the same time you read Virginia Woolf's diary, thrilled at what she wrote about proceeding at a "random, haphazard gallop, . . . sweeping up accidentally stray matters which I should exclude if I hesitated, but which are the diamonds in the dust heap." You were looking for diamonds too.

Holly, with her blond hair backlit by sun streaming through the window from her round walled garden with the little witch's gate, talking about what she called "a sense of possibility" in poetry. How many Tuesday mornings did you spend in her workshop? How many long drives from Claremont into L.A. did you make, the San Gabriel Mountains so sharp against the blue you could cut your hand on them if you touched them? Where would you be if you had not had those mountains? Where would you be if you had not met Holly? As lost, you think, as the tiny sugar ant that skitters across your page as you write this seems to be, though perhaps it knows exactly where it is going.

Holly validated something in you, simply by believing, by intimating that there was and is another way of understanding the world than what you'd learned in school. You'd forced yourself to be analytical there, though it felt like being locked in a cage, your mind a wild mustang that had never known a bridle, the bit cold and sharp in your soft mouth. And meanwhile on the other side of the fence lay a landscape filled with all the surprises that happen if you loose the strictures linear reasoning places on the mind, shucking them off like a too-tight dress, peeling the green husk of life back from the pearly kernels of sweet corn underneath.

Even in your grief, even in your sadness over losing Annabelle, your beautiful female collie, all wind-rush and fur-silk and jingling tags you think you hear down the hall at night, your mind moves in its reliable motions, and this is comforting. Out and out and out, your mind swims into the surf, riding the waves back in, the way you did one afternoon at San Onofre beach, your body aligned so perfectly with the music of the earth you could have died then, water spangled on your skin, your bikini top off because the beach was so empty. Waves and mountains—they are your favorite forms of prayer—the scent of salt air and California bay laurel steeped in sunny canyons just two of your many homes.

Digressions, tangents, intuitive through-lines, spines. When you were a teacher, you drove your students crazy, making them laugh, making them say, "Oh, no. Here we go again. Danger, danger, Will Robinson! We're going *off* topic!" One minute you'd be talking about James Baldwin's magnificent and heartbreaking story "Sonny's Blues." Then you'd say, "Okay, chickadees. Let's look at how many times windows occur in the story." And you were off, hopscotching from Baldwin's windows to the hundreds of windows Andrew Wyeth painted (looking in and looking out), to the intrinsic nature and purpose of windows, to "Let's get out pen and paper and write for five minutes about what you see from the window you look out of most, and then five more on what characters in the story see."

And then it was time to hear some of their words, halting and shy, and then back to the story again, diving into its beautiful and terrible complications of race and art. There was one passage you always read aloud, voice shaking at the loveliness of Baldwin's words, remembering how one of your own professors cried once when reading, her pearl earrings trembling. Then you had the students read it too, word by word, the circle you'd required them to sit in suddenly magic, a ring of light held together by sound of their voices: "Then Creole stepped forward to remind them that what they were playing was the blues . . . and the music tightened and deepened, apprehension began to beat the air. Creole began to tell us what the blues were all about. They were not about anything very new. He and his boys up there were keeping it new, at the risk of ruin, destruction, madness, and death, in order to find new ways to make us listen. For, while the tale of how we suffer, and how we are delighted, and how we may triumph is never new, it must always be heard. There isn't any tale to tell, it's the only light we have in all this darkness."

"I thought we were talking about windows," one husky boy said as you left class that afternoon. "But we were really talking about

race, weren't we?" You remember him still, a young man who perhaps traveled farther than any student you ever had, from his conservative upbringing in northern Wisconsin to your English class.
Where he found himself in a small discussion group with two feisty
African American girls from Milwaukee. By the end of the year
they were housemates. "College really opened my eyes," he said
once, during a conference over a paper. "What if I hadn't come
here? What if I hadn't changed?"

You wanted to weep at what can happen, at what the human
heart can open and hold. There are miracles everywhere. Even at
a land-grant school in what felt to you like the middle of nowhere
but was of course a place like any other, beloved to your students
because it was theirs. You cared about your students so fiercely it
hurt, learned more from them than they ever did from you. You
were there unwillingly, through circumstances of love and work,
but determined to do your best by them. The Midwest was never a
place where you ever planned to land, the yearning for somewhere
else a permanent lump in your throat, an irritation, an itch you
can't scratch, a question you can't ever answer.

But you've made a home here, on the north side of drumlin,
haven't you, learning the flowers, trees, animals, the mineral scent
of snow in winter, the scent of sweet earth turned over in spring?
Last night you sat on the deck with your husband, eating arti-
chokes and arborio rice in the soft May air, the oaks just opening
their tiny fists of green leaves, May apple parasols shining beneath
them, and Island Lake shimmering in the distance, its waters a
mirror lit pink by setting sun. So many evenings you've sat out
there with the collies, both dogs rushing out, excited, barking like
wild things the instant you opened the door. Now there is just one
who lies quietly at your feet, head on his paws, looking out toward
the hill where Annabelle is buried beneath the mulberry tree.

It's almost your birthday. Your husband asks if you remember
the year when he inquired what you wanted and you said, "All I
want is the pink lake." And he gave it to you, in a photo that hangs
in your bathroom, and in so many other ways, the two of you sitting on this deck more evenings than you can remember, dogs at
your feet, Annabelle's ears always perked, alert triangles of black
velvet you loved to stroke. The pink lake was all you needed, then
and now. Pink lake and a pink sky. In summer you will sit here, sip-

ping rosé, remembering the vat your father made when you were a child, and the essay he wrote about it called "Pink Wine."

And even as you answer your husband, you remember more. Your mind slides to your first kitchen at Wild Run Farm. You mother says, "I'm in the pink," explains what it means, and then waltzes around on the old-fashioned rose-patterned linoleum, singing, "Brown paper packages tied up with string, these are a few of my favorite things." She holds in her arms a puppy with orange eyebrows like those on the dog you just buried. The puppy will be dead in a few weeks, hit by a car as you walk together down the road to Perkiomen Creek. Your mother will die of cancer two years later. Your beautiful collie is dead now, her suffering over, heaven for dogs an endless green field where they can run and run. "Dog years," another of your teachers, Mark Doty, calls them in a book remembering Arden and Beau. These have been your years, the animals who companion us a measure of our time on the planet.

The next morning your throat constricts at the sight of Togo lying near Annabelle's favorite spot beside the front door. A half wall by the door makes the area denlike; it was always, indisputably, hers. The last month of Annabelle's life the dogs often lay there together, Togo watching her, gazing into her eyes when she woke, the two of them communing about something you are not privileged to know. There's a mark on the wall where she'd brush it with her fur, turning in her dog-circle before lying down. You will never wash it away. How to go on without her?

And yet somehow we all do go on, don't we, the ever-present question of what to make for dinner and where to go next sometimes one and the same. Life keeps opening up before you, like all those blue-gray highways you have traveled, moving from one place to another in this big country. The names of states pile up inside you, like the drawer in your grandfather's mahogany secretary desk, crammed with a life's worth of photos you've never had time to arrange. Every instant is a sandalwood-scented mala bead you run through your fingers to remember. Woolf called them "moments of being." How to string them together, how to hold joy and sadness cradled in your palm at the same time? You wrote a line about this once, published it in a book of poems. But when you look you cannot find it. Does this mean you are meant to learn it all again?

"I meant to write about death," Woolf writes in her diary, "only life came breaking in as usual."

And all those moves, what do they mean? You always intended to stay in one place, didn't you? A friend who was born here laughs and says your sensibility is bicoastal, not midwestern at all. You wonder how a sensibility can be shaped by a place and what that means. Is there a way to map it, and if so, what would it look like? Would it be like nineteenth-century ribbon maps, unfolding in long, interconnected scenes, or the spiral-bound TripTiks you used to get from AAA before driving cross-country? You loved how the agent would print the TripTik maps out, highlighting the trail of your journey with a fluorescent orange Magic Marker.

You think you understand the mystery of place for a moment as you lie on the ground beside your dog's grave, letting earth hold you as it holds her. Always, no matter where you have been, you have known to do this. The scent of the herb called sweet Annie floats all around you, rising from its dried boughs you piled upon her grave. You've grown sweet Annie for years but just learned just the other day that its proper name is artemisia. It is beautiful, from the name of one of your favorite Greek goddesses, patroness of animals. But you like common names best for the folklore they reveal. Sweet Annie is perfect for your Annabelle, and you are glad you never got around to making all the fragrant wreaths you planned on as gifts at Christmas, glad the boughs are here, spilling their green seeds into her black fur.

Sitting up, you notice that the cat's grave beside your dog's new one has, in just two years, been covered by violets. You remember a pet cemetery you saw once on an estate in Wales, and then a line from a poem you wrote your sister years ago. "At home, violets open their blue lamps," you said. And then: "In the spring rain, even the cut branch blooms." You were talking about boughs pruned from the apricot tree in your California yard, which bloomed even after they were cut. The sight of those pale pink stars was so startling you felt something ripple inside you, like the first faint inklings of the child you would later lose. You were shocked that the severed limb persisted in blooming, nature profligate and elemental. It hurt to look, though you did. You made jam from the tree's fruit that year as you did every summer, stirring up great vats of the sweet gold on your Western-Holly stove, ladling it into Kerr's canning jars. That apartment over a carriage house was like the inside of a roll-top desk. The first home of your adulthood, you lived there for ten years. You loved it so much you paid rent on it when you and your first husband went to Texas for a year. You wanted to be sure it was there to come back to.

The real wonder is that we can (and do) go on living, even when we lose what we love most, even as you pick your way carefully around the slippery, tar-pit edges of clinical depression, afraid you'll be pulled in again, tugged under into the black slick of it, forgetting the way home to joy, that undervalued commodity you forget so easily because happiness takes care of itself.

Woolf again, in *To the Lighthouse:* "What is the meaning of life? . . . The great revelation perhaps never did come. Instead there were only little daily miracles, matches struck unexpectedly in the dark; here was one."

Tonight your miracle is a window cranked open on the May evening, cool air moving over you in waves as you lie down beside your man, wearing a summer nightgown for the first time this season, its worn cotton batiste delicious against line-dried sheets that smell of wind and sun and new beginnings. All night the window stays open on the garden that smells of rain and possibility, that thing Holly taught you to look for in poems. All night, when you wake, so sad about Annabelle you cannot sleep, still listening for the sound of her breathing, you pick the stars out as they hang in the still mostly bare branches of the oaks like lanterns guiding the way. Years ago your father read a story to you with the line "When you love someone who lives on a star it is lovely to look at the sky at night." Is your dog a star now, like your father and mother?

You count your stars. You "count your blessings instead of sheep," the way Bing Crosby advises Rosemary Clooney to do in *White Christmas.* The bed is a boat that carries you through darkness, everyone you love aboard ("It's the ark of us," you said to your husband), even if you can't see them on Earth anymore. Your beloved dog lies down in the den of your heart, her brother curled on the green braided rug beside your bed. The window is open on frog-song and Canada goose-murmur, crane-call and coyote-yip, their voices stitching the air together in an invisible quilt of sound you pull over your shoulders, everything connected to everything else—as it always has been, as it will still be, come tomorrow, come morning.

DAVID L. ULIN

Bed

FROM *Another Chicago Magazine*

December 4, 2014

THE NIGHT BEFORE I go to the desert, I sleep in our old bed for
the last time. I, we . . . Rae is here beside me, although as usual, or
often, she is turned head to foot, Molly Bloom, *yes I said yes I will
Yes*. This is a strategy she developed years ago, reaction to my snoring, when she doesn't abandon the bed altogether, sleeping on a
mattress in Noah's room to evade the noise. That is where this bed
will go, Noah's room, once the new one is delivered, the remaking of our house in increments, time pursuing its slow passage, its
incursions, conditional yet also lasting, small ripples begetting big
movements, change upon change . . . But I digress.

No, the bed, the old one: we have had it for more than twenty
years. Our first substantial purchase in California, and if I can't
remember when exactly we switched over from our futon, I do
remember it as the heart (or at least the ventricle) of everything.
Both our children were conceived in this bed, and both were
nursed here; both climbed into it when they were sick or couldn't
sleep. In February, on the afternoon we realized Noah's eating
disorder was going to require more help than we alone could offer, he wept (wept? more like thrashed and wailed and rent his
garments) here on this mattress in his mother's arms. I holed up
in this bed, wrote books and essays, read hundreds of novels, hid
from the pressing insistence of the world. *There is an alternative to
war*, John Lennon once declared. *It's staying in bed and growing your
hair*. He's not talking about disengaging, and neither am I. For me,
bed—*this* bed—is the place where the purest, most engaged life

has taken place, where we reveal ourselves, our vulnerabilities and deepest trustings, where we show each other who we are. I think of John and Yoko, in their pajamas, those hotel rooms in Montreal and Amsterdam, singing songs and painting slogans, and what this tells us about how we mean to be. Private and yet also public . . . or perhaps the point is that in our public lives our private selves are revealed. It is in this bed, after all, our bed, that I have most exposed myself, that I have been both sick and happy: secure, protected, and yet in the next moment utterly, existentially alone. *In a real dark night of the soul*, Fitzgerald writes, *it is always three o'clock in the morning, day after day.*

Three o'clock in the morning . . . Fitzgerald's issues were not the same as mine, but this is something we share. I am often awake at this hour, wrested from sleep by my bladder or my conscience, insistence of an anxiety so deep and pervasive it never quiets even in my dreams. I have trouble falling asleep, have for as long as I can remember, find it not only difficult but also treacherous to navigate that boundary between waking and not-waking, between being here and not. Sleep is like a shore—or no, not a shore, more like the water that laps upon it, an ocean in which I must submerge. At times it feels like drowning, a backward tumbling, my head, my face, going under, unable to breathe. We've all known this: the startle awake, the sensation of having caught yourself in the midst of falling, disquieting certainty that there is no air in your lungs. I gasp, I swallow, I twist and flail, uncertain for the moment whether I am coming back or falling, now and forever, into something deeper, the slipstream that will carry me to the farther shore.

This is a cliché, I know it, framing sleep in terms of death, *le petit mort* (which is, of course, a different sort of trope). And yet there is something, I think, a sense of surrender or loosening, that terrifies me about both. *Terrifies?* It's a strong word to describe my relationship with sleeping—not entirely accurate, but more so, perhaps, than I might want to let on. Some nights it captures precisely the way sleeplessness metastasizes, as a rising pressure, heightened by the ticking of the clock. My insomnia—if we can call it that; I always get to sleep eventually, always feel the water fold over me like a pair of hands—is at its worst when I have a commitment the next morning, some reason I have to be up and out of the house.

It's not as if I sleep in most other days; usually I'm awake by 6:30 and writing, trying to take advantage of the quiet hours. But the knowledge that I could were I to need to do so is like a get-out-of-jail-free card. Those other nights . . . I go through a series of rites and rituals to allay my anxieties. I avoid caffeine, make sure to have a drink, sometimes smoke a little weed. I try to avoid screens, the stimulation of their light, their electricity, their promise that there is something out there that requires my attention, some connection that I need to make. Sleep is about severing connection, from yourself, from the world. Once, a decade and a half ago, I wrote a long piece about dream research, tracing the dynamics of the mind at rest. This was before I began to dread, or worry about, my own sleep, back when I could still routinely slumber the whole night through. This was, in other words, before I created (or exacerbated) the problem by naming it, by giving it a shape and presence in my psyche. Dreams are either meaningless or they aren't, random expressions of neurons firing or the manifestations of a deeper set of longings and desires. The same might be said about the waking world. I suppose this could be reassuring, the notion that the line between waking and sleeping is indistinct, blurry, but for me it only makes the apprehension worse. At times I can hardly tell the difference, slipping into sleep so shallow I never quite lose sight of myself as a body tossing in a bed.

It's worse, of course, when I am not in my own bed, when I am in a hotel or a guest room, when I can't allow myself the consolations of what let's frame as safety, or at least the comfort of familiar space. I never sleep well the first or last night in a new location: the one a matter of acclimatization, the other of its inverse. I turn off the lights, arrange the pillows—one between my knees, one in my arms, one underneath my head—kick out the covers so they are not tucked in. I push my feet through, leave them uncovered, an emblem of freedom or escape. I am in bed right now, feet crossed in the open air, blanket clustered around my waist. I am tired but it doesn't matter; were I to roll over, get comfortable, shut my eyes, and wait for drift, I would be wide awake in a moment's time. Awake as in alert, mind moving, tracing, scanning, seeking an idea on which to settle, a worry to work over like the rough edge of a stone. Awake, as in aware of the minutes as they pass, slow collapse of distance until morning, the darkness of the night looming like a blank space, an expanse I cannot get across. Partly, I suppose, this has to do with getting older; we sleep less as we age. Still, it is not sleep that concerns me, so much as the moment consciousness lets go. *Lets go?* No, not this either, for sleeping, dreaming, is a form of consciousness. In that sense it is utterly unlike death, which I cannot imagine because there is nothing there, I think (fear), to imagine, not a space to traverse but rather an endless emptiness.

On the one hand, it is about control, this back-and-forth of sleeping, not unlike my unwillingness to be put under by anesthesia. Control, control, control—this is the great deception, and how to give it up? How do we fall asleep? What is the mechanism? I lie in bed and wonder, even as I know that this will keep me from my rest. The paradox: the more I worry about sleeping, the more it eludes me, the more I toss and turn and slip into anxiety, as midnight yields to 1 a.m. I remember my father, when I was a teenager and would come home late, or wander into the kitchen at three or four in the morning, sitting in a wing chair by the window in the study, reading by a kind of hooded half-light, wide awake in his underwear. *Sometimes you just have to give in,* he told me one night when I asked what he was doing out of bed. He was right, of course, although this giving in, it cuts both ways. Sometimes you have to give in to not sleeping, sometimes to allowing sleep to come. I want to say that it's a matter of comfort, shelter, and it is true that I (almost) always sleep better at home. In bed with Rae, even head to toe, steady whisper of her respiration, warmth of her back, her breath, yeasty smell of her at rest, I feel protected, even from my dreaming, know she will save me (for the moment, anyway) from myself. In a hotel, or someone else's house, I am alone, but even more than that I am unguarded, left to reveal myself in ways I don't intend. Sleep is among the most intimate of gestures; it is where we let down our guard. No wonder, then, that I feel most secure in my own bed, girded by the solace of familiars: on the mattress where, in all the ways that matter most, the essence of my adult life has been imagined into being.

And yet that bed is gone now, moved into Noah's room (he has moved into his own apartment) while I've been away. When I return, it will be to a new mattress, new box spring—higher off the ground, Rae says, and firmer: a new adjustment, familiar and unfamiliar at once. I don't mean to make too much of physical things, since they, I know, desert us. What else, however, is the physical if not a manifestation of our memories? I feel safe in my bed *because* it is my bed. Even when I cannot sleep, I feel a touch of (no other way to put it) certainty. That this is an illusion goes without saying, but then, so is everything. It is why I have such trouble letting go.

JERALD WALKER

Breathe

FROM *New England Review*

ONE CAUSE OF your son's seizure, the doctor says, could be syphilis. Ask what's the basis for such speculation, given that no physical exam was conducted, no bloodwork drawn, no urine sample taken, and that your son, who is lying on the hospital bed before you looking bewildered, is twelve. "Obviously it's not unheard-of for twelve-year-olds to have this disease," she responds, which is impossible for you not to hear as "You're black, so I shouldn't have to tell you this."

But it is possible, apparently, not to lose your temper. Be grateful for the article you read last month about the benefits of breathing exercises in times of high stress, because the one you're doing now is actually working. Before speaking, take another deep breath, followed by a slow exhale, focusing all the while on the air passing through your lungs. There. Now tell your family it's time to leave. Marvel at the calmness of your voice and wish you'd discovered this exercise years ago, long before your high blood pressure and reputation for being angry. Pat your son's shoulder as you nudge him upright. Take him home.

Once home, in your study, do some Google searches. Start with syphilis. Tell yourself you know your son doesn't have syphilis but you're curious to see if the doctor was racist and dumb or only racist. Find it hard to decide; syphilis left untreated for a decade can cause meningitis, which can cause seizures. Forget the doctor and just search "adolescents and seizures," but when you reach the part about brain tumors turn off the computer and work on your breathing some more. Come up with your own diagnosis; the seizure was a fluke, a random occurrence, like hiccups or warts. Try to convince yourself there's no need to worry.

There is need to worry, though, because your wife is in the kitchen screaming. Run there to find her standing next to your son, who is seizing again, his thin quivering arms bent at odd angles like a scarecrow's. Choke up tomorrow as you recall how your ten-year-old gently placed a hand on his brother's lower back to steady him, but for now keep it together. You need to be strong. You need to be wise too, which is problematic; the seizure has run its course and your son looks at you with fear in his eyes and says, "Daddy, why is this happening?" You cannot answer this. Believe a good father could. A good father, if you think about it, would not have bought a house in a small white town so that when medical emergencies arise paramedics take you to the nearby small white hospital instead of to Boston, thirty miles away, where the world's best hospitals receive black people all the time. And a good father would have just said, "We're driving him to Boston Children's" before his wife beat him to it. Agree with her, at least. At least get the phone so she can arrange a sitter.

It is Saturday, shortly after 9 p.m. Very few cars are on the highway. Conclude, in other words, that there's nothing to prevent you from showing your resolve to get answers by driving ninety miles an hour, except for your wife, who thinks she can do so by calling you a lunatic. She can't. She doesn't even know what a genuine lunatic looks like. Let a cop stop you; then she'll know. Just let one stop you. Let a white cop stop you, damn it. A white cop, with some weird-ass sunburn in December, probably, and his mouth full of tobacco. Between the tobacco and a southern drawl you will barely understand him ordering you to step out of the car, boy, and keep your hands where he can see them. He'll see your hands, all right. He'll see them as they're going upside his goddamn head . . .

Snap out of it. You're getting worked up and so is your wife, who's now demanding you to slow down. Go ahead and do it and while you're at it remind yourself that stress kills. You don't want to end up like your father, after all, who only lived to be sixty-eight, although that was much longer than your brother, who only made it to forty-seven. You've outlived your brother by two years but outliving your father will be harder. You are even more high-strung than he was, a trait greatly exacerbated by fatherhood, or rather by the inadequacy fatherhood often makes you feel, especially when you think of your duty to protect your sons from harm, including, needless to say, racism. You think of this duty all the time. Lately, when thinking of it, your mind plays tricks on you by swapping out your sons' faces with the face of Travyon Martin, the recently slain black teen. When this happens your breathing exercises do not work. They only work on things like being told your twelve-year-old has syphilis.

It's 10:15 when you arrive at Boston Children's. Even at this hour the place is packed. Fill out some paperwork at the receptionist's desk and then sit in the waiting room with dozens of other people, many of whom are black, which is good to see, but wish they were not here. Wish there were no white people either. Or Asian. That woman and infant of dubious ethnicity can stay because there are only two of them, but in a perfect world they would not be here either. The bottom line is you'll be here a while, maybe all night, unless, that is, your son has another seizure. Hope that he does. A brief one. No more than ten seconds or so, just long enough to get the receptionist to call triage. Or maybe he can fake a seizure. That would be better, now that you think about it, since who knows what kind of damage the seizures are causing his brain, or who knows, as you think about it more deeply, what kind of brain damage is causing the seizures.

If he has brain damage that's not a tumor assume it occurred at Mercy General, another small white hospital, where your wife's seven-hour labor culminated in him being stuck in her birth canal. The doctor held off for so long to have a C-section that it became more of a life-threatening proposition than continuing to try to suck your son out with a vacuum. When the vacuuming presented itself as the greater threat, an emergency C-section was ordered, but right before your wife was rushed to the OR the doctor made one final attempt, yelling *push, push, push* as you whispered *please, please, please* and with that your son plopped free with a blue face and his head smushed into a cone. Now he's having seizures. And now, unlike then, when you wept with gratitude while hugging the staff, let this thought enter your mind: if your family had been white, a C-section would have been performed at the first sign of trouble.

"Are you okay?" your wife is asking.

"I'm fine."

"Then why are you doing your breathing exercise?"

Tell her it's precautionary. Tell her that even though Boston
Children's is one of the world's premier heath institutions, the
doctor you get could be a screwball, a real nut job who somehow
slipped through the cracks, and then notice your son's wide eyes
and realize this was the wrong thing to say. Put your arm around
his shoulders. Tell him not to worry. Assure him that the doctors
here are as sane as you are and that if he wants this proved sooner
rather than later, he must fake a seizure. He chuckles, because he
thinks you are joking.

Two hours pass before a nurse calls his name and leads your
family to an examination room. After she takes his vitals, your wife
describes the seizures from earlier today before mentioning another, the one that occurred when he was two because, you later
learned, of a temperature spike. You hadn't thought of that for
some time but the memory returns with awful clarity, the way his
body went rigid as you were buckling him into his car seat, how
his eyes rotated in their sockets until only white remained. You
yelled for your wife to call 911 and while you were snatching your
son into your arms you pictured your father, who was epileptic,
thrashing about on the floor with blood oozing from his mouth
as he involuntarily bit his tongue. You will never forget that blood.
You were still thinking of it when the paramedic admonished you
for risking being injured by forcing a finger between your son's
clamped teeth, but you knew, if necessary, you would do it a thousand times more. You would have done it today. You would have,
but all your son did was tremble, his mouth slack but also—as if
he were trying to keep you from stressing out, from completely
losing it, from dropping dead like your brother of a massive stroke
—fixed into a sad little smile. You will never forget that sad little
smile either.

Your wife finishes giving his medical history. The nurse, before
leaving, says a neurologist will be in shortly. Wonder what she
meant by that two hours later. Your son is asleep. You are angry.
Your wife is legendary for her patience but she is getting angry too.
Do not bother suggesting she join you in doing a breathing exercise because when you first mentioned its benefits she said it was

not for her. It is for you, though. It's helping you stay alive. Decide that all it needs is a modification. Leave the room.

There are no nurses at the nurses' station but two clerks are sitting there talking. When you reach them, inhale deeply, and then slowly exhale. Do this once more. Now tell them you have been waiting to see a doctor for three goddamn hours. Tell them this is unacceptable, this is some bullshit, and then insist on seeing someone *right now,* just as you should have insisted that the paramedics bring you here and you should have told that syphilis doctor to fuck herself and you should have, all those years ago, demanded a C-section as soon as there was trouble. The clerks are speechless. They look aghast. They are staring at you with gaped mouths as if you're a lunatic but they have no idea. You could show them what a real lunatic looks like. You definitely could. Instead, as you back away, show them more deep breathing.

A moment after you return to the room a doctor bursts in, already apologizing. There was a mix-up, he says, at the change of shift; no one informed him that you were here. Maybe this is true, maybe it's not. Decide for the time being it doesn't matter. All that matters is that he's here now and your son is having seizures and you want to know why.

In five days you will. One referral will lead to another, which will lead to a diagnosis of paroxysmal kinesigenic dyskinesia, a neurological disorder that can trigger petite seizures when the body is suddenly thrust into motion. It strikes pubescent children and can last through their late teens or early twenties. It's a rare disease, largely unknown to the medical profession, and next week, standing before you in this very room, as fate would have it, will be the neurologist credited with its discovery. There are medicines to control the seizures, he will say. He will say everything will be fine. The neurologist standing before you now does not say everything will be fine, but he knows enough, after thoroughly examining your son, to say this: "The seizures themselves, while frightening to experience, and no doubt even more so for parents to witness, are harmless."

Look at your wife and son. See how their faces have broken with relief. Yours has too, but only for an instant before stiffening again, the result of another modification you add to your breathing exercise. From this point on, whenever you are under high stress, after you have blown off a little steam between deep breaths and slow exhales, think of something you have done as a father that is worthy of the title. Right now think, once again, of your son's first seizure. Picture yourself clutching his rigid little body. See yourself staring into the void of his eyes. "I'm here, I'm here," remember whispering, as his teeth bore into your skin.

STEPHANIE POWELL WATTS

The Unfound Door

FROM *Oxford American*

THE HOUSE LOOKS friendly and familiar, like the homeplace in a holiday reunion movie. Its wide porch holds two rows of black rockers nodding in the breeze; small plaques on the tops of the chairs list the names of the famous Carolina writers who donated them. Even without entering you know that the floors will sag in places, many rooms will feel tacked on and haphazard like the architect made up the plan as he went along. More than once you will whiff the faintest smell of rot, but that's part of the charm too.

A bank flanks the house on one side, with a good-sized hotel practically in the front yard and a community theater and large all-day parking lot on the other side. The only formerly private residence on the block, the Thomas Wolfe Memorial House looks like the last stubborn holdout to Asheville's progress. The Wolfe family called it the Old Kentucky Home. Not the home where Wolfe was born—that place was leveled long ago—but the boardinghouse his mother, Julia, owned and operated. In *Look Homeward, Angel,* Wolfe called the house Dixieland—not exactly a place an African American woman would choose to stay. Who am I kidding? I'm sure few black guests ever stayed in the Old Kentucky Home or its fictional counterpart.

I have wanted to visit this house for years. Like many North Carolina kids, I grew up with the broad strokes of Thomas Wolfe's story, the prolific small-town genius who became one of the most revered writers of his generation. I lived in North Carolina for most of my life, but I never took the opportunity to visit. Not enough money, not enough time, too much to do: that's an old story, I know, and a true one. It is also true that we seldom value the places where we live, not enough anyway.

My own father's house, where I grew up, is about ninety minutes down the mountain. Like anything not loved enough, it has no name. When I visit, I usually go to my father's place to see it or maybe to witness it, though no one lives there now. My father stays instead in the house where my grandmother lived, a mile away. She died a few years ago, but that house was hers and contains her mixing bowls and her teddy bears and her high, high bed and too-large kitchen table. It comforts him to see her things and sit where she sat to watch television or watch the kudzu overtake the ravine at the edge of her property. My father and grandmother worked together on a furniture factory line for decades. They ate together at her house nearly every Sunday. We did not take vacations when I was a child; we staycationed long before it was a thing. We took day trips to Lake James near Morganton, or Grandfather Mountain near the Boone area, or to Carowinds, a Charlotte amusement park we all adored. We did not leave town much, is what I'm saying. For all of these reasons, I can say with great confidence that they saw each other nearly every day of his life.

Old Kentucky Home was Julia's business, and she ran it with ferocity and skill. While her husband and all of her children except for Wolfe stayed in the family home just down the street, Julia attended to the needs of travelers. People on the road want food. They want a bed that appears clean. At Julia Wolfe's they could get two hots and a cot for a dollar a day. Compared to the needs of eight children and a husband, the boardinghouse might have seemed like the better deal. But who knows? Maybe she wanted money and didn't want to depend on her husband for it, or maybe the hard work of caring for travelers made her difficult marriage less hurtful or important, or maybe she needed to keep her mind off the children that preceded her in death, including her infant firstborn. Who can say for sure? Any lived experience reveals that our true motives are complex and strange and often contradictory even to ourselves.

You enter the dark hallway of the Wolfe house into the formal parlor, and it's all there: polished wood furniture and antimacassars on the upholstery, hurricane oil lamps. Stories ping-pong around my head, and I expect the white patrons to materialize as characters from improbable romantic scenarios. Where is the lovely towheaded hired girl? When will she catch the eye of the handsome, wholesome stranger? Shouldn't the young widow be stepping into the dining room any minute? All the regulars can see that she makes a special effort with her curls when that certain salesman passes through. I know from his writings that Thomas Wolfe was unhappy here in this dirty-yellow house, with the dreaded strangers, with his life sleeping on a pallet on the floor at his mother's feet, away from the world of his siblings. He was angry for his unconventional life—angry at his mother and his father too, but mothers bear the brunt of their children's disappointment. Perhaps he forgot or else didn't know yet that you can't get from people what they don't have to give you. Julia did what she knew how to do and that's the best you can expect. That's life's immutable law.

My father has six brothers and a sister and my mother was one of nine children, and family members often dropped by the seventies ranch-style house. They never came to the front door, though, preferring the door off the carport and entering through the kitchen. Few people ever stayed overnight with us, except my uncle—my mother's older brother—after his divorce. We kids loved having another presence in the house, the shine of our own company faded long ago, and we treated him like he was an exotic pet, remarking on his large curly 'fro, his hysterical barking laughter at his own jokes, the hint of a gold tooth that flashed when he smiled big. He did nothing extraordinary, but his effect was enormous. Our parents were calm with us then and almost nice to each other during his stays. We children made every effort to keep quiet and attempted statue-stillness so we were allowed in the room with the adults. We felt real pain when my uncle got his own trailer and stopped spending the night at all.

I go through the side door whenever I enter the house. The kitchen still has the round table my father made himself while working at Bernhardt Furniture. His fridge is gone, probably sold, and the doors of the cabinets under the sink haven't been opened in years. There is a smell of dust and decay and too-long-of-nobody-stirring. No traces of anyone who ever made oatmeal, or stretched a wall-mounted-telephone cord down the hall for privacy, or fought with a wet mop the endless battle between the white linoleum and the red Carolina clay. Some places feel like their people. In their stuff and their messes you get a sense of what and who they valued. I do not believe in spirits, but even if I did, there is nothing shimmering or alive that suggests anybody ever loved here at all.

In Julia Wolfe's kitchen I covet the long rectangular oak table low enough to work seated while she peeled potatoes or apples for pies. A small bedroom off to the side of that room is where Julia and young Thomas slept. Thomas was her last child, her baby, and she was already in her forties when he was born. We are sisters in our old motherhood, Julia and I, though she had many more pregnancies than I—at least seven. I have only one child but had two pregnancies. That's the bloodless way to say it. My body hasn't forgotten the first one even more than a decade later. I do not believe in spirits.

Perhaps Julia couldn't stand to be apart from her baby. Maybe she thought her husband and surviving older children were ill-equipped to care for a young child. Whatever her reasons for having Thomas with her at the boardinghouse, I'm sure she did not imagine that she would live to bury him. I wonder, since Thomas lived much of his adolescence and adult life away from Asheville, if, when he died at the age of thirty-seven, she imagined him overseas or on some ship headed someplace temporarily unreachable. When people are far away you don't have to believe in death. Death is simply distance, a few hours in a car, a dreaded flight. When you live apart, you can believe your people live still. It is your schedules that don't synch. Any day you will see them again.

Down the short hall at my father's house on the left is the only bathroom. Three small bedrooms are on the right. Three of my brothers slept in bunk beds in the first room. I was the only girl and had my own room, and the baby boy slept (probably not much) in a bassinet beside my parents' bed. When I visit the house, I do not open the bedroom doors. This is not from the pain of remembrance of things past but because those rooms are now crammed full of stuff bought from yard and estate sales and thrift stores for my father's flea market business. God only knows what vermin might lurk there. Any variety of spider or rat or snake might be nesting in all that junk. Yes, I said snake. How can you tell the difference between a southerner and a northerner? The southerner is the one with the snake story. I have enough of those stories to last a lifetime.

Julia turned big rooms into much smaller ones, landings into sleeping spaces, and the second floor of the Old Kentucky Home is a jumble of bedrooms stashed in every available nook. Thomas slept in a side bedroom when he returned to the house as a grown man, though nothing here announces it as the room of a writer. No papers or books or journals. Nothing that appears to be his, not even a comb on a bedside table. There is a bed, a dresser, and a large window with white curtains that I'm sure billow like a cartoon ghost at the slightest breeze. On the other side of the house, facing the street, is the room where Ben, Thomas's beloved brother, died. Ben's room is the best of the bedrooms, large, with a fireplace and a small picture of him in an oval frame on the mantel. A fictionalized version of Ben Wolfe's death is reimagined in Wolfe's first novel, *Look Homeward, Angel.* Ben of the novel is joined with light, and at the last moment all the confusion of life slips away, passing "scornful and unafraid, as he had lived, into the shades of death."

In a very literal way, all of the rooms in the house are death rooms. It is highly unlikely that anyone who ever stayed there as a guest, and certainly none of the Wolfes' immediate family, is still alive. Probably more than a few people died in the house. I have been in the rooms of the dying and dead. I don't linger there.

The public rooms in my dad's house have the delightful wood veneer paneling so popular in the seventies. (They say everything comes back with time, but I will believe this revival when I see it.) I used to wish that we had an upstairs so we could race dramatically down to the tree at Christmas, or sit on the steps to overhear adult conversations. But like most of the kids we knew lucky enough to have a house at all, we had a ranch. When my parents built it, it was a dream to them. I can remember my mother polishing the walls with a cloth that smelled like lemon, though what feels like a memory could be a TV commercial I have stuck in my head. I do know that nothing of my mother survives here to summon her to the room. My parents divorced decades ago. She remarried and her home is somewhere else. An old story, I know. I have not seen her in years. That is an old story too. Motherhood does not suit everyone, and there are many reasons for this—my mother's motives are no less complicated than Julia Wolfe's. This is the way of the world. I am no longer ashamed.

When I leave the Wolfe House I must reacquaint myself with the current century, with the galleries, fantastic bookstores, white people with impressive dreadlocks, good buskers on every corner, and many, many places to eat fancied fried chicken. Wolfe called it Altamont in his writing, which is so much more lofty and grand than "Asheville." Wolfe must have loved it too. But I know from his writings that he never cared about the town in the same way after Ben died. Of course he didn't. Wolfe got back to Asheville in 1937, just months before he too died. But in that final view, that house he hated must have looked just fine with time's fuzzy focus. Love is not static in any circumstances.

Like everyone who has ever visited Asheville, I want to stay. Haven't you heard about those people who become marathoners, or master chefs, or move to houses they foolishly renovate themselves? I could be one of those shakers, those movers. I could be an overcomer too. When I was a child my mother and her sister took us kids with them to a tent revival. I saw people give testimony to the enormous crowd about their healed bodies. I saw grown men fall backward, faint dead away when touched on their foreheads by the bouncing preacher. I wanted to feel what they felt—that renewal, envelopment—though I was very afraid. Yet I still want revelation. Wolfe wrote in *Look Homeward, Angel* that "we seek the great forgotten language, the lost lane-end into heaven, a stone, a leaf, an unfound door." We are always looking for revelation—even in our most known places and our most loved people. We hope to find the undiscovered in ourselves—the window into everything. I feel the open window in beautiful spaces. I start to think about myself differently and imagine that I can become new. I travel to remember this. I travel to forget that my foundation is set and unmovable.

PHILIP WEINSTEIN

Soul-Error

FROM *Raritan*

THE SOUL AS twinned to error? I begin by way of Freud. In his essay on "The Uncanny," Freud explores a spatial confusion: a state of mind in which one sees "out there" something palpably shaped from "in here." Freud's most striking vignette in "The Uncanny" rehearses how, some years earlier, he found himself wandering through an unknown Italian village, looking for the train station. He perused his map, made the appropriate right and left turns—and found himself in the red-light district. Time for reconnoitering: he rechecked his coordinates so as not to make the same mistakes again, set out once more for the station, via a different sequence of streets and turns—and ended up in the red-light district. Quite frustrated by now—what was wrong with his village map?—he tried a third time. Scrutinizing the map with an attentiveness never required before, he plotted a foolproof course and set out once more for the station. Need I say where he ended up?

Some would scratch their heads at this point and write off the search for the train station as simply failed, or try to find a taxi to take them there. They'd know they were lost beyond self-correction. Freud—and, I suspect, anyone else who shares his sense of the deviousness of the mind—began to realize that he was not getting lost but being found. Against his conscious intentions, he must all along have been looking for the red-light district.

This essay, though not drawn to the red-light district, returns repeatedly to the traffic that unpredictably occurs between us ("in here") and the world ("out there"). Because we are endowed with stunningly intricate minds, we move through space and time interestingly, circuitously, mistakenly. With respect to time, we look not only straight ahead but forward and backward too. What we see from either end of the temporal telescope differs greatly from what we see here, now, in our presence. As for space, we are—surprisingly for a species so cerebrally gifted—susceptible to wandering; we easily get lost. Or if not lost, subject to altering takes (mistakes) on what lies before us.

Some three centuries before Freud, Michel de Montaigne was fascinated by kindred aspects of the human comedy of misperception. His phrase for how we stubbornly insist on misreading our world is "soul-error." By this he means an ineradicable tendency, seeded deep within us, to get things wrong. Because we enjoy but also suffer from what Montaigne insists on calling "soul," we tend to fall into error. Montaigne's phrase may strike us as surprising, perhaps even contradictory. We tend to ascribe to the soul (if we use the term at all) that dimension of ourselves that we deem deepest and truest. To characterize the soul as a faculty inseparable from error requires some unpacking. Here is the gloss Montaigne himself supplies, from "On Presumption":

> I feel myself oppressed by an error of my soul which I dislike . . . I try to correct it, but uproot it I cannot. It is that I lower the value of the things I possess, because I possess them, and raise the value of things when they are foreign, absent, and not mine . . . The housekeeping, the house, the horse of my neighbor, if equal in value, seem better than my own, because they are not mine.

I came across this passage while reading commentary on Marcel Proust. But the resonance of soul-error did not begin with Montaigne, nor does it end with Proust. When Groucho Marx avers that he would never join any club that would take him in, we see that soul-error is alive and well in the midtwentieth century. It is true that Groucho's ego preoccupations—a mix of self-promotion and self-loathing—may predispose him to this condition. The half-Jewish Proust—part Catholic bourgeois, part Jewish homosexual pariah—may likewise be susceptible for related reasons. But the roots go deeper, touching down on an ensemble of predilections that beset identity itself.

Montaigne's French terms—*erreur d'âme* rather than *erreur de l'âme*—denote a constitutive bond between the two elements, not a remediable error. Like *chemin de fer* (French for "railroad"; liter-

ally "path of iron"), where there is no "road" unless there is iron
for making its "rails," so there is no soul without error that permanently affects its conditions of operation. Soul tends to move
on rails of error. This is hardly how the Judeo-Christian tradition
speaks of soul. What might it mean to regard soul as the dimension of our inner being most intractably committed to mistaking?

Montaigne's examples shed further light. Soul is that faculty in
us that registers an ongoing spatial comedy. I covet from a distance
what you have in your possession because . . . you have it and I do
not. Your house, your horse, your spouse (he does not mention
this last but that is his logic) are desirable because I do not have
them. No one knows better than Montaigne that if he had your
house, your horse, your spouse, they would at once lose their aura.
Their appeal is inseparable from their being *not-his*. Bring them
into his realm of possessions and they reduce to only what they
are. This is the comedy of presence/absence. We denigrate the
value of what is materially here and ours. We inflate the value of
what is immaterially not here and not ours.

It is no surprise that the opposite is sometimes also true. What I
possess may appear to me to be the best, not because of any intrinsic value but because it is mine. I have a friend whose wife, wines,
house, cars, dogs, and travel plans are all the best: because they
are his. But devaluing what one has—and longing for what one's
neighbor has—is probably more widespread. Desire can hardly
function without it, and desire seems in no danger of ceasing to
fuel the gambits of social life.

Proust's huge novel endlessly replays the drama of soul-error,
beginning with its opening scene: the ordeal of the good-night
kiss. The little boy (Marcel) at the center of the novel has been
lying in bed for hours, waiting anxiously for his mother's kiss; he
cannot fall asleep without it. So, staying up until his parents' dinner party is over, he waylays her coming up the stairs. Against all
parental rules, he will have that kiss. His father—fatigued and half
grasping his son's misery—allows the mother to spend the night
in her boy's bedroom.

Let's pay close attention to the spatial/temporal framing of
that good-night kiss. The kiss—passionately anticipated while his
mother is downstairs at her dinner party—becomes anticlimactic
when he actually receives it. Taking place now (and securely *his*),

it feels like what it merely is: just her kiss. Next, that bedroom he is in feels like a prison (because he is in it) separating him from what he desires outside it.

The actual place we are in pales in comparison to the siren call of the places we have been in *before* or are not in *yet*. Such fantasy logic underwrites a vexing dimension of Marcel's lifelong relation to place itself—and perhaps of ours as well. Where we actually are (once we've familiarized it) tends to shed its intricacy, to become boring, taken for granted. It becomes boring because we've made terms with its contours, put it to sleep. But finding ourselves in unfamiliar places can be menacing: settings we do not (yet) know. Such places are ones we can (at first) do nothing with. I trust I am not alone in needing help from sleeping pills, now and then, when I travel to unknown places, more often than when I remain at home. Unfamiliar space—the situation of me somewhere unknown, right now—can feel unsettling enough to keep me awake long into the night.

These same new places, however, may be powerfully attractive, prior to our actually engaging them. Is this because—absent rather than present—they come to us as purely mental images, shaped to immaterial configurations we have learned to desire? In Proust's novel, soirées and ballroom parties elsewhere are exciting so long as anticipated, yet anticlimactic when later experienced. The basic energy that fuels social climbing is the desire to escape from where we are (a little world we have domesticated, put to sleep) and get ourselves admitted into the fantasized space of where we are not yet. In his fictional world always—and in our real world all too often—the allure of what is sought disintegrates on being possessed. Such disenchantment sounds the bass note of Montaigne's soul-error.

What mandates such disenchantment? Is it that the immaterial image of what we seek and the materiality of what can be actually encountered exist in realms that never meet? What can be encountered must take on embodiment—be extensive in space and time—in order to be engaged. But what we passionately seek escapes these limitations; it gets its seductive lineaments by way of images saturated in our thoughts, feelings, and desires. Such an ensemble has no material basis at all. Proust's most memorable instance of this irreducible difference is the boy Marcel's feverish desire to travel to Florence and Venice. So feverish, in fact, that when his father says they are going next week to Florence—and time now to pack his bags—the boy (faced with a clash between actual places and his gorgeous vision of them) falls into a swoon. The trip is postponed. Put better, the trip is aborted. The Florence and Venice that Marcel dreamed of visiting were lovingly constituted by way of books and paintings devoted to these cities. He had absorbed the images arising from these sources, taken them into himself like mother's milk. They are the stuff of dreams.

Taken into himself, yet not only himself, and not taken in by mere personal caprice. The multibillion-dollar tourism industry battens on its promise to collapse the difference between images of the exotic (as the mind caressingly envisages it), on the one hand, and unfamiliar places we can actually encounter, on the other. As people age, as their tenure on the globe grows shaky, their desire to visit the places they have only dreamed about increases. Vast hordes of retired people fill the buses, airplanes, and cruise ships committed to transporting them, bodily, to these long-envisaged exotic places. The cruise ships exploit this desire with an unbeatable formula. They will provide their elderly clientele with pseudo-engagements, reductively staged rituals standing in for more intricate encounters with the otherness of unfamiliar sites. Yet the travelers need abandon no familiar bodily comforts along the way. It may be dreamed-of images that get them onto the cruise, but it is the copious meals and familiar activities on board the ship that make them likely to return for more. Fueling this industry is the pathos of a shared, largely speechless hunger. These elderly voyagers would like to know more about the earth they inhabit before departing it for good. They half grasp how tenuous their contract with place actually is. Pseudo-engagements with the desired unknown are better than none.

Not just the old are susceptible to the allure of travel. How many younger people have dreamed—for months or years—of going to Paris? Finally they purchase their plane tickets, climb aboard the jet, and during the night (six hours that are so long, so short) they cross the huge Atlantic. The moment I focus on comes next, at seven or eight o'clock in the morning, after Charles de Gaulle Airport and in the bus or taxi taking them into the awakening city. Sleep-deprived, anxious, and eager, they look all around. Can this be *Paris?* Where is *Paris?* What they mainly see on the way in are graffiti-chalked billboards, highways crowded with trucks and cars, nondescript warehouses and office buildings on their left and their right: not so different from the city they left! This whirl of incessant material activity hardly has them in mind. They are eventually deposited at their hotel in the fantasized city, and (obscurely troubling their week of scheduled activities) a wordless suspicion may continue to gnaw at them. The sprawling ensemble that is Paris—the material city they've been industriously crossing on foot and by bus and metro—keeps refusing to merge with the gorgeous images of the city lodged inside their heads. Even the Eiffel Tower —replete with long queues before going up, various concession stands surrounding the entry, numerous clusters of unruly tourists speaking foreign languages as their leaders try to shepherd them into docility, and a visible smattering of wary policemen—is not *the Eiffel Tower.* These two realms—one material and indifferent to subjective desire, the other immaterial and embroidered by subjective desire—do not coincide.

When I was struggling through my years of graduate school, a fellow student sought to describe our pervasive sense of not being in control of our situation, unable to access the imagined center of operations. We were condemned, he proposed, to remain in the "antechamber." It might be next to the main room, but it was not that room and could never become that room. The big decisions (the ones affecting our futures) were ones we imagined taking place elsewhere, in the real chamber where things that matter got decided.

That phrase—*antechamber*—has stayed with me over the years. Whenever I teach Kafka, I feel again its resonance. Joseph K (in either *The Trial* or *The Castle*) cannot make his way out of the antechamber. His fate turns on finding and entering the main chamber, where the Court considers his case, where the Castle reveals its bureaucratic logic. Kafka's readers eventually realize he will never get there. The logic of his defeat is simple. Every room K enters is, by virtue of his entering it, an antechamber (Groucho: "I'd never join a club that would allow a person like me to become a member"). Kafka's fiction unnerves us because something deep inside half recognizes our incapacity to make exterior space our own, once and for all. We stubbornly intuit that our internalized images of place fail to coincide with the maps of what is materially outside us. At the beginning, as infants, we had to work hard to learn those outer maps. At the end, growing senile, we find that the maps have become opaque again. Space seems, uncannily, not to be meant for us, at the beginning and near the ending. The far-from-senile Kafka suffered the defects and insights of something like senility throughout his life. "I have experience," he declared, "and I am not joking when I say that it is a seasickness on dry land."

I have no data supporting my next claim, but I would hazard that up to half of our nightmares revolve around becoming physically lost. Or if not lost, then no longer in charge of what remains familiar but has become uncanny. Dream settings slip their manageability, turn resistant to our organizational will; space goes gamey. This spatial slipperiness is true not only of dreams. Tolstoy long ago realized that battles do not radiate from some organizing center, that the elaborate plans that precede them—like the authoritative accounts that come later—are equally false to the unmasterable chanciness of the material event itself. Anyone reading through the voluminous materials about Nixon's Watergate White House (in the early 1970s) would eventually recognize as well that despite an awesome will to control the outer damage, *there was no commanding master plan*. No single mind was coordinating all the messy, many-peopled machinations. New events spilled out as unanticipated consequences of earlier ones; the left hand didn't quite know what the right hand was doing. This is no less true of Trump's chaotic White House. No master blueprint controls the incoherent yet interrelated maneuvers spasmodically taking place. This despite our desire—no less than the president's—to unify them all (by a misleading shorthand) as "coming from the White House."

Soul-error: the comedy of the mind's altering relation to objects and others and events in time and space. We see them differently according to whether they are materially here or imagined as elsewhere. No less, we see them one way if part of our present moment but otherwise if remembered from the past or fantasized into the future. Montaigne, Kafka, and Groucho Marx reveal the warp besetting our optic, reminding us that to see at all is to see with bias: from somewhere more like an antechamber than a fantasized Command Central.

Such distortion only intensifies if we consider how often "seeing the other" is unknowingly inflected by the self who does the seeing. Take that precious moment all parents are familiar with: their screaming child, with whom they've been quarreling for what seems like hours, is finally in bed and has fallen asleep. The parents tiptoe into the child's bedroom, batten on the becalmed spectacle, and their hearts swell with love—their child, so troublemaking earlier, so precious now. Yet reconsider the optics at play, the perceptual slippages in time and space. The troublemaking child, obstreperous and demanding an hour earlier, has been replaced by the image of a tranquil, sleeping one. This sleeping one, mentally absent though bodily in the room, finally quiescent, has become wholly accessible to the parents' conception of it. Silent, unresisting, the child is now *theirs*—again. What they are so moved by is less the actual child than the magnitude of their feeling for their offspring. Tomorrow they will quarrel again—embodied players in present time again, active wills opposed to each other—but for now the child has been subsumed into its parents' precious image.

That image will in time be replaced by subsequent images. Indeed, the parents will live out their lifelong relation to their child mainly by way of such images. Do we ever grant the extent to which others in our lives—the others we care for most—are accessed by way of our images of them? How else can we keep them with us? Whenever we depart from the materiality of the present moment —whenever we remember, whenever we look forward and project —we are thinking and feeling and seeing in reference to images. Images of substantial beings, yes, but made immaterial now. They become housed spectrally inside us, and they take on in countless ways the imprint of that housing. This is how they become *ours*. More, this endless substitution of the immaterial image for the substantial being characterizes present experience as well. Partners living in the same house engage each other on a daily basis by way of images, each in another room doing what he or she wants to do, each thinking now and then of the other. Or even in the bedroom together, each one's eyes closed during or after a moment of intimacy, it is the images that predominate. That is how others continue to matter to us at all.

Soul-error: Montaigne's term implies that acts of misperception, affectionate or otherwise, are beyond correction. They reveal irremediable distortions in our traffic with our world. To be a self is to exact a price: to reckon others and objects and in so doing often to reckon them wrong. Finally, soul may be, in addition, that inner energy that not only tends to get others wrong but that over time lets us see that we have done so—and gotten ourselves wrong as well. Milan Kundera has claimed more than once that the Czech word closest to *soul* is *litost*. In *The Book of Laughter and Forgetting*, Kundera defines *litost* as "a state of torment caused by a sudden insight into one's own miserable self." In a later essay, asserting that it is impossible to approach the idea of the soul without centering it on "regret," he returns to *litost:* "Litost," Kundera writes, "is an untranslatable Czech word. Its first syllable, which is long and stressed, sounds like the wail of an abandoned dog. As for the meaning of this word, I have looked in vain in other languages for an equivalent, though I find it difficult to imagine how anyone can understand the human soul without it."

Insight into one's own miserable self, regret, the wail of an abandoned dog: these dimensions of soul come together comically, darkly, yet suggestively. (You don't have to be a self-exiled Czech writer living out his life in Paris to grasp the drama of displacement and reinvention that Kundera is referring to.) Soul would be that capacity in us that accompanies our creaturely, self-altering trajectory over time. Accompanies, not transcends. In the Jewish and Christian traditions, thinkers may insist on hypothesizing soul as something precious that is beyond time, but Kundera has his eye on the pathos of our inescapable becoming. It is only later (if at all) that one catches glimpses of one's former "miserable self"—only later that this recognition engenders regret, even as one senses, only later, the wailing of abandoned beings (selves and others), the sorriness of earlier, once-proud choices. T. S. Eliot is mapping kindred territory in "Little Gidding" when he speaks of unwanted later recognitions—of moments when one grasps the damage one has done to others, "Which once you took for exercise of virtue. / Then fools' approval stings, and honour stains."

Soul-error seems to betoken an incorrigible mis-taking—of others and ourselves—that pervades our lives in time. To learn of such error is bad news (it is no fun to discover how wrong one has been), yet it *is* funny, inexhaustibly so. As Keaton, Chaplin, and comedians before and after have known, few things are funnier than a sudden slippage of the gears, wherein you land on your back rather than giving orders on your feet. "Nothing is funnier than unhappiness," Nell says to Hamm in Beckett's *Endgame*. Condemned to live the remainder of her life in a trashcan, Nell ought to know. Whenever I have seen the play performed, she does not laugh as she utters the line.

The job of rueful reckoning may in fact be soul's elemental task: soul as the dimension of our being that registers our falling, that looks back and reassesses. In the West—at least since Sophocles's Oedipus plays—we have the highest regard for retrospective reassessment. We tend to call it recognition. The stuff of epiphany, it may well be priceless. Who could bear to pass a life in time without ever looking back and seeing more? This essay testifies to my drawing on insights (or what I take to be such) that were not available earlier. Life without the possibility of revision, as Dante knew, is experienced as hell.

Yet the countertruth is no less telling. In rewriting the past we erase its stubborn texture and reality—and our own, as players in it when it was actually unfolding as an intricate and unfinished present. How often a man who divorces a wife of thirty years' standing will then say (to himself, to others), "I never loved her after all." A friend of mine said to me just this, some twenty-five years ago. When I urged him to be more generous toward what had been good in their union—the abundant moments of shared humor and intimacy, the rearing of children in common—he refused to budge. It was taking all of his courage to make the case against his marriage. He could not at the same time make the case for it.

He eventually remarried, and his former wife struggled to remake her life; the gaping hole left in it by the failed marriage never disappeared. Each went on to develop new narratives about who they were and needed to become. Antechamber: Do we ever escape it? Indubitable assessment and authority may reside in the main chamber, where those who seem to know beyond time make their unerring calls. But our lives unfold in a harder-to-map, obscurely altering elsewhere bedeviled with incompatible options, each (for a time) seductive in its own fashion. What we do not know now will later affect our choices—for good or for ill—more than what we do know now. "Never again are you the same," Jorie Graham writes. "The longing is to be pure. What you get is to be changed."

Proust refers to our incorrigible changeableness as "intermittence": the fact that in time, we are never altogether there. We are instead intermittently there, ourselves for now, and our different selves for later. *On ne se réalise que successivement,* so Proust puts it: one becomes oneself only over the course of time. We will not look the same to ourselves later, and it will be cause for regret. Not a regret, moreover, that if we were wiser we might have avoided. Passage through our cumulative time zones (the image is temporal, not spatial) does not permit the sustaining of heroic integrity. As error and its revision—and sometimes as undignified as the wail of an abandoned dog—the soul perseveres.

ELIZABETH WINKLER

Was Shakespeare a Woman?

FROM *The Atlantic*

ON A SPRING night in 2018 I stood on a Manhattan sidewalk with friends, reading Shakespeare aloud. We were in line to see an adaptation of *Macbeth* and had decided to pass the time refreshing our memories of the play's best lines. I pulled up Lady Macbeth's soliloquy on my iPhone. "Come, you spirits / That tend on mortal thoughts, unsex me here," I read, thrilled once again by the incantatory power of the verse. I remembered where I was when I first heard those lines: in my tenth-grade English class, startled out of my adolescent stupor by this woman rebelling magnificently and malevolently against her submissive status. "Make thick my blood, / Stop up th' access and passage to remorse." Six months into the #MeToo movement, her fury and frustration felt newly resonant.

Pulled back into plays I'd studied in college and graduate school, I found myself mesmerized by Lady Macbeth and her sisters in the Shakespeare canon. Beatrice, in *Much Ado About Nothing*, raging at the limitations of her sex ("O God, that I were a man! I would eat his heart in the marketplace"). Rosalind, in *As You Like It*, affecting the swagger of masculine confidence to escape those limitations ("We'll have a swashing and a martial outside, / As many other mannish cowards have / That do outface it with their semblances"). Isabella, in *Measure for Measure*, fearing no one will believe her word against Angelo's, rapist though he is ("To whom should I complain? Did I tell this, / Who would believe me?"). Kate, in *The Taming of the Shrew*, refusing to be silenced by her husband ("My tongue will tell the anger of my heart, / Or else my heart concealing it will break"). Emilia, in one of her last speeches in *Othello* before Iago kills her, arguing for women's equality ("Let husbands know / Their wives have sense like them").

I was reminded of all the remarkable female friendships too: Beatrice and Hero's allegiance; Emilia's devotion to her mistress, Desdemona; Paulina's brave loyalty to Hermione in *The Winter's Tale;* and plenty more. ("Let's consult together against this greasy knight," resolve the merry wives of Windsor, revenging themselves on Falstaff.) These intimate female alliances are fresh inventions —they don't exist in the literary sources from which many of the plays are drawn. And when the plays lean on historical sources (Plutarch, for instance), they feminize them, portraying legendary male figures through the eyes of mothers, wives, and lovers. "Why was Shakespeare able to see the woman's position, write entirely as if he were a woman, in a way that none of the other playwrights of the age were able to?" In her book about the plays' female characters, Tina Packer, the founding artistic director of Shakespeare & Company, asked the question very much on my mind.

Doubts about whether William Shakespeare (who was born in Stratford-upon-Avon in 1564 and died in 1616) really wrote the works attributed to him are almost as old as the writing itself. Alternative contenders—Francis Bacon, Christopher Marlowe, and Edward de Vere, the seventeenth earl of Oxford, prominent among them—continue to have champions, whose fervor can sometimes border on fanaticism. In response, orthodox Shakespeare scholars have settled into dogmatism of their own. Even to dabble in authorship questions is considered a sign of bad faith, a blinkered failure to countenance genius in a glover's son. The time had come, I felt, to tug at the blinkers of both camps and reconsider the authorship debate. Had anyone ever proposed that the creator of those extraordinary women might be a woman? Each of the male possibilities requires an elaborate theory to explain his use of another's name. None of the candidates has succeeded in dethroning the man from Stratford. Yet a simple reason would explain a playwright's need for a pseudonym in Elizabethan England: being female.

Long before Tina Packer marveled at the bard's uncanny insight, others were no less awed by the empathy that pervades the work. "One would think that he had been Metamorphosed from a Man to a Woman," wrote Margaret Cavendish, the seventeenth-century philosopher and playwright. The critic John Ruskin said, "Shakespeare has no heroes—he has only heroines." A striking number of those heroines refuse to obey rules. At least ten defy their fathers, bucking betrothals they don't like to find their own paths to love. Eight disguise themselves as men, outwitting patriarchal controls—more gender-swapping than can be found in the work of any previous English playwright. Six lead armies.

The prevailing view, however, has been that no women in Renaissance England wrote for the theater, because that was against the rules. Religious verse and translation were deemed suitable female literary pursuits; "closet dramas," meant only for private reading, were acceptable. The stage was off-limits. Yet scholars have lately established that women were involved in the business of acting companies as patrons, shareholders, suppliers of costumes, and gatherers of entrance fees. What's more, 80 percent of the plays printed in the 1580s were written anonymously, and that number didn't fall below 50 percent until the early 1600s. At least one eminent Shakespeare scholar, Phyllis Rackin, of the University of Pennsylvania, challenges the blanket assumption that the commercial drama pouring forth in the period bore no trace of a female hand. So did Virginia Woolf, even as she sighed over the obstacles that would have confronted a female Shakespeare: "Undoubtedly, I thought, looking at the shelf where there are no plays by women, her work would have gone unsigned."

A tantalizing nudge lies buried in the writings of Gabriel Harvey, a well-known Elizabethan literary critic. In 1593 he referred cryptically to an "excellent Gentlewoman" who had written three sonnets and a comedy. "I dare not Particularise her Description," he wrote, even as he heaped praise on her.

> All her conceits are illuminate with the light of Reason; all her speeches beautified with the grace of Affability . . . In her mind there appeareth a certain heavenly Logic; in her tongue & pen a divine Rhetoric . . . I dare undertake with warrant, whatsoever she writeth must needs remain an immortal work, and will leave, in the activest world, an eternal memory of the silliest vermin that she should vouchsafe to grace with her beautiful and allective style, as ingenious as elegant.

Who was this woman writing "immortal work" in the same year that Shakespeare's name first appeared in print, on the poem "Venus and Adonis," a scandalous parody of masculine seduction tales (in which the woman forces herself on the man)? Harvey's tribute is extraordinary, yet orthodox Shakespeareans and anti-Stratfordians alike have almost entirely ignored it.

Until recently, that is, when a few bold outliers began to advance the case that Shakespeare might well have been a woman. One candidate is Mary Sidney, the countess of Pembroke (and beloved sister of the celebrated poet Philip Sidney)—one of the most educated women of her time, a translator and poet, and the doyenne of the Wilton Circle, a literary salon dedicated to galvanizing an English cultural renaissance. Clues beckon, not least that Sidney and her husband were the patrons of one of the first theater companies to perform Shakespeare's plays. Was Shakespeare's name useful camouflage, allowing her to publish what she otherwise couldn't?

But the candidate who intrigued me more was a woman as exotic and peripheral as Sidney was pedigreed and prominent. Not long after my *Macbeth* outing, I learned that Shakespeare's Globe, in London, had set out to explore this figure's input to the canon. The theater's summer 2018 season concluded with a new play, *Emilia,* about a contemporary of Shakespeare's named Emilia Bassano. Born in London in 1569 to a family of Venetian immigrants—musicians and instrument-makers who were likely Jewish—she was one of the first women in England to publish a volume of poetry (suitably religious yet startlingly feminist, arguing for women's "Libertie" and against male oppression). Her existence was unearthed in 1973 by the Oxford historian A. L. Rowse, who speculated that she was Shakespeare's mistress, the "dark lady" described in the sonnets. In *Emilia* the playwright Morgan Lloyd Malcolm goes a step further: her Shakespeare is a plagiarist who uses Bassano's words for Emilia's famous defense of women in *Othello*.

Could Bassano have contributed even more widely and directly? The idea felt like a feminist fantasy about the past—but then, stories about women's lost and obscured achievements so often have a dreamlike quality, unveiling a history different from the one we've learned. Was I getting carried away, reinventing Shakespeare in the image of our age? Or was I seeing past gendered assumptions to the woman who—like Shakespeare's heroines—had fashioned herself a clever disguise? Perhaps the time was finally ripe for us to see her.

*

The ranks of Shakespeare skeptics comprise a kind of literary underworld—a cross-disciplinary array of academics, actors (Derek Jacobi and Mark Rylance are perhaps the best known), writers, teachers, lawyers, a few Supreme Court justices (Sandra Day O'Connor, Antonin Scalia, John Paul Stevens). Look further back and you'll find such illustrious names as Ralph Waldo Emerson, Walt Whitman, Mark Twain, Henry James, Sigmund Freud, Helen Keller, and Charlie Chaplin. Their ideas about the authorship of the plays and poems differ, but they concur that Shakespeare is not the man who wrote them.

Their doubt is rooted in an empirical conundrum. Shakespeare's life is remarkably well documented, by the standards of the period —yet no records from his lifetime identify him unequivocally as a writer. The more than seventy documents that exist show him as an actor, a shareholder in a theater company, a moneylender, and a property investor. They show that he dodged taxes, was fined for hoarding grain during a shortage, pursued petty lawsuits, and was subject to a restraining order. The profile is remarkably coherent, adding up to a mercenary impresario of the Renaissance entertainment industry. What's missing is any sign that he wrote.

No such void exists for other major writers of the period, as a meticulous scholar named Diana Price has demonstrated. Many left fewer documents than Shakespeare did, but among them are manuscripts, letters, and payment records proving that writing was their profession. For example, court records show payment to Ben Jonson for "those services of his wit & pen." Desperate to come up with comparable material to round out Shakespeare, scholars in the eighteenth and nineteenth centuries forged evidence—later debunked—of a writerly life.

To be sure, Shakespeare's name can be found linked, during his lifetime, to written works. With *Love's Labour's Lost,* in 1598, it started appearing on the title pages of one-play editions called quartos. (Several of the plays attributed to Shakespeare were first published anonymously.) Commentators at the time saluted him by name, praising "Shakespeare's fine filed phrase" and "honey-tongued Shakespeare." But such evidence proves attribution, not actual authorship—as even some orthodox Shakespeare scholars grant. "I would love to find a contemporary document that said William Shakespeare was the dramatist of Stratford-upon-Avon written during his lifetime," Stanley Wells, a professor emeritus at the University of Birmingham's Shakespeare Institute, has said. "That would shut the buggers up!"

By contrast, more than a few of Shakespeare's contemporaries are on record suggesting that his name got affixed to work that wasn't his. In 1591 the dramatist Robert Greene wrote of the practice of "underhand brokery"—of poets who "get some other Batillus to set his name to their verses." (Batillus was a mediocre Roman poet who claimed some of Virgil's verses as his own.) The following year he warned fellow playwrights about an "upstart Crow, beautified with our feathers," who thinks he is the "onely Shake-scene in a countrey." Most scholars agree that the "Crow" is Shakespeare, then an actor in his late twenties, and conclude that the new-hatched playwright was starting to irk established figures. Anti-Stratfordians see something else: in Aesop's fables, the crow was a proud strutter who stole the feathers of others; Horace's crow, in his epistles, was a plagiarist. Shakespeare was being attacked, they say, not as a budding dramatist but as a paymaster taking credit for others' work. "Seeke you better Maisters," Greene advised, urging his colleagues to cease writing for the Crow.

Ben Jonson, among others, got in his digs too. Scholars agree that the character of Sogliardo in *Every Man Out of His Humour*—a country bumpkin "without brain, wit, anything, indeed, ramping to gentility"—is a parody of Shakespeare, a social climber whose pursuit of a coat of arms was common lore among his circle of actors. In a satirical poem called "On Poet-Ape," Jonson was likely taking aim at Shakespeare the theater-world wheeler-dealer. This poet-ape, Jonson wrote, "from brokage is become so bold a thief,"

At first he made low shifts, would pick and glean,
Buy the reversion of old plays; now grown
To a little wealth, and credit in the scene,
He takes up all, makes each man's wit his own

What to make of the fact that Jonson changed his tune in the prefatory material that he contributed to the First Folio of plays when it appeared seven years after Shakespeare's death? Jonson's praise there did more than attribute the work to Shakespeare. It declared his art unmatched: "He was not of an age, but for all time!" The anti-Stratfordian response is to note the shameless hype at the heart of the Folio project. "Whatever you do, Buy," the compilers urged in their dedication, intent on a hard sell for a dramatist who, doubters emphasize, was curiously unsung at his death. The Folio's introductory effusions, they argue, contain double meanings. Jonson tells readers, for example, to find Shakespeare not in his portrait "but his Booke," seeming to undercut the relation between the man and the work. And near the start of his over-the-top tribute, Jonson riffs on the unreliability of extravagant praise, "which doth ne'er advance / The truth."

The authorship puzzles don't end there. How did the man born in Stratford acquire the wide-ranging knowledge on display in the plays—of the Elizabethan court, as well as of multiple languages, the law, astronomy, music, the military, and foreign lands, especially northern Italian cities? The author's linguistic brilliance shines in words and sayings imported from foreign vocabularies, but Shakespeare wasn't educated past the age of thirteen. Perhaps he traveled, joined the army, worked as a tutor, or all three, scholars have proposed. Yet no proof exists of any of those experiences, despite, as the Oxford historian Hugh Trevor-Roper pointed out in an essay, "the greatest battery of organized research that has ever been directed upon a single person."

In fact, a document that does exist—Shakespeare's will—would seem to undercut such hypotheses. A wealthy man when he retired to Stratford, he was meticulous about bequeathing his properties and possessions (his silver, his second-best bed). Yet he left behind not a single book, though the plays draw on hundreds of texts, including some—in Italian and French—that hadn't yet been translated into English. Nor did he leave any musical instruments, though the plays use at least three hundred musical terms and refer to twenty-six instruments. He remembered three actor-owners in his company, but no one in the literary profession. Strangest of all, he made no mention of manuscripts or writing. Perhaps as startling as the gaps in his will, Shakespeare appears to have neglected his daughters' education—an incongruity, given the erudition of so many of the playwright's female characters. One signed with her mark, the other with a signature a scholar has called "painfully formed."

"Weak and unconvincing" was Trevor-Roper's verdict on the case for Shakespeare. My delving left me in agreement, not that the briefs for the male alternatives struck me as compelling either. Steeped in the plays, I felt their author would surely join me in bridling at the Stratfordians' unquestioning worship at the shrine

—their arrogant dismissal of skeptics as mere deluded "buggers," or worse. ("Is there any more fanatic zealot than the priest-like defender of a challenged creed?" asked Richmond Crinkley, a former director of programs at the Folger Shakespeare Library who was nonetheless sympathetic to the anti-Stratfordian view.) To appreciate how belief blossoms into fact—how readily myths about someone get disseminated as truth—one can't do better than to read Shakespeare. Just think of how obsessed the work is with mistaken identities, concealed women, forged and anonymous documents—with the error of trusting in outward appearances. What if searchers for the real Shakespeare simply haven't set their sights on the right pool of candidates?

I met Emilia Bassano's most ardent champion at Alice's Tea Cup, which seemed unexpectedly apt: a teahouse on Manhattan's Upper West Side, it has quotes from *Alice in Wonderland* scrawled across the walls ("OFF WITH THEIR HEADS!"). John Hudson, an Englishman in his sixties who pursued a degree at the Shakespeare Institute in a midcareer swerve, had been on the Bassano case for years, he told me. In 2014 he published *Shakespeare's Dark Lady: Amelia Bassano Lanier, the Woman Behind Shakespeare's Plays?* His zeal can sometimes get the better of him, yet he emphasizes that his methods and findings are laid out "for anyone . . . to refute if they wish." Like Alice's rabbit hole, Bassano's case opened up new and richly disorienting perspectives—on the plays, on the ways we think about genius and gender, and on a fascinating life.

Hudson first learned of Bassano from A. L. Rowse, who discovered mention of her in the notebooks of an Elizabethan physician and astrologer named Simon Forman. In her teens she became the mistress of Henry Carey, Lord Hunsdon, the master of court entertainment and patron of Shakespeare's acting company. And that is only the start. Whether or not Bassano was Shakespeare's lover (scholars now dismiss Rowse's claim), the discernible contours of her biography supply what the available material about Shakespeare's life doesn't: circumstantial evidence of opportunities to acquire an impressive expanse of knowledge.

Bassano lived, Hudson points out, "an existence on the boundaries of many different social worlds," encompassing the breadth of the Shakespeare canon: its coarse, low-class references and its intimate knowledge of the court; its Italian sources and its Jewish allusions; its music and its feminism. And her imprint, as Hudson reads the plays, extends over a long period. He notes the many uses of her name, citing several early on—for instance, an Emilia in *The Comedy of Errors*. (Emilia, the most common female name in the plays alongside Katherine, wasn't used in the sixteenth century by any other English playwright.) *Titus Andronicus* features a character named Bassianus, which was the original Roman name of Bassano del Grappa, her family's hometown before their move to Venice. Later, in *The Merchant of Venice*, the romantic hero is a Venetian named Bassanio, an indication that the author perhaps knew of the Bassanos' connection to Venice. (*Bassanio* is a spelling of their name in some records.)

Further on, in *Othello*, another Emilia appears—Iago's wife. Her famous speech against abusive husbands, Hudson notes, doesn't show up until 1623, in the First Folio, included among lines that hadn't appeared in an earlier version (lines that Stratfordians assume—without any proof—were written before Shakespeare's death). Bassano was still alive, and by then had known her share of hardship at the hands of men. More to the point, she had already spoken out, in her 1611 book of poetry, against men who "do like vipers deface the wombs wherein they were bred."

Prodded by Hudson, you can discern traces of Bassano's own life trajectory in particular works across the canon. In *All's Well That Ends Well*, a lowborn girl lives with a dowager countess and a general named Bertram. When Bassano's father, Baptista, died in 1576, Emilia, then seven, was taken in by Susan Bertie, the dowager countess of Kent. The countess's brother, Peregrine Bertie, was —like the fictional Bertram—a celebrated general. In the play, the countess tells how a father "famous . . . in his profession" left "his sole child . . . bequeathed to my overlooking. I have those hopes of her good that her education promises." Bassano received a re-markable humanist education with the countess. In her book of poetry, she praised her guardian as "the Mistris of my youth, / The noble guide of my ungovern'd dayes."

As for the celebrated general, Hudson seizes on the possibility that Bassano's ears, and perhaps eyes, were opened by Peregrine Bertie as well. In 1582 Bertie was named ambassador to Denmark by the queen and sent to the court at Elsinore—the setting of *Hamlet*. Records show that the trip included state dinners with

Rosencrantz and Guildenstern, whose names appear in the play. Because emissaries from the same two families later visited the English court, the trip isn't decisive, but another encounter is telling: Bertie met with the Danish astronomer Tycho Brahe, whose astronomical theories influenced the play. Was Bassano (then just entering her teens) on the trip? Bertie was accompanied by a "whole traine," but only the names of important gentlemen are recorded. In any case, Hudson argues, she would have heard tales on his return.

Later, as the mistress of Henry Carey (forty-three years her senior), Bassano gained access to more than the theater world. Carey, the queen's cousin, held various legal and military positions. Bassano was "favoured much of her Majesty and of many noblemen," the physician Forman noted, indicating the kind of extensive aristocratic associations that only vague guesswork can accord to Shakespeare. His company didn't perform at court until Christmas of 1594, after several of the plays informed by courtly life had already been written. Shakespeare's history plays, concerned as they are with the interactions of the governing class, presume an insider perspective on aristocratic life. Yet mere court performances wouldn't have enabled such familiarity, and no trace exists of Shakespeare's presence in any upper-class household.

And then, in late 1592, Bassano (now twenty-three) was expelled from court. She was pregnant. Carey gave her money and jewels and, for appearance's sake, married her off to Alphonso Lanier, a court musician. A few months later she had a son. Despite the glittering dowry, Lanier must not have been pleased. "Her husband hath dealt hardly with her," Forman wrote, "and spent and consumed her goods."

Bassano was later employed in a noble household, probably as a music tutor, and roughly a decade after that opened a school. Whether she accompanied her male relatives—whose consort of recorder players at the English court lasted ninety years—on their trips back to northern Italy isn't known. But the family link to the home country offers support for the fine-grained familiarity with the region that (along with in-depth musical knowledge) any plausible candidate for authorship would seem to need—just what scholars have had to strain to establish for Shakespeare. (Perhaps, theories go, he chatted with travelers or consulted books.) In *Othello*, for example, Iago gives a speech that precisely describes a fresco in Bassano del Grappa—also the location of a shop owned by Giovanni Otello, a likely source of the title character's name.

Her Bassano lineage—scholars suggest the family were conversos, converted or hidden Jews presenting as Christians—also helps account for the Jewish references that scholars of the plays have noted. The plea in *The Merchant of Venice* for the equality and humanity of Jews, a radical departure from typical anti-Semitic portrayals of the period, is well known. "Hath not a Jew hands, organs, dimensions, senses, affections, passions?" Shylock asks. "If you prick us, do we not bleed?" *A Midsummer Night's Dream* draws from a passage in the Talmud about marriage vows; spoken Hebrew is mixed into the nonsense language of *All's Well That Ends Well*.

What's more, the Bassano family's background suggests a source close to home for the particular interest in dark figures in the sonnets, *Othello*, and elsewhere. A 1584 document about the arrest of two Bassano men records them as "black"—among Elizabethans, the term could apply to anyone darker than the fair-skinned English, including those with a Mediterranean complexion. (The fellows uttered lines that could come straight from a comic interlude in the plays: "We have as good friends in the court as thou hast and better too . . . Send us to ward? Thou wert as good kiss our arse.") In *Love's Labour's Lost*, the noblemen derisively compare Rosaline, the princess's attendant, to "chimney-sweepers" and "colliers" (coal miners). The king joins in, telling Berowne, who is infatuated with her, "Thy love is black as ebony," to which the young lord responds, "O wood divine!"

Bassano's life sheds possible light too on another outsider theme: the plays' preoccupation with women caught in forced or loveless marriages. Hudson sees her misery reflected in the sonnets, thought to have been written from the early 1590s to the early 1600s. "When, in disgrace with fortune and men's eyes, / I all alone beweep my outcast state, / And trouble deaf heaven with my bootless cries, / And look upon myself and curse my fate," reads sonnet 29. (When Maya Angelou first encountered the poem as a child, she thought Shakespeare must have been a black girl who had been sexually abused: "How else could he know what I know?") For Shakespeare, those years brought a rise in status:

in 1596 he was granted a coat of arms, and by 1597 he was rich enough to buy the second-largest house in Stratford.

In what is considered an early or muddled version of *The Taming of the Shrew,* a man named Alphonso (as was Bassano's husband) tries to marry off his three daughters, Emilia, Kate, and Philema. Emilia drops out in the later version, and the father is now called Baptista (the name of Bassano's father). As a portrait of a husband dealing "hardly" with a wife, the play is horrifying. Yet Kate's speech of submission, with its allusions to the Letters of Paul, is slippery: even as she exaggeratedly parrots the Christian doctrine of womanly subjection, she is anything but dutifully silent.

Shakespeare's women repeatedly subvert such teachings, perhaps most radically in *The Winter's Tale,* another drama of male cruelty. There the noblewoman Paulina, scorned by King Leontes as "a most intelligencing bawd" with a "boundless tongue," bears fierce witness against him (no man dares to) when he wrongly accuses Queen Hermione of adultery and imprisons her. As in so many of the comedies, a more enlightened society emerges in the end because the women's values triumph.

I was stunned to realize that the year *The Winter's Tale* was likely completed, 1611, was the same year Bassano published her book of poetry, *Salve Deus Rex Judæorum.* Her writing style bears no obvious resemblance to Shakespeare's in his plays, though Hudson strains to suggest similarities. The overlap lies in the feminist content. Bassano's poetry registers as more than conventional religious verse designed to win patronage (she dedicates it to nine women, Mary Sidney included, fashioning a female literary community). Scholars have observed that it reads as a "transgressive" defense of Eve and womankind. Like a cross-dressing Shakespearean heroine, Bassano refuses to play by the rules, heretically reinterpreting scripture. "If Eve did err, it was for knowledge sake," she writes. Arguing that the crucifixion, a crime committed by men, was a greater crime than Eve's, she challenges the basis of men's "tyranny" over women.

"I always feel something Italian, something Jewish about Shakespeare," Jorge Luis Borges told *The Paris Review* in 1966. "Perhaps Englishmen admire him because of that, because it's so unlike them." Borges didn't mention feeling "something female" about the bard, yet that response has never ceased to be part of Shakespeare's allure—embodiment though he is of the patriarchal authority of the Western canon. What would the revelation of a woman's hand at work mean, aside from the loss of a prime tourist attraction in Stratford-upon-Avon? Would the effect be a blow to the cultural patriarchy, or the erosion of the canon's status? Would (male) myths of inexplicable genius take a hit? Would women at last claim their rightful authority as historical and intellectual forces?

I was curious to take the temperature of the combative authorship debate as women edge their way into it. Over more tea I tested Hudson's room for flexibility. Could the plays' many connections to Bassano be explained by simply assuming the playwright knew her well? "Shakespeare would have had to run to her every few minutes for a musical reference or an Italian pun," he said. I caught up with Mark Rylance, the actor and former artistic director of the Globe, in the midst of rehearsals for *Othello* (whose plot, he noted, comes from an Italian text that didn't exist in English). A latitudinarian doubter—embracing the inquiry, not any single candidate—Rylance has lately observed that the once heretical notion of collaboration between Shakespeare and other writers "is now accepted, pursued, and published by leading orthodox scholars." He told me that "Emilia should be studied by anyone interested in the creation of the plays." David Scott Kastan, a well-known Shakespeare scholar at Yale, urged further exploration too, though he wasn't ready to anoint her bard. "What's clear is that it's important to know more about her," he said, and even got playful with pronouns: "The more we know about her and the world she lived in, the more we'll know about Shakespeare, whoever she was."

In the fall I joined the annual meeting of the Shakespeare Authorship Trust—a gathering of skeptics at the Globe—feeling excited that gender would be at the top of the agenda. Some eyebrows were raised even in this company, but enthusiasm ran high. "People have been totally frustrated with authorship debates that go nowhere, but that's because there have been two hundred years of bad candidates," one participant from the University of Toronto exclaimed. "They didn't want to see women in this," he reflected. "It's a tragedy of history."

He favored Sidney. Others were eager to learn about Bassano, and with collaboration in mind, I wondered whether the two women had perhaps worked together, or as part of a group.

I thought of Bassano's *Salve Deus,* in which she writes that men have wrongly taken credit for knowledge: "Yet Men will boast of Knowledge, which he tooke / From Eve's faire hand, as from a learned Booke."

The night after the meeting I went to a performance of *Antony and Cleopatra* at the National Theatre. I sat enthralled, still listening for the poet in her words, trying to catch her reflection in some forgotten bit of verse. "Give me my robe, put on my crown," cried the queen, "I have / Immortal longings in me." There she was, kissing her ladies goodbye, raising the serpent to her breast. "I am fire and air."

Contributors' Notes

*Notable Essays and Literary
Nonfiction of 2019*

Notable Special Issues of 2019

Contributors' Notes

RABIH ALAMEDDINE is the author of a story collection, *The Perv*, and the novels *Koolaids; I, the Divine; The Hakawati; An Unnecessary Woman* (a finalist for the National Book Award 2014), and *The Angel of History*. His novel *The Wrong End of the Telescope* is forthcoming in 2021.

Born in Bosnia, ELVIS BEGO left that country at the age of twelve and now lives in Copenhagen. His fiction and essays have appeared in *Agni, The Common, Kenyon Review, New England Review, Threepenny Review, Tin House,* and elsewhere. He is at work on a novel and completing a book of stories.

RACHEL CUSK is the author of ten novels and four works of nonfiction, which have won and been shortlisted for numerous prizes. In 2015 Cusk's version of *Medea* was staged at the Almeida Theatre.

BARBARA EHRENREICH is a contributing editor of *The Baffler*. Her newest book is *Natural Causes: An Epidemic of Wellness, the Certainty of Dying, and Killing Ourselves to Live Longer.*

GARY FINCKE's latest collection of personal essays, *The Darkness Call,* won the Robert C. Jones Prize for a book of short prose (2018). Winner of the Flannery O'Connor Prize for Short Fiction and the Wheeler Prize for Poetry for earlier collections, Fincke has published thirty-four books of nonfiction, fiction, and poetry. He founded and then directed the Writers Institute at Susquehanna University for twenty-one years.

RON HUETT graduated from Kurt T. Shery continuation high school in June 1995; he received a BA in creative writing from Columbia University's School of General Studies in May 2018. An alumnus of the CRIT writing workshop, Ron teaches third grade in Brownsville, Brooklyn. He is working on his first novel.

LESLIE JAMISON is the author of *The Recovering,* a critical memoir; two essay collections, *The Empathy Exams* and *Make It Scream, Make It Burn;* and a novel, *The Gin Closet.* She directs the graduate nonfiction program at Columbia University.

JAMAICA KINCAID is a writer, novelist, and professor. Her works include *Annie John, Lucy, The Autobiography of My Mother,* and *Mr. Potter,* as well as her classic history of her Antigua, *A Small Place,* and a memoir, *My Brother.* Her first book, the collection of stories *At the Bottom of the River,* won the Morton Dauwen Zabel Award from the American Academy of Arts and Letters and was nominated for the PEN/Faulkner Award for fiction. Kincaid's last novel, *See Now Then,* was published in 2013. Professor of African and African American studies at Harvard University, Kincaid was elected to the American Academy of Arts and Letters in 2004. She has received a Guggenheim Award, the Lannan Literary Award for Fiction, the Prix Femina Étranger, the Anisfield-Wolf Book Award, the Clifton Fadiman Medal, and the Dan David Prize for Literature in 2017.

JOSEPH LEO KOERNER is the Thomas Professor of the History of Art and Architecture and Senior Fellow at the Society of Fellows at Harvard University. He is the author most recently of *Bosch and Bruegel: From Enemy Painting to Everyday Life* (2016). His film *The Burning Child* was released in 2019.

ALEX MARZANO-LESNEVICH is the author of *The Fact of a Body: A Murder and a Memoir,* which received a Lambda Literary Award, the Chautauqua Prize, and awards in France and Canada and was translated into nine languages. The recipient of fellowships from the National Endowment for the Arts, MacDowell, Yaddo, and the Bread Loaf Writers' Conference, as well as a Rona Jaffe Award, Marzano-Lesnevich has written for the *New York Times,* the *Boston Globe, Oxford American, Harper's Magazine,* and many other publications. They live in Portland, Maine, and are an assistant professor at Bowdoin College. They are at work on a book about gender, from which "Body Language" was adapted.

CLINTON CROCKETT PETERS is an assistant professor of creative writing at Berry College. He is the author of *Pandora's Garden* (2018) and *Mountain Madness* (forthcoming in 2021). He has been awarded literary prizes by *The Iowa Review, Shenandoah, North American Review, Crab Orchard Review,* and *Columbia Journal.* Peters has been noted four times in the Best American series. He holds an MFA in nonfiction from the University of Iowa, where he was an Iowa Arts Fellow, and a PhD in English and creative writing from the University of North Texas. His work also appears in *Orion, Southern Review, Utne Reader, Catapult, The Threepenny Review, Electric Literature,* and elsewhere.

SUSAN FOX ROGERS is the author of *My Reach: A Hudson River Memoir* and the editor of eleven anthologies, including *Solo: On Her Own Adventure* and *Antarctica: Life on the Ice,* which was created while in Antarctica on a National Science Foundation award for artists and writers. Her most recent collection, *When Birds Are Near: Dispatches from Contemporary Writers,* celebrates the birding life. "The Other Leopold" is part of a longer work, *Learning the Birds: A Mid-life Journey,* to be published in fall 2021. Rogers has taught the creative essay, nature writing, and bird-related classes at Bard College since 2001.

MATTHEW SALESSES is the author of three novels, *Disappear Doppelgänger Disappear, The Hundred-Year Flood,* and *I'm Not Saying, I'm Just Saying,* and two forthcoming books of nonfiction: a craft book, *Craft in the Real World* (2021), and a collection of essays. He has written for NPR's *Code Switch,* the *New York Times's Motherlode, Gay Magazine, Vice,* and many others. He is an assistant professor of English at Coe College.

PETER SCHJELDAHL has been a staff writer at *The New Yorker* since 1998 and is the magazine's art critic. He came to the magazine from *The Village Voice,* where he was the art critic from 1990 to 1998. Previously he had written frequently for the *New York Times's* Arts and Leisure section. His writing has also appeared in *Artforum, Art in America, The New York Times Magazine, Vogue,* and *Vanity Fair.* He has received the Clark Prize for Excellence in Arts Writing from the Sterling and Francine Clark Art Institute; the Frank Jewett Mather Award from the College Art Association, for excellence in art criticism; the Howard D. Vursell Memorial Award from the American Academy of Arts and Letters, for "recent prose that merits recognition for the quality of its style"; and a Guggenheim fellowship. He is the author of four books of criticism, including *The Hydrogen Jukebox: Selected Writings,* and *Let's See: Writings on Art from The New Yorker.* His latest book is *Hot, Cold, Heavy, Light: 100 Art Writings, 1988–2018.*

A. O. SCOTT has been a critic at the *New York Times* since 2000, writing mostly about film and sometimes about books, music, television, and other subjects. He is the author of *Better Living Through Criticism: How to Think About Art, Pleasure, Beauty, and Truth* and a distinguished professor in the College of Film and the Moving Image at Wesleyan University.

A prolific journalist with columns in *The Spectator* and *Harper's Magazine,* LIONEL SHRIVER has published one short story collection and fourteen novels, including the bestsellers *The Mandibles: A Family, 2029–2047; Big Brother; So Much for That; The Post-Birthday World;* and the Orange Prize winner *We Need to Talk About Kevin* (a 2011 feature film starring Tilda Swinton). Her latest novel is *The Motion of the Body Through Space* (2020). Her work has been translated into more than thirty languages. She lives in London and Brooklyn, New York.

MARK SULLIVAN is the author of a collection of poetry, *Slag,* and his poems, essays, and reviews have appeared in many publications, including *Alaska Quarterly Review, New England Review,* and the *Southern Review.* He has received a number of awards for his writing, including a fellowship from the National Endowment for the Arts.

MARK SUNDEEN is the author of five books, including *The Unsettlers* (2017), *The Man Who Quit Money* (2012), and *The Making of Toro* (2003). His work has been translated into seven languages and has appeared in the *New York Times, Believer, McSweeney's,* and many other publications. A contributing editor for *Outside* magazine, he has held the Russo Chair in Creative Writing at the University of New Mexico and teaches fiction and nonfiction at the Mountainview Low-Residency MFA Program. He lives with his wife and son in Albuquerque, New Mexico.

ALISON TOWNSEND is the author of *The Persistence of Rivers: An Essay on Moving Water, Persephone in America,* and *The Blue Dress.* Emerita professor of English at the University of Wisconsin-Whitewater, she lives in the farm country outside Madison, the inspiration for her essay collection, *American Lonely: A Natural History of My Search for Home* (forthcoming in 2021).

DAVID L. ULIN is the author or editor of a dozen books, including *Sidewalking: Coming to Terms with Los Angeles,* shortlisted for the PEN/Diamonstein-Spielvogel Award for the Art of the Essay, and *Writing Los Angeles: A Literary Anthology,* which won a California Book Award. The former book editor and book critic of the *Los Angeles Times,* he has written for *The Atlantic, Virginia Quarterly Review, The Paris Review,* and the *New York Times,* among other publications. He has received fellowships from the Guggenheim Foundation and the Lannan Foundation and teaches at the University of Southern California. Most recently he edited the Library of America's *Joan Didion: The 1960s & 70s,* the first in a three-volume edition of the author's collected works.

Recipient of fellowships from the National Endowment for the Arts and the Michener Foundation, JERALD WALKER is a professor of creative writing at Emerson College. His essays have appeared in publications such as *The Harvard Review, Mother Jones, The Iowa Review, The Missouri Review, Oxford American,* and *Creative Nonfiction,* and he has been widely anthologized. He is the author of *The World in Flames: A Black Boyhood in a White Supremacist Doomsday Cult; Street Shadows: A Memoir of Race, Rebellion, and Redemption,* winner of the PEN/New England Award for Nonfiction, and *How to Make a Slave and Other Essays,* which includes "Breathe." This is his fifth appearance in the *Best American Essays* series.

STEPHANIE POWELL WATTS won the Ernest J. Gaines Award for her short story collection *We Are Taking Only What We Need.* Her novel, *No One Is Coming to Save Us,* was the inaugural American Library Association selection by Sarah Jessica Parker and the winner of a 2018 NAACP Image Award.

PHILIP WEINSTEIN, the Alexander Griswold Cummins Professor Emeritus at Swarthmore College, has published widely on nine-teenth- and twentieth-century fiction. The Society for the Study of Southern Literature chose his *Becoming Faulkner* (2010) for the C. Hugh Holman Award. "Soul-Error" is the signature essay in his current manuscript of the same title.

ELIZABETH WINKLER is a journalist and book critic based in New York. Her essays, profiles, and reviews have appeared in the *Wall Street Journal,* the *Times Literary Supplement,* the *Economist,* the *New Republic, and* the *Washington Post,* among other places. She holds a BA in English literature from Princeton University and an MA in English literature from Stanford University.

Notable Essays and Literary Nonfiction of 2019

SELECTED BY ROBERT ATWAN

MARILYN ABILDSKOV
    Confetti, *The Cincinnati Review*,
    16/1
ALICE ABRAHAM
    Holding Patterns, *n+1*, #34
KIM ADRIAN
    Ten Conversations About My
    Struggle, *The Gettysburg Review*,
    32/1
MARCIA ALDRICH
    Trina's Voice, *Zone* 3, 34/2
TARA MCCARTHEY ALTEBRANDO
    What's a Good Playlist for
    Fighting Cancer? *Slate*, July 11
HEATHER ALTFELD
    A Scribe from the Double
    House of Life, *Conjunctions*,
    #72
ABE AMIDOR
    Diary of a Triage Patient, *The
    Antioch Review*, 77/3
STEPHANIE ANDERSON
    Atlas, *Hotel Amerika*, #17
ANNA ANDREW
    Five Ways to Eat Termites, *The
    Bare Life Review*, #3
DONALD ANTRIM
    Everywhere and Nowhere,
    The New Yorker, February
    18 & 25

CHLOE ARIDJIS
    Insomnia Begins in the Cradle,
    Harvard Review, #54
DAVID ARMAND
    Mirrors, *Belmont Story Review*, #4
JASON ARMENT
    Flame and Fortune, *Eclectica*,
    23/3
CHRIS ARTHUR
    Voice Box, *The Dalhousie Review*,
    99/2
TIMOTHY AUBRY
    To Be Continued, *The Point*, #20

KAREN BABINE
    Little Houses, *Ascent*, October 13
C. MORAN BABST
    The House of Myth: On the
    Architecture of White Supremacy,
    Oxford American, #104
POE BALLANTINE
    Nomads, *The Sun*, January
TANEUM BAMBRICK
    Sturgeon, *Booth*, #13
RITA BANERJEE
    Birth of Cool, *Hunger Mountain*,
    #23
DANIEL BARNUM
    Natality: Moon/Sun/Stars,
    Hayden's Ferry Review, #64

Notable Special Issues of 2019

The Antioch Review, Writing and Reading, ed. Robert S. Fogarty, 77/1

Ascent, Special Issue, ed. W. Scott Olsen, November

The Baffler, Body Shots, ed. Jonathon Sturgeon, #48

The Bare Life Review, This Is the Language That Was Given to Us, ed. Nyuol Lueth Tong, #3

The Believer, The Borders Issue, ed. Joshua Wolf Shenk, 16/5

Bellevue Literary Review, A Good Life, ed. Danielle Ofri, #37

Belmont Story Review, Out of Place, ed. Richard Sowienski, #4

Booth, Nonfiction Prize Issue, ed. Robert Stapleton, #13

Chautauqua, Moxie, ed. Jill Gerard & Philip Gerard, #16

Conjunctions, Earth Elegies, ed. Bradford Morrow, #73

Creative Nonfiction, Intoxication, ed. Lee Gutkind, #69

Daedalus, Why Jazz Still Matters, guest eds. Gerald Early & Ingrid Monson, Spring

Foreign Affairs, The New Nationalism, ed. Gideon Rose, March/April

Freeman's, The Best New Writing on California, ed. John Freeman, October

Hayden's Ferry Review, Magic, ed. Joel Salcido, #64

Image, 1989–2019: Thirty Years, One Hundred Issues, ed. James K. A. Smith, #100

Iron Horse Literary Review, Apocalypse, ed. Leslie Jill Patterson, 21/1

Kenyon Review, Literary Activism, eds. Rita Dove & John Kinsella; journal ed. David H. Lynn, 41/6

Lapham's Quarterly, Night, ed. Lewis H. Lapham, 12/1

The Massachusetts Review, Celebrating Sixty Years, ed. Jim Hicks, 60/4

Michigan Quarterly Review, Iran, guest ed. Kathryn Babayan; ed. Khaled Mattawa, 58/2

The New Atlantis, The Ruin of the Digital Town Square, ed. Ari N. Schulman, #58

The New York Times Magazine, The 1619 Project, ed. Jake Silverstein et al., August 18

Notre Dame Magazine, Do You Believe It?, ed. Kerry Temple, Spring

Oxford American, Southern Music Issue Vol. 21, ed. Eliza Borné, #107

The Point, What Is the Earth For?, editorial staff, #18

Room, Sports, ed. Meghan Bell, 42/3

Ruminate, What Sustains: 50th Anniversary Issue, ed. Brianna Van Dyke, #50

Salmagundi, Debating Belief & Unbelief, ed. Robert Boyers & Peg Boyers, #200 & 201

Slice, Time, ed. Elizabeth Blachman, #24

Sport Literate, Fight Club 2019, ed. William Meiners, 12/1

Territory, Extremes, ed. Nick Greer & Thomas Mira y Lopez, #10

The Threepenny Review, A Symposium on Desire, ed. Wendy Lesser, #159

Vice, Truth and Lies, ed. Ellis Jones, 26/1

Washington Post Magazine, Prison, ed. Richard Just et al., November 3

The Yale Review, 200th Anniversary Issue, ed. Meghan O'Rourke, 107/4

Yellow Medicine Review, Language & Identity/Bodies & Borders, guest eds. Angela Trudell Vasquez & Millissa Kingbird, Spring

ZYZZYVA, The Bay Area, ed. Laura Cogan, #117

Note:

The following essays should have appeared in "Notable Essays and Literary Nonfiction of 2018":

BRENT BARBER, Sketches of Spain (Four Sounds in a Friendship), *Harmony,* 2018

ANITA GILL, Hair, *The Iowa Review,* 48/3

SONJA LIVINGSTON, Miracle of the Eyes, *The Cincinnati Review,* 14/2

DW MCKINNEY, In All, There I Am, *Stoneboat Literary Journal,* 8/2

LARA MESSERSMITH-GLAVIN, When Blue Walks Away from Green: The Mathematics of Synesthesia, *Stoneboat Literary Journal,* 9/1

CLAUDIA SMITH, The Bones: A Letter to My Daughter, *The Texas Review,* 39/3 & 4

One of the Notable Essays of 2018 was mistitled. The correct title is

CARLA SAMETH, If This Is So, Why Am I?, *The Nervous Breakdown,* February 26

THE BEST AMERICAN SERIES®

FIRST, BEST, AND BEST-SELLING

The Best American Essays

The Best American Food Writing

The Best American Mystery Stories

The Best American Science and Nature Writing

The Best American Science Fiction and Fantasy

The Best American Short Stories

The Best American Sports Writing

The Best American Travel Writing

Available in print and e-book wherever books are sold.

Visit our website: hmhbooks.com/series/best-american